THE CHAIN HOUSE

Also by J.H. Markert

Dig
Spider to the Fly
Sleep Tight
Wicked Games
Mister Lullaby
The Nightmare Man

Writing as James Markert

The Strange Case of Isaac Crawley
Midnight at the Tuscany Hotel
What Blooms from Dust
All Things Bright and Strange
The Angels' Share
A White Wind Blew

THE CHAIN HOUSE

A NOVEL

J.H. MARKERT

CROOKED LANE

NEW YORK

Published in the United States by Crooked Lane Books, an imprint of
The Quick Brown Fox & Company LLC.

Crooked Lane Books and its logo are trademarks of The Quick Brown Fox & Company LLC.

Library of Congress Catalog-in-Publication data available upon request.

ISBN (hardcover): 979-8-89242-675-6
ISBN (paperback): 979-8-89242-676-3
ISBN (ebook): 979-8-89242-677-0

Cover design Emily Mahar

Printed in the United States.

www.crookedlanebooks.com

Crooked Lane Books
34 West 27th St., 10th Floor
New York, NY 10001

First Edition: October 2026

The authorized representative in the EU for product safety and compliance is eucomply OÜPärnu mnt 139b-14, 11317 Tallinn, Estonia,
hello@eucompliancepartner.com, +33757690241

10 9 8 7 6 5 4 3 2 1

To all the booksellers out there, and librarians, and readers, and to all who play a part in the process of making a manuscript into a book, from agents and editors to designers and marketing and sales, thank you.

This one is for you.

"Believe me, with as many books as that mystery man has sold over the years, I'm flattered so many people think he is me. But I promise, I am not Mallard Malone."

Ben Bookman, New York Times
best-selling author of ***The Pulse***

The Mallard Malone Novels

(in order of publication)

Book 8: *Long Pale Moon*
Book 7: *Crown and Crows*
Book 6: *The Pandemonium Flux*
Book 5: *Feast or Famine*
Book 4: *Hammer and Nails*
Book 3: *Wastelands*
Book 2: *Phoenix Rising*
Book 1: *The Breakout (upcoming)*

BEFORE

May 28, 2006

Louisville Courier
9 Found Dead at the Hawthorne House
Several more wounded
Investigators say a local cult is to blame

EARLY SUNDAY MORNING, Louisville Metro Police were called to the home of Deron Hawthorne, CEO of Bridgerton Technologies and heir to Hawthorne Brothers Bourbon Distillery, after the Hawthorne's golden retriever arrived at a neighbor's house with a torn fabric in his mouth. The fabric, they soon realized, was from a shirt and it was soaked with blood. What began at dusk the night before as a lavish party to celebrate the publication of Deron and Clarice's youngest son Justin Hawthorne's first novel, The Craze, *had, by dawn, turned into a senseless tragedy of unspeakable horrors, and a scar on a community that, surviving family members say, might not ever heal . . .*

June 3, 2006

Louisville Courier
Louisville Man Arrested as Mastermind Behind the Hawthorne Massacre Manson as Possible Inspiration

Louisville native Sal Batise, 35, was arrested on the property of his 200-acre wooded compound known as Freedom, in southeastern Jefferson County, as a suspect in last week's heinous murders at the Hawthorne house. Leader of the cult known as The Collective, Batise is believed by the FBI and the Louisville Metro Police Department to be the mastermind behind the attack. Batise, known by his 500-plus followers as "The Breaker of Chains," submitted willingly to authorities. Batise has yet to comment publicly on the crimes, but after securing evidence from the "Freedom" compound, eerie parallels to Charles Manson have already been drawn. Three other cult members, Nancy Tanner, Sylvia Purell, and Annie Blackburn, have been detained for further questioning . . .

June 4, 2006

Louisville Courier
4 Children Found in Locked Bedroom Closet on Batise's Freedom Compound

Four children, ranging from age four to seven, were found by Louisville Metro Police yesterday morning, locked inside a bedroom closet in what is believed to be Sal Batise's main residence during their continued search of the Freedom Compound in the Hawthorne murder investigation. The four children, two boys and two girls, aside from obvious shock and hunger, all appeared to be in good physical health, which leads the authorities to believe they were hidden not long before the June 2 raid and subsequent arrests. Detectives are in the process of identifying all four children, but it is likely they belong to various cult members, and possibly to Sal Batise himself, as it has been rumored that he had as many as five wives . . .

June 6, 2006

Louisville Courier
Evidence of Cannibalism Found at Batise's Freedom Compound

Only days after the four children were found inside what we now know to be Sal Batise's main house at the Freedom Compound, cooked remnants of human flesh was found in what at first appeared to be a stew on the stove's front right burner, showing evidence of possible cannibalism.

PROLOGUE

"DEAD MAN WALKING!"

At the sound of the guard's booming voice, Warden Adrian Wren shifted in his office seat inside the prison's central tower for a better view of the window overlooking the yard below, as two armed guards escorted Sal Batise down a sidewalk that bisected a meticulously maintained lawn.

"Dead man walking," the guard shouted again.

There were currently three dozen inmates in the yard, doing anything from talking in groups to playing basketball or pickleball or cards, and every one of them had stopped what they were doing, as they'd been told, and turned away from the death row inmate, one of forty now currently on the row.

Even the two stray cats that roamed the state prison at Twisted Tree turned their backs on the dead man walking. Everyone knew the routine, and the display of discipline made Warden Wren smile with pride.

"Dead man walking!"

Sal Batise and the two guards disappeared from view down below.

A heavy door clicked shut and one by one the inmates turned back around and resumed what they'd been doing in the yard before the guards had interrupted them. Several inmates stared at the door through which Sal Batise had just entered the tower, probably wondering which dead man had just passed through their hour in the sun. The warden suspected some of them had figured it out. Sal Batise, after nearly twenty years on death row, carried an aura of energy some swore they could feel like a subtle, low-level current that made arm hair stand erect and brought all senses to celebrity-like attention.

Warden Wren turned in his chair and faced the door. It wasn't protocol for any inmate to be delivered into his office, but Sal Batise wasn't the everyday run-of-the-mill prisoner. And with less than forty-eight hours to live, the warden figured he'd allow him a quick nature stroll through the yard. But that wasn't the only reason Batise had been given this special privilege, and the privilege they were about to discuss for tomorrow, which to the warden still screamed as outlandish. But what was he to do? Blackmail was real, and the picture sent to his phone as a threat two weeks ago had been sent by a real person. Only God, and Sal Batise—who had often thought of himself as a god—knew who sent it. And the actual sender, of course, who Warden Wren assumed was one of Batise's followers. He still had thousands of them who—God only knew how he'd reached them from his isolation cell—were still willing to do his bidding.

But while Warden Adrian Wren was known to be an upstanding citizen and father, he'd evolved, ashamedly, over the past year into a horrible husband who'd begun an affair he'd only ended two weeks ago, when a compromising photo of himself and his mistress had landed in his texts from an anonymous source—and Sal Batise somehow knew about it.

And here we are, Warden Wren thought as he awaited Sal Batise's arrival in his own personal office like he was a friend, because that's what Sal had demanded.

Like the family and friends of Sal Batise's wildly branched victim tree, Warden Wren wanted Batise in the ground, and, like Governor Hawthorne, he'd made no secret of it. But now he especially couldn't wait for Batise to be executed, and the blackmail to be over and done. Sal, with a whisper into the warden's ear two weeks ago, had promised the picture would never see the light of day.

Just grant me this one last wish, he'd said.

And the warden had agreed.

The personal meeting inside his office was a show of solidarity, and deep down, perhaps, a smidge of respect. Although he wanted the psychotic son of a bitch in the ground, he secretly admired Batise's uncanny ability to stay alive, to delay the inevitable, to continue kicking the can down the road like some death-dodging magician, pulling one trick after the next from sleeves that, for the past five years in particular, had seemed endless. With all his appeals exhausted years ago, he'd become the king of the last-minute—and in once instance, last-second—stays of execution. He'd had four last meals, and in one case had made it as far as the needle in his arm when the call came in to halt things.

Always one more trick up his sleeve.

One more buried body he claimed to know about.

One more murder he claimed to know about.

And they always checked out.

Warden Wren knew this could be one more trick, but what else could he do?

He wanted to stay married, and he wanted to keep his family intact, and Sal Batise—a man who'd never shied away from the fact that he'd had multiple wives—had made the warden promise he'd never cheat on his wife again.

Warden Wren straightened upon a heavy knock on his door. "Come in."

The door opened and there stood Sal Batise in the red prison garb the Twisted Tree death row inmates wore every day. Chains connected his wrists. Chains connected his ankles. He shuffled instead of walked, but with his trademark grin, which was sometimes a full smile, as if constantly giving off the vibe that none of the daily grind bothered him in the least bit. And despite the fact that he now had less than two days left to live and weeks ago had dismissed the last of a long string of lawyers, he still carried himself like he had no doubt he'd one day walk away from the Kentucky State Penitentiary at Twisted Tree a free man. He took the chair Warden Wren had left for him on the opposite side of his desk.

Sal Batise was a relatively young man upon his arrest and sentencing, and while he was not old in his fifties, his hair, cut short to his scalp, was completely gray, as was his neatly trimmed beard. His skin had barely seen the sun in two decades, yet any hint of paleness somehow evaded him. But it was the sky-blue eyes that never failed to own a room and mesmerize even the most unshakable of men or women. And now, even as the warden had mentally prepared himself for this moment, as he did every time he'd met Batise face-to-face over the years, cold chills still crawled like icy spiders up and down Warden Wren's spine.

To mask his nerves, the warden leaned forward with his elbows on his desk, hands together. Doing his best not to stare into the bottomless depth of those piercing eyes, he cut right to the chase. "Well, Sal, who will it be?"

Sal ignored the question, and instead surveyed the warden's office with a sense of nonchalance that belied his nature. "Nice place you got here, Warden." And then he nodded toward the framed picture of Warden Wren's family on the corner of the desk. "That your family? Your wife sure is a looker."

Warden Wren gently placed the picture frame face down and remained calm, but he could feel the guards' stares and he could hear their question in his mind—*Are you going to stand for this, Warden?*

And the answer to that was yes, for two more days he would.

Then Sal said, "Got a pen, Warden Wren?"

One of the guards, the tall dark-haired one with a smiley-face tattoo on the top of his left hand, Billy Boyle, said, "Just spill it, Sal."

But Warden Wren said, "It's okay, Billy." The warden removed an index card from a drawer and grabbed a pen from the cup at the corner of his desk and slid both in front of Sal Batise.

Sal clutched the pen in his left hand, turned the index card at an angle, and started writing like any left-hander the warden had ever seen write. But Sal used his right hand as a shield, covering the card as he wrote. Other than the heavy scrawl of pen on paper and the eerie sound of his chains moving across the desktop, the office was silent.

They waited and watched.

The bastard had perfected the art of calligraphy over the years, and the warden could tell that's what Sal was doing now. Making a show of it.

It didn't take long, as the warden knew it wouldn't. It was his final answer to a simple question they'd been waiting on for fourteen days now. The result of the blackmail. The one wish Sal asked to be granted—one last interview, and the interviewer would be chosen like a contest—something Warden Wren would never have agreed to otherwise. The decision Batise had finally made after two weeks of going through snail mail—because that had been one of the rules he'd made for what he called the final contest: old-school, mailed-in pitches from all the major news networks, from Fox to MSNBC and *Rolling Stone* to *People* and every outlet in between, all practically begging to have Sal Batise's final interview.

His first interview in nearly a decade.

Warden Wren, up until the dreaded picture was sent to him via text, had been adamant that Sal Batise receive no interview before his death. When asked by reporters why he'd reversed his decision, he told them after receiving so many requests daily, now that the execution was on their doorstep, that he'd had a change of heart, pure and simple. Quickly adding, with a smile that even to him felt phony, that he'd *prayed on it*. And now here they were.

With his right hand covering what he'd written, Sal playfully slid the card back toward Warden Wren, who plucked it out from beneath the weight of Sal's fingers.

It was written in calligraphy, just as he'd assumed, but instead of a major network or news outlet or famous reporter, Sal had written two words. A name.

Sam Harper.

Warden Wren said, "Is this a joke?"

"I don't joke, Warden Wren." He leaned back in the chair, smiled. "You know that."

"Who is Sam Harper?"

Sal shrugged. "I guess we'll find out soon enough."

CHAPTER

1

THERE WERE PERKS to being the governor's wife.

Too many, in fact, Beth Hawthorne remembered thinking several nights ago, tipsy from Moscato, in the final hours of their yearly August clambake on the grounds of the governor's mansion, standing atop the bluff overlooking their in-ground pool and trellised flower gardens as fancily dressed guests roamed about with cocktails.

She too often felt guilty because of the perks, wondering if it was all too much, when so many still lived paycheck to paycheck, or in poverty, or even on the streets.

The ever-widening divide between the haves and the have-nots.

It was also why she was such a beloved First Lady.

She cared. Not only for the well-being of the people in their state of Kentucky, whether left wing or right wing and everything in between, but for people in general, and because of it she'd never been viewed in public or online as anything other than wholesome and genuine.

She and her husband, Governor Gavin Hawthorne, both Independents, were as middle of the road as politicians could get—she a psychiatrist originally from Boston, and he a former Major League baseball player from Louisville. But while the governor, at fifty, was known for his rakish good looks, his charm on the campaign trail, and his cheeky charisma during speeches, it was Dr. Bethany Brooks Hawthorne who often took the spotlight, and was, as Governor Hawthorne often admitted, not only the quarterback behind it all but his *better* in every way. For them, it truly was their teamwork that made their dream work, and their recent popularity as good-vibes-only vocal centrists in a country so divided by right and left had them rumored, now in their final year in their second term as Governor and First Lady, to be likely third party candidates for a presidential run in 2028.

Gavin's answer, whenever asked about a possible White House run, was always the same: *Sure, I think I'd make a pretty darn good First Gentleman, don't you?*

And for that reason, as Dr. Bethany Hawthorne liked to tease the security guard now tasked with accompanying her on morning runs, she had to stay in shape. Who knew what their future might hold? But the security guard, who'd begun to accompany them damn near everywhere they went, was a perk she'd grown tired of long ago. While she tended to win most arguments with the governor, discussion over her safety was a fight in which she didn't engage. Gavin was protective of her to a fault, and the same went for their two grown children, Thomas and Sarah, if not more so.

And who could blame him?

Gavin Hawthorne knew tragedy all too well—back in 2003, in a three-year span, it had come at him as an unrelentingly cruel two-headed monster. Gavin was a rookie for the Cincinnati Reds, while he and Beth had two children in diapers, when his younger sister Emily, living the life of a happy, single twenty-five-year-old in Manhattan, disappeared a month after her promotion as a fiction acquisitions editor at the prestigious Stanton Publishing House. Emily, who had been Beth's matron of honor at their wedding, had last been seen running through Central Park on a sunny Sunday afternoon in June—and was never seen again. Three years later, when Gavin was toiling through his floundering baseball career and becoming increasingly homesick from being away from his young family, a horrible attack left four of his family members dead and Beth grievously wounded in what would come to be called the Hawthorne murders.

On a warm Saturday evening in May 2006, members of Sal Batise's cult, The Collective, had emerged soundlessly from the surrounding woods masked in balaclavas and swarmed a private party at the Hawthorne mansion armed with machetes, murdering nine in a matter of minutes. The list of dead included four from Gavin's family, including his cousin Justin Hawthorne, who had been the man of the hour that night, celebrating the publication of his debut novel, *The Craze*, a horror thriller—which went on to hit the *New York Times* best-seller list and stayed there until Sal and three other cult members from The Collective were found guilty nearly a year later. Sal, even though not present that night, was sentenced to death. Nancy Tanner, Sylvia Purell, and Annie Blackburn were sentenced to life in prison without parole. The fourth cult member's identity that evening was unknown, with only one of the survivors remembering seeing a man in a tuxedo wearing white gloves and a Guy Fawkes mask, his weapon of choice the sharpened corkscrew end of a wine bottle opener.

Beth Hawthorne still had scars from that encounter—she was the survivor of the mystery cult member's attack that night, seeing him casually walking through the house as chaos reigned all around, his boots, big and dirty and brown, in contrast to the slick black pants of his tuxedo, his footfalls heavy on the old wood floors, all as dozens of guests screamed in panic, attempting to flee as the three women in balaclava masks butchered anyone within reach. But while Nancy Tanner, Sylvia Purell, and Annie Blackburn seemed to be killing at random, this man moved with cold, calculated purpose, stopping only when he spotted Beth hiding behind a fancy sofa in the cigar room as if she had been his lone target. He'd grabbed her by the ankle and started stabbing relentlessly with the corkscrew, first in her left calf, and then her right thigh, before moving upward with near-fatal blows to her abdomen and chest and the left side of her neck. The last she remembered was him straddling her waist, pinning her hands to the hardwood floor. She'd lost too much blood by then to fight, and he was too strong. His face lowered to within inches of hers, his eyes dark as coal, gleaming wet through the holes of the Guy Fawkes mask.

That was when she blacked out, only to wake up the next morning in the ICU, connected by wires and IV drips to machines, her husband bedside and holding a hand she could no longer feel.

At trial, when asked about the fourth member of their crew that night, Sylvia Purell and Annie Blackburn both categorically denied anyone other than the three of them—who called themselves Sal's Angels—being at the mansion. Nancy Tanner, historically considered the weakest link of the Angels, mentioned a man by the name of Justice Minks. *He was a wisp*, Nancy had said on the stand under oath, adding, almost playfully, that *Justice Minks was like fire smoke, in a way. One minute he was there and the next he was gone, with only a hint of him remaining, like a smell just to remind you something just got burned.* She later recanted that part of her testimony, admitting she was under the influence of drugs somehow sneaked into the prison. By the time the authorities infiltrated the Freedom Ranch to arrest Sal Batise and his Angels, most members of The Collective had fled, but no evidence of the existence of the mystery man, Justice Minks, was found. Of the dozens of cult members who stayed behind to fight for their cause or for questioning, not one admitted to knowing a man named Justice Minks. And in each of the dozens of interviews during Sal Batise's time on death row, he either denied the man's existence or referred to him as "fire smoke," just as Nancy Tanner had at trial.

Beth, a thirty-year-old doctor at the time of the attack, had nearly died before the ambulances arrived, and had suffered deeply from survivor's guilt, going to great pains to make sure none of her scars could be seen in public. But in recent years, and especially during Gavin's early campaign trails, she began to wear dresses and outfits that didn't conceal her scars, as reminders to never forget that horrifying evening. Gavin had been on the road pitching that night in Atlanta, and sat bedside at the hospital for two weeks as Beth convalesced, then retired abruptly from baseball. A year later, he began his career as a politician, and he never shied away from his outspoken views in favor of capital punishment while Sal Batise continued to live and breathe on death row, as flippant and unapologetic as he'd been when he was first convicted and sentenced.

With Batise set to die in less than two days by lethal injection, Beth didn't fight the extra security her husband demanded. The ramped-up media coverage nationwide had brought out the protesters at the new Kentucky State Penitentiary at Twisted Tree, including some vocally active crazies with threats on the family. Governor Hawthorne didn't want to take any chances.

Due to a judge-issued injunction blocking executions back in 2010, no death row inmates had been executed in Kentucky since 2008. But during the first year of Governor Hawthorne's first term, the injunction was lifted on the grounds that the previous concerns had been revised and addressed, and the wheel of capital punishment started rotating again. Sal Batise, the psychotic cult leader, the so-called Breaker of Chains, became the face of it.

But with no more apparent tricks up his sleeve and with all appeals exhausted, Batise, for the first time since his arrest, appeared to have lost the flair that had kept him alive. He appeared, according to Warden Wren at the Twisted Tree State Penitentiary, to *finally be ready to meet his Maker, almost contently so*. Beth had heard he'd agreed to one last interview, and if rumors were true, Sal was to pick which network as early as today. But with Governor Hawthorne repeatedly refusing clemency no matter how many threats he received from the thousands of Sal Batise's fans from across the country, it appeared Batise would finally die by lethal injection.

So Beth no longer took her morning jog alone.

She only wished the security could keep up.

Today it was Agent Nathan Sparks, an officer twenty years her junior. None of the rotating guards would be able to keep up if she were to really start running, she knew. Granted, they were armed and not in attire conducive for exercise, but as a former college athlete, four years running cross-country at Harvard, Beth craved the wind in her face. She wanted to let loose and really stretch her legs, as she'd been doing, alone, through the familiar trails in the woods on the outskirts of the governor's mansion, for years. But she held back, allowing Nathan to save face as they jogged side by side under leafy boughs and moving shadows and spots of filtered morning sunlight, their footfalls sometimes in rhythm, sometimes in unison, and occasionally soporific.

And peaceful.

Until Beth suddenly heard footsteps trailing behind them that hadn't been there seconds before.

Agent Nate was the first to look over his shoulder, quickly moving in front of Beth as a man in full camouflage gear and wearing a Guy Fawkes mask moved toward them with careful purpose, only twenty yards away, with a gun raised.

The man fired before Nathan could raise his gun. The gunshot echoed and birds flew from trees. The bullet hit the agent between the eyes, dropping him lifelessly to the trail.

Beth screamed, sprinted in the opposite direction.

The next bullet found her right calf, and she went down hard, rolling from the trail and into a thicket of brambles and tall weeds. She crawled like a wounded soldier over jagged deadfall, away from her attacker, but it was futile.

He was on her in seconds, his knee on her back, her face pressed to the ground, the mask inches from her ear, his deep, familiar voice, "Remember me?"

CHAPTER

2

WHO IS MALLARD Malone, anyway?

This was what Sam Harper thought as he entered his childhood home and noticed the stack of hardcover Mallard Malone novels on the end table beside his father's recliner.

He called out, "Hey, Dad, it's me," over the sound of The Who's *Tommy* coming from the kitchen, but his father didn't answer. Dr. Trevor Harper liked his music loud when he cooked, and it smelled like chicken alfredo, his son's favorite.

Sam had never been drawn into the global hype of who exactly Mallard Malone was, other than an unknown novelist probably sitting on enough money to support a small country, but the question had been on Sam's mind of late.

Who *was* Mallard Malone?

The question popped up organically, even with the most who-gives-a-shit readers out there, upon the publication of each subsequent Mallard Malone novel, of which there were now seven, with an eighth and final book quickly approaching.

But why was there a stack of Mallard Malone novels in his father's house?

Dr. Trevor Harper, a fifty-year-old history professor at the University of Louisville, was an avid reader, but he despised popular fiction in general and the Mallard Malone novels in particular, even though, to Sam's knowledge, he'd yet to read that first page.

Sam didn't care one way or another; he wasn't necessarily a Mallard Malone fan either. He'd hurried over with fresh career news that had him busting at the seams, but seeing the stack of Mallard Malone novels had been jarring enough to give him pause.

Pinball Wizard played loudly from the kitchen.

It was one of a million songs that, to Sam, encapsulated his childhood.

He'd grown up in a music-lovers household, but since his mother's death sixteen years ago after a grueling yearlong battle with ovarian cancer, it was a rare time when his father wasn't playing music, either on vinyl from the dining room or CD in the five-disc changer in the living room, or, of late, Alexa in the kitchen. Sam chalked it up to his father's perpetual loneliness without her, and the fact that any type of *quiet* made his father sad.

Sam had warned his dad he couldn't stay long, but wanted to tell him the news in person, and agreed to stay for a quick dinner. Sam had spent the five-mile drive from his apartment contemplating how best to break the news to his father, who not only wished his son had chosen a career other than filmmaking but had already made his feelings on Sam's latest project quite clear.

Sam, nothing good can come from doing a documentary on Sal Batise, his father had said of the former cult leader, sociopath, and rumored cannibal. *Nothing good can come from you diving too deep into that cesspool of filth and senseless carnage*, he'd said, with venom Sam still didn't understand. *And*, his father added, *too many sensationalized documentaries have already been done on the man, and . . . and done poorly, I might add, because no one, even after going through the countless hours of taped interviews with that monster, can decipher what's true and what's not, Sam, because there has never been a better liar who ever walked the earth.*

His father wasn't wrong.

Sal Batise, a.k.a. the Kentucky Cannibal, the Breaker of Chains, may have admittedly drawn inspiration from the infamous cult leader

Charles Manson, but it was the opinion of most that Sal, on his near two-decade stint on death row, had not only surpassed even Manson in his innate ability to so convincingly lie in front of a camera, but in every sensationalized way possible.

But shit was about to get real, Sam thought, suddenly hesitant to enter the kitchen, where Pete Townsend and Roger Daltry brought back comfortable feelings of nostalgia, of home, a sensory embrace of safety he could easily bury himself into and under, if only to escape the anxiety now suddenly hitting him like a ton of bricks. The realization that, yes, he might be in way over his head, and what was he thinking, reaching out to the state penitentiary about that asinine contest?

Because deep down, you didn't think they'd respond.

Deep down, you were hoping *they wouldn't respond.*

Because there was no way in hell Sal Batise would pick you over a real news network.

And now what, Sam?

In less than twenty-four hours, he'd be sitting face-to-face with a bona fide monster, the man who, upon his arrest at his Freedom Ranch, had taken the time as the authorities drove down the meandering gravel driveway of his wooded property to spray paint in red the words *The Kentucky Cannibal Was Here* above the stove, where a certain and now infamous "stew" was cooking in an old Teflon pot.

Sam's hands started shaking. His heart raced. He was no longer nervous about telling his father the news but terrified of what might happen tomorrow, on the very day Sal was set to be killed, at midnight. Sal was anything but predictable; he'd grown up early, on the streets, and whether or not he'd been born with hints of it, his life had helped turn him into a well-seasoned psychopath by his midtwenties, which was Sam's age now.

Twenty-six years old and a late bloomer at every stage of his life.

Sam forced his feet to uproot from the carpeted living room floor. His reasons for hurrying over were multipronged, with the *I-told-you-so* being the least of them. And it had nothing to do with his father not believing in him; his father had *always* supported him, even his filmmaking, but as more of a hobby, something to do on the side while he pursued a more stable career. But it was news of *this* current project, a documentary Sam had been working on for nearly a year now because of his infatuation with Sal Batise and his cult, that had Sam on the verge of throwing up. He'd only decided on a title for the doc on the drive over: *The Last Interview.* It was perfect, right? He knew what his father would say.

But do I tell him right away? Do I wait until we're eating? Wait until we clear the table?

"Hey, Sam, I didn't hear you come in."

Sam looked up from the Mallard Malone novels.

Trevor Harper stood in the threshold to the kitchen, wiping his hand on a dish towel, dressed like he always did, a button-down shirt rolled to the elbows and tucked into jeans, a worn belt cinched to a hole he'd had to add to the leather with a knife.

"Hey, Dad." Sam gave him a quick hug and let go. Unlike Sam, who stood close to six feet tall and 180 pounds, his father was a small man at five foot five, thin-framed, and a 150 pounds fully dressed. "Smells good."

"You sounded excited over the phone," Trevor said, "and I thought, better make his favorite. It's been a while, right?" Sam couldn't tell if that was a jab at him and instantly got him wondering how many days it had been since he'd visited. The guilt came fast when his father patted his shoulder and said, "I know how busy you are, son."

And it dawned on Sam that it hadn't been days, but longer. "Yeah, still no excuse." He followed his father into the kitchen and sat in one of the four chairs positioned around the square wooden table at the bay window, where Trevor ate all his meals, overlooking a small vegetable garden he tended to daily. The dining room had been used maybe five times since Annie Harper had passed away, not so much because the three of them often ate there, but more so, at least from what Sam could remember from his early childhood, that they'd had more parties when his mom was alive. He could vividly remember the dining room filled with music and drinks and laughter, all ghost swirls of memory, but as readily there as the dust bunnies now coating the baseboards.

His father put a full plate of pasta in front of him, poured two glasses of red wine, and joined him across the table. "Cheers."

They didn't clink glasses, but his father made eye contact before digging in.

Sam watched him eat. For a small man, he could put the food away, eating with gusto to perhaps mask the elephant in the room, which made Sam think his father already had an idea what the news might be. Or, at least, what the news was about—the hated documentary.

For the same reason, Sam had lost his appetite. He took periodic bites and engaged in awkward small talk. "Grass looks good."

"Cut it yesterday." His father wiped his mouth with a cloth napkin and took a swig of wine. God love him. But his father was a man of such monotonous routine and simplicity that Sam often couldn't help thinking of him as anything but boring. Trevor Harper continued, "Got a new mower. Self-propelled. Practically runs itself."

"Where was that when I used to cut it?" Sam asked jokingly.

To which Trevor shrugged, dug back into his plate of pasta, and continued the small talk—about their hot, rainless August, about the addition he wanted to put on a deck Sam already thought was too big, about the stack of Mallard Malone novels next to his recliner, about which his father said, "I finally caved, just wanted to see what all the hype is about." Which Sam didn't believe for a minute. And then in a quick subject change, his father asked about Sam's latest online date that, to Sam's chagrin, didn't lead to a second, before telling Sam about a new course he was teaching in the fall on how Nazi Germany turned ordinary men and women into murderers.

Sam wondered if that was his father's way of segueing into whatever his news was. Of casting the line and trying to hook him with the passive-aggressive bait Sam was accustomed to. His father had, more than once, drawn the correlation between how Hitler had brainwashed so many to murder, just as Charles Manson had done with his cult, albeit on a much smaller scale, culminating in the Tate-LaBianca murders. Just as Sal Batise had done with the even more gruesome Hawthorne murders decades later.

His father stood from the table and carried his empty plate to the sink.

Sam stared at his father's back as he rinsed the plate under the tall swan-necked faucet. This was another way he had of opening the door, turning away so two introverts wouldn't have to look at each other at the start of what Sam knew could be an uncomfortable conversation.

And Sam went for it. "I reached out to the Tree House, Dad. I entered that contest, for the interview." His father, the last time they'd spoken over the phone, had called that contest *the dumbest fucking thing I've ever heard of.* Proof that Sal Batise, even behind bars, was still pulling strings. When Trevor Harper didn't answer, Sam felt the need to explain. "The Tree House. That's the nickname for the State Peni—"

"I know what it is," Trevor said abruptly.

"In Twisted Tree," Sam finished, deflated. His father added Dawn to the running water, making suds, and busied himself with the dishes. Sam said, "I didn't think I'd hear back. It was such a long shot. But I did." When his father didn't respond, he added, "He picked me." Sam let out a nervous laugh. "They gave me permission to interview him, Dad. Sal Batise. One last interview, on the day he's to die. I know you don't approve of the doc—"

"Are you going to do it?" his father asked, interrupting him.

Sam saw the tension in his father's shoulders, heard the anxiety and anger in his voice as suds grew in the sink. "Yeah . . . tomorrow morning."

Sam watched his father, waited as his old man said nothing and instead continued with the dishes, even though they had a perfectly fine dishwashing machine right next to him.

Even during his teen years, when the two of them standing side by side at the sink might have been construed by his classmates as dorky or uncool or whatever, for them, it was always a time of meaningful conversation. Doing the dishes was something they'd done together since Sam was a little boy. He had only been ten when his mother passed away, but one of his more indelible memories was seeing his parents at the kitchen sink, the glow from the evening's twilight framing them like a painting as his father washed and his mother rinsed, as their post-dinner ritual, the two of them talking, laughing, occasionally flicking suds on each other—what Sam, in hindsight, would later realize was flirting. Sam recalled a morning in the weeks after his mother's funeral, after the dishes had been piling up for days, when he'd entered the kitchen to find his father quietly sobbing at the sink, the spot beside him vacant. Sam had grabbed a stepping stool from the pantry, placed it beside his father, and without preamble stepped up and started handing him the dirty plates and bowls and cups they'd neglected for days. His father, as if by rote, wordlessly began stacking the dirty dishes to his left while Sam squirted liquid soap into the sink and billowy suds started to form, and soon doing the dishes also became *their* thing too.

Sam stood from the table, carried his plate to the counter, and made as if to take his spot beside his father at the sink, but before he could get into position, his father said, "I think you should leave."

"Dad? Really?"

And Trevor Harper, who had never raised his voice at Sam in all their years, howled without looking at his son, "I said go!"

Sam thought about arguing, because this wasn't fair. But, like his father, Sam Harper wasn't a fighter. Not only was it not fair, but so over-the-top, in Sam's opinion, that his father's reaction didn't make any rational sense. Hating Sal Batise for what he did was one thing, but this, as far as Sam's filmmaking career, was a game changer. A chance of a lifetime. While Sal Batise had given a dozen high-profile interviews during his time on death row, it had been nearly ten years since his last one, which had been with CNN on prime time and ended abruptly with Batise refusing to answer a question about being referred to as the Kentucky Cannibal. And he swore he'd never give another.

And while this interview was intended for the documentary alone, and Sam didn't even know now if it would end up being on live television or not, the fact that a twenty-six-year-old no-name filmmaking upstart had managed to snag an interview on the day Batise was set to be killed was big-time news. Why couldn't his father see that?

Sam backed away slowly, as if to give his father a chance to reconsider, to come to his senses. But instead of doing the dishes, Trevor watched out the window above the sink, to the house next door, where their neighbor Lizzie Hall sat on the top step of her concrete porch, battling her own emotions as she gazed out toward the street.

His father's right hand was clenched into a fist.

Sam said, "You're in love with a married woman, Dad. You know that, don't you?"

He didn't think his father's fist could clench any tighter, but it did, his knuckles so white it looked like they might pop through the freckled skin. Sam knew he shouldn't have said it. He'd had no right to go there, didn't matter that it had been on his mind now for years, and recently, on the tip of his tongue—the fact that, for his father, seeing Lizzie Hall, whether it be for a quick chat over the fence line or her bringing over a plate of cookies or brownies she'd just baked, never failed to bring about a smile on his face. And that was no easy task.

But on the heels of Sam's humiliation and disappointment, it just came out. You didn't have to be a fighter to deliver a low blow. Lizzie was crying out there, which wasn't uncommon. And it appeared she had a bleeding cut over her left eye, along with a visible bruise. Unfortunately, those weren't uncommon either. Her husband, Jake, was probably inside their home right now, pacing, slowly coming down from whatever burst of rage he'd been in to have Lizzie outside looking like she did.

The sight of all of it pissed Sam off so much, he couldn't stop the next words flowing from his mouth. "At least I'm not all talk, Dad."

CHAPTER

3

TREVOR HARPER STOOD frozen at the sink until he heard Sam's car start up outside.

The front of the car scraped the curb at the end of the driveway, which told Trevor that Sam was backing out too fast. It wasn't the way he'd taught him as a sixteen-year-old, when Trevor had been on pins and needles every time Sam got behind the wheel. That anxiety hadn't waned with time. He'd also told Sam to never drive angry, but here they were, both fuming, him still clenching his fist and Sam speeding away with angry tires.

They didn't argue often, and things rarely, if ever, got heated, but when they did, silence prevailed after, sometimes for days, because neither of them knew how to break it, the result of their innate inability to simply speak their minds.

Except Sam had certainly spoken his just now, and the truth of it had hit home so hard it hurt more than just his heart, but rattled his bones and sent sparks of unease flashing across his vision as he watched Lizzie Hall out the window, her eyes following Sam's car as it backed out of the driveway and sped down the street. Her eyes then briefly captured Trevor's in the window, as if she'd known he'd been watching her all along. She waved, but it was quick and hard to read, and only then did he unclench his fist and wave back, but of course by then she'd already stood from the porch and retreated toward the door of her own house. He couldn't take his eyes away from the curves beneath her cut-off jeans shorts, not because he was a pervert or a voyeur but, because, goddammit, Sam was right. Lizzie was at least ten years younger than him, but he had feelings for her, and they were strong, and he wasn't man enough to do anything about it. Plus, he had no right. As madly dysfunctional and violent as their relationship seemed to be, Lizzie and Jake Hall were married.

So, what good would it do?

And what would Annie think? Even sixteen years gone, what would Annie Harper think of his eyes finally roaming again, of his heart finally warming again?

Trevor turned away from the sink and the window because both were too chock full of bad memories. But what had him reaching for the wine bottle and refilling his cup with merlot had less to do with Lizzie Hall than Sam would ever know.

At least, he hoped Sam would never know.

Because there was so much Sam *didn't* know.

He should have been happy for his son, the potential career break of a lifetime, but all Trevor felt was fear.

No, the word *fear* was too simplistic; he was terrified.

Oh, Sam, if you only knew what you were about to do.

Trevor drank a large gulp of wine and closed his eyes as it warmed his chest. He considered turning *Tommy* back on and listening to The Who as he did the dishes, but he knew that would only be stalling. What Sam didn't know was that Trevor's mind had been completely preoccupied even before the phone call, and that had everything to do with what Sam had mentioned during dinner and Trevor had, he hoped, cleverly evaded—the stack of Mallard Malone novels beside his recliner.

Trevor had meant to hide them before Sam arrived, but Sam's *I'll be right over* rarely meant he'd be right over, and he'd thought he'd have more time.

Of course he'd hurried over, Trevor thought after another gulp of wine, he couldn't wait to tell his stubborn father the news—that his documentary on Sal Batise was indeed a tree that could bear fruit. *He couldn't wait to see me proud*, Trevor thought, hating himself more with every passing minute for not giving his son that. *You squashed the opportunity with perfect clarity, Professor.*

He finished the wine, poured more, and took the glass with him into the living room, where his recliner awaited. Where the seven Mallard Malone novels waited. What Sam hadn't seen, apparently, was the box they'd arrived in, resting empty now at the foot of his recliner.

A box with no return address, the only marks on it at all being his name in black Sharpie: *Professor Harper.* That was enough to tell him it was possibly from a student, and by the scrawl of letters, he could tell it had probably been written by a girl, knowing, by that point, to a near certainly who it was—the clever young woman with the strawberry blond hair from his World War II Foreign Relations class, who had, near the end of spring semester, despite the fact that she'd always sat in the front row making periodic eye contact, finally approached him after a lecture to ask him what she must have been wanting to ask for much of the semester.

Do we know each other? She'd asked him the final week of school.

And his clumsy response had been, *Of course we know each other, you've been in my class since January, Miss Daley.*

Then what's my first name? She'd asked with a smile.

Jennifer, he'd said too quickly, much too quickly, because while they didn't know each other exactly, he knew who *she* was—he'd noticed her the first day of the semester—and at that moment instantly feared she'd one day recall who *he* was. So, when she'd finally come up to him with her question—*Do we know each other?*—Trevor had panicked, just as he'd warned himself not to do if Jennifer Daley were to ever approach him outside the boundaries of class.

Because there's no way she could remember, right?

If only she would have left it at that. If only she'd taken him at his word, however false it had been, and let it go. But she hadn't. The next class she'd confronted him again, hammering it home how distinctly she remembered his face from somewhere, specifically his narrow blue eyes. And even as a line of eager students with real questions waited behind her in the lecture hall, she'd continued with what to him seemed like an interrogation but was really only one more question—*Who do you think Mallard Malone is, Professor Harper?*

He'd tried to play it off, laughing as he'd said, *Well, I wouldn't have the foggiest clue, Miss Daley, as I've never read those books.* Quickly adding, *And I don't plan to.*

He assumed she'd asked because the name of the anonymous author had come up during class and Trevor Harper had scoffed at the mere mention of him. Or her. Or they, or them, or who really knew.

Why not? She'd asked, following in his wake even as he'd turned from the podium. *Why wouldn't you ever read them?*

Because I don't read popular fiction, he'd answered over his shoulder, again with that nervous hitch in his voice, crushing any attempt at nonchalance.

And then she'd gone right for the jugular. Wait . . . *Are you?*

Am I what?

Are you . . . Mallard Malone?

Now *that* had caught him off guard, and he'd had no problem unmasking his genuine shock over the question. *No, dear*—and in hindsight, if he'd done anything wrong, he wished he hadn't said *dear*—*I am certainly not Mallard Malone.* Instead of leaving it at that, he'd had to ask: *Why would you ever think that? I've seen the numerous lists of guesses of possible authors over the years, and I can tell you I've never come close to landing on any of them. I don't even write fiction.*

But you do write, she'd responded.

I've published one book, fifteen years ago, on the rise of Nazi extreme groups.

I know, Jennifer Daley had said so matter-of-factly it had frozen him. *I just finished reading it. And that's why I asked the question. There are similarities in how you described the nineteen twenties and thirties in Germany with some of the white nationalist groups now, with the nation-building in Mallard Malone's fantasy novels. There are many similarities between Adolf Hitler and Mallard Malone's main character*

Oliver Crown, who, in my opinion is both the protagonist and antagonist.

To which he smiled and said, *I'm sure this Oliver Crown is quite the character, but all this seems like a stretch. Although I've never heard anyone refer to Hitler as the protagonist type.*

To his followers he was, she'd said. *Until of course, he wasn't. You should read the novels. You'll notice the similarities.*

Coincidence, I'm afraid.

You refer to Hitler and the Nazis as a cult . . . in your book.

And your point?

Most Mallard Malone enthusiasts believe the apocalypse and genuine breakdown of the world order in those novels happened because of a cult. At least that's what they predict will be unveiled in the final book. I mean, Book One. You know the books are written in reverse order, that the timeline goes backward?

So I've heard.

And we'll finally learn how Oliver Crown became the evil leader he is. You do know who Oliver Crown is?

I don't live under a rock, Miss Daley. I hear he's the most popular fictional character since Harry Potter.

He hoped her pause meant she was finished, but it only proved to be a diving board into her next question. *You know who else was in a cult? Sal Batise*, she said. Professor Harper smiled, as if amused, but he was fighting the fury bubbling up from the pit of his stomach—it had only been a few days since his son had finally told him about the documentary he'd been working on, and the revelation, with him, was still raw. And as if reading his mind, she said, *I heard your son is doing a documentary on him.*

Is that so?

Word gets around.

I don't see your point, Miss Daley.

If anyone knows about cults, it would be Sal Batise. He seems to know a lot about everything . . . You know, "Just Ask Sal"?

He knew all about "Just Ask Sal." Batise was popular for many reasons, most of them horrible, but in his four stays of execution, he'd conveniently told authorities each time, and in the final days before he was set to die, where a missing person's body could be found buried. Each time, bodies were found, and families of the missing gained closure. And while Sal swore up and down that he had nothing to do with said bodies being in the ground, his answer to the inevitable question—*How did you know the body was there?*—was always the same: *Little birdie told me.* Bottom line was that Sal Batise showed an uncanny ability to simply know things no one else did, as well as an even more uncomfortable ability, nearly on par with *The Simpsons* TV show, to predict things that had yet to come, whether it be sports games or stock market swings or future presidents—he predicted President Trump from his death row isolation unit as early as 2008—or the scoop on P-Diddy years before it started to come out. And it didn't take long for the meme "Just Ask Sal" to start all over the internet.

But Trevor Harper didn't know what this had to do about anything now, and said to Jennifer Daley, *I still don't see your point with all this.*

I don't really know anymore, she'd said. *It's just that . . . I'm not sure why no one has ever thought to ask him before.*

I don't have an answer to that. He showed her a kind smile and said, *Now if you'll excuse me,* and sidestepped her on the way to the next student in line, one whose name he did not know but who had a genuine question about the final exam. Meanwhile, Jennifer Daley walked out of the lecture hall with a clearly prideful bounce in her step.

For nearly two months now, Trevor had managed to push the lecture hall encounter to the back of his mind, not forgetting her entirely—that, for reasons Jennifer Daley would never know about, would have been an impossibility—but at least enough so he didn't think about it daily anymore.

Until the box had arrived on his porch hours ago.

The quick knocking on the door had drawn his attention from the model airplane he'd been working on in the dining room—a replica of the RAF's Spitfire. But by the time he'd opened the front door, secretly hoping it would be Lizzie from next door asking to borrow an egg or some sugar, whoever had knocked had already run off, or driven off—there had been a small red car turning the corner down the street—and at his feet was a cardboard box with his name on it. He'd carried it inside and opened it immediately, knowing even more immediately who it was from, and here he was now, swallowing the rest of the merlot in his glass in a pathetic attempt to conjure the strength to open that first book.

Or Book Eight, rather, he thought, as he opened the cover and turned the page and read the first line—*Oliver Crown was a man of faith but believed in no God*—him thinking all over again, how stupid this all was.

A heavy stack of commercially written crap.

A series in reverse order.

The final book coming soon from an author whose identity was still unknown.

It was a gimmick, and nothing more. Mallard Malone was out there somewhere, laughing on a pile of money.

But why had Jennifer delivered these books now, weeks after their conversation?

Trevor Harper read the first page with the utmost skepticism, but was soon turning page after page, his narrow blue eyes tracking words and lines and paragraphs as rapidly as if following the flight of a dazed gnat, his mind as glued to the story now as so many millions of others across the globe had been for nearly a decade.

But, he thought, as a stab of recognition coursed through him as powerfully as a lightning strike, for a very different reason.

CHAPTER

4

SAM FOUGHT NAUSEA as he drove home.

He nearly pulled over twice in fear of throwing up inside his car. He held the steering wheel as tight as vise grips to quell the shaking in his arms.

At least I'm not all talk, Dad.

He couldn't believe he'd said it. He and his father had said things to each other they probably shouldn't have over the years, but they'd never gotten cruel.

And that had been cruel.

But it was true, right? If his father had said it once—*if that son of a bitch hits her one more time, I'm going over*—he'd said it a hundred times, about Lizzie Hall and her abusive firefighting husband, Jake, who Sam knew could pummel Trevor Harper with one punch. But still? Either shit or get off the pot.

Be a man, Dad. Sam laughed as he drove, but with tears in his eyes because that was like the pot calling the kettle black. What did that even mean, *be a man*? Did it mean tough? Did it mean restraint? It was extra ironic now, as he recalled the drunken conversation he'd had with his roommate Carl and a group of their friends last week, over which of them was the most and least manly of their crew—and they'd all hands-down voted Sam Harper as the least.

As he drove, Sam recalled the one time, several years ago, his father had at least tried to stand up to Jake Hall. The morning after a time when the cops had been called, when Trevor had gone out to get the morning paper and on his way in saw Jake on their front porch drinking coffee. Sam had eavesdropped, listening to their brief conversation through the screen window, and his antenna had immediately gone up because neither he nor his dad had ever said more than a few words to the uber alpha male, Jake Hall. Jake, unprompted as far as Sam knew, saying, *I see you watching our house, Travis.* And Sam's father at least having the balls to say, *It's Trevor.* And then going another notch by adding *Dr. Trevor Harper, actually*, like he was trying to intimidate the big goon with his brains.

And then his father must have somehow conjured the nerve to ask, *Everything okay over there, Jake?* Sam thinking, at the time, *No, everything's not okay, Dad. He beat the shit out of her again and the cops came and the question you should be asking is why Jake Hall is still there drinking coffee and not behind bars by now.* That was also the instant Sam realized his father cared more than just for Lizzie Hall's well-being, because it then really dawned on Sam how often his father *did* glance at their house, how often he'd look out the window whenever Lizzie Hall was out in the yard, or watch the front of the house every time he got out of his car after returning home from work or the grocery or wherever, like he was secretly hoping she'd come out right then and there and say, *Hello, Trevor. Or hey, Trev. Or howdy do, Professor Trevor Harper, you studly little man.*

Sam pulled into the parking lot of his apartment complex and recalled how that conversation between his father and Jake Hall had gone that day—with Jake warning the professor to *mind his own fucking business and to not play hero*, and then adding, *Although I doubt heroes even come in pint-size.*

Guilt came at Sam with enough force to make him nauseous again.

He parked his blue Honda Civic beside the apartment pool and hurried across the lawn toward the outdoor stairwell that led to the second-floor apartment he shared with Carl, now going on two years. His father that day, completely unaware Sam had heard it all through the window, had stormed back inside to mind his own fucking business, just as Jake Hall had warned him, taking his anger out on the drawers and cabinets as he opened and closed them preparing for dinner, mumbling under his breath, *I'll show you heroes come in pint-size, you ignorant fucking ape. Roger Daltry is five foot seven. Paul Simon five three. Prince was five two. Bono, five six, Michael Stipe, fine nine . . .*

And he just kept going on naming short rockers.

Thinking of his dad mumbling the names that day made Sam feel sorry for him.

But Trevor Harper's reaction back at the house today had been bizarre, nothing he'd ever expect from his father.

He'd expected a reaction, probably negative, because what parent would want their kid, no matter their age, within striking distance of Sal Batise? But kicking him out had been over-the-top. Sam understood it, a little—his father's generation, especially the locals, had lived through it all, the proximity of the cult and the madness that climaxed the night of the Hawthorne murders. The men and women and children of that generation had lived it through the news, through stories and gossip and rumors to firsthand accounts of what had gone on for nearly two years inside the cult ranch now infamously known as Freedom. Most from his father's generation knew someone who'd lived there, or someone who knew someone who'd lived there, or had known one of the eight who'd died there trying to defend it on the day the authorities had moved in with full riot gear, what Sal Batise, in an interview with NBC years later, had called *foreign military invading his sovereign territory.*

Sam opened the door of his apartment planning on grabbing a beer from the fridge and taking it to his room to regroup while he drank it. It wasn't a shock to find Carl on the end of the sofa facing their big screen TV—he'd been in the same spot when Sam left earlier, in a D&D T-shirt and '90s basketball shorts that landed below his knees—but the young woman on the other end of the couch was unexpected, and about as jarring as seeing the Mallard Malone novels inside his father's house. The girl stood immediately upon Sam's entrance. She was tall, five nine, at least, Sam thought, with striking green eyes and curly strawberry blond hair gathered loosely in a braid that rested atop her bare left shoulder. Her skin was tan enough to make a strong contrast against the white spaghetti straps of her crop top. He caught himself staring at her long legs and black-painted toenails, and feared she had too; when their eyes met, neither of them looked away, but unlike her, he felt himself blushing like he always did in the company of an attractive female, someone he immediately tagged as out of his league.

Carl, without moving from his end of the sofa, said, "Sam, meet Jennifer. Jennifer, Sam." And then he grabbed his laptop from the cushion beside him and started in on his work, which must have been what he was doing before Jennifer arrived.

Jennifer stepped closer, offered her slender hand; her fingernails were painted to match her toes, except each black nail had a distinct dot in the middle, all colored like the colors of the rainbow. He shook her extended hand and worried his palm was too sweaty.

"Jennifer Daley," she said.

Sam said, "How long have you known Carl?"

She glanced over her shoulder toward his roommate. "Ten minutes."

Carl, without looking up from his typing, said, "True." And then, "She's here to see you, bro."

"I wanted to talk to you about your documentary on Sal Batise?" she said.

"Uhm . . . yeah," Sam said hesitantly, not wanting anyone to know yet he was going to interview the man in less than twenty-four hours, and wasn't close to being prepared.

"Carl here told me you're actually interviewing him tomorrow?"

Sam flashed Carl a *what-the-fuck* look.

Carl shrugged, resumed typing. "Sorry, man. Just came out. I have no filter when it comes to attractive women. My brain goes to complete mush."

"How flattering," Jennifer said, seemingly amused, but without taking her eyes from Sam. She was waiting for an answer.

"Yeah . . . it's true." He couldn't deny it now. "Ten o'clock tomorrow morning."

"That's like . . . incredible," she said. "So, you won that contest?"

"If that's what you want to call it, yeah."

"Do you mind if we talk?"

"Isn't that what we're doing?"

"She means without me, bro," Carl said. "Maybe show her the balcony. It's either that or your bedroom cuz I'm firmly planted on this couch for the day."

Sam said, "He works remotely."

"I work from this cushion, bro," Carl said.

Sam looked to his right, where a sliding glass door that was perpetually off the slider was already half-open and crooked in the frame. A humid breeze filtered in. He gestured for her to follow him toward the tiny balcony beyond.

When Jennifer headed that way, Carl said, under his breath, to Sam, "Offer her a drink, dumb-fuck."

Jennifer was already out on the balcony, hands on the rail, watching over the in-ground pool below.

Sam called out, "You want a drink or something?"

"Got beer?" she asked without turning around. "Amazing view out here."

Sam couldn't tell if she was being serious. He and Carl spent a lot of time out there, camped out in the two mesh lawn chairs that barely fit in the six-by-four–foot platform, with a cooler of iced beer wedged between them, but it was far from an amazing view. The pool was big, with plenty of chairs around it, and the water looked clean, but the pool lining, Carl liked to say, looked like it had leprosy. Sam grabbed two Landshark bottles from the fridge, popped the tops, and met Jennifer Daley out on the balcony. He handed her a beer. She clinked her bottle with his like they were friends, and the casual move helped calm his nerves.

He glanced over his shoulder toward the glass door behind him. "Door's broken."

"I see that." She swallowed from the bottle and stared at him, like she was analyzing him from head to toe, not too unlike he'd visually done with her upon entering the apartment, but somehow her doing it didn't seem improper. Maybe she thought he dressed like a dork, in his cargo shorts and threadbare Led Zeppelin T-shirt and flipflops, and then that made him wonder what he was going to wear tomorrow at the prison. He must have passed her quiet analysis, because she returned her focus back to the pool, where two college-age girls had just walked through the creaky metal gate to sunbathe. Jennifer said, "You saw the news today? About the governor's wife?"

"Saw it on Instagram."

She chuckled. "That where you get your news?"

"Better than TikTok."

"Fuck TikTok," she said. "And Twitter."

"You mean X?"

"Fuck X," she said. "Fuck all them, actually."

"Either way," he said, taking a drink of his beer. "It's terrible. I heard one security guard dead?"

"And Beth Hawthorne is missing," Jennifer said. "I can't stop thinking about it."

"Do you know her, the governor's wife?"

"More like the governor is *her* husband," she said, with venom, and then she softened her tone after another swig of beer. "No, I don't know her. But I'd like to. She was always kind of a role model, you know, from afar. She has a lot of fans out there." They both watched the pool water for a few seconds, and then Jennifer said, "You think Batise had anything to do with it?"

"With what happened to Beth Hawthorne?"

"Yeah, that," she said. "Don't tell me it hadn't crossed your mind."

It honestly hadn't; he'd been so engrossed in the sudden news of the interview that he hadn't had time to focus on anything else.

She said, "You know he has a history of delaying his inevitable death. He has something up his sleeve, you watch."

"He lives every day in an isolation unit with no access to the outside world," Sam said, hearing the naivety in his own words.

"He spins a wide web, Sam."

She said his name with such ease it was like they'd known each other for years.

"Ask him," she said.

"Ask him what?"

"Ask him tomorrow, since you're about to become the man of the hour, if he had anything to do with what happened at the governor's mansion this morning," she said. "I'd ask him first thing. Boom. Right out of the gate. Mention Beth Hawthorne being abducted on her morning run. On the grounds of her own home. I think this is all some stunt."

They drank beer through a good thirty seconds of silence before he gathered the courage to ask, "Is that why you're here?"

"Is what why I'm here?"

"The interview? You want to sneak in a few questions?"

She watched him long enough to make him uncomfortable.

"What?"

"No," she said. "But that should be one of your questions. NBC would do it. CNN would do it. Fox would—"

"Fine," he said. "I get it."

"And if you can remember back to when we met ten minutes ago, I had no clue about the interview until your roommate told me."

"Carl."

"Carl, fine. Whatever," she said. "I mean, I knew about the potential interview itself, who didn't know, unless you're living under a rock. Even social media wasn't wrong on that, but I had no clue it would be *you*." She sipped her beer, watched him. "No offense." She turned back toward the pool. "I know your dad. That's really why I'm here."

Sam digested this. "How do you know my dad?"

"I was in his class last semester."

"History major?"

"Not really," she said. "I graduated from SCAD a year ago, in Savannah. I'm an artist."

"No shit."

"No shit," she said. "Does that surprise you?"

"No. Just that I almost went there myself. You like it?"

"Loved it," she said. "But I'm home now."

"And taking random history classes?"

"Creeping, more like." She swallowed more beer. "You know what you want to do with your life, Sam?"

"Make films."

"I mean, like, really?"

"You sound like my dad."

"Well, I don't totally know what I want to do," she said. "But honestly, I love history. I was considering getting another useless degree, so I started scrolling through the history program at U of L. I came across your dad's professor photo and . . ."

"And?"

"I recognized him. I know him, Sam," she said. "From somewhere."

The way she said *somewhere* made Sam think she had an idea where that somewhere was, but she was maybe feeling him out and so didn't verbalize it.

"So you joined his class because you think you know him . . . from somewhere?"

She took another drink of her beer. "Have you read the Mallard Malone novels?"

A cold chill went up Sam's spine. He watched her, wondered where this was coming from, and so soon on the heels of seeing the complete series in his father's house. "I've read *Long Pale Moon*," he said. "And then the next two, I can't remember the titles."

"So you've read up to *The Pandemonium Flux*?"

"Sure."

She laughed.

"What's so funny?"

"I questioned your dad after class one day."

"About?"

"I asked him if he was Mallard Malone."

Sam nearly spat out his beer.

"Why's that so funny?"

"If you truly knew my father, you wouldn't have to ask," he said. "But why in the world would you think he might be Mallard Malone?"

"I don't know," she said, appearing defeated by something that weighed on her. "In hindsight, it was stupid. I was drawing correlations between how he spoke of Nazi Germany in class to modern-day cults. And how he wrote about it in his book."

"He's been known to do that, yes."

"And with the theories going around that Oliver Crown and that entire world Mallard Malone has created in his books, that it was all started by a cult . . ."

"I suppose we'll find out when the final book comes out," he said. "Although I've heard rumors the release date has been moved back. And that Malone hasn't even given the book to his editor yet."

"I took the entire series to your dad," she said matter-of-factly. "I placed the box on his porch, knocked on his door, and ran. I'm sure he knows it was me, though."

"I saw the books at my dad's," he said. "Why'd you do it?"

"I don't know," she said.

"You don't still think he's Mallard Malone, do you?"

"No," she said. "Just trying to stay connected, I guess."

"Why?"

"Like I said . . ."

"You think you knew him from somewhere?"

"Not just that." She turned sideways, leaned an elbow on the railing and faced him. "I'm good at reading people."

"Most artists are."

"I'd like to think I'm an expert at reading reactions, facial expressions. Like right now," she said, taking another swig of beer. "The confused look on your face tells me you're wondering where in the hell I'm going with this."

"You're not wrong."

"The day I confronted him after class," she said, "I could tell right away that he recognized me from somewhere too. He was shocked to see me."

"How so?"

"Like, even though I was trying to place him from somewhere, he knew exactly who I was. And because of it, I think he couldn't wait for me to go away. I made him nervous."

"Doesn't take much to make him nervous." Sam glanced at her; she was studying him again. He said, "What?"

"You really don't know who I am?"

"You're Jennifer Daley? Unless you were lying earlier."

She shook her head incredulously and laughed. "What kind of a filmmaker are you?"

Again, he couldn't tell if she was joking and said nothing.

"How far have you gotten in your documentary?" she asked.

"Mostly covering Sal's history, the forming of the cult itself," Sam said. "I was just starting to dive deep into the Hawthorne family when I got the email from the prison, giving me the go-ahead on the interview."

"Don't you think that's weird?"

"What?"

"I mean . . . you're a twenty-six-year-old amateur filmmaker, a virtual no-name, and you land an interview every news channel on the planet is trying to score?"

Suddenly defensive, he said, "I made a good pitch."

They both laughed at that, and Sam said, "Trust me, I've been thinking the same thing."

"And with Beth Hawthorne being one of the survivors from the cult murders back then . . . and she's suddenly missing now, like a day before he's set to be executed?"

"I'll ask him," Sam said.

"Pinkie promise."

He stuck out his right pinkie and she playfully swatted it away.

"Kidding," she said. "But seriously. Make that one of your questions."

He took a big swallow of beer, suddenly feeling the need to be tipsy. "It's gonna be a long project. The doc. There's a lot I haven't covered yet. I don't even know if I'm ready for this."

She turned toward him quickly. "You need help?" And then, "I think I can help. Okay, so I'd really like to help with this, Sam."

"The interview or the doc?"

"The doc," she said. "But both, now, I guess."

He did, he desperately needed help, but so far, he'd done it all on his own.

Unlike her, though, he wasn't good at reading people, and right now he couldn't see her angle on this. "Jennifer . . . why are you really here?"

She shrugged, watched the pool again. "So, in your doc, you haven't gotten to the part where the four children were found inside the closet of Sal's house . . . on the Freedom Ranch."

"No . . . I know about them, of course, and they're on my list to hunt down, but no, not yet. Why?"

"I'll save you the trouble of hunting one of them down."

"How?"

She looked at him like he was dense. "I was one of them, Sam. I was one of the four children locked inside that closet."

CHAPTER

5

Before

THE LITTLE GIRL didn't understand why it was called the Freedom Ranch.

She knew what it meant to be free. Birds were free. They could fly over the treetops. The deer and raccoons and squirrels were free. They could run through the woods and nobody hunted them down. Therefore the birds and the animals, aside from those that got hunted and cooked in the Kitchen House, all had their freedom.

She just didn't know what it *felt* like to be free anymore. Because even though she was only six and had only been here for a month, she knew the rules, and one of the biggest ones was that nobody was allowed to leave the Freedom Ranch.

Nobody could leave The Collective.

She knew what a prisoner was, and if you weren't free, you were a prisoner of something.

A prisoner of some*one.*

And she wasn't too young to know who that someone was—the man who lived in the main house. The man with the beard and long hair who she thought looked like Jesus and who her mother—wherever she was—thought looked like Jared Leto, the lead singer from her favorite band, Thirty Seconds to Mars.

The man with the cold blue eyes who called himself the Breaker of Chains.

The man who once told the four kids that demons lived in the woods, and to never enter them. And that the ranch was like a beehive, and they were all bees, and that bees always return to their hive.

He was the only male on the ranch with facial hair, the girl noticed, to which Markie, one of the three boys on the ranch, explained: *He's the only one allowed to, because he makes the rules*. Markie was only five and had big ears, but he seemed to know things, so she'd buddied up to him on day one. And she'd buddied up even more after he and Iris and Peter told her that anyone who goes into the woods, unless it's with a gun to hunt, never comes back. That had made her instantly sad and scared, and she'd decided right then not to tell them why she'd brought the woods up in the first place. Her mother had disappeared into the trees on their second night on the Freedom Ranch, and she'd never come back. Which meant maybe there *were* demons out there. The girl had knelt on her bed and watched out the window as her mother sprinted into the woods that night, her bright red hair trailing like fire flames, and then gone. Nobody had seen her since, although her mother's parting words were still fresh in the girl's ear, as clear as if they'd been whispered last night and not a month ago.

I think we made a mistake coming here, Jennifer, her mother had whispered, after sneaking into the children's barracks in the middle of the night. She was crying softly and looking over her shoulder every few seconds, and completely terrified of something, or someone, or all of it. *I think we made a mistake*, she said again, kissing her daughter's forehead and smoothing her hair back with a hand that shook so much the girl thought it might fall off.

And also thinking: *It wasn't my idea to come here, Mom*.

And thinking now, as she looked out the same window next to her bed at the morning sunlight and green leaves on the trees, that she definitely wasn't free.

And it *was* a mistake to come here.

She couldn't believe the rest of the kids had been here for almost two years, and they weren't frightened, or even complaining.

The morning bell chimed three times for breakfast. Unlike her three roommates, she didn't run toward the door of their barracks, even though she was starving and her stomach had been growling all night. She was too busy spying across the compound toward the main house, where the man with the beard lived. There was a boy up there in the window. She'd taken her gaze from the woods, which was where she stared every morning waiting for her mother to come back, when movement in the upstairs window of the main house had caught her eye. From her distance and vantage point, he wasn't much more than a shadow. She waved. The shadow—no, it was a boy, it was definitely a boy, and he looked their age too—raised his hand to the glass and waved back.

And then he was gone.

She imagined someone must have told him, *Get away from that window, boy, somebody might see you.* Or something like that.

And that somebody, she thought, *was me. Jennifer.* And her middle and last name had once been Rae Hamilton. Jennifer Rae Hamilton. Except once they entered the gate at Freedom, their names had gone away. All remnants of their past had to be eliminated, all ties to family and friends completely severed.

At least that's how her mother had explained it, right before she'd informed her that *her* new name was Red, which made complete sense to Jennifer, because of her hair. Although the kids were stripped of their surnames, they got to keep their first names, for now. A young, auburn-haired women who went by the name Yellow said it was because kids weren't old enough to have chosen The Collective on their own, so they weren't ready for new names. A young, dark-haired man whose name was The Raven, or simply Raven, said it was because *he* didn't like kids on the ranch at all, and that kids didn't deserve new names.

As Jennifer watched the main house, hoping the mystery boy would reappear in the upstairs window, she recalled what else The Raven had said that afternoon as a warning: *Steer clear of the main house. It isn't a place for kids.*

Jennifer had asked The Raven at that point, *If the main house is so bad, then why did I see you going in and out of it several times today?*

Business, The Raven had said bluntly, with enough sadness in his eyes to keep her from pushing for more truth.

She wondered now if the boy in the upstairs window had a name.

And what was he doing inside the main house if it wasn't a good place for kids?

Did this mean there were five kids on the ranch and not only four? But if so, why wasn't he with them in the barracks? And why was she only now seeing him, after four weeks on the ranch? And, most importantly, why hadn't her roommates told her there was another? Maybe they were liars. Unless they didn't know, in which case, she looked forward to being the bearer of interesting news at breakfast.

"Jennifer, are you coming?" Iris asked in passing.

"I'll be there in a minute," she said without taking her eyes off the upstairs window of the main house. The boy had yet to reappear, which made her wonder if indeed he had been a figment of her imagination. But she didn't think so, and she made a mental note to sketch him on her drawing pad before she went to sleep, just a quick picture of the boy standing at the window.

The door to the barracks opened and closed.

Seconds later, Markie, Iris, and Peter ran past her window outside toward the Kitchen House. Peter was last because he ran with a limp. But what he lacked in speed he made up with goofiness. He flashed Jennifer a funny face and then disappeared from her view at the window, just as the door to the barracks creaked opened again and an adult voice said, "Jennifer, you coming?"

It was Yellow.

"Yes." She hurried along to the door, grabbed Yellow's outstretched hand, and together they walked out into the warm morning sunshine.

Yellow often acted like her new mother, and Jen was grateful for it, especially now that her real mother was gone. She'd picked the name *Yellow* because it was her favorite color and it reminded her of sunshine. The name was fitting because Yellow was bright and cheery and warm, and even sometimes burning hot when she got mad, which wasn't often, and mostly at the men on the ranch, who seemed to make the rules. One of which was: *It was wrong to show anger toward another member of The Collective.* So, Yellow had to bite her tongue a lot.

Yellow was an adult but still a kid at heart. Together they skipped and swung their arms as they approached the Kitchen House. But underneath Yellow's smile Jennifer saw the same worry she'd been seeing for weeks now. The same worry Yellow only seemed to speak about to The Raven, and in whispers, and always in the shadows. Jennifer considered bringing it up, but instead stayed quiet, and stole frequent glances at the main house as they skipped along; it was the only house on the ranch that had any color other than gray. The clapboard siding had been painted deep blue but was already peeling under the sagging gutters.

The man with the beard, the man who called himself the Breaker of Chains, Jennifer thought, apparently never did any touch-ups. Maybe he wasn't even handy. And then because she couldn't hold it in, she asked, "Is there a little boy living in that house?"

"What house?" Yellow asked in return, although Jennifer knew she knew what house. She was just stalling. "The main house," Jennifer said. They'd stopped skipping. They'd stopped swinging their arms. But they continued walking with their hands locked.

"No," Yellow said, squeezing Jennifer's small hand. "No little boy lives in that house." But then, as if genuinely curious now, she said, "Why do you ask?"

"Because I saw him standing in the window a few minutes ago."

"Maybe it was the sunlight playing tricks."

"It wasn't," Jennifer said. "He waved at me."

They walked a few more steps. Jennifer felt Yellow's hand growing sweaty and warm. And when she said, "Jennifer," it sounded like she had a frog in her throat.

"Yes," Jennifer said. Yellow was still holding her hand but had stooped to eye level. Jennifer saw tears in her eyes. "Why are you crying?"

Yellow wiped her eyes and cheeks and looked at her wet fingers like she didn't know she was crying. "What did the boy look like? Jennifer? What did the boy look like?"

"He was kind of tall. He had a red shirt on."

Yellow bit her lip, closed her eyes, opened them, like maybe *He was kind of tall and had a red shirt on* wasn't the answer she was looking for. Or maybe it was, and that's why she now looked extra stressed, and her jaw was clenched so tight she could have chewed nails. She said, "Are you sure he waved to you?"

Jennifer nodded, but she was getting scared of the conversation and now wished she hadn't started it. Now she only wanted to eat breakfast.

Yellow then let go of her hand and placed both of hers on Jennifer's shoulders. "Jennifer, look at me. Was it a wave? Or did the boy place his hand on the window. On the glass." She splayed her right hand out like a starfish. "Like this. On the glass. Jennifer? It's important."

Jennifer swallowed hard. "Like that. His hand was on the glass, just like that."

"Son of a bitch," Yellow said under her breath. She wiped her left cheek with her right hand, a hand that shook as violently as her mother's hand had on the night she'd run into the woods. "Go on into the Kitchen House, Jennifer."

"What's happening?" Jennifer asked, teary-eyed now. "Did I do something wrong?"

"No, you didn't do anything wrong."

"Why are you mad? We're not supposed to show anger on the ranch."

"Just go inside, Jennifer. And tell The Raven I said to come out here. Now."

CHAPTER 6

SAM AND CARL's dining room table was a ping-pong table.

When they had parties, they'd take the net off and use it as a buffet table. He'd removed the net an hour ago to spread out the years of research he'd collected on Sal Batise.

The full names of the four children found in that closet were Jennifer Hamilton, Mark "Markie" Staphanski, Iris Erickson, and Peter Moore. After none of the parents—assumed cult members—showed up to claim their children, they all went into the system and were eventually adopted. When they'd been discovered, a dead flashlight was found inside the closet with them, and no one knew at which point during their twenty-four to thirty-six hours inside the closet things had gone completely dark for them. But the bigger story was what had been drawn on the closet wall.

"And that was you?" Sam asked Jennifer as they sorted through his research. It was a stupid question, he knew, but he had to officially confirm; it was well-known that Jennifer Hamilton, now Daley, had been the artist inside that closet, which had made her the key target for the questioning authorities.

"Yes," she said without giving him glance. "That was me. And no, I don't remember drawing it. I barely even remember being inside that closet. It was a long time ago, Sam."

They worked in silence for the next few minutes, but Sam couldn't stop thinking about that collage, or mural of sorts, authorities had found on the interior closet wall, sketches ranging from the Freedom Ranch's wooded landscape and barracks to Sal Batise's main house, and interspersed throughout were depictions of who authorities assumed were various cult members. Photographs of the lone closet wall had been in every true crime book ever written on Batise and the ranch and The Collective, and it had been analyzed to death by writers and art therapists and psychologists ever since. One aspect of the wall drawing that had always stood out to Sam were the four children drawn as stick figures inside what was assumed to be the ranch's main house. The four stick figures were the only part of the wall art that appeared to have been drawn by a child; the rest of the mural had been expertly done. That had initially caused investigators to believe one of the children maybe had drawn most of the wall while another had drawn the stick figures. But the kids had all been so shell-shocked upon being freed that they barely had any recollection of their time inside the closet, and when asked which child, if any of them, had drawn the mural on the wall, the other three all pointed to Jennifer, like they all knew they weren't supposed to draw on walls. But the real interrogation resulted from the detectives' disbelief that any of the children could have drawn something so sophisticated and intelligent, something that would later give credibility to Bethany Hawthorne's mysterious, masked attacker during the night of the massacre, who everyone now believed was a man named Justice Minks.

Sam wanted so badly to ask Jennifer about Minks, but feared her reaction, when suddenly she looked at him and said, "What's your question? I know you have one."

Sam froze like a deer in headlights.

"Sam, if we're going to work together, you can't be afraid of me."

Afraid wasn't what he felt; it was more like awe, but he couldn't admit that. They'd called her a prodigy back then, and here she was, inside his apartment. "How did you do it?" Sam asked. "I mean, the vision. The skill. You were six years old."

Jennifer said, "I don't remember much from my mom, but she liked to tell people I was born with a pencil in my hand. Although now it's a brush. I paint, mostly."

She returned to the files she'd been digging through.

Sam lifted a file that held a photocopied picture of the closet's mural and held it so Jennifer couldn't see what he was looking at. It was one of those things that once you saw it, you couldn't *unsee* it. He'd first looked at it as an eighth grader and hadn't initially seen the image of the Guy Fawkes mask staring up at him from the photograph. He hadn't even known who Guy Fawkes was, or what he looked like, and later googled the historic figure when he got home. It was only after staring at the photocopied mural inside the confines of his bedroom with the door closed that he'd finally noticed it, and he'd been mesmerized how all those smaller, individual sketches of various things could all come together to form one larger picture.

While Bethany Hawthorne had been the only survivor from the massacre to recall seeing the man in the Guy Fawkes mask that evening, no one, inside or outside The Collective, would speak to his existence at all. But the mural—and this was what had started the talk of the girl's artistic genius—held much more in store for the detectives than initially thought. At first it wasn't noticed because the closet was small, and they couldn't stand far enough away to see it, but once clear pictures were taken and studied, the mural itself, when viewed from afar, had indeed shown a creepily accurate image of the Guy Fawkes mask itself.

The detectives had been blown away at how a six-year-old could have the foresight and vision to draw *that* inside a dark closet with only the aid of a flashlight that eventually lost power. The pencil found on the closet floor had been used all the way down to within an inch of the eraser. Jennifer's fingers showed no blisters, and in fact were calloused, which told them she was no novice. She'd soon admitted to drawing the mural, but they'd gotten very little else from her after that, and as time went on, she seemed to remember and understand less of her time in that closet. But in the coming days, after searching the Freedom Ranch barracks, they'd found dozens of sketches under Jennifer's bed, many of them later used at trial, a handful ending up as vital in the defense's case on the three women known as Sal's Angels.

Sam would eventually ask about those sketches, but right now he couldn't step away from the mural in the closet. "Did you know when you started drawing on that wall, what it would look like in the end?"

"I don't remember, Sam."

"But you must have seen the man Beth Hawthorne saw the night of the massacre," he said, with caution. "I mean, you must have seen him at some point on the Freedom Ranch, to have drawn what you did. To disguise that face in those sketches."

"Yeah," she said. "That's the assumption."

"But you don't remember him?"

"Do you remember much of anything from when you were six, Sam?" She waited, then said, "I didn't think so. As time goes on, it's like those memories don't count. Whatever happened didn't happen. They aren't *me* anymore."

Sam could tell by the sorrow in her eyes that she didn't believe her own words, because those memories, for her, *did* count. *Or you wouldn't be here,* he wanted to say. But whoever it was in that mask—and most thought it was the mystery man Justice Minks—he'd had such a profound effect on her that she drew what she did in such a secretive way that few people, if any, had noticed it initially.

She'd feared that man back then and she still feared him now, and Sam couldn't let it go. "On the wall," he said, "you wrote . . . 'The Raven was here'?"

"Yes," she said. "Evidently so. And no, I don't remember who The Raven was. Or why I then must have written, 'The Raven is a liar.' Except I spelled it wrong."

"L-Y-E-R," Sam said, glancing down at the open file in his hand.

"Thanks for the reminder," she said, with a nod toward the concealed file folder in his hand. "And I know what you're looking at, dork. You don't have to hide it."

He lowered the file now that he'd been outed. "What about the stick figures?"

"What about them?"

"Why did you draw them like a normal kid would?"

"So I'm abnormal?"

"Not what I meant."

"I don't know," she said, looking away. "Maybe because we were kids and we were scared, so that's how I drew them."

"Why don't you admit you're a badass?" Sam said, unable to contain his smile.

"Same reason you don't admit you're a dork."

"But I am."

"Thank you," she said. "Is that all?"

"No."

"I didn't think so," she said. "Go ahead and ask it, Sam. The fifth child?"

"Now that you bring it up."

"Same as the rest of it," she said, in reference to what was generally thought of as an erased fifth stick figure on the wall. "I couldn't answer it then, and I can't answer that now."

It had drawn the obvious question back then over whether there had actually been five children in the closet and not just four. Or maybe it had meant there were five children on the ranch at one time, but only four remained. Regardless, it was universally agreed that there had been five stick figures on the wall and one of them at some point had been erased. "Or maybe I just lost count," Jennifer added. "Or maybe it was full dark by then."

Jennifer was right, memories from that young of an age *were* fleeting. Or maybe they'd been in full flight mode. But what most therapists agreed on was fear. The children were afraid to talk about anything pertaining to the ranch or Sal Batise. The fear of the repercussions. The fear of someone coming back to punish them. The fear of what Iris, during one interview let slip, of someone she called the bad man finding them and cutting out their tongues. When asked who the bad man was, she clammed up and never spoke of him again, and the same went for the other three children. Markie was on record in the days after their discovery saying, *We're not supposed to talk about The Collective.*

Sam asked her, "Did you really believe there were demons in the woods?"

"Look at the mural," she said in a way that made him feel stupid.

He looked down at the photocopy, although it had long ago been engraved in his mind, and the six-year-old Jennifer *had* drawn what appeared to be ghosts or demons throughout the wooded areas of the mural.

She said, "Of course I believed it."

"And now?

She looked at him incredulously. "No, Sam. I don't. Although *something* must have stolen my mother," she snapped. And they went quiet again. They both knew that no cult members or other family members ever came back to claim the four children. "But that's when I became Jennifer Daley. I was adopted into a loving family. I have two stepbrothers, and my parents are as vanilla as it gets. I'm not complaining," she said. "Could have been a lot worse."

Sam thought of his father at home, right now, and how'd uncomfortably they'd parted a few hours ago. He said, "My mom . . . she died when I was ten."

"I'm sorry." Jennifer ran her index finger through some light dust on the table. The painted dot on that black nail was purple. She blew the dust from her fingertip. "Do you remember her? Your mom?"

"A little bit," he said. "Sometimes I get out her picture and look at it so I don't forget what she looked like. She was kind. She smiled a lot."

"Yeah . . . I think my mom was too," Jennifer said. "I mostly remember her red hair. Green eyes. But she must have been pretty stupid to have brought us into that cult."

"I don't think *stupid* is the right word," Sam said. "Vulnerable, maybe. Lost. Confused."

"Okay, I get it."

She was ready to get to work, but Sam didn't feel finished with the conversation. "And you haven't . . ." He couldn't bring himself to finish the question. "Never mind."

"He's going to eat you alive and pick his teeth with your bones tomorrow, Sam." Jennifer folded her arms and stared at him, waiting as if daring him to finish the question, her black nails tapping the smooth flesh of her arm. "You can't be afraid to ask questions, Sam."

"Fine," he said. "So you haven't ever heard from your mother after that night she fled?"

"No."

"What do you really think happened to her?"

"Oooh, a quick follow-up, nicely done." She chewed her bottom lip, kept her eyes on him. "I think she couldn't take her life choices and ran. And she's a coward."

"And you haven't tried to find her?"

"No, next question," she said, snapping her fingers.

"And the other children."

"That's not a question, Sam."

"Have they heard from their parents?"

"I don't know," she said, with an expressive sigh. "I haven't spoken to them at all since then. But I've kept tabs, so when it comes time to hunt them down for the documentary, Peter is in a rehab center in Ransom. Drugs *and* alcohol. He's had a rough time of it. Markie Mark got married to his longtime boyfriend last year and they live in Lexington. And Iris is in her second year of law school in Virginia and engaged to a future doctor."

"You sound jealous."

"Wouldn't you be? And good observation. Maybe you won't totally suck tomorrow."

Sam laughed; he was starting to read her better. She was quirky and smart, and it didn't hurt that she was pretty, but her just-don't-give-a-fuck no-filter attitude made him want to hug her. He pulled his phone from his pocket. He'd felt it vibrate several times while they were talking. He'd secretly hoped he'd gotten a text from his father with a change of opinion, but the text was from Carl in the other room, close enough to them that Sam could see his legs stretched out from the sofa as he worked.

Carl had texted: Howz it going

Sam typed: good

You ask her out yet

No

If u dont I will

FU

"What's so funny?" Jennifer asked.

Sam looked up from his phone. "Just that Carl's an idiot."

"I picked up on that," she said. "But he seems like a teddy bear. I like him." She looked around the cluttered table. "I need a pen and paper."

"For what?"

"Have you even started a list of questions for Sal?"

"In my head."

"If you don't write them down, Sam, you'll freeze like a storefront mannequin when the lights come on."

He slid a pen and legal pad across the table to her. She snatched both with the graceful skill of a hockey goalie and immediately started writing questions, one after the next, and he was grateful for her proactiveness. While she wrote, and without looking up, she said, "I do remember the smell sometimes. From the closet . . . We had no choice but to piss and shit ourselves. And that's the memory that sometimes hits me. Not only the smell of that closet, Sam, but . . . shame. They might have called us heroic, but I don't think so."

"Jennifer?"

She wrote two or three questions before looking up. "What?"

"Did you know Sal?"

She seemed to be carefully thinking this over, and said, "I have a few slight memories of seeing him on the ranch. Back when he had long hair and a beard. But I don't think anyone really knew Sal Batise. Not really. And he's never shied away from talking about how he'd never wanted any kids on the ranch."

"Why?" Sam asked, although he already knew why.

"They're a distraction," she said. "From him. Because parents love their kids, and that's where their main focus would be, on their kids."

"And not him," Sam said, "the Breaker of Chains."

"The chains we forged in life, yes. You were supposedly free of them once you lived on the ranch." She wrote down another question. "Sal wanted everyone's attention and focus and loyalty directly on him."

He nodded, because that all checked out with what he'd read and presumed.

And then Carl shouted from the living room, "Dude, get in here!"

Sam and Jennifer shared a brief look before hurrying into the next room, where Carl had placed his laptop on the couch cushion beside him and had scooted up to the edge of his seat. He pointed toward the TV with the remote; it was on the local news, and Carl cranked up the volume.

"Now that's the fuck," Carl said, a phrase he'd coined years ago that still secretly annoyed Sam. "Look at you, bro."

"Holy shit," Jennifer said from beside Sam. She squeezed his arm in excitement.

Sam stood speechless, though, as he stared at his picture on the TV, one they'd dug up from his senior year at DeSales High School, in his clean white button-down shirt and brown tuxedo jacket and tie and the zit on his forehead.

The picture went away, thank God, and a brunette news anchor stood there in studio, talking about how Louisville's own young filmmaker Sam Harper had landed the coveted "last interview" with Sal Batise, who was now just over twenty-four hours away from his execution at the State Penitentiary in Twisted Tree.

On the screen, the news anchor, Shaffer Swanson, continued: "Mr. Harper will be conducting the interview with Sal Batise live tomorrow morning at ten o'clock with us here at WDRB News hosting from a designated space at the State Penitentiary."

"What?" Sam said under his breath, just as Carl said, "Now that's the fuck, bro. We gotta make sure you wear a good outfit."

And Jennifer, gently shaking his arm, said, "This is good, Sam. This is good."

Is it? Sam thought. *For who? Good for who?*

He removed the phone from his pocket. "It was supposed to be me and my tape recorder and camera. Just for the doc." He scrolled, searching for the earlier email from the prison, but it was difficult because his phone was blowing up with text messages. He didn't even know that many people. And then the first call came through from a number not in his contacts, so he let it go to voice mail. He found the original email, but it had been followed by two more he'd yet to read, both of which, as he skimmed, spelled out exactly what they'd just heard Shaffer Swanson say on television—that Sal wished for the interview to be broadcast on TV. And he'd chosen one of the local channels to *help get it out to the masses.*

Because Sal would never do anything just for the documentary, even though that had been Sam's main pitch in the letter he'd sent weeks ago—suggesting an unobtrusive conversation between just the two of them—and he assumed that's why he'd been picked.

But it was also the exact reason he figured he'd never be picked. He couldn't have been more wrong. He should have known Sal Batise would never go quietly into the night.

CHAPTER

7

HEAD SWIMMING FROM wine, Trevor Harper closed the first Mallard Malone novel, already halfway through the five hundred pages, and tossed it toward the couch cattycorner to his recliner.

He'd been reading for hours. The sun was already setting. He downed what was left in his glass of merlot and resisted going back into the kitchen for more of the second bottle he'd opened. *But it was all too much.* The morning news of Bethany Hawthorne's abduction and the murder of her bodyguard had shaken him. Sam's news about the interview had shaken him even harder. But these Mallard Malone books. *This damn novel,* he thought, staring at the back of the book jacket, where plenty of blurbs and testimonials filled the page, but no picture of the author.

Trevor couldn't read another page.

The book wasn't bad; in fact, the entertainment level was top-notch and the writing solid, but something about the world building, just as Jennifer Daley had suggested, hit too close to home, and *everything* about the language—what novelists and agents and editors would call *the voice*—made his skin crawl. Because he knew that voice. Some hidden part of him knew that voice. At least a dozen different passages, he'd looked up from the book to see his arm hair standing on end.

Because he knew. Deep down, he knew who Mallard Malone was. Or might be.

But then again, maybe he didn't. Not for sure. But he knew at least where Mallard Malone had come from. It's the only thing that made sense, and if Jennifer Daley had sent him these books, it meant that deep down she knew something too.

No, he warned himself, *don't go there, Trevor*.

There, meaning his past. Because his past wasn't pretty. His past was a story best left buried—every tragic part of it—and only Annie, God rest her soul, knew it, and she'd taken that to her grave. But even Annie didn't know *all* of it.

Trevor had been too ashamed to tell her all of it.

But if he were honest, Annie wasn't the only person who knew his past.

There were at least two more people who knew, and one of them was set to die by lethal injection at midnight tomorrow night. And the world couldn't get rid of him fast enough.

I can't get rid of him fast enough, he thought, and that was the crux of the matter. Trevor hadn't truly had a good night's sleep since Sal Batise's arrest, looking over his shoulder like he had been doing now for two decades. Even with the bastard in prison, in isolation, on death row. It didn't matter.

Only when Sal Batise was in the ground would Trevor truly be free.

But would he?

Because Sal's not the only one, he thought. Sal was a monster, but he wasn't the worst. Not by far. He grabbed his wine glass and started to tip it back again before noticing he'd already finished it. He glanced at the Mallard Malone novel he'd tossed to the couch, and thought of the main character in it, the main character in every book in the series, Oliver Crown, and he felt sick with nauseating dread. Oliver Crown might be a fictional character, but he was based on somebody. No, in fact, he knew. If not just based on one person, Trevor thought now, Oliver Crown might just be the perfect blend of two. Of *both* of them. Both of his monsters.

A memory flashed at him without warning. Him, an adult, on his hands and knees, a strong hand clutching his hair, yanking his head back and laughing, one hand forcing his mouth open while the other held the handful of . . . of . . .

Trevor pinched his eyes closed to block the rest of the memory, but it had come on so fast and strong it had brought back with it a smell, a horrid memory of a stench, and he gagged, gagged again, and . . .

. . . no . . . no please no, he pleaded in the memory, his scalp on fire from how forcefully his hair was being pulled back, straining every tendon in his awkwardly arched neck . . . and the handful of horrifying mush crept closer to his forced open mouth, both of them laughing now, and the stench . . . and that fucker's evil eyes gleaming down at him through the mask holes . . .

Trevor's eyes flashed open. He fought rapid breaths, fought the panic attack, the first he'd had in years, in sixteen years, in fact, the last one occurring in the days after Annie's death when he'd looked upon ten-year-old Sam sleeping in his bed and realized it was up to him and him alone to raise that boy now, and the pressure had come crashing down on him like a ton of bricks.

He considered calling Sam now to apologize for earlier.

He considered telling Sam that he had secrets, so many secrets no one would believe them, but with the weight of them now just under the surface, he felt like they were urgently pleading to come out.

One day when Sam was a teenager and he'd begun to grow his hair long, he'd said to Trevor, *You know, Dad, I bet you'd look good with long hair. We should grow ours out together.* It was a sweet thing to say, and Trevor had nervously laughed it off, hoping Sam would drop it, but he didn't. *Come on, Dad,* Sam said, *me and you. Let's grow it out like rock stars.*

And Trevor had overreacted so instantly he still occasionally, even years later, felt the emotional pain from it. *I'm not growing my hair out, Sam, and that's that,* and he'd stormed from the room, silently crying about it later that night inside his locked bedroom.

But he couldn't tell Sam he'd sworn to never let his hair grow out after that night on the Freedom Ranch. After that night he'd been on his hands and knees on the kitchen floor, with Minks's strong hand gripping his hair so tightly his scalp felt like it was on fire and he'd later found it crusty around some of the follicles from having bled during the worst of it. He couldn't tell Sam that. He couldn't tell him he'd never grow his hair out long enough for someone to grab again, because of that.

So he'd overreacted then just like he'd overreacted today—because PTSD is real and when it comes it hits you like a truck, with little to no warning—but he'd only acted out of love, he thought.

And ultimately, out of fear.

Constant fear.

Trevor felt the urgent need to hear Sam's voice, even if it was on voice mail. He dug around in his pockets, couldn't remember where he'd left his phone. He'd been in such a zone reading that he didn't even know what time it was. He was too buzzed to talk to Sam anyway. Maybe in the morning, after he slept this off. Sam had never seen him drunk, because it had happened only a few times in his life. Sam had rarely even seen him buzzed.

Because you don't drink that much, Trevor.

You don't fucking open a second bottle.

He leaned forward in his recliner and attempted to rub the alcohol buzz from his eyes, but that only made him dizzier when he opened them.

Dizzy and nauseous and woozy. He swallowed over the heavy lump in his throat, which was dry and felt thick and in need of another glass.

Someone knocked on the door and he nearly jumped from his seat.

For the first few steps toward the front door, he felt unsteady on his feet, but by the time he opened it, he'd somewhat regained his bearings.

He never got visitors, other than Sam, but Sam, he knew, wouldn't have knocked, even after their disagreement. He didn't expect to find his next-door neighbor, Lizzie Hall, standing on his porch, wearing the same clothes she'd had on earlier, the short, cut-off jean shorts and yellow tank top. At first, he thought he was dreaming, but he wasn't. Aside from the lurid, freshly stitched cut above her right eye, Lizzie was even prettier up close. Not only pretty, he thought, as he stood there like a fool, but innocent and plain, in that what you see is what you get kind of way, not too unlike his late wife Annie, a woman who rarely felt the need for makeup or fake nails or lipstick.

"Sorry to bother," Lizzie said. "But I think I just saw your son on TV."

Trevor did his best to sound sober, and it was only then that it dawned on him that he really was drunk. Really drunk. One bottle of wine, for him was over-the-top, but the sudden impulsiveness of downing half of another had been unnecessary and unlike him. "Hey . . . hi," he said, holding on to the door to keep steady.

"Are you okay, Mr. Harper?"

He closed his eyes, nodded, and fought back a wave of nausea.

"I tried calling," she said. "But you didn't answer."

"Phone's charging," he said, thinking, *somewhere. My phone is somewhere. And how do you even have my number?* But then he remembered, they'd exchanged numbers early on, when the Halls had first moved in, just in case of emergencies, back when Trevor had no clue that Jake Hall was such a motherfucker. Maybe he should have guessed at it, when Jake had shaken his hand that day and smiled and squeezed Trevor's hand so hard he'd felt the bones in his hands shift like they were little bird bones. It was a sign of dominance, Trevor knew, in hindsight. Like, *Feel how strong I am*, that handshake had said. *Look how much bigger my hand is than yours.* And Trevor finally said to Lizzie Hall, "Sorry . . ." And didn't know exactly what he was apologizing for.

"Are you okay?" Lizzie Hall asked again.

He smiled, hoped it didn't come off as too goofy because that's how he felt now, goofy and giddy, like he often felt when he'd first met Annie, but without the alcohol. He never thought he'd love again, and then Annie had come along.

And now . . .

Trevor forced focus. "Did you say my son?"

"Yes," Lizzie said, excited all over again. "On CNN. On Fox. On MSNBC. I had no idea he was . . . I can't believe he's going to be interviewing Batise." She paused. "Wait, you knew, didn't you? I mean . . ."

"I knew," he said. "I just didn't know it was on the news." *But I should have known*, he thought. *I should have anticipated it, and any real father would have watched it unfold* with *his son.* He looked past Lizzie Hall toward their driveway and didn't see Jake's massive truck.

"You worried about Jake?" she asked. When he didn't answer, she said, "He's at the firehouse all night. Not that it matters. Just a friendly visit between neighbors, right?"

"Yeah," he said, thinking, *Why had she even brought that up?* And then he realized she seemed as nervous as he was. And then he thought back to his son's parting jab earlier in the day, before he'd stormed off . . . *You're in love with a married woman.* And then: *You're all talk, Dad.* And Trevor Harper said to Lizzie, "You're welcome to come in for a few. I suppose we can catch up on some breaking news?"

She didn't answer verbally, but with a cautiously innocent nod and a quick glance toward her house, she stepped inside.

Trevor closed the door behind her, carefully balancing himself as he did so. His head was still swimming, and now his heart was thumping inside his chest like an enraged animal in a cage. He knew she worked but had weird hours, just like her husband, and then remembered she was a nurse. *Jesus, Trevor, how drunk are you?* He turned toward her. She was standing with her arms folded against her yellow top.

"Annie's favorite color was yellow," he said.

And she nodded, looked a little uncomfortable, and who could blame her, because what kind of icebreaker was that? Lizzie had never known Annie. Annie had been dead a couple of years before the Halls had moved in next door. And why would he need an icebreaker, anyway? Why was she even here, in his house, just the two of them? Sam. That's right. She's here because she saw Sam on the news and . . . He asked Lizzie, "Care for a glass of wine?"

She checked her watch, said without any further hesitation, "Sure. I'd love a glass."

"Merlot?"

"Perfect."

CHAPTER

8

Beth Hawthorne imagined she was floating in space.

And the sparks zipping across her blurry vision were stars and not her brain fizzling out, signs of her own imminent death.

She opened her eyes at the sound of a creaking gate.

The room was dark, but not dark like before. *You're inside a garage, Beth.* She remembered now. A thin line of daylight shone across the floor beneath the garage door.

She'd awakened hours ago inside this hot, stuffy place, handcuffed to a metal pole that stretched from floor to ceiling in the middle of the garage. Her wrists had been rubbed raw beneath the cuffs. She remembered desperately trying to escape at some point, before passing out. The blood on her wrists had clotted. The space was large and mostly empty, like it wasn't even his garage, but maybe a storage unit. But that would be stupid, keeping her in a storage unit, where so many others could be walking the premises at any point to hear her cries for help.

Her throat was raw too.

She remembered screaming until her lungs were weak, until her throat felt inflamed, and then his voice was in her ear, the mask inches away, "Scream away, Beth, nobody is gonna hear you. I promise you that."

It was revolting, hearing her name in his mouth.

And that mask. The same one he'd been wearing twenty years ago when he'd tried to kill her inside the Hawthorne mansion. If indeed it *was* the same man. But she knew it was. Had to be. His voice had changed slightly over the years, and he'd grown thicker all over, but who, after so many years of aging, hadn't changed? It was him. Unless he *had* been a ghost swirl back then, when he'd nearly killed her with the corkscrew, with her being the only survivor to remember him.

She repositioned herself on the hard floor.

Her right calf throbbed like it was on fire.

That's right, I was shot. Shot fleeing in the woods after her security guard was gunned down on her morning run. How many days ago? She heard footsteps approaching on gravel outside the garage door. Her right calf had been wrapped. Carefully wrapped. And no blood stained the bandage. A hint of hope came upon her like a blessing. If he'd taken the time to dress her wound, perhaps multiple times, it meant he might not kill her.

Not yet, at least.

But then all hope faded into an avalanche of fear, of what he could do to her while she was alive and vulnerable and chained to this pole.

The door started to open with a loud mechanical groan, his sunlit silhouette growing larger as the door rotated up into the ceiling, first revealing his boots and jeans and T-shirt and the mask on his face.

He stood there, his head angled slightly toward his left shoulder, as if analyzing her.

"Good morning, sunshine." His voice was muffled by the mask. She used her bare feet to push herself away from him, but she couldn't go far because of the pole. He pulled an overturned milk crate from the nearby wall and sat on it. His legs were long. The bottom of his jeans rose as he sat, revealing crisp, clean white socks and black hard-soled shoes. He leaned forward with his elbows resting on his knees. She'd initially wondered if this was the same person who'd nearly killed her back then. Anyone could have remembered her description of him at trial and used the same mask to scare her. But those eyes, she saw now, up close, were his.

She was sure of it now.

"You . . . know . . . my . . . name," Beth said, every word a painful exhale.

"And so you'd like to know mine," he said, his large hands hanging so casually limp from his wrists it made her want to scream. "How about you just call me Oliver."

"Oliver . . ."

He leaned closer. "Oliver Crown."

CHAPTER 9

SAM DIDN'T SLEEP all night.

After seeing his face plastered on the news, nervous adrenaline kept him awake.

He eventually turned off his phone. A half dozen neighbors from the apartment complex, none of whom he'd ever talked to but at least recognized either from bump-ins in the parking lot or laundry room or fitness area, knocked on his door to let him know he'd been on TV, or had asked him, *Was that you?*

After the sixth visitor, Carl locked the door and closed the blinds.

Sam had yet to hear anything from his father, but maybe he was knee-deep in the fictional world of Oliver Crown by now, completely unaware his son had become a celebrity overnight. But while Sam hated the sudden attention, Jennifer appeared to take it in stride. Of course, it hadn't been her face on the TV screen, but, at the same time—as she'd reminded him—she'd had her unfortunate time in the spotlight as a child. She'd eventually turned her phone off as well. While it wasn't yet known she was helping Sam Harper, her closest friends knew her past connection with Sal Batise, so it was only natural for them to reach out to see how she was doing. She'd told them all, *Yeah, I heard the news, and yes, I'll be watching*, telling Sam, as she responded, how hard it was to bite her tongue and not reveal to them all that she'd be at the interview too.

That was the exact moment when Sam decided that, yes, he needed Jennifer Daley by his side tomorrow, and after three more hours of preparation, he'd concluded there was no way he could do it without her. Even Carl had bypassed his weekly D&D game to stay and help however he could. And because Sam simply couldn't stop shaking, and it had only grown worse as the night moved along, they'd begun loading their Landshark beers with tequila in the throat of the bottle. By the time Jennifer left, well after midnight, Sam wasn't far from being drunk but remembered her telling them she'd be back in the morning, and they'd show taillights by eight o'clock sharp. Twisted Tree was a thirty-minute drive east of Louisville and even though the prison had sent directions on where to park and a list of bullet points on visitor protocol, they weren't taking any chances of being late.

Carl had slept like the bear he was. Sam tried, but never went to sleep. Maybe he'd dozed off a time or two, but at most for only a matter of minutes, and by the time Jennifer knocked on their door—freshly put together in a black sleeveless blouse and white pants and black shoes, with her strawberry blond curls clasped and flowing down to her slender shoulders—Sam was already yawning and exhausted. He felt inadequate and completely not up for the daunting task ahead.

Plus, she was fifteen minutes early.

The first thing she said to Sam was, "Your shirt's wrinkled."

He looked down at his shirtfront. *Damn it.*

"Told you, bro," Carl said, emerging from the kitchen in a blazer and tie and jeans and eating from a disposable cup of probiotic yogurt.

Jennifer eyed Carl and whistled. "Looking good."

"Snappy casual." Carl slow-spun in a circle, graceful in his white Nikes.

"Don't know what *snappy casual* means, but I like it." Jennifer flicked lint from the shoulder of Carl's blazer, and then faced Sam. She checked her watch. "We have ten minutes. Take the shirt off."

"Why?"

Carl said, "It's wrinkled as a fucking prune, bro."

Jennifer said, "Unless you got another shirt that looks better, off with that one. What about an iron?"

"Coming up." Carl disappeared into the hall, his voice trailing him. "No ironing board, though."

"I'll use the ping-pong table." Jennifer looked at Sam. "Let's go, time's running. And are you sure about those pants?"

"Only ones I have." Sam began plucking at his shirt buttons, but his hands were shaking like a meth addict in withdrawal, so Jennifer stepped in to help, her fingers moving as nimbly as a concert pianist, and the next thing he knew he was standing bare-chested and self-conscious.

They left the apartment at eight sharp, with Carl driving his Ford 150 and Jennifer and Sam going over their notes in the back seat. Jennifer had a habit of scouring the news every morning, both local and national, and as Carl drove, she spouted off headlines. So far there were no leads on yesterday's apparent abduction of Beth Hawthorne, with no ransom demands. As Jennifer read off the numerous national news outlets reporting on the morning's interview with Sal Batise, Sam feared they'd come for him as soon as they pulled onto the prison grounds.

"You're not gonna get out of this without giving a few interviews yourself, Sam," Jennifer said, reading from an article in the *Twisted Tree Gazette*, whose headline told of a fire last night at the mansion of James McFee, the multimillionaire owner of the Old Sam Bourbon Distillery. "Suspected arson," she said. It was common knowledge that the McFee family owned practically all of Twisted Tree. "No deaths, thank God," Jennifer said, reading to them how outspoken James McFee had been in recent weeks of Sal Batise's imminent execution, clearly in favor of the *sick son of a bitch finally getting what was deserved*. The state penitentiary's property, the writer stated, was only three miles from McFee's largest Old Sam distillery, and the distillery owner was tired of the extra traffic the impeding execution was bringing, people starting to camp out in his woods weeks before the needle was set to enter Batise's vein.

"You think they could be connected?" Sam asked. "That fire and Hawthorne's abduction?"

"Could be a good follow-up question," Jennifer said, writing it down on their legal pad. "They were both clearly in favor of Batise meeting his Maker."

Halfway there, with Carl cruising casually down the westbound lane of I-64, he spoke over his shoulder like a tour guide. "Remember the Spider Murders? We're right on that stretch of road where the bodies were found."

Sam said, "He brings that up every time we're on this interstate. He's infatuated with it."

"No different from you and Batise, bro."

"I'm actually a member of the Spider Web," Jennifer said, referring to a popular online true crime community

"No shit?" Carl said with a glance over his shoulder. "Same. I joined soon after it all went down, and they finally caught the bastard. I'm on the Web about every night."

"He's in love with Ellie Isles," Sam said, glad for the sudden diversion.

Carl grinned large as he drove, and said under his breath, "Now *that's* the fuck."

Sam folded his hands in his lap so Jennifer wouldn't notice his nerves. But she must have because she casually placed her left hand on his right forearm. She left it there for a few miles, and damn if it didn't help to calm him.

She said to Carl, "So that's the fuck?"

"What?" he asked as he drove, nearing the main exit for Twisted Tree. "What about it?"

"You've said it several times," she said. "Just never heard the phrase before. Doesn't make much logical sense."

"So there's a story," Carl said.

Sam saw Carl eyeing him from the rearview mirror, and just knew Carl was begging him with that stare to let him tell it. "Don't," Sam said.

"Come on," Carl pleaded.

"What?" Jennifer eyed them both. "Tell me."

"It's stupid," Sam said, "She doesn't need to know. Carl's just an asshole."

That didn't stop Carl. "So Sam here, this is back during our senior year at U of L, and he's studying for a physics final and I'm on the couch binging *Breaking Bad* and eating corn nuts."

"That checks," Jennifer said.

"And Sam, he's got this thing . . . people chewing, especially crunching on something."

"You know that's actually a medical thing, like a condition," Jennifer said.

"See, Sam, you can be medically explained." Carl glanced back over his shoulder. "But you really can't get louder than corn nuts, right? But I'm just chilling while he's studying. I have no clue how riled up he's getting, but all of a sudden he's standing right next to me—"

Sam said, "Carl, come on, she doesn't need to know."

Carl said, "And I'm like, what? And he goes, can you stop chewing those fucking things? I'm trying to study. I say sure, and he goes back to work. A minute later I throw a handful in my mouth and start crunching those bastards. I'm like, putting extra umph into it, just to see if I can really piss Sammy off, you know, and he comes back over . . . and he punches the corn nut bag on the coffee table." Carl laughed. Jennifer was too amused for Sam's liking, so he watched the passing trees and rolling hills of Twisted Tree out the window, still ashamed of that entire event. Carl said, "I started laughing, because, at that point, I'd never seen him get mad. I mean, he's completely unhinged. So, I finish crunching what's in my mouth and he goes apeshit. He just starts pummeling the corn nut bag on the table, just punching it like it's his worst enemy's face, over and over, until everything in that bag is dust and his knuckles are bleeding. I'm not kidding, his knuckles were *bleeding*. It was like he went somewhere else, and that wasn't Sam anymore."

"Just finish the damn story," Sam said.

Carl said, "So I stood from the couch, and I yelled, *What the fuck, dude!* Huh? I mean, I love corn nuts, and they'd been reduced to dust bits. And I'm all, like, what the fuck!" Carl laughed again. "And Sam points to the bag he'd just pulverized and screamed right back at me. *That's* the fuck! *That's* the fuck, dude. He was practically psycho."

Jennifer nudged Sam's shoulder with her own; he figured she was trying to lighten him up. "This guy?" she asked. "Him? This Sam Harper who I've known since . . . yesterday?"

"The same," Carl said, slowing down to take a sharp, hilly curve.

But within seconds, and after another glance toward Sam in the rearview, his smile faded. Carl's tone changed.

Jennifer's laughter subsided as well.

The entire vibe in the car had been altered on the heels of the story. Sam didn't know if it was because the first of four massive guard towers now loomed over the treetops, and they'd all just noticed, which meant it was almost go-time.

Or maybe Carl and Jennifer realized they'd gone too far, and their sudden silence stemmed from guilt.

Carl said, "You good, bro?"

Sam nodded but kept his gaze out the side window.

He used their stupid phrase as often as Carl did, but what Carl didn't know was that he felt a stab of horror every time it was used by either one of them, even years after the fact.

Because right before he'd started punching the corn nuts that day, he'd considered punching Carl in the same way, with the same barbaric ferocity.

With the same unknown rage.

His best friend.

Because he *had* been a different person in that moment; he'd smiled at the sight of the blood on his knuckles and for the briefest of moments craved more of it.

And remembered thinking minutes later, after he'd cooled off, *Where had that rage come from? That burst of violence?*

And that's what scared him still.

The hidden origin of some things.

CHAPTER 10

TREVOR HARPER AWOKE with a gasp, breathing heavily, heart racing, head swirling as remnants from the dream drifted away like smoke trails.

Lizzie Hall . . . naked and bare-chested and sitting atop of him, her eyes locked on his as she moved gently up and back, her hips in his hands and her hair hanging down like curtains on either side of her pretty face . . . shhhh, she said, placing a long, slender index finger to his lips like a tease . . . shhh. . . .

As much as Trevor enjoyed the vision, a memory from the dream he'd just had, the feeling of confused anxiety in him now needed it gone. Guilt surged, and he needed to right the ship. What was going on? He closed his eyes in hopes of pushing away the disorientation, and when he opened them seconds later, the sexual memory was gone. Long gone to where most dreams went whether the dreamer wanted them to or not. But what were dreams, he thought, if not the seeds of some previous thought, unconscious or not, fully fleshed out into a cleverly revealed conclusion whenever the eyes were closed.

And why did his bedroom smell like a woman's perfume?

Why did it smell like *her*?

How do you know what she smells like, Trevor? Was that Annie's voice coming out as his guilty conscience? *What was another woman doing in our bedroom, Trevor? What was another woman doing in our bed?*

His vision swirled, his brain felt loose inside his skull, afloat on violent ocean waves with no shore in sight. He sat up against the headboard, closed his eyes again. Opened them. His underwear was cold and wet and clinging to his skin. He wore nothing else beneath the coiled bed sheets. He typically slept in pajama bottoms and a T-shirt, and he knew what Lizzie Hall smelled like because . . . because she'd stopped by last night. He'd smelled her perfume when he'd closed the door behind her, just before he'd asked her if she liked wine . . . and the last thing he remembered was . . .

Jesus, he thought, his fingers massaging his temples, remembering he'd opened a third bottle of merlot at some point.

He'd been in his recliner. She'd been sitting on the couch catty-corner to him, and at one animated moment when she'd leaned forward laughing to touch his arm, their knees had touched, and they'd locked eyes, and it had gotten momentarily quiet and awkward.

And that's when she started crying.

And she apologized profusely for doing that in front of him because they barely knew each other and then damn if he didn't recall maybe crying too, because she wasn't the only one with baggage. She wasn't the only victim of horrible abuse.

Damn, he thought now . . . had he really said that to her?

He had.

Because *sometimes victims have to get practically murdered before anything is ever done about it.*

Had he said that? No, that had been her, and he'd agreed so wholeheartedly they'd locked eyes again. The understood sympathy was there between them, hard and true, but the empathy . . . that had linked hitch and trailer and from there their conversation . . . had gotten deep.

Cathartic, he remembered thinking at one point and recalled cloudily now.

He'd passed out at some point.

He'd *blacked* out.

It was something that had never happened to him before, at least not with alcohol. With a punch to the head, yes, multiple times in his younger years, which made him wonder if that had made him more susceptible to blacking out last night, not only the overindulgence with the wine but with the painful conversation itself.

But how did I end up undressed in bed?

Trevor swung his feet from the sheets and touched his toes on the hardwood floor; he wasn't tall enough for his full foot to touch. He looked at his underwear, the clear wet stain on the crotch. He'd had a wet dream, the first since God only knew when, and it shamed him. He was a fifty-year-old man who had, long ago, after Annie's death, mentally and emotionally turned off those nether region waterworks. At least he thought he had. But it made him feel dirty. Made him feel like a teenager again, which was a time in his life to which he never wanted to return, because no years had been worse. The cold sensation reminded him of the years he'd wet the bed, and the cruel ridicule his brother gave him for doing so at that age.

Shame.

Ashamed.

You're a disgraceful little pussy, Tommy, the voice screamed at him from the past. *Who does that, Tommy? Huh? What twelve-year-old pisses himself like a little baby?*

Trevor stepped out of his underwear and grabbed a clean pair from his top drawer, thinking, *If only Sam knew about me. The real me. What would Sam think if he knew that Trevor wasn't even my real name?* And neither was Harper.

Although both had been necessary to save lives.

You aren't a coward, Trevor. Lizzie had said that last night.

Christ, what had he told her?

Every movement brought with it pangs of nausea, and even though he was on the verge of throwing up, he managed to get on a pair of shorts and a T-shirt, and only then did he notice the note on his bedside table, the edge of it tucked under the lamp stand.

The bottom of it signed simply, ***Talk soon, Lizzie***.

His first thought was, *What did I do?* So she *had* been in the bedroom at some point. But had she come in here for certain reasons that had led to his dream? Had the dream really been a memory? Or had he been so drunk . . .

Jake, Trevor thought suddenly of Lizzie's husband, *he's gonna kill me. He'll find out his wife was over here, and he'll tear me limb from limb.*

Not if you kill him first, Trevor.

Across the room, next to the windowsill, leaned his Louisville Slugger baseball bat. That was his weapon of choice in case of a home invasion. He might be pint sized, but at one time, in another life, he'd had a solid swing at the plate. He remembered his father telling him that much, right before he'd thrown the next baseball right at his head.

But he could use that on Jake Hall, if it came to it. He had a history of having to defend himself from bullies.

He pulled the note out from beneath the lamp and read it.

Hey, thanks for listening last night. Please know that wasn't the reason I came over. What happened was the LAST thing I would have expected, but I guess we both needed it in a way. You know? To talk. To listen. Who would have thought there'd be that many tears? And I promise, I'll keep everything you told me in confidence. I know you were worried. You can trust me. Hope you don't remember this as an awkward evening, as I think it might have done us both some good? As long as we aren't too hungover—Ha! I'll see you around and hopefully we can catch up again sometime? Best of luck to your son tomorrow . . . actually today! Look at the time! Anyway, your love for Sam was so apparent in everything you said that I often felt jealous last night, of that kind of love. It gives me hope that someone who endured all you did could turn out so loving and put-together. You are a good man, Trevor Harper. And by all I can tell, an even better father. P.S. You did get sick on your shirt and pants near the end of the night. So I tossed them in the washer for you and ran it through. Might want to run it again when you wake up. Talk soon, Lizzie.

Trevor lowered his arm but continued clutching the note. At least that explained why he'd awakened nearly naked, with the scent of her perfume in his nostrils. She must have helped him into bed. He could still smell the scented shampoo in her hair.

But what had he told her last night?

He had a vault full of secrets and now feared he'd willingly opened it to a virtual stranger.

Could he trust her?

He looked at her note again and the line, ***please know that wasn't the reason I came over***, jumped at him. And then he recalled what *had* been the reason she'd come over.

Sam.

He'd been all over the national news, and she'd come over to ask him about it. The alarm clock on his bedside table read 9:55 in the morning, and the interview was set to start at 10:00.

Head throbbing, Trevor unsteadily made his way into the living room, using walls for support, swearing he'd never drink again. The first Mallard Malone novel he'd tossed aside last night was back atop the stack next to his recliner. He turned on the TV to WDRB, which showed a large crowd outside the Twisted Tree prison and his son, escorted by two prison guards, making his way through the throng of eager reporters. He at first thought it was live, but then a female voice sounded over the visual, *This was the scene moments ago as young Sam Harper entered the prison . . .* Trevor's eyes grew large when he noticed the young woman beside Sam: Jennifer Daley. What was she doing there? How had she involved herself in this? The news anchor's voice continued over the scene . . . *We now know that the young woman by his side is Jennifer Daley, who aside from apparently being his partner on a true crime documentary on Sal Batise, is also one of the four children found locked inside the closet of Batise's bedroom on his cult ranch twenty years ago . . .*

Trevor scooted up to the edge of his recliner as he watched his son move closer to the prison gates. The crowd pinched in on them. Trevor said softly, "Stay back, vultures." And to the security guards: "Do your job. Do your job." On the screen, a balding man in glasses reached from the crowd, almost desperate to get closer to Sam, and even managed to grasp his shirt sleeve before the guards eased the man away. Trevor breathed, "Get off my son." He stood from the recliner and approached the TV. "*Get the fuck off my son.*"

And just as the man in the glasses made eye contact with Sam, the news anchor's voice-over continued: *You can see there, the gentleman who just briefly touched Sam Harper, we now know to be Harold Martin, the author of the bestselling true crime novel* Mastermind, *based on the life of Sal Batise and the forming of his cult . . .* The picture froze. The voiceover continued . . . *looks like we're ready inside the prison and we'll be taking you there momentarily. . . . Hold on, wait, okay, we're taking you there right now . . .*

The picture changed to the interior view of a windowless room somewhere inside the prison. Trevor's heart lurched when he saw Sam sitting next to Jennifer Daley. They were surrounded by lights and a camera crew, and across from them was an empty folding chair he assumed would soon hold Sal Batise.

A door opened.

On camera, Sam looked toward an off-screen door and shifted in his seat.

Jennifer's hand touched his forearm as if to calm him, and Trevor wanted to hug her like he had when she was a little girl.

The voiceover: *And here we see Sal Batise entering the room, escorted by three guards, and here we are, handing it over, going live with our very own Shaffer Swanson . . .*

The camera zoomed, and instantly the scene became more intimate. Sal Batise, wearing his red death row fatigues, sat casually in the empty chair, folded his tattooed hands on his lap, and instead of first looking at Sam, his interviewer, he peered directly into the camera and smiled as if reunited with a long-lost friend.

Trevor flinched—he knew it wasn't the case, but it seemed that Batise had just somehow spotted him.

CHAPTER

11

OLIVER CROWN LEANED forward in his folding chair, turned up the volume on the television sitting atop the cart he'd rolled inside the garage moments ago. He listened as the young upstart, Sam Harper, on screen, nervously introduced himself and his partner, Jennifer Daley, to Sal Batise, who eyed them both like he was a jackal and they were about to become his prey.

Oliver grinned, because this *was* a reunion of sorts.

And much of what was said during this interview would determine his next course of action. What to ultimately do with the bitch sitting in the shadows behind him.

He looked over his shoulder at her. "Can you hear?"

"Go to hell," Beth Hawthorne hissed, yanking at the chain that tethered her to the homemade anchor back in the shadows.

He turned up the volume so loud the governor's wife had to cover her ears.

Once he assumed she got the message—nobody can hear us out here—he returned his focus back on the television, on Sam Harper, thinking, *Oh, how much you've grown.*

CHAPTER

12

SAM HATED WHEN athletes on TV during post-championship interviews said the word *surreal*, telling himself that if he was ever in that situation, he'd pick a different word.

But surreal was exactly how it felt the moment Sal Batise entered the room and took his seat in the chair across from him. Sam felt like it wasn't real. Like he was in the middle of a dream. Sal Batise was barely five foot ten, and slender, but his presence loomed larger than life, and even though this was Sam's interview, everyone in the room—the security guards, the warden, and the professional news crews alike—watched Batise like there was no doubt to whom this room now belonged.

Sal's blue eyes settled hawkishly on Sam and Jennifer.

Feeling the heat from the lights, Sam nervously wiped at his brow and fidgeted in his seat. "Mr. Batise, my name is—"

"I know who you is, Sam Harper." Sal had taken an IQ test in prison years ago and scored 150; he liked to play it off sometimes that he wasn't intelligent. He'd also been on record referring to himself as an uneducated genius. He said, "But because I know who you is, that means I also know who you ain't."

Sam replied softly, "And who would that be, Mr. Batise?"

"Cal me Sal, please." Sal clapped once, and then wiggled his fingers in Sam's direction, like he'd put some kind of voodoo curse on him. His unpredictable movements and quirky mannerisms had often been compared to Charles Manson, who Sal admitted he admired. And when Chet Sage at ABC had brought it to his attention in an interview in the spring of 2015, that Batise seemed to be almost mimicking Manson's crazy, off-the-wall mannerisms and inflections and reactions, Sal had said with joyful pride, *Of course I do, Chet Sage. Because part of him is in me, you dig?* And then he'd famously added, *When Charlie died in prison at the ripe old age of eighty-three, his spirit came to me and we had ourselves an important convo, Chet Sage, like a passing of the torch, you might say.* At which point Chet Sage reminded Sal that Charles Manson was still very much alive across the country. To which Sal, feigning surprise and placing a hand over his mouth for effect, said, *Oopsie.* The entire exchange was brought up again two years later, adding more fuel to the fire of "Just Ask Sal" when, in 2017, Charles Manson did die of natural causes in prison at the ripe old age of eighty-three.

"Now that's better." Sal leaned back in his chair and crossed his legs at the knees. "I need this last interview to be all casual like. Like a morning rainstorm, a calm and peaceful conversation and not some Nazi interrogation. And who you ain't, Sam Harper, is all those big fancy TV networks out there watching. They envy you right now. They want to *be* you. Now tell me how does that feel?"

"I don't know yet, Mr. . . . Sal."

"Does it make your toes curl? Does it make you heart palpiTATE?"

"I suppose so, yes."

Sal waved toward the camera and then focused again on Sam, but only briefly, because his eyes then moved to Jennifer, who stiffened in her seat.

It was the first sign of fear Sam had seen in Jennifer, but it was only momentary. She quickly regrouped and went on the offensive, first with her posture, leaning forward in her chair, elbows on her knees, and then with her abrupt question: "Did you have anything to do with yesterday morning's disappearance of Bethany Hawthorne?"

"Well, hello to you, too, Miss . . ."

"Daley," she said. "Jennifer Daley."

"Don't recall ever hearing your name in Sam Harper's letter to me," Sal said, leaning forward in his chair again, as if mirroring her aggressive pose.

"I was a late addition," she said. "Can you please answer the question?"

The room went silent as Sal folded his arms and seemed to be pondering how best to respond. He smirked and said to Sam, "Have you fucked her yet, Sam Harper?"

The warden stood from his chair, motioned for the camera to be shut off, and told Sal, "We're finished here. I warned you."

But Sal wasn't done. He quickly said to Sam, "How about a threesome? I used to love me some threesomes on the ranch, Sam Harper, but the only time I come close to a threesome anymore is when I get both of my hands involved." He laughed. "You dig?"

The guards moved in.

The news crew acted like they didn't know what they were supposed to do, sharing looks that said, *This can't be it. This can't end before it barely started.*

Sal locked eyes with the warden and shook his head, as if to say, *Don't even think about it. Don't you dare take this interview from me.*

And damn if Warden Wren didn't stop the guards from removing Sal. Sam didn't know what he'd just witnessed other than some apparent power Sal had not only inside the walls of the prison but over Warden Wren himself. Warden Wren leaned down and whispered into Sal's ear and Sal nodded, grinning but nodding, perhaps even obediently, which wasn't a facet of his personality he showed often, if ever. Sal then whispered something back to the warden and Warden Wren's eyes grew large. Sam didn't know what threat had been made or what kind of compromise they'd come to, but Warden Wren then motioned for the camera crew to ready themselves again, and said to the room, "I'm giving him ten minutes. Not one second longer."

Sam didn't think his anxiety level could go any higher; this wasn't how things were supposed to go, this wasn't what they'd practiced last night. They'd agreed to ease into the interview for Sam's sake, to allow him stable footing and solid ground before he would then begin to ramp up the questions.

As if reading Sam's mind, Jennifer whispered, "I'm sorry, Sam. He was staring right through me, and the question just came out."

"It's okay," he said. "But ten minutes. What do we do now?"

"First we get him to answer my question, or we'll look weak," she said. "And then . . . I don't know, skip right to the Kentucky Cannibal question."

"Really?"

"Yes."

They both knew, as did most of the country, that *that* had been the last question ever publicly asked of Sal Batise, during the CNN interview, when he'd refused to answer and then abruptly asked to be escorted back to his cell. So this wouldn't be the first Sal Batise interview with fireworks, and it wouldn't be the first interview suddenly cut short.

But ten minutes, Sam thought. *Why even allow him to continue at all, after what he'd just said to Jennifer?*

As the camera crew readied themselves again and the makeup woman stepped up to dab at the sweat on Sam's brow and re-powder a portion of his forehead, Jennifer leaned in again, even as they adjusted her hair. "What do you think they just discussed? The warden and Batise?"

"I don't know," Sam said, watching Warden Wren frantically write something on a ripped piece of paper. "But he looked shocked by something."

Sam figured the ultimate punishment for Batise would have been to cancel the interview. This had all been Sal's doing anyway. He'd turned down interview requests for years before asking for this moment. And whether you were in the camp that believed Sal had changed and had finally stopped fighting and delaying his imminent death and this was truly some type of parting swan song, or if you believed like so many that this was just another publicity stunt and stall tactic because the man had proven time and time again he was willing to do and try anything to stay alive, everyone could get on board with the fact that Sal Batise was a narcissistic showman who had never settled for anything other than the spotlight. What was happening now shouldn't have shocked anyone.

But the warden hadn't pulled the plug. He'd given the man ten more minutes, and Sam couldn't help wondering why.

Warden Wren finished writing whatever note he'd been working on, and before he allowed the camera to start rolling again, his eyes homed in on his "dead man walking."

Sal must have gotten the clue, because he then turned to Jennifer Daley and said, "*Miss* Daley. I do apologize for my outlandish behavior and blundering vulgarity. I do hope you can find it in your lovely heart to forgive me."

Jennifer nodded but said nothing.

And from behind them, the cameraman said, "We're rolling again in five, four . . .

Warden Wren took those few seconds to hand Sam the note he'd written.

He claims to have the whereabouts of another buried body, so I'm giving him a little rope. He also claims to know who the author Mallard Malone is. This is out of left field, I know, but he insisted you work that into your ten minutes.

After quickly reading it, Sam showed the note to Jennifer.

Once the camera started rolling, the lights seemed even brighter, but unlike before the interruption, Sam felt a sense of calmness now that he hadn't before. He sat up straight in his chair and said, "Before the break, you were asked a question about the disappearance of Bethany Hawthorne."

Sal wasted no time answering, Sam thought, because he knew now that his time was limited and whatever game he'd planned would have to be adjusted. Sal said, "I knew nothing of Mrs. Hawthorne's disappearance until now, and therefore I had nothing to do with it."

"But you have to admit the timing of it all seems sketchy?" Jennifer asked.

Sal watched her, delaying his answer, Sam mused, not so much because he didn't know what to say, but in the way his facial expression had just changed from puzzlement to revelation, and in the way he was now studying Jennifer, Sam guessed Sal may have just realized exactly who Jennifer was. And then, with a knowing grin, Sal said, "I know you. You're from Freedom, aren't you? Which would have put you as a little girl back then on the ranch."

"Would you admit that the timing of the abduction—"

Sal cut her off: "Of course it may seem sketchy, but I assure you, with coincidence and fate and all those colorful conundrums set aside, I had nothing to do with it." He held up an index finger. "Yet, as the good Christian I am, I hope and pray that the good governor's wife will be returned soon to her house, home, and family." This last part, Sam noticed, Sal had said directly into the camera, like he was speaking to whoever was responsible.

Sam scanned his list of questions, skipping over most, settling on one in the middle. "Are you afraid to die?"

Sal leaned forward, elbows back on his knees, twiddling his thumbs. "I'm afraid of pain, Sam Harper. I'm afraid of the not knowing. I'm afraid of death, of what's waiting on the other side, but no . . . I ain't afraid to die. Cuz I ain't afraid of nothing." He leaned back, crossed his legs again and laughed. "Look at me, Sam Harper. I look afraid of anything to you? Maybe of aliens . . . of Bigfoot . . . of the Loch Ness Monster. Or maybe the needle not properly going into my vein. Maybe I'm afraid of the Helter Skelter race wars my man Charlie spoke of. But you know what I'm really afraid of?"

Before Sam could stop it, the words came out: "You're afraid of any talk of the Kentucky Cannibal."

Sal froze like he wasn't expecting this. Like Sam Harper had just got him good. Like he'd just been interrupted on a major point he was about to make and he didn't appreciate it none.

Sam held strong. "Are you the Kentucky Cannibal?"

This was the exact question on which Sal had gotten up to leave during the CNN interview, but here, he answered definitely and without hesitation. "No. I am not. I have not, and never will, dine on human flesh. The thought of it revolts me."

Sam said, "There was a pot of stew found on the kitchen stove of your house on the Freedom Ranch, and after it was analyzed, it—"

"Oh, I've heard all about the famous stew, Sam Harper, so don't waste my time." Sal shifted in his chair. "Or, as my mother used to say, before she was beaten to death by some vagrant on the streets of your fine city, Sam Harper, quit dilly-dallying."

"Why did you write on the wall above the stove, the words, *The Kentucky Cannibal was here*?"

"Because he was."

"Who is the Kentucky Cannibal, Sal?"

"That's for me to know and for you to perhaps one day find out."

"So the Kentucky Cannibal is real?"

"Yes."

"And you know who he is?"

"Yes," Sal said. "And I think you do too."

Sam froze long enough for the tension in the room to grow amped.

"What do you mean?" asked Jennifer.

Sal said, "I mean Sam Harper here, as evident in his letter to me weeks ago, pitching this very interview, knows a lot about me and my so-called cult. And, therefore, knows all the players in the game. So use your noggin, son, keep digging, it'll come to you."

Without giving thought to whether it made sense, Sam asked his next question: "Did the Kentucky Cannibal abduct Bethany Hawthorne?"

"I truly don't know," Sal said. "But as I stated earlier, I hope and pray—"

Jennifer cut Sal off, and her urgency was an instant reminder to Sam that they only had a couple minutes left. "You were saying earlier . . . what are you afraid of, Sal?"

And it dawned on Sam then that a few minutes earlier, before he'd brought up the Kentucky Cannibal, that Sal had been about to transition to something important. Something to open the door for them and segue into what would have been an otherwise very blunt and off-the-wall question about Mallard Malone.

And then Sal said it: "I'm afraid of a class war. A class war between the haves and have-nots. Between the elite and downtrodden. Between the disenfranchised and the millionaires. Between those behind bars and the crooked society that helped put them there. Between—"

Jennifer cut him off again. "It sounds like you're referencing a lot of the rumors circulating about a certain final book in a popular fiction series."

And Sal smiled large, showing pearly white teeth that somehow appeared perfectly maintained.

Jennifer said, "In the Mallard Malone novels, everyone suspects that's all what led to the earth's undoing. A massive war between the classes. And that the character Oliver Crown rose like a phoenix from those ashes."

Sal fidgeted, looked like he might suddenly come out of his seat, and then sat on his hands like a little kid might, grinning like a chimp, hopping slightly up and down like he had to pee, hamming it up like the actor he was.

Sam asked, "Have you read the Mallard Malone novels, Sal?"

"Yes. Cover to cover and back again. Every one of them."

Sam scooted up to the edge of his seat. "Sal, do you know who Mallard Malone is?"

Sal nodded, smiling, and said, "Just ask Sal, right? Just ask Sal."

Jennifer said, "Does Mallard Malone have something to do with the disappearance of Bethany Hawthorne?"

Sal pointed to his nose and then at Jennifer.

Sam said, "Are you saying Mallard Malone has Bethany Hawthorne?"

"No, Sam Harper. Listen to the details."

Jennifer corrected Sam. "He's saying Mallard Malone has something to do with it. Like . . . he's responsible for the abduction?"

"You could say that, yes," Sal said.

Sam said, "Tell us then, Sal. It's obvious this is why you called this party. Tell us . . . Who is Mallard Malone?"

Sal started laughing, clapping.

The warden had had enough. "Answer the question."

"Who is he, Sal?" Sam surprised himself by growing angry, louder. "Who is Mallard Malone, Sal?"

Sal laughed and clapped right in Sam's face.

"Why is this funny?" Sam asked.

"Because you just don't get what's right in front of your face, Sam Harper," Sal screamed at Sam. "I wrote those books. I *am* Mallard Malone."

CHAPTER 13

THE NEXT HOUR there at the prison, for Sam, was a whirlwind.

Warden Wren had stopped the interview seconds after Sal's Mallard Malone revelation, after his *claim*, what everyone in the room had assumed to be a lie, because it made no sense.

Did Sal have the time to write those books? *Yes.*

But the means and opportunity and outreach? *No way.*

Sal was quickly escorted from the room by the same guards who'd brought him in, and Sam could tell Warden Wren, as he watched them all go, was wondering—if the Mallard Malone claim *was* true—which of the guards had been an accomplice. Because Sal couldn't have managed it alone.

After Sal was gone, Warden Wren stood stupefied and seething; it was obvious he'd been duped. To which Jennifer had said, "Do we believe him . . . sir?"

"Whether we believe him is irrelevant now," said Warden Wren. "I'd convinced myself he was finished playing games." He left the room, slamming the door behind him.

The news crew was next to leave, and Shaffer Swanson, the WDRB news anchor, promised Sam they'd be in touch soon and asked if he could keep them informed of any new developments.

Sam agreed, still stunned and speechless, as a guard escorted them from the building. Just like that, it was over. But it couldn't be.

Sal couldn't make that claim without proving it. The next thing they knew, Sam and Jennifer were swarmed by the rest of the news outlets with questions. Sam, on instinct, reached out his hand to Jennifer and she took it, and together they navigated through the crowd. They couldn't have been outside for more than a couple minutes when the crowd began to part and another prison guard approached.

"Sam Harper," the guard shouted. "Warden Wren needs you back inside."

Sam stopped, and then gently tugged Jennifer that way.

"Only Mr. Harper this time," said the guard.

Sam said, "What is this about?"

"He didn't say. But he was adamant I find you before you left the premises."

"Sam, it's fine." Jennifer pulled her hand free from his grasp. "Go on. I'll find Carl. We'll wait in his truck."

Sam watched her disappear into the crowd and then followed the guard back into the prison, where he'd been waiting for the past ten minutes, alone, inside Warden Wren's tower office overlooking the prison yard, without any explanation as to what he was doing there.

How had this happened right under Warden Wren's nose? A man known for running a tight ship. *If it was true*, Sam thought, *how had this prison harbored perhaps the most popular novelist of their generation without anyone knowing?* If it was true, then *someone* had to know. Someone helped. Someone *from* the prison. Maybe more than one someone.

The door opened.

Sam sat up from his slumped position in the cushioned chair as Warden Wren entered his office and closed the door behind him.

"Sorry about the confusion, Sam." The warden took a seat behind his desk and motioned for Sam to scoot his chair closer. "I urgently need to get to the bottom of a few things, and for that I need answers from Sal, and Sal . . . and I don't know why this surprises me anymore . . . said he, and I quote here, 'won't say another word to anyone about anything unless Sam Harper is present.' So here we are."

"Me?" Sam said. "Why me?"

"I don't know. Perhaps it's the same reason he picked you to begin with."

"Dead man walking," a prison guard shouted from the yard outside the tower office.

"He's on his way," Warden Wren said.

Sam turned in his chair to see Sal Batise moving across the yard between two armed guards. "They really say that? 'Dead man walking'?"

"Yes, they do."

Sam's nerves ratcheted up again while he awaited Sal's arrival for the second time of the morning. There was an empty chair on the opposite side of Warden Wren's desk Sam assumed was for Sal. A minute later, the guards escorted Batise inside and he sat in the chair as casually as a dear friend might. The warden was furious at Sal, Sam could tell, be he also sensed a deeply hidden connection that bordered on camaraderie between the two men. While Sal had a history of obnoxious and often toxic behavior during interviews, Sam knew Batise otherwise had never been a problem in his two decades here, with Warden Wren having been quoted in the newspaper calling him a model prisoner. It was immediately clear to Sam that away from the cameras, Sal seemed like a different person. The larger-than-life persona was still there, but now that it was just them, he'd clearly dialed down the antics.

Sal sat with his hands folded. Hash-mark tattoos ran like train tracks across the top of every knuckle. He'd been on record saying each mark stood for a year his father spent in prison, with a total of twenty-three hashes on Sal's skin. He must have noticed Sam looking, because he moved his hands closer, so the marks were more visible. "He didn't do it, Sam Harper."

"Who didn't do what?" Sam asked.

"My daddy," Sal said. "He didn't kill that man like they said he did."

"He didn't rob that store?" Sam asked. He knew the history. "He didn't put the gun to the back of the clerk's head and pull the trigger?"

"No. They got the wrong man. And my daddy spent most of his life behind bars for a crime he didn't commit."

"That's not why we're here, Sal," said Warden Wren.

Sal scooted back in his seat and interlocked his fingers on his lap. "*He* was the one staring, Warden Wren. Just wanted to let the boy know two things."

"What two things then, Sal, and then we're getting down to business."

"That my daddy was innocent," he said. "And that maybe if he hadn't been so unfairly incarcerated for most of my childhood, mayhap I would have turned out a little different."

Warden Wren wasn't having it. "You get that out of your system, Sal?"

Under his breath, Sal started singing Cher's "If I Could Turn Back Time." After he must have realized the warden wasn't amused, his words faded to silence.

Warden Wren leaned forward, elbows on his desk. "I don't know what game you've started, Sal, but I'm getting to the bottom of it. We're going to start with this: Why are you insisting Sam join us?"

"Because it's Sam and Sal, Warden. Sal and Sam. Sam and Sal. You dig?"

"Stop wasting my time," said Warden Wren.

"And stop wasting mine," Sal said in retort. "I got another book to write."

"So we're starting there?"

"No . . . in fact," Sal said, "we're ending there. Last book of the series and all."

"Prove you are Mallard Malone, Sal. Quit fucking around and tell me what I need to know. If this is true, I need names. I need to know how and when you wrote those books and how you got them out of my prison without me knowing."

"Without *anyone* knowing, Warden Adrian Wren. Not just you."

Sam's eyes flicked back and forth, mesmerized by the exchange. Couldn't believe he was here for it. His mood changed from nervous anxiety to a buzzing opportunistic delight. He only wished Jennifer was by his side to witness it.

Sal continued: "The when is easy. I got all day in my cell. I don't think I need to remind you, Warden Adrian Wren, that—"

"Could you stop that please, with the full names?"

"Sam Harper here doesn't mind. Ain't that right, Sam Harper? You don't mind if I call you Sam Harper, do you, as that is your name?" After a beat, he said, "Or is it?"

"It's my name," Sam said with a quick glance toward the warden, hoping he didn't come off as taking Sal's side. "And I don't mind."

Because Sam and Sal. Sal and Sam . . .

"Good," Sal said, before finishing for the warden. "I spend twenty-three of my twenty-four hours a day in lockdown inside my cell. By myself. In isolation."

"And how?" asked the warden.

Sal made typing motion with his fingers. "Like this."

"I'm not opposed to moving your execution up a few hours."

"If there is an execution."

Warden Wren clenched his jaw. "You're dying on schedule, Sal."

"We'll see about that," he said. "I now have millions of fans across the globe who are dying to read the final book in the series."

"How clever of you," said the warden, his face expressionless.

"And I'm not opposed to leaving the whereabouts of another body buried in the ground. Of having another family continue to grieve because they never found their loved one."

Warden Wren said, "If you're banking on a groundswell of support across the globe to plead for your life, you'll lose."

"No . . . well, maybe. But you're going to have a hard time finding the book if I die. In which case you just might have a revolution on your hands. And an easy mark on your head."

"Are you threatening me, Sal?"

"Wasn't my intent, no."

Sam felt like he was waiting to jump into a circling jump rope, and took the brief lull to ask, "So the book is written?"

"The book is written," Batise said to Sam while staring daggers at the warden. "And it's in a safe place outside of this prison."

They watched each other coldly. Warden Wren swiveled in his seat and removed from the floor a two-foot-tall stack of typing paper he then dropped with a heavy thump atop his desk.

"My papers," Sal said. "You kept them."

The warden said to Sam: "For good behavior, believe it or not, Sam, ten years ago we allowed him, under supervision, to have a typewriter wheeled into his room for a few hours a day."

"Heavy son of a bitch," Sal said. "Old-school typewriter with the keys plopping up to the paper. Love the sound of it, Warden Adrian Wren, and so do the rest of the dead men on the row. Soporific almost, like rainfall, and I'm fast too." He air-typed with his fingers. "I use the home keys, no chicken pecking."

The warden placed his hand atop the tall stack of paper and fanned through a few inches of it just to show Sam they weren't blank. "He types out his thoughts. Mostly incoherent gibberish. And then the typewriter is removed, as well as what he'd written. If you can call this writing." He homed in on Sal again. "So tell me, if it's as you claim, Sal, how did you write the books?"

Sal smiled. "It wasn't rocket science. The top several pages of the pile I gave the guard was, as you say, incoherent gibberish, but the rest of it, the glorious world of Oliver Crown." He tapped his head with an index finger. "It's a story I've been writing up here for years. And years. My incarceration simply allowed me the time and focus to get it done."

"And how then did the manuscript pages get pulled from the bullshit?"

"You mean who aided and abetted?"

"That's exactly what I mean."

"It wasn't like writing a book was illegal," Sal said.

"But sneaking anything out of the prison is."

"I sneaked nothing out of the prison."

The warden's face had grown red. "If it wasn't illegal, then why didn't you just tell us you wanted to write a book, Sal?"

"Then I doubt it all would have blown up like it has," Sal said, pointing at Sam, as if gesturing to write this down. "Foresight, Sam Harper. Vision."

"Not too unlike the forming of your cult," Sam said.

"If you want to call it that."

"What else would you—"

"Can we get back to the manuscript?" Warden Wren said forcefully to Sal. "I need the name of the guard who smuggled your manuscripts out of the prison."

"I'm not a rat, Warden Wren."

"Is it Billy? CO Billy Boyle? I see you all talking often enough."

Sal said nothing, but his body language spoke volumes.

Warden Wren pressed a button on his desk. A few seconds later a young man in glasses, presumably his secretary or assistant, poked his head in the door. "Jeffrey, find me CO Billy Boyle." When Jeffrey didn't do just that, and in fact kept his head in the door like he didn't know how to respond, Warden Wren said, "What is it?"

"Mr. Boyle," Jeffrey said. "He, uh, didn't report for work today, sir."

"Did he call in?"

"No, sir."

"Did we call him?"

"Yes, sir. No answer."

"Send someone to his house. I want him here ASAP."

"Yes, sir."

The door closed. Warden Wren studied Sal, who wore an eager-to-please grin. "Who did Billy Boyle get the manuscript to? Editor? Agent? What was the chain, Sal?"

"If I feel the need to divulge such info, Warden Wren, I shall do so in the coming hours with Sam Harper, and Sam Harper alone."

"Why?" Sam asked. "Why me?"

"Because we've got a documentary to work on."

Sam straightened in his seat at the mention of his documentary. An interview was one thing, but whatever bonus hours he could grab with Sal before his execution would be gold.

"Before I agree to anything," Warden Wren said, "give me *something*."

"I'll give you two things at the same time," Sal said. "Proof I am who I say and also the whereabouts of a body."

"A body?" Sam asked. "Are you implying there's more than one body you know about?"

Sal smiled. "How's this for a start, Sam Harper. Mallard Malone, book four, *Hammer and Nails*. In chapter seven on page seventy-seven, I believe, you will find that a character . . . a character, mind you, who was not all that important to the plot, is buried. And I go into great, perhaps unnecessary detail of exactly where that character is buried . . . In the book, in the small town of Georgetown, Indiana, there's a red barn a hundred yards down the hillside from the tennis courts of Boyd Central High School, and fifty paces northeast from the front doors of that barn a certain unimportant character is buried. I've seen reviews, Warden Wren. I often get hammered for such extraneous detail, but I assure you now they'll all come in quite handy to the authorities in the coming days."

Warden Wren's face went pale. "Are you telling me there's a body buried in that same location in real life?"

"Yes, that's exactly what I'm telling you."

"Who? Who is it, Sal?"

"Fifteen-year-old Miranda Knox went missing from southern Indiana in the fall of 1999 and her body was never found," Sal said. "Follow those exact directions, with shovels, and start digging. And there you will find her bones."

"Did you kill her?" Sam asked, hoping he wasn't overstepping his bounds, but why else was he here other than to ask questions?

Sal answered, "Of course not, Sam Harper. I don't murder."

"Because you get others to do it for you."

"Touché."

Warden Wren said, "But you know who did, Sal? You know who killed this girl back then?" He referred to the name he'd written on a notepad in front of him. "This Miranda Knox?"

"Yes."

"Who?"

Sam asked, "Is it the Kentucky Cannibal?" Sal smiled, but answered neither yes nor no. After studying past interviews, Sam knew whenever Sal Batise didn't initially answer a certain question, then the question itself was off the table and would go unanswered.

Instead, he altered the question. "Was he a member of your cult? Was he a member of The Collective?"

"Yes."

"Did he live on the Freedom Ranch?"

"Yes."

Sam felt himself gaining steam, like this was the interview he'd been promised earlier in true form. "Has this person murdered more people than just Miranda Knox?"

"Many more."

"And do you know where those bodies are buried too?"

"Yes, and so does Mallard Malone."

Sam paused, shared a look with the warden, who then asked, "Are you telling me there are more buried bodies described in detail, in those books?"

"*My* books . . ."

The warden continued undeterred, "That point to where bodies are buried in real life?"

"Have you not read the Mallard Malone novels, Warden Adrian Wren?"

"I have not."

"Sam Harper?"

"A couple of them."

Sal scoffed. "A couple of them." After a beat, where Sal watched out the window as a bird flew by, he said, "Out of the seven Mallard Malone novels, there are eighteen instances where I refer to burials. In detail."

"Jesus Christ," said Warden Wren. "Eighteen victims?"

"Unfortunately," Sal said. "Their bodies are buried all over the country."

"And you know this how?" asked Sam.

"He told me."

"Who?"

"The man who killed them."

Warden Wren pounded his desktop. "Stop fucking around, Sal. What's his name?"

"I'm not a rat."

Sam looked up. "Justice Minks?"

Sal looked at him and pointed to his nose.

"So he *does* exist."

"You've done your homework, Sam Harper."

Warden Wren scribbled on his notepad and looked up at Sal. "Eighteen victims. All murdered and buried by a man named Justice Minks?"

"Although I seriously doubt that's what he calls himself nowadays."

"When did he join The Collective?" Sam asked.

"I don't recall exactly when."

"But he told you of his previous murders?"

"He was a bit of a braggart once he came out of his shell."

"And he told you where he buried eighteen victims?" asked Warden Wren.

"Yes," said Sal. "And that was *before* I was incarcerated. There's no telling how many he's killed since then."

"Wait," Warden Wren said. "Are you telling me he's still out there?"

"Yes."

"How do you know?"

"Because I believe that's who has taken Mrs. Bethany Hawthorne."

Sam felt like his throat was constricting, and his nerves had returned tenfold. "And how do you know this?"

"Because he's Mallard Malone's biggest fan."

CHAPTER 14

Beth Hawthorne awoke, groggy, on a hardwood floor.

She wasn't inside the garage anymore, but she couldn't remember being moved.

She was inside a large room with a tall, coffered ceiling and a single globe light. By the size of the spacious room, she guessed it was the master bedroom inside an actual house. A large house. From the view of the trees out the lone window across the room, she guessed she was on the second floor, perhaps even a third. The window had six vertical bars on it, spaced just wide enough so no prisoner could slither through, and beyond it, there was no glass.

No windowpanes; just a tease of freedom out there.

Breeze circulated freely into the room and ruffled the pictures that covered every square inch of the walls like a collage.

Beth stood with a painful grunt. Her legs and back were sore, and the bullet wound on her right calf, covered with fresh gauze, still burned like fire, although not as badly as before. The wound seemed to be on the mend.

He was keeping her alive for a reason.

Her vision was blurry. She wobbled as if drunk. Drugged, more like; he'd made her take antibiotics to stave off any chance of infection, but she felt sure that wasn't all she'd been given, wasn't all she'd been forced to take—she recalled, vaguely now, him forcing pills down her throat, forcing her to swallow the water he poured into her mouth.

It was apparent now that he needed her alive, and the mere notion worked to calm down her racing heart. The question was why? And finding the answer motivated her.

She managed to balance herself in the center of the room, her eyes more focused now. She was still in her running clothes from . . . she didn't know how many days ago. Maybe only one, or two, yet the time spent under this man's control had felt like a lifetime of hell already.

Where was he?

Where was *she*?

These walls . . . those weren't pictures attached to them. They were book covers. Hardcover book jackets removed from the books and attached to the walls. All of them Mallard Malone novels, from baseboard to ceiling, every inch had been covered as if the book jackets were wallpaper. Covers from all seven books. Covers from different editions and covers from different translations and the bizarreness of it all nauseated her.

The heavy chain around her left ankle clinked as she turned in a slow circle, noticing two things immediately on the wall behind her. One, the chain around her ankle not only ran directly toward that wall but disappeared into a dark hole in the middle of it. A hole no bigger than one on a golf green. Big enough for the chain to fit through but not an arm. But the wall itself, from corner to corner and floor to ceiling, instead of the book cover collage that concealed the other three walls, was a painted mural of the United States. But it wasn't the United States she knew. It wasn't the fifty states she'd become accustomed to and had taken pride in visiting throughout her lifetime. On this wall, the United States' boundaries had been divided into what appeared to be eight different sections, or zones, two of which reached well into Canada to the north and Mexico to the south. It reminded her of a map one might see at the beginning of a fantasy novel, showing the land of whatever world the reader was about to devour, page by page, chapter by chapter. This was a fictional rendering of the United States years in the future, the world of Oliver Crown. The world of Mallard Malone.

And this man—if it was the enigmatic Justice Minks—was a true psychopath.

A psycho fan.

The thought kickstarted her into a panic. How did she get here? She didn't remember being moved from the garage, certainly not walking on her own two feet. She backtracked mentally, to the last minutes she remembered, him rolling the television cart inside the garage and making her watch the Sal Batise interview with that poor young man, Sam Harper, who looked barely older than her two sons. And the young woman with him had looked like a kid herself. *What were they doing in there with that monster*, Beth remembered thinking during the interview, *knowing that monster had orchestrated the nine murders inside the Hawthorne mansion that night, and no one knew his true motive.* Of course, the interview had nearly ended before it truly got started, because of the horrible thing Sal Batise had said about the young woman. *Have you fucked her yet, Sam Harper?* Beth's captor, still in his Guy Fawkes mask, had found enjoyment in what Batise had asked. *The pig*, Beth had thought then, and again now. To ask that question of him, with the girl sitting there like . . . like she didn't matter. Like she was a mere sex object.

And in the end, as soon as Batise made the wild claim that he was the mysterious writer Mallard Malone, her captor had stood from his seat and clicked off the TV, seemingly not surprised in the least bit by the revelation, and in fact nodding like he'd known all along. Or, even more, like he'd been hoping Batise would admit it. And that perhaps his only goal in bringing the television in was to make sure she knew too. To make sure she heard the news that was now, no doubt, spreading like wildfire across the globe.

And here she was now inside a room that could have doubled as a Mallard Malone shrine, held captive by a man who called himself Oliver Crown.

But why would it matter to her? She'd never read the Mallard Malone novels. She knew the gist of the series: a postapocalyptic future where the world was run by the Have-Nots, a lawless world of class systems where the millionaires and billionaires were put into concentration camps and later sold out as slaves, a violent world ruled by a man named Oliver Crown. The series ran in reverse, she knew, with the intent of raising suspense by slowly revealing how Oliver Crown became the ruthless ruler he was. She knew, because people talked and she'd followed it in the news and on social media, that in *Phoenix Rising*, Mallard Malone's latest book, published almost a year ago, officially as Book Two, but in the series was really the seventh book, told of Oliver Crown as a young man, rising from the ashes of whatever event had caused the world to crumble, first in the United States before spreading north and south to Canada and Mexico, and then across the Atlantic Ocean to Europe and beyond.

Looking at the map on the wall made her knees wobbly.

She visually followed the length of the chain snaking from her ankle, roughly eight feet across the floor, before rising four feet up to the hole in the middle of the wall, a hole, she figured, that would have been somewhere around Kansas in the real world but in this one was the dead center of an amoeba-shaped zone called The Untrustables.

Beth lifted the chain in both hands. The brace around her ankle was tight, and her skin around it was red and swollen. She shuffled toward the wall, holding the chain as she went. It was heavier than she'd imagined, or maybe she was weaker than she thought.

Four paces from the wall, she felt resistance on the chain, and wondered what it was connected to on the other side of that wall.

She tugged.

And immediately heard a male voice from the other side of the wall say, "Jesus, what the fuck?"

Beth froze. "Who's there?" Her throat was raw from yelling during her initial hours inside the garage, and she felt now like she'd survived the first stage of a video game and this was the next level.

"Who's over there?" the male voice asked from the other side of the wall.

Beth shuffled the remaining distance to the wall and squatted low enough to put her right eye to the opening and peer through the hole to the other side, where the chain disappeared into another room. The walls of that room were covered as well, not by book covers but by drawings and sketches of what Beth assumed were characters from all the Mallard Malone novels.

A shadow approached from the other room.

The chain shifted inside the golf-hole-sized tunnel connecting the rooms, and then another eye filled the hole on the other side. Beth flinched but didn't back away from it.

"I asked who are you?" the male voice said.

"Beth," she said. "Bethany Hawthorne."

"Holy shit," said the voice. "The governor's wife? You're still alive?"

"Yes," she said, and for whatever reason, perhaps to combat her nerves, felt the urge to joke with this apparent stranger and fellow captive. "But Gavin is better known as *my* husband."

His laughter appeased her. Her shoulders relaxed.

And then he said, "I'm Billy. Billy Boyle."

CHAPTER 15

Before

RAVEN WASTED NO time contemplating.

As soon as Jennifer told him that Yellow needed him outside, and then adding the word *now*, just as Yellow had moments before, Raven, without hesitation, rushed from the Kitchen House. Raven was small for a man, but he looked mad enough at that moment to lift a house. Jennifer watched them out the window as they talked animatedly, with Yellow pointing repeatedly at the house where Batise lived, pointing more accurately, Jennifer thought, at the now vacant upstairs window of that house, where she'd seen the boy standing earlier. Yellow appeared to be holding Raven back, calming him down.

What was the big deal? she wondered, as her friends called her over to their table for breakfast, the three of them laughing about something because they didn't know what was going on *out there.* And Jennifer had yet to tell anyone about what she'd witnessed the other day, too, and then later that night, after they returned from wherever they'd gone—the three women Jennifer first thought were nice but weren't, and Mister Mean. Who Iris called the bad man. The man with the scar running down from the inside corner of his left eye and across his nose and onto his right cheek like a crooked jack-o-lantern mouth.

Or who Jennifer now referred to as the man in the mask.

She'd yet to tell anyone about any of it, because there were parts of her brain still trying to tell her it never happened. That she never saw what she saw around that campfire. But then what were those pictures under her bed? Pictures she'd drawn from memory, pictures she'd drawn in such scary detail and in such a hurry that they couldn't have been from a dream. Or, in this case, a nightmare.

She'd been building up the courage to tell Yellow, but then seeing the boy in the window had sidetracked her. And now, something *else* was going on. Jennifer sat beside Peter and across from Iris and Markie at the small wooden table inside the Kitchen House, and when she mentioned the boy she'd seen in the upstairs window, her three friends went eerily quiet. Iris started crying and Peter was on the verge of it.

Markie sucked in a deep breath, as if to conjure some needed toughness. "It must have been a ghost."

"Don't," said Iris. "Steven isn't a ghost."

Jennifer watched them. "Wait, who is Steven?"

Peter shook his head and covered his ears. "We aren't supposed to talk about Steven. They warned us."

Markie must have sensed Jennifer's confusion, and said, "There were four of us. Before you came."

Iris started crying harder. Markie shushed her and gently patted her back, glancing over his shoulder toward the line cook refilling eggs into the container at the buffet. They didn't need an adult they didn't trust walking over and getting into their business. It was no secret that, as children on a ranch full of adults, they felt isolated and unwanted. The rest of the adults believed wholeheartedly in the "No Children" rule at Freedom, either coming here without them or, in some drastic cases Jennifer had heard of, giving their children or child up for adoption before entering. Children, to them, were chains, Sal Batise preached, just one more chain keeping them tethered to a world of burdens. He was the Breaker of Chains, because at Freedom, you truly were free of everything that may have bound you. And Jennifer couldn't help but think that the rest of the adults eyed them like they secretly all hoped they were gone.

Jennifer had made it known days ago that the only two people on the ranch she trusted were Yellow and Raven, and sometimes the bald guy who did magic tricks and called himself Clown, and after some careful, perhaps even cautious contemplation, the other three had agreed.

Yellow and Raven were their comfort zone.

Yellow and Raven were different. In a way, with how they watched over them, mostly in secret, they'd become parents to all of them. And because of it, weeks ago, the children had made a pact to stick together no matter what.

Jennifer, as quietly as she could, demanded they tell her who Steven was.

Markie leaned over his pancakes. "He wasn't here as long as we've been, but longer than you. He lived with us in the barracks. He . . . died . . . a couple weeks before you came."

"How?"

Iris wiped her eyes, somewhat composed now, and said, "He went into the woods."

"And the demons got him," Peter said.

Jennifer watched them all, and it immediately registered how serious they were. Of course, the demons got him, just like they'd gotten her mother. "But I saw a boy in that window. He was wearing a red shirt. He had brown hair. Did Steven have a red shirt and brown hair?"

"Yes." Markie's voice shook, and his right leg wouldn't stop moving under the table. "His favorite shirt was a Cincinnati Reds baseball shirt."

Jennifer noticed the three of them exchanging glances. She took it as them questioning what they'd previously believed—what they'd been *told*—and asked them, while they appeared vulnerable, "Did any of you see Steven enter the woods that night?"

Again, they shared looks, before Markie seemed to answer for all of them: "No." It was like deep down they'd all questioned it but were always afraid to admit it. "He went to sleep when we did one night, just like always, and when we woke up the next morning, he was gone."

"And you assumed he ran away . . . into the woods?"

They all nodded, one by one, but, Jennifer noticed, from Markie's lead, like he was telling them by his expressions that it was okay to open up. Like it was about time they finally faced this, and then Markie suddenly looked as mad as she'd ever seen him. "They told us he ran away," he said. "We asked where he was, and they told us he'd run into the woods. And that the demons got him. And we believed them because . . ."

"Because why?" Jennifer asked.

"Because we're stupid kids," Markie said.

And Peter said, "He was talking about running away for weeks."

"Why?" Jennifer asked, although she could guess why—she'd been contemplating running away herself since she arrived under the cloak of darkness with her mother weeks ago.

"Because he hated this place," Iris said as she bit into her biscuit with butter and jelly. Her tiny hands were shaking.

Peter said, "They were extra mean to him."

"He got special attention since the day he arrived," Markie said. "He didn't want it, but sometimes he'd get called away and taken into the main house." He said to the other three, "So maybe she did see him. Maybe he didn't die like they said."

Jennifer agreed but couldn't get past what Markie had said about special attention, and even now, as they spoke, she saw Yellow and Raven out the window, no longer talking but walking toward the main house like something was about to go down, and her three friends were now noticing it too. Raven was so often around Yellow that the two of them might as well have been connected at the hip. Like a couple. And that's how they were approaching the main house now, like a couple. She'd heard whispers of it, of late, about Yellow and Raven being secretly married, which was illegal on the Freedom Ranch. *Partners* weren't a thing here, Jennifer knew, because everybody was free to *do it* with anybody at Freedom.

Especially with Sal Batise.

Every female on the ranch wanted to *do it* with him.

Jennifer wasn't so young she didn't know what *doing it* was, even though she'd never seen it being done; the sounds of it were bad enough. Anytime, day or night or any hour in between, she could hear adults *doing it* inside various barracks as she walked by. Men coming outside afterward and buckling their belts and women straightening out their dresses, staring at them, like this was no place for a child, and Jennifer thinking, *No shit*, all while their innocence leaked out of them daily. Because, as Jennifer had heard more than one of them whisper, there wasn't much else to do at Freedom once their chores were done, aside from getting high on the limitless supply of gummies Sal handed out to the adults like daily vitamins.

And as Yellow and Raven disappeared into the main house, Jennifer conjured up the nerve to bring up what had been heavy on her mind since she'd left Yellow outside the Kitchen House. "I told Yellow that he waved at me. The boy. And she got all scared or something, or mad, and asked if it was a wave or if he placed his hand on the glass. I mean, what's it matter?"

Markie said, "It matters. Which did he do?"

"He put his hand on the glass," she said, recalling it clearly now. "Just like this." She showed them her right hand, fingers splayed out like a starfish. When Markie nodded, knowingly, Jennifer said, "What's that mean?"

Markie said, "Like we said. Steven got picked on. He often had to go into that house and when he came back, he was always sad. Sometimes it would take us hours to calm him down. Raven knew it. So did Yellow. They did the best they could to protect him. But there was a special connection between Steven and Raven. Every night at bedtime, they'd sneak in and tuck us all in. Steven's bed . . . it's your bed now. Right by the window. Every night after Raven and Yellow would go, Raven would stop by that window, on the outside looking in. Steven would kneel on the bed and reach over the headboard and put his hand up to the glass, and Raven would do the same on the other side. It was like a special connection." He nodded toward the Kitchen House window. "Raven was extra sad when he heard Steven went into the woods. So was Yellow. They cried for days, but in secret. And then they got mad. And that's when they really started teaming up. Talking to each other in whispers. In the shadows of the trees."

Iris said, "They're planning something."

Markie nodded in agreement but kept his eyes out the window, maybe looking at the upstairs window of the main house, just as Jennifer had done earlier, and then he said, "I'm with Jennifer. I think she saw Steven. I think he's still alive."

"What do we do?" Peter asked.

Markie said, "I don't know . . . wait and see."

"But until then," Jennifer said, "can you all keep a secret?"

They nodded in unison.

"I've got something to show you, under my bed."

CHAPTER

16

TREVOR HARPER WAS on his third cup of coffee when Lizzie's text came through.

Hey I'm assuming you saw that interview???

I did, he typed, sitting at his kitchen table with REM playing softly in the background, his hangover headache and all-around funk finally beginning to wane enough for him to realize the level of attention his son had garnered from that bizarre interview.

Crazy, right?

Yes, he sent. It was crazy. I'm still not sure what to think. He'd yet to reach out to Sam to congratulate him. He'd call him instead of sending a text, but wanted to give him time to get back home and decompress.

Another text came through from Lizzie, and Trevor couldn't contain his schoolboy smile. At least we know who Mallard Malone is!!!! Ha! I mean no way right? I'm sure he's lying . . .

"He isn't," Trevor said to himself, thinking of the stack of books in the other room. "It's him."

But he sent: Thanks for taking care of me last night. Hopefully I didn't embarrass myself too much?

He waited, and then her next text came through: Not at all. Everybody has something, right? But I was thinking the same thing. I really poured it out to you. I'm sorry. But I'm gonna do it. I'm really gonna do it this time.

He didn't know what she was talking about; he barely remembered last night. He was still terrified he'd revealed too much to her about his own life—but did she mean leaving Jake? Had he encouraged her to do it?

At the sound of car tires and a loud engine outside, he looked up toward the window above the kitchen sink, and through it saw the forest-green hood of Jake's truck.

The truck door opened and closed.

Maybe Lizzie heard it, too, because she sent another text: Gotta go

And Trevor instantly sensed fear. For Lizzie next door, and for himself. He stood from the table, paced the kitchen, tossed the rest of his coffee in the sink. He'd been imagining different scenarios all morning, and most of them ended with Jake rearranging his face after learning his wife had practically spent the night there last night.

Anytime the fear reflex was stoked, PTSD swarmed like a cluster of angry hornets and had him now on high alert. It didn't matter that he was a successful fifty-year-old college professor with tenure; when he began to sense fear, especially in the form of violence and pain, he instantly became a kid again. He was that tiny boy on the schoolyard who hid in the shadows during recess. The little pipsqueak they'd line up against the brick wall and hurl kick balls at his head. He was the boy who, after his cheek was rubbed raw that day they'd made him lick a line of marching ants from the asphalt, who then lied to the principal, as they'd bandaged him up, that he'd just fallen on the playground. He was the boy who got good at lying to protect himself. The boy who was an afterthought to every one of his mother's male dalliances, and a punching bag to most of them, and a cigarette ashtray to one—he still had the circular scars on the underside of his left bicep to prove it.

Sam's parting words from last night came back with a vengeance now, with screaming purpose, like a steam kettle about to blow.

At least I'm not all talk, Dad.

Those words hurt more than Sam would ever know. Those words translated to *coward*, except now, after witnessing his son's bravery on TV moments ago, the words struck like a lash from a whip dripping with so much truth his knees nearly buckled and he had to brace himself on a kitchen chair—the reality that Sam's bravery had not come from him. And that their entire lives were a lie. The same boy Trevor had bathed in bubble baths and read books to and carried on his shoulders. Trevor had never felt so tall as when Sam would view the world from up there, thinking his daddy was tall because he was taller than him, thinking his daddy was a hero because he took him places and provided and kissed his forehead at night and played him music and worked tirelessly every day to fill the hole Annie's death had left, gaping and raw, right in the middle of their lives. That same boy now thought him a coward, and Trevor couldn't help but wonder how long his son had thought it before he'd said it.

Hands trembling, Trevor looked at his phone, saw the last text from Lizzie again.

Gotta go

And thought: *If that son of a bitch touches her again . . .*

As if on cue, Lizzie screamed next door. Trevor faced the window above the sink, hoping he'd misheard, but screams like that—full of terror—pierced him like a fiery sword to the gut. He felt Lizzie's fear now because he knew it and had lived it and wore it as intimately as he wore his own skin. Because the anticipation of being hit was a fear even worse than the pain that followed.

What? What are you gonna do? If that son of a bitch touches her again, then what?

Except that wasn't his own voice and it wasn't Sam's, either, asking that question—what are you gonna do?—but a blast from the past voice he thought he'd buried years ago, back when he was Tommy and not Trevor.

What are you gonna do, Tommy? Huh? You chickenshit little mouse . . . run to big brother?

"Fuck you," he said to it, that memory voice in his head, to that face the voice belonged to, that lumpy head with the jagged scar running like a diagonal jack-o-lantern mouth across his face, over the ridge of his nose. "Fuck you . . . Justice Minks . . ."

Because goddamn it, kids who got bullied weren't supposed to be bullied still as adults. But nobody told the world that, did they? And things were supposed to get better after his mom died by the needle and he went to stay with the half brother he barely knew he'd had, the two of them sired from a man who lived most of his life in jail for a murder he swore he never committed.

Lizzie Hall screamed again from next door and Trevor said, "Fuck you, too," to Jake Hall, and with a hidden lifelong bottled-up rage crushing in on him from every direction, he saw blood. With the sudden irrational fear that he was about to lose his son, his Sam, he saw blood. He saw blood and stars and ants marching. He felt the hand against his throat, pinning him to the wall, his feet dangling above the floor. He saw himself on the floor and gasping for air. He saw dark rooms and locked doors and demons in the trees. He heard them laughing and felt the gut-wrenching pain when the Whistle-or-Lose-It game became a nauseating reality, and they laughed at Tiny Tommy and when he cried it only made it worse . . . and he smelled the stew bubbling on the stove, and he thought, fuck you, fuck you, *fuck you*, as he walked out of the kitchen and down the hallway to his bedroom and grabbed the Louisville Slugger baseball bat leaning next to the window and stormed from his house. He rhythmically beat the barrel of the bat into the palm of his left hand, crossing the driveway toward the Halls' house just as Lizzie screamed *GET AWAY FROM ME*, from inside the house, and Trevor bounded up their porch steps in one single leap, just like he imagined the lead singer of a rock band would have done it, just like Roger Daltry would have, shirt unbuttoned and flapping in the wind to show off his chest, and Trevor kicked at the door that was already open and thought, *Here's Trevor, you cocksucking motherfucker, here's pint-size Tiny Tommy.*

And there Jake was, looming over Lizzie in the middle of the living room, her pleading for him to stop as she cowered on the floor, him as large as King Kong, arm cocked, fist raised like he was about to strike, or maybe he already had because the cut above her eye was open again and running blood down the side of her face, and Lizzie screamed, "Trevor, don't!"

And Trevor only then realized he was about to, when Jake Hall, in full firefighter uniform and buzzed hair and thick mustache, turned to face him. And Trevor heard Lizzie's voice from last night telling him how much she hated kissing Jake with that stupid mustache and they'd laughed about it over wine, and oh how she hated him, hated her husband and wished him dead . . . her asking if that was terrible of her to think that and him saying without hesitation that it wasn't, and then thinking that he'd often wished her husband was dead, too, along with a lot of other people from his past, but he didn't go there . . . because right now he had a job to do.

And maybe it was Jake's smirk that put Trevor over-the-top, the smirk that said Trevor was more of a nuisance than a threat. But Trevor knew what it really was that sent him into full- fledge attack mode with that Louisville Slugger, and it had everything to do with Jake's left hand clutching Lizzie's hair, because that was a feeling of PTSD, that scalp-burn from the pressure and strain of a fist clenched with hair, that hit home hard and true.

Trevor said, "Let her go, Jake."

And when Jake laughed and said *Or what?*—Trevor's brain started pulsing and his heart went full-on rabid dog inside his chest.

Because it just dawned on him that Lizzie was naked. She'd had a towel on when Trevor had burst into the house seconds ago, but the wet towel was on the floor now. Her hair was still wet from the shower and there was a tiny water trail on the hardwood leading from the bathroom, like he'd chased her out of there, and you can't get more vulnerable than unclothed.

Trevor raised the bat.

And Jake said, "Did you fuck my wife last night?"

And Lizzie shouted, "No, Jake. We didn't do anything, I swear . . ."

Jake yanked on her hair, and she grabbed at his wrists and wrenched painfully along with his movement, her bare chest exposed, and Trevor—he so wanted to cover her up—with tears of rage and sorrow in his eyes, swung that bat with the full jagged force of his past. Maybe it was because Jake didn't think he would do it. Maybe he thought Trevor Harper was all talk too. But Jake was slow to react and the barrel of the bat struck the side of his head with enough steam to crack something in his skull.

Jake Hall went down like a sack of grain, one solid thump that shook the house when he hit the floor. Face sideways on the carpet. Eyes open, unblinking.

Trevor thinking, *What did I just do?*

CHAPTER

17

JENNIFER DALEY KNEW all about delayed reactions.

As whip-smart fast as she was, she was joke-slow, always last to a punchline, and therefore, among friends, known for her delayed reaction. She laughed late, laughed last, and most the time awkwardly, because by then the joke was long past.

But what she'd experienced inside that prison had been no joke.

Sal Batise was a monster in human skin. A beast hiding behind a charismatic smile.

Have you fucked her yet, Sam Harper?

The thought of those words gave her chills. Because how dare he even think it, let alone say it right in front of her? Like the fucking of her would be up to Sam Harper. So even as she'd taken Sam's hand earlier as the two of them navigated the postinterview crowd—more like a mob—outside the prison, she'd been thinking of how she'd like to cut Sal's balls off and shove them down his throat.

Thankfully Sam Harper was a gentleman and was equally mortified, if not more so.

Jennifer took pride in her toughness, a trait she got honest from the wonderful family who had taken her in. But while the Daley family was kind and loving and hardworking, for lack of a better word, they were poor. Her adoptive father, who she'd immediately bonded with over art, was a sculptor who often went months looking for projects. Her adoptive mother ran her own daycare out of their house and spent too much of the little they had on other peoples' children, baby food and clothes, to make sure they were comfortable. Jennifer had been telling them for years that neither of them charged enough for their services—they were too nice. And she still wondered how they'd managed to pay for her college at SCAD in Savannah, yet every year her tuition got paid, and back to school she'd go. But the frugal life they all lived—along with her two new older brothers, who were both weirdly innocent, even as teenagers—had further instilled in Jennifer a level of toughness she readily added to what had been forged from her barely remembered life on the Freedom Ranch.

She'd used every bit of that toughness inside the prison, under the camera lights, sitting that close, again, after so many years, to Sal Batise. The way he'd stared at her with those cold, blue eyes—she knew he'd recognized her, which made her wonder if her existence had never been far from his mind. The girl who'd drawn that mural on the closet wall. The girl who'd drawn those incriminating pictures the detectives had found beneath her bed inside the children's barracks. The girl whose artistic ability and genius-level foresight had made the mystery man, Justice Minks, more real in everyone's mind, her convoluted mural helping solidify Beth Hawthorne's claims that there *had* been another killer in that house that night in a Guy Fawkes mask.

So she'd kept her shit together through the brief ten-minute interview, which was already a blur. She'd kept her shit together outside the prison, even as she let go of Sam's hand and she told him she'd be fine, watching as he was suddenly ushered back into the prison without her. She'd kept her shit together as she fought through the crowd on her own, and eventually found Carl's truck in the parking lot, and even managed to keep it together as reporters hurried toward them as Carl pulled away and drove—to where, he didn't know—because she'd told him, *Drive, Carl . . . just drive . . . just get us out of here.*

But finally, after a few miles of distancing themselves on the open roads of Twisted Tree, the delayed reaction, as noticeable as her laughing late on punchlines, hit her first full force as a painful, rib-wrenching sob, and then as a quiet flood of tears. She heard a knocking sound, and at first looked around the truck before realizing it was internal. Not so much inside her head, but a knocking that resonated throughout her body, like a low-level thrum in her bloodstream before gaining steam through her bones and into her heart toward a fist-pounding crescendo of fear, of knuckles on wood, of a closed fist on wood, a wooden door rattling inside a wooden frame and her heart beating so hard it knocked against her rib cage. She leaned forward and hugged her chest but the *knock-knock-knock* continued.

Carl, after checking his rearview mirror, must have felt like it was safe to pull over to the side of the forested road. None of the reporters had followed them.

Jennifer looked around at the trees on either side of the road, grateful Carl had stopped; the motion was making her nauseated, the internalized knocking sound driving her mad.

"Do you hear it?" she asked Carl.

His reply was muted, but the shaking of his head was clear, and it said, *Hear what? Do I hear what?*

She shook her head, *I don't know.*

She cried. She covered her face and cried.

Carl squirmed in his seat; he clearly didn't know how to comfort her, or even if he should. Instead, he let her be, and even in the middle of whatever this was, she was grateful for that too. Because even she didn't know what this was—this emotional outburst from someone who typically wasn't a crier. Some kind of emotional dam had broken. This was so unlike her it might as well have been someone else sitting in the parked truck, and as her tears waned, her brain somehow cleansed and clear, she knew exactly who this other person was. And the knocking . . . she knew that too.

It was her, as a girl. It was her then, and the same girl knocking to come out now.

The same girl she'd unconsciously locked away twenty years ago, locking her inside the closet of her mind in the hours before they'd physically been rescued from the closet inside that house. She'd buried that girl inside as a start-over, thinking they were all inside the closet because of what she'd seen. Because of what she'd witnessed, and it was all her fault. Her thinking, *Maybe if I put her—the old me—inside her own closet, and hush her up*, that only then would someone come save them. Because The Raven didn't. The Raven wouldn't.

"The Raven was here," she said aloud in Carl's truck, recalling not only what she'd written on that closet wall twenty years ago, but somehow seeing herself write it all over again, now, but as the terrified child she'd been back then. "The Raven is a liar."

She turned, wiped her eyes and cheeks, saw Carl watching.

"Who's The Raven?" he asked. "Jennifer, what are you talking about?"

"I don't know," she said, to stall, to kick the can down the road until her mental clarity was restored. Mostly she did know; she thought she did but wasn't yet sure. The only thing she was sure of was that seeing Sal Batise again in person had triggered something within her, and this was the delayed reaction. It had opened a door within her, because a small fist had been knocking on it. For years perhaps the knocking had been muted, but now it was loud and clear, and the floodgate had opened wide.

They'd tried when she was a little girl.

Her new parents were amazed by how well she'd adapted. Since the circus surrounding the finding of the children, and the subsequent months of questions from detectives, from child therapists and psychologists, and later, when her new parents had tried bringing in an art therapist, as cautiously curious as they'd been about her lack of memory, what they'd referred to as *lack of baggage*, they'd been so concerned she was harboring something deep down that one day could damage her.

She laughed at the thought of that now, and Carl might have thought she'd lost her mind, but in truth it was her mind being returned to her, maybe not in full, but whatever it was . . . she felt the intense urge to put a clean pencil to fresh paper and draw. The little girl inside her was coming out from the closet to breathe fresh air, her little hand hurt from holding the pencil, from drawing with it so hard and for so long without stopping that her fingers cramped. Her friends were locked inside with her, and they were crying in the dark because the flashlight had burned out hours ago. She remembered putting her cheek to the dusty closet floor to get her nose closer to the crack at the bottom of the door, to get a whiff of cleaner air out there, air that wasn't polluted with the stench of their own urine and feces.

She said to Carl, "Take us back home, please."

"What about Sam?"

She checked her phone, saw a text she'd missed from Sam that said: I might be longer than I thought. Batise wants me to stay

Jesus, Jennifer thought, *how can you spend another minute inside the same room with that man?* Her urge to get as far away from the prison as possible was now as strong as her urgent need to draw the face her mind was now revealing.

She said to Carl, "Find a Target. Or a CVS. Walgreens, whatever. I need a pencil and paper."

One thing she was beginning to love about Carl was that he didn't ask too many questions and mostly did what he was told. He pulled back out onto the road, typed into his Maps app, and drove off in the same direction they'd been going before he'd abruptly pulled over. But she was better now and eager to move on.

She texted Sam as Carl drove: We'll be around when you're ready. Just let us know. What else have you learned? Is he really Mallard Malone?

Carl took a right turn and followed his navigation prompts through country roads edged by equal parts woodlands and fields.

Sam responded with a long text: Can't call right now but he's given us the coordinates for another body he claims to know about. Police are quietly looking into it. If it checks, he might really be Mallard Malone. And I think Justice Minks is real. Batise thinks that's who took Beth Hawthorne. Said something to do with Minks being Mallard Malone's biggest fan?

Jennifer typed: Wow please keep me posted

Will do

And be careful, Sam

U2

By the time she pocketed her phone, Carl was pulling into a corner-lot Walgreens. As soon as he parked, she opened her door and jogged into the store. She found a pack of pencils, a sharpener, and typing paper in the Back to School section, paid with her debit card, and hurried back out to Carl's truck. From the passenger seat, Jennifer ripped open the pencil pack and ream of paper and started sharpening one of the pencils with Carl curiously watching beside her.

Before putting pencil to paper, she closed her eyes, sucked in a deep breath, and was relieved and terrified simultaneously to find his face still vividly etched in her mind.

She opened her eyes and started drawing.

Ten minutes later, she'd filled out the page with a face that had at one time haunted her dreams on the Freedom Ranch. The man's short dark hair was parted down the middle so cleanly the line in his scalp resembled a straight road. His face was wide, his lantern jaw stubbled with a cleft at the chin. His eyes dark and bottomless, his nose crooked, flat, with wide nostrils. But it was the scar she spent the most time drawing, raised like a mountain range on a map and running diagonally from the inside corner of his left eye, across the bridge of his nose, and ending in a puckered mass of scar tissue that took up much of his right cheek.

By the time Jennifer finished drawing, she was panting, gasping for air and close to hyperventilating. She began to calm only after she placed the pencil down.

Beside her, Carl said, "Who is that?"

"Justice Minks."

"The mystery man?"

"Yes."

"Ugly motherfucker."

She nodded, thinking he looked like a modern-day Frankenstein. "I saw him when I was a girl. On the ranch. He always wore a mask, but one night, I saw him without it."

CHAPTER

18

SAM STILL COULDN'T believe he was here.

Inside the warden's personal office. Inside the State Penitentiary. With Sal Batise, for what might be the rest of the day? The rest of Sal's life, in fact, which was due to end in less than twelve hours.

He felt guilty for feeling enthralled, and reminded himself he was sitting only a few feet away from a man responsible for the murder of at least nine people, and probably more.

From everything Sam knew about death row, that he was here at all was unorthodox. A last meal was one thing, or maybe a final hour in the sunlight or watching the stars, but this was something else altogether. The relationship between Batise and Warden Wren seemed not only unconventional and at times contentious, but like Batise was the one in charge and somehow pulling strings. When Warden Wren was in the office, Sam noticed him constantly checking the wall clock or his watch like he was counting down the hours.

Sam felt sure Batise was holding something over the warden.

Two armed guards remained in the room with them, and Batise was in shackles and chains as he sat in the middle of the room, his chair an island to itself.

"What's going through that head of yours, Sam Harper?"

"Nothing," Sam said from his chair, five feet away from Batise.

"Not true," said Batise. "Although when everything is going through one's mind it can often be construed as nothing at all. What to do next, what to pick first, it all becomes too much, and we end up sitting and doing nothing at all. Twiddling our thumbs."

In other words, Sam thought, *quit wasting time. Show him the sketch.*

Jennifer, via text message a minute ago, had sent Sam a sketch she'd apparently just drawn—had just remembered, in fact—of Justice Minks, and he'd been reluctant to show it to Batise, fearing any negative reaction at this point might shut him down.

When he'd asked Jennifer: Why are you just now remembering this?

She'd responded: Seeing Batise was a major trigger. Will explain later.

If Jennifer was with him, she would have had half of Batise's life story from the man by now.

Show him the picture, Sam.

He ignored his inner voice and instead asked one of the preplanned questions from their initial list for the interview. "The motive for the Hawthorne murders has been discussed from every angle. Why did you send Nancy Tanner, Sylvia Purell, and Annie Blackburn to the Hawthorne mansion that night in May 2006?"

Batise watched him coldly. Sam immediately felt uncomfortable, then fearful he'd already closed him off, when Batise said, "Answering that question might incriminate me into admitting I had anything to do with it."

"All three of them, Nancy, Sylvia, and Annie—Sal's Angels, they were called—testified, under oath, that they'd been given direct orders. By you."

"Because they, themselves, were trying to avoid the death penalty."

"Were they your wives, Sal?"

"Marriage was not allowed at Freedom, Sam Harper, you should know that."

"Except for the leader. The Breaker of Chains. You made the rules, right? Can you at least tell me that, were they or weren't they—"

"They were," he said. "I married Sylvia first. Nancy months later. And then Annie a year to the day of the unlawful invasion of my sovereign territory."

"And they lived in the main house with you?"

"They did."

"Why did you send them on that murder spree?"

"I plead the Fifth."

"Was it like they say, all the journalists and detectives and writers, that *that* was your Tate-LaBianca murders? Or at least the beginning of it."

"I was an infant at the time," Batise said. "Had nothing to do with those either."

"That's not what I—"

"I know what you meant, son. I'm not thick. Spit it out."

"You've never shied away from your . . . idolization of Charles Manson," Sam said. "With your use of drugs on the ranch. You spent time as a pimp. You had your closest disciples. He took his followers out to the desert to protect them and told them they'd one day be rulers of the world, and you took yours to a wooded ranch. You even took his term 'Creepy Crawling' and you sent members of The Collective out wearing all black, into homes, to vandalize, eat their food, move furniture around, just to mess with people's minds, their sense of security."

"And to gauge their obedience to me," he said, although it was clear he wished he had kept that in. *But the narcissist in him wouldn't allow it,* Sam thought.

"And, like Manson, you eventually turned your followers into deadly weapons."

Batise closed his eyes and pretended to snore.

"Manson was trying to convince the world of an impending race war, black versus white, that he called Helter Skelter. It didn't take off, so he took matters into his own hands with the Tate murders. And the next night, LaBianca . . ."

Batise's eyes flashed open. "Get to your point, Sam Harper, so I can shoot it down."

"Were you hoping to start a culture war? A class war. The Haves and the Have-Nots?"

Batise said, "Like in my Mallard Malone series?" Sam knew as much, and now, in hindsight, couldn't believe that no one, in all the time the books had been out, had connected those dots. That no one had thought of Sal Batise as the possible author. Batise added, "But I honestly can't say why those three women did what they did that night."

"You're lying," Sam said.

Batise grinned, chewed on a fingernail, spat it out toward one of the guards.

Sam said, "Were you planning a second attack somewhere like Manson did with LaBianca?"

"Next question."

Sam glanced at his legal pad, but his next question came organically and with sudden rage: "Where does your anger come from?"

"What anger?" Batise asked calmly.

Sam leaned forward. "The anger I see in your eyes, right now."

"The same anger I see now reflected at me, in yours, Sam Harper?" Chains rattled as Batise leaned forward, mirroring Sam's pose. "Huh? Where does *your* anger come from?"

Sam leaned back, having taken an obvious blow, because he'd asked the same question of himself too often. And had he really just nearly come out of his seat challenging the Breaker of Chains?

He had. Sam did his best to ignore Batise's satisfied grin, and tried again.

"What was your *failure*, Sal? Most cult leaders failed at something. Jaime Gomez failed at everything from acting to dancing to porn. Manson failed at music. He wanted to be a rock star and failed. What was your great failure? Where does your anger start? *When* does your anger start?"

"In the womb," said Batise, with an undercurrent of menace that chilled Sam's blood.

He took a few seconds to regroup. *Time to get to the picture Jennifer sent.* "At trial, you played off any notion that Justice Minks was a real person. But now, you're claiming he does exist, and that you believe he has taken Bethany Hawthorne."

"Is there a question in there, Sam Harper?"

"Why now? When back then, you and every follower were interviewed . . ."

"Interrogated."

"Fine," said Sam. "Interrogated. Not one person admitted under oath to knowing someone named Justice Minks. Beth Hawthorne was made to look like a fool, as if she'd imagined him in delirium. Except Nancy Tanner, at trial. What did she call him, a wisp?"

"Fire smoke."

"Because he vanished in the wind, but you could still smell the remnant of something having been burned."

"Something like that," Batise said. "But she recanted. Said she was under the influence of drugs."

"Until the mural was found inside that closet," Sam said. "You've seen it?"

"I've seen it. I saw it at trial, and yes, I saw the image of the mask. That girl is a special talent. And she's grown into quite the beautiful woman. You failed to answer my question of her during the interview, Sam Harper, because it has dawned on me that you just might be a true . . . gentleman. But you do like her, right? I mean, I can tell."

"I just met her yesterday," Sam said.

"Are you sure?"

"Yes, I'm sure." But the fact that he'd been asked the question now had Sam asking it of himself. Jennifer was convinced she'd seen his father before, and now he wondered if she had thought the same of him. He pushed on. "But you're saying Minks *does* exist."

"Yes."

"But he didn't back then?"

"Oh, he did. It was just that everyone was afraid of him."

"Even you?"

Batise raised a finger in warning. "Don't test me, son. Sal Batise is afraid of no one. Not then and not now."

Sam swallowed over the lump in his throat. "Then why the change of heart?"

"Quite simple . . . I only have hours to live, and therefore much more to lose."

Sam opened his phone, got permission from the guards to approach Sal Batise. He showed Batise the sketch Jennifer had just drawn of Justice Minks.

"Where'd you get that?" Batise asked abruptly.

Sam returned to his seat and didn't answer.

"She drew that, didn't she? How?"

"From memory."

"Impressive memory from a girl as young as she was."

"Nightmares have a way of embedding."

"Don't they ever."

"Is it him?" Sam asked. "Is that Justice Minks?"

"Yes," Batise said. "Although even I only saw him a few times without his mask."

Bingo, Sam thought. "Did he always wear the Guy Fawkes mask?"

"No, he had several others. That was just his favorite."

"Who was he to you?"

"He was part of The Collective."

"Was he in your inner circle?"

Just when Sam thought he wouldn't respond, Batise said, "Yes."

"Did he live in your house, on the ranch?"

"Yes."

"For how long?"

"He arrived four months before . . ."

"The massacre?" Sam asked. Batise nodded, solemnly almost, maybe as close as he'd get to ever admitting his involvement. "Some called him your Bruce Davis. Or Tex Watson. Was he your right-hand man?"

Batise extended his right arm, wiggled the fingers on his right hand theatrically. "Oh, I don't know about that. But we did have our talks, he and I."

"What would you talk about?"

"Life," he said. "The future."

"And what does this have to do with Mallard Malone?"

"Because Minks must have gotten his hands on the book. The final one," Batise said. "Book One."

"Why does this surprise you?"

"Because he's not in the chain."

"Billy Boyle smuggled the manuscripts from the prison. Who was next? What did Boyle do with them? Who handled the correspondence with the publisher? With the editor? Who handles the money, Sal?"

"Now we're in overload, Sam Harper. Too many questions at once. Don't be a novice."

"How could Justice Minks have gotten his hands on the final book if he's not in the chain?"

"He's clever. And ruthless. And he won't stop until he gets what he wants."

"What do you think he wants?"

Batise leaned back in his chair, as if to think, but Sam couldn't tell if his movements and mannerisms were coming from a true place or were just amusing theater to him. He tried again, *knowing* he was getting close to something, knowing Batise would stop talking when the warden returned. "You said earlier that Minks must be Mallard Malone's biggest fan. Why?"

Batise leaned forward again, as if to speak out of the guards' earshot. "Because in the final book, Sam Harper, Oliver Crown abducts the governor's wife."

Sam glanced toward the office door. "Why? Why, in the book, does Oliver Crown abduct the governor's wife?"

"Because in the last book, *The Breakout*, there's a certain someone on death row. The leader of a famous cult he called The Collective. And they lived on a ranch known as Freedom. And he's made a career on death row of . . . of . . . finding ways to stay his execution. But he's due to die in less than twenty-four hours, when . . ." he gestured toward Sam, as if asking him to finish his thought.

"When the main character, Oliver Crown," Sam said, a hard chill going down his spine, "kidnaps the governor's wife, and there's a ransom demand—"

Batise smiled, moving his hand in a rolling motion, like, *You're almost there, Sam Harper, keep reeling it in . . .*

"And Oliver Crown wants this cult leader dead?"

"Yes."

"In the books," Sam said, talking faster now. "What is the cult leader's name?"

"Malcolm. Malcolm Dodd."

"Your father's name was Malcolm."

"Yes."

"You never got over not having a father in your life?"

"So says the world."

"You visited him once a month for years."

"You're sidetracking yourself, young man. My time is running short as we speak. Back to Oliver Crown."

Sam said, "Oliver Crown was said to have risen from the ashes like a phoenix. In this final book, *what had caused* the world to become what it is in the series?"

"Let's not get too far ahead of ourselves, Sam Harper."

"Disease?" Sam asked. "A virus? An uprising?"

Batise chewed on his lower lip.

"Did you write the series or not, Sal?"

"I'm trying not to show all my cards," Batise said with an angry edge.

"Why not? You're dying in less than twelve hours," Sam pointed out, his voice rising just a touch. "And a woman this state adores has been taken by a human monster and you know more than you're telling."

"I'm trying to stay alive," Batise hissed.

"So you're using me to stay alive? That's what this is about?"

"Did you think I'd roll over and die, Sam Harper? Sail quietly into the sunset?"

"But why me?"

"Next question."

"Why did Minks abduct Beth Hawthorne?"

"Think about it."

And Sam did: "Because he knows you'll do anything to stay alive."

"And?"

"And you've exhausted all your appeals."

"And?"

"At this point, the governor is the only one who can stay the execution."

"Bingo." Batise sat back, looking satisfied. "Minks knows I have a final card up my sleeve for the governor."

"This is your final card?" Sam asked. "The bodies they're looking for right now? The ones mapped out in your books? Because you've already played it."

"I'm no rookie, Sam Harper. That was just to let everyone know I'm serious. And that I am who I say I am."

"Then what is your final card?"

"That's between me and the governor," Batise said. "And it's not yet time to play it. When I do, I'll get my stay of execution."

"You're confident?"

"Yes."

"And Minks?"

"That's when he'll make his ransom demand."

Sam sat up straight. "Your death for Beth Hawthorne's life?"

"Yes. He wants to make sure I die tonight, as planned."

"Why?"

"Because that's exactly how it plays out in the book," said Batise.

CHAPTER 19

BETH HAWTHORNE SAT with her back to the wall, the hole just above her head to the right.

Occasionally, she'd feel a tug on the chain around her ankle, which meant Billy Boyle was shifting his own position on the other side of the wall.

On one hand, she felt hope because she wasn't alone inside this Mallard Malone–inspired house of horror, but on the other hand, considering that they were connected by a chain that ran through the wall between them, she saw no way out of this level of macabre insanity.

Earlier, after they'd exchanged names through the hole in the wall, a door had opened inside Billy Boyle's room and he'd gone instantly quiet. She heard footsteps over there, and Billy breathing like he was terrified. Billy begging quietly for his life, to be let go, promising he'd never tell anyone anything, but his words were ignored. Something was placed on the floor, the footsteps trailed away, and the door closed.

They'd been quiet now for a few minutes, when Billy said, "Have you tried this yet?"

"Tried what?" Beth asked in a hushed whisper.

"This food," Billy said. "I assume that's what it is. He just put a bowl on the floor like I'm a dog. Fucking flies in it. Jesus." She heard a scooting noise and a rattle, like he'd just shoved the bowl away with his foot. The chain moved above her shoulder. He must have realized the tug. He said, "Sorry."

"It's okay."

Billy gagged like he might throw up, like it was taking great effort to compose himself.

She was starving, but by the putrid stench coming from the hole in the wall, if it was from the food Billy had just been delivered, she didn't want it. She'd rather starve.

Billy said, "Are you hurt? I saw on the news . . . they thought you'd been shot."

"In the leg," she said. "It's not bad. I think I'm on pain meds. He's been forcing pills down my throat."

"How long have you been in here?" Billy asked, his voice sounding closer to the hole now.

"Hours, I think," she said. "I was in a garage before. Or something like that. Did you get a look at the surroundings when he brought you in?"

"No," he said. "He knocked me out. I woke up here. Do you know what's going on?"

"No," she said. "Other than my worst nightmare coming to life."

"I know about you and . . ." Billy trailed off like he didn't know how to attack the topic. "I always believed you, by the way. I always believed in the fourth killer that night."

"Thank you," she said. "But what's going on? Has something happened?"

"Yeah," Billy said. "A lot has happened. You heard about Sal Batise's last interview?"

"He made me watch it."

"So you know Batise announced to the world that he's Mallard Malone?"

"Yes," she said. "Do you believe him? You said you were a guard there?"

"Yeah. It's him. I'm the one who's been smuggling the manuscripts out of the prison for the past eight years."

Beth couldn't believe what she was hearing, but at least another piece to the puzzle had just snapped in place. "Justice Minks. That's who's holding us prisoner, you know that, right?"

"Yeah, I guessed that with the mask. Or at least someone impersonating him."

"No, it's him," Beth said.

"He told me his name is Oliver Crown," Billy said. "This place, I mean, what the fuck? Oh . . . sorry."

"It's okay, Billy. I'm scared too."

"He's psycho, right? I mean, he has to be. Have you read the books, Mrs. Hawthorne?"

"No. You?"

"All of them," Billy said. "Only I waited until they came out. I have the entire collection at home. I was low man on the totem pole. I got the manuscripts out of the prison and into a secure PO box. Usually within a week of putting them there, I'd find money left for me. Money for the job, but mostly to keep my mouth shut. You wouldn't believe how much . . ."

"It's okay, Billy. I don't need to know."

He lowered his voice. "I'm a millionaire, Mrs. Hawthorne." It was like he couldn't help himself. "I've been counting down the days until I could put in my two weeks. But I was locked in until the last book came out. I had to stay until then, that was the deal I signed."

"With who?" she asked, still trying to wrap her mind around it all. "Who did you sign the contract with, Billy?"

"I don't know," he said. "Nobody is supposed to know anybody in the chain. That's how it's worked for so long. That, and keeping quiet. The money kept me quiet. It was easy money. And the threats, of course. Whether they ultimately came from Batise or whoever in the chain, I wasn't about to test it."

"So you all called it the chain?" Beth asked.

"Yeah, ironic, right . . . coming from the guy who calls himself the Breaker of Chains."

"Is that why you're here, Billy? Did you break the chain? Did you tell someone?"

"No, that's the thing. I didn't do anything. For years I did my job, and I've been waiting and waiting for Sal to write the last damn book, but it never came."

"You mean he hasn't written it?"

"Not to my knowledge," he said. "And then the interview this morning. He announces who he is. I get ambushed on my way into work, and here I am."

"I'm sorry, Billy."

"Yeah, maybe not as sorry as I am. I knew all along I was playing with fire." He was quiet for a minute, and then it sounded like he was fighting tears. "I think we're gonna die in here, Mrs. Hawthorne."

"No, we're not," she said, but deep down she didn't believe it. "How old are you, Billy?"

"Thirty-two. I'll be thirty-three next week. Got a wife and two kids." He choked up again, composed himself. "They didn't know anything about anything. I took the threats seriously, because they weren't all against me, they named my family too. That's why I toed the line. Always. I don't know why I'm here. I just don't. But I was counting down the days and weeks, you know? I was out of there, and all my money, you know . . . offshore accounts, all that. I was going to take my family and go . . . just sail off into the sunset somewhere. On a beach. Rum drinks every night. Bloody Marys every morning. And I don't even drink that much, Mrs. Hawthorne." After another beat, he said, "I mean, why couldn't he just finish the fucking series already? Sorry . . . language, I know."

"It's fucking okay, Billy," she said.

He laughed at that, and then said, "Say, what's on your side of the wall?"

"A map," she said. "Looks like a map of . . . the world of Oliver Crown."

"Yeah, same," he said. "Does the chain come through over there inside the area marked *Untrustables*?"

"Yes."

"Same," he said. "Figures."

"What does?"

"Malone goes into detail about it in one of the books," he said. "*Crown and Crows*, I think. Or maybe *Feast or Famine*. But this is how they imprison everyone in the world of Oliver Crown. Special houses, like prisons, they call Chain Houses. Two to three floors high, and all the prisoners are connected by chains through the walls and ceilings and floors. It's brutal."

Beth closed her eyes, too tired to fight, but knowing at some point her life would depend on her ability to do so. But her mind kept going back and forth between looking for a way out now or conserving her energy for an escape at the right moment. She longed to look out the window across the room and breathe the fresh air coming in between the bars, but knew her chain wouldn't allow it, not with Billy on the other side of the wall.

Her eyes flashed open at the sound of movement directly below her. A door opened down there, followed by footsteps, and then a chain rattling.

"What's going on over there?" Billy said.

"I don't know," Beth said. "It's coming from the room below me."

Seconds later she heard a power drill churning, and then louder as it appeared to be coming through her floor. She screamed when the drill bit emerged in a tiny mound of splintered wood and dust.

The drill bit disappeared into the floor, and then emerged again seconds later, and bit by bit, the hole in the floor grew larger.

Not stopping, she knew, until it was big enough for another chain to fit through.

CHAPTER 20

SHIT, THOUGHT TREVOR Harper.

Shit, shit, shit.

What did you do? he thought as he stared at Jake Hall's felled body in the middle of the living room floor, standing, Louisville Slugger still in his shaking hands, inside a house he'd never entered until now, a house he'd often wondered about, what it looked like inside, what it smelled like inside, what it sounded like inside when the two of them weren't fighting.

Jake's eyes were open, but they weren't moving.

His eyelids weren't blinking.

That's because you killed him, Tommy.

I'm not Tommy, he thought. *I'm Trevor now, just as I have been for twenty years. Dr. Trevor Harper, PhD, and I should be home right now prepping for my fall course load.*

"What did you do?"

It wasn't his voice this time, or even Tommy's from yesteryear, but Lizzie's voice from across the room, because that's where she'd crab-walked, backward, into the wall, as soon as he'd come in swinging.

"Trevor, what did you do?"

I don't know, he said, or thought he'd said, but the words never came out, not really.

"I think you killed him. Jesus Christ, you killed Jake . . ."

"No . . ." he said, not so much as an answer to what she'd said, but in general. Everything right now was a *no*, because this couldn't be happening.

Long time coming though, Tommy. About time you fought back.

"Fuck you," he said aloud, but in a whisper, because the last one had been the voice of Justice Minks. "Don't ever touch me. Don't ever touch me again," he told the voice.

And Lizzie Hall reached for the towel that had come off during the scuffle with her husband—her dead husband—like she was no longer comfortable being naked in front of her neighbor. And the way she was looking at him now crushed his soul, eyeing him like she was full of fear of *him*, like *he* was the monster and not the dead sack of bones on the floor. She should be thanking him. That was crazy talk, he knew, but didn't it hold a bit of truth?

Quit looking at me like that, he wanted to tell her, but instead said nothing because there was blood running from Jake Hall's head, staining the carpet in a shape that looked a little like Texas; he'd split it good and wide just over the left temple.

His arms were shaking like he could still feel the impact in them through the bat.

There's no way he'd swung hard enough to kill the man. But then again, hadn't that been his intent all along? Maybe not all along, but in that exact moment—Jake Hall had been a bully beating on a defenseless woman, and in that instant, he'd wanted the man off this earth.

He needed to be taught a lesson.

He didn't deserve to play the game of life because he didn't follow the rules.

"Trevor . . ."

He wasn't civilized.

"Trevor . . ."

He was a total asshole.

"Trevor!"

He turned and screamed, "What?"

And she cowered against the wall again, crying even harder now, and he felt like he'd really done it now. Severed any hope of remedying this situation. Maybe deep down he'd planned this out, killing Jake Hall and the two of them running off into fairytale land, but screaming at the one person now he wanted so badly to hug wasn't the way to go.

"I'm sorry," he said to Lizzie. When she didn't respond, he said it again, but with more desperation, because he just realized he'd protected her from violence by using violence.

By going one step further.

By turning his bat into a weapon. A murder weapon.

What she didn't know, and he couldn't take the time to rationalize now, was that it hadn't been just Jake he'd hit, but all of them, every one of the bullies who'd beat on him and ridiculed him and tortured him for being Tiny Tommy.

What's done was done. After the brief thought of checking Jake's pulse and deciding what was the point, he backed away from the scene, slowly at first—like maybe if he walked in reverse he could pretend none of it had happened—before turning from Lizzie and her dead husband and running out the door.

The cops would probably come soon. Maybe an ambulance.

He could either stay at home and wait and take whatever punishment was coming, or he could run. He'd run before, and he could run again.

And as he entered his house, all he could think of was Sam.

Everything he'd ever done in his life, for better or worse, had been for Sam.

And as he opened his dresser drawers and threw in clothes and underwear and socks, he said, "I'm sorry, Sam." He grabbed a toothbrush and deodorant and his cholesterol meds and shoved them into the bag. The television was on in the living room. He'd left in such a hurry earlier he'd forgotten to turn it off, but truthfully, he didn't even remember turning it on. The entire morning had been a hangover-induced blur. Below the TV was a row of shelving that held their photo albums. Sam often kidded them that nobody *did* photo albums anymore, and he'd tried to explain to his son that photo albums weren't something someone *did*. But maybe he wasn't totally wrong, because every one of the photo albums was full of pictures of things they'd done. Memories they'd made. As a family. And yeah, maybe he hadn't added to the photo album collection since Annie died, maybe he'd gotten lazy, but the truth was it had hurt Trevor too hard to open them ever again. They were dusty even now, just like the baseboards in the dining room.

Trevor removed one album from the shelf and turned the pages, looking for one picture in particular. It wasn't in that album, or the next, but halfway through the third one he found it, a picture of himself and Annie and Sam from twenty years ago, one they'd gotten a stranger to take of them in front of the chalet they'd rented in Gatlinburg. It was his favorite picture because he felt it was a trip, as far as pure happiness went, that could never be duplicated, and maybe it never was. But in it, Annie was beaming, her smile broad and honest and full of relief, and Sam stood between them, each of them with a hand on his shoulders, his smile equally as large and full of pure joy, because they were fresh off eating ice cream cones and they'd promised him an hour in the pool and then pulled pork, his favorite, for dinner.

Trevor was crying as he removed the picture from the clear plastic sleeve of the photo album, the surrounding pictures all from the same trip but not as special to him as that one. He stood from the floor, slid the picture into his shirt pocket, and faced the TV just as whatever program was on was interrupted by breaking news about Bethany Hawthorne. The news anchor's voice-over said something about authorities now believing they knew who may be behind yesterday's abduction of Beth Hawthorne and the murder of her security guard, about history coming back to haunt the Hawthorne family yet again in the name of Justice Minks, and they now had a sketched rendering of what the man may have looked like twenty years ago behind the infamous mask . . .

But it was mostly bee buzz to Trevor, because he couldn't take his eyes off the TV screen and the sketch of a man Trevor knew all too well. Very few people, if any, had seen Justice Minks without his mask, and Trevor was one of them. He'd seen the face up close and personal, too close, so close, in fact, that Trevor could still see the raised ridge of the jagged scar across his face, could still recall the smell of his breath on his skin and the brownish-yellow hue of his coffee-stained teeth, when he'd grabbed Trevor by the collar and hissed, *You forget me, Tommy. You got that. You forget I exist. I was never here. Or I'll find you. I'll find you and whatever life you manage to make after this, and I'll ruin it. I will hunt you down and end you and everyone you love. The only question will be how many pieces I cut you into. And I won't give a fuck who your brother is anymore.*

CHAPTER

21

WITH THE SKETCH of Justice Minks now out across the news outlets, Jennifer's hope that the man would be recognized by someone was dampened by the sudden fear of her vulnerability.

The fear Minks would see the sketch, know she'd drawn it, and then come to hunt her down. If he could get to Bethany Hawthorne, he could get to her.

Carl told her she was being paranoid, but she didn't think so. It wasn't that she knew Minks well, but she knew him enough, and as the minutes passed since sketching Minks's horrid face from the resurfaced memory of her time at the Freedom Ranch, she knew there were more memories in there, and snippets were beginning to stir up like dust devils on a windswept floor.

Most she couldn't yet pinpoint, and therefore they made no sense, but because of the intense feeling of unease she'd experienced since leaving the prison, she knew they were in there lurking, waiting for the next trigger. She had a notion to draw them out, just like the art therapist her parents had arranged had wanted her to do twenty years ago, but she didn't know how—how to draw something out without a clear vision of what that something might be. But one thing that was clear to her was that they needed to return to Louisville.

When Carl protested that he didn't want to leave Sam at the prison, she promised him they'd come right back. Reminded him that Sam had his hands full and, according to his last text, may even be there with Batise until his execution.

Carl was full of obvious anxiety on the thirty-minute drive west back to Louisville. "This is way more than Sam bargained for," he said. "It's like he made a deal with the devil getting that interview, and now look."

Jennifer said, "This was exactly what he wanted, Carl. He's a filmmaker."

"He's Batise's prisoner."

"How about we agree to disagree," she said, although she didn't totally disagree with him. Batise couldn't be trusted, especially in his last hours, and she feared for Sam's well-being as deeply as Carl, but right now there was nothing they could do about it but find their own answers. *It's better*, she'd told Carl before leaving Twisted Tree, *than sitting here jerking off in your truck*. He'd laughed at that, and said, *You're one cool chick*, before putting his truck in gear and driving on, and now here they were, approaching Sam's childhood home. "Turn here."

"I know how to get there," Carl said.

"Yeah, my bad," she said. "It's my nerves. I get bossy when I'm nervous."

"You must be nervous all the time, then," he said. She smiled. Carl glanced at her as he turned the corner toward the house. "You still want to do this?"

"Yes."

"And you don't think we should warn Sam?"

"No."

He turned into Trevor Harper's driveway. "I still don't get why you need to see his dad all of a sudden. He's kind of boring."

"Maybe not as boring as you might think," she said, sure now she knew him from somewhere, and had a strong idea of where and when that somewhere had been. And she wasn't going to let the professor off the hook this time.

As soon as Carl put the truck in park, she opened the door and hurried toward the porch. She smelled smoke. Over her shoulder, she asked Carl if he smelled it, too, and he said he did, but neither of them saw where the smoke was coming from. Maybe she did need to slow down and think this through, but she couldn't. Her insides were thrumming. She opened the screen door and was about to knock when the wooden front door, already ajar, creaked open wider. She took that as her invitation to go in.

Carl, behind her, said, "What are you doing? You gonna freakin' knock?"

"Mr. Harper?" she called out from the foyer. Music sounded from the kitchen, "Stairway to Heaven."

"Professor Harper," she called out again.

"This is breaking and entering," Carl said from behind her.

"Did you see his car in the driveway?" she asked.

"No."

"Then why was his door open?" she asked. "And why is the music playing?" She wasn't expecting an answer. "He left in a hurry, Carl."

"Yeah," he said, "Maybe you're right."

I am right, she thought, peeling off toward the living room as Carl continued toward the kitchen, toward the music. The TV was on across the room, but the screen was paused on the news. The sketch she'd drawn of Justice Minks was frozen on the screen, as if Trevor Harper had paused it there on purpose before he'd taken off. On the table next to the recliner, she saw the Mallard Malone books she'd dropped off yesterday. Photo albums had been left on the floor in front of the TV stand, one of them open. Averting her eyes from the frozen sketch of Justice Minks on the television—it was like he was watching her—she knelt by the open photo album and studied the pictures inside the plastic sleeve. One of them was missing, and she felt sure Trevor Harper had removed it before leaving, but the rest, as she studied them one by one, justified her reason for coming. Because she instantly recognized the young man in all the photos. This was Trevor Harper as a young man, and the young woman smiling next to him, Jennifer recognized her too. It must be Trevor's late wife, Annie. Although those weren't the names she knew them by.

And the boy standing between them . . .

Jennifer swallowed hard, closed her eyes, opened them again, begging her mind for clarity and focus, because she knew the little boy from somewhere, too, and felt sure that it was Sam, but she just couldn't connect the dots.

Her hands trembled as she removed the family photo from the album sleeve.

A man, woman, and a little boy.

They're from the Freedom Ranch, Jennifer. But there were only four kids on the ranch, and that boy was not one of them. *Think. Think.* Even though she still had no recollection of drawing it, she pictured the mural on the inside of the closet wall and the erased fifth stick figure now loomed large. Because there were five kids on that ranch, not four.

Five. And this boy was one of them. *Sam* was one of them.

She closed her eyes, tight, and saw a boy waving to her from the second-floor window of a blue house. A blue house in need of painting. No, he's not waving, he's putting his hand on the glass, because . . . because that's what he does with . . .

"The Raven," she said, looking again at the picture she now held in both hands because it was shaking too much in one. "Yellow."

Trevor Harper was The Raven. Annie Harper was Yellow.

Her mind flashed back to the closet wall and what she'd written on it.

The Raven was here.
The Raven is a lyer.

Why?

"Jennifer . . ." Carl said behind her.

She studied young Trevor Harper in the picture—he was such a small man. *What did you do? Why were you a liar?*

"Jennifer," Carl said louder.

She turned around to find Carl standing with a foot-tall stack of what looked like booklets in his hands, folded pages stapled and colored with Crayons and markers. "What are those?"

"Comic books," he said. "Homemade. Looks like a kid drew them. They're old. They were left on the kitchen table."

Jennifer stood from her crouch, plucked the top comic book from the stack, and read the title: *The Raven & The Mongoose. Adventure #1.* The cover featured a colored picture of what she assumed was a raven holding a baseball bat and swinging it at a faceless bad guy, with what she assumed was a mongoose chewing the bad guy's right leg.

Underneath the picture were the words: *Written by Tommy Batise.*

CHAPTER

22

Before

JENNIFER FELT LIKE she'd started a ball rolling and there was no way now to stop it.

Showing Iris, Markie, and Peter the sketches she'd drawn and hid under her bed was one thing, but showing them to Raven and Yellow was another. But she knew she had to do it, even while the doing of it brought along with it a sense of doom that made her want to cry. She'd seen the three women come back from the woods last night and burn what they'd been wearing in a fire. She knew she shouldn't have been out of the barracks, but she hadn't been able to sleep, and she'd heard commotion outside on the ranch. She'd been curious, so she'd sneaked outside and hid behind a tree, just as the three women emerged from the woods, wobbling a little and laughing a lot, like she'd often seen the adults do after eating the gummies. At first, she'd been shocked because they'd come from the woods, and she remembered thinking, *Good thing the demons didn't get them*. But then she noticed the large knives they were holding, larger than any knives she'd ever seen, like swords almost, and wondered if maybe they *were* the demons. The three women then approached an outdoor fire where Sal Batise sat on a log, like he was waiting for them to come from the woods. Waiting for them to come back home. He stood when he saw them and kissed them all one by one. He said something and they giggled. They tossed their big knives into the fire and then immediately started taking their clothes off and throwing them into the flames. The flames went *whoosh*, licking toward the trees, growing as each item of clothing went in and disappeared into spirals of smoke and floating ash. Jennifer had really started trembling when she'd seen who came from the woods next—the mean one, the big bad wolf, the man in the weird mask, and in his right hand was something sharp and twisted and he used it to open a bottle of wine he held in his other hand. They all shared the wine, passing the bottle around and talking in whispers and laughing, and then the man in the mask and the Breaker of Chains began taking their clothes off too and the giggling women walked into their arms.

That's when Jennifer turned away and hurried back to the barracks, praying she hadn't been seen or heard or sensed, or whatever bad guys did to know somebody was watching. And as soon as she retreated to her bed, where the other three were still sound asleep, she took her papers and pencils from beneath the bed and started drawing everything she'd just witnessed outside around the fire. She'd studied them, their faces, their hair, their bodies, the way they walked, which one was tallest, and which one was shortest, and which one was in between. She'd seen them before, all three women, and had once heard Yellow refer to them as Sal's Angels, except she'd said it in a way that made Jennifer think Yellow didn't like them very much. And so she drew them coming from the woods and she drew them holding those knives and she drew them undressing into the fire, and now here she was, having just told Yellow and Raven all about it, and even though they'd not brought up the boy she'd seen earlier in the window, she had a feeling they both believed her now, and the boy was in that house, and now Yellow and Raven acted like they were planning to do something about it. And now that she'd told them about what she'd seen last night and showed them the pictures, they were dead set on doing something about that, too, because Yellow said, "It's time," and Raven agreed, with tears in his eyes, like they'd maybe been planning to do something even before tonight and this had been, what Jennifer's mother used to say, the final straw. And it looked like Raven was trying to muster up courage and strength, and that's when he sat Jennifer and Iris and Markie and Peter down in the shadows and told them that things on the ranch were about to change. That the people here weren't who they thought they were, and they'd made a big mistake in coming—just like Jennifer's mother had said before she'd gone into the woods—and they'd made an even bigger mistake by staying for as long as they had.

Because something bad had happened. Really bad. And Jennifer, they said, was somehow a witness to it.

"But we will take care of you and make sure you're safe," said The Raven. The Raven was calm and gentle and soft-spoken, and Jennifer trusted him with her whole heart. He gathered the kids closer and said, "Let me tell you a story I started writing when I was your age. It's about a raven and a mongoose who fight bad guys. . . ."

CHAPTER

23

"Hello, this is Sam Harper," he said into the cell phone the guard handed him outside Warden Wren's office.

Half of Sam couldn't wait to get back inside with Sal Batise, while the other half considered running from the prison with whatever he'd learned thus far and never coming back. It seemed almost comical, how he was suddenly the center of attention as Sal's lone go-between, and now Governor Hawthorne was on his way to the prison, and here he was on the phone with Mallard Malone's editor.

"Mr. Harper, this is Donna Hanson from Quiver and Bow. Mallard Malone's editor."

"Hi," Sam said. "Nice to meet you."

He felt like an unprepared fool and didn't know what else to say but also couldn't imagine what the publishing house felt now that it had all but been confirmed, in the most disturbing of ways, that Sal Batise was Mallard Malone. Of the eighteen burials referred to throughout his series, potentially mirroring where real victims had been buried around the country, three had been unearthed in the past two hours: the one in Georgetown, Indiana; another in Waco, Texas; and a third in St. Louis, Missouri. By now, it was clear Sal Batise had a photographic memory; he'd named all three victims who'd been unearthed. DNA tests would have to be done, but with the given names all matching missing persons from decades past, authorities—and now the FBI—assumed, at this point, that Sal wasn't lying.

Over the phone, Donna Hanson said, "We've been following on the news, Mr. Harper. As we've told the media and local police and the FBI, we knew nothing about any of this being secretly written into the Mallard Malone series. And believe us or not, we, until this point, never knew who Mallard Malone was. The first book in the series arrived on our desk nine years ago. It was literally left in a box on the porch at our offices at Quiver and Bow, here in downtown Manhattan. Obviously, we agreed to publish it. It said it was an exclusive submission, but we had a week to decide before the book would be left on a competitor's doorstep. We loved the concept and the writing. It was flawless. But because the whole thing was a bit sketchy, we offered a low advance. It was accepted." She spoke quickly, as if her time on the phone with him was limited, or maybe she just couldn't wait to get it over with. "At first, the correspondence was done over regular mail, with warnings that any detective work trying to learn of his identity would be considered a breach of the contract signed with Mr. Mallard Malone, proprietor. Understand, Mr. Harper, that Quiver and Bow, at the time, was an indie press. We, as you probably know, have blown up since, with houses now in multiple countries, due to our success with Oliver Crown and Mallard Malone. We now have seven other publishing imprints. The book blew up on its own merits, but part of the book's ultimate rise to superstardom had to do with the idea of the anonymous author. I probably don't need to tell you the rest, but that's how it started."

Sam said, "I'm referring to this correctly by calling it the chain?"

"Yes, it was called the chain. There were many links in the chain as far as payments and royalties and correspondence."

"And no one ever dove deep into reversing the chain?" Sam asked.

"No," Donna said with a sigh that sounded regretful. "Books were all delivered on time. Correspondence, which eventually turned to secure emails with frequently changing addresses, was always prompt. We were all making money. A lot of money. And the bottom line is, Mr. Harper, that the entire thing was fun. We had fun with a mystery that constantly revolved around Mallard Malone and Oliver

Crown." She paused for a deep breath. "But this . . . what's coming out now, is deeply disturbing, and as you can imagine, we're scrambling with how best to deal with it."

Sam was so mind-blown he didn't know how to respond, other than saying, "I'm sorry, Mrs. Hanson." And remembering why she was speaking to him in the first place—because Batise refused to talk directly to her—Sam said, "What is it I can do for you?"

She let out a laugh that wasn't really a laugh, but an expression of disbelief and perhaps annoyance at the current situation. "All things as they are, and we don't even know yet what the status will be going forward on the final book, other than a worldwide revolt if we *don't* publish it, we'd still like to know where the final book is."

Sam was shocked. "You mean you don't have it?"

"No, we don't."

"But . . . I thought it was due out in a few months?"

"We were already in panic mode here even before the news came out this morning," she said. "And when you're in a panic, Mr. Harper, you . . ." Her voice cracked with obvious emotion. "Desperation leads you to do things you wish you could take back."

"What . . . what did you do?" Sam asked, his heart revving right back up again.

"I asked . . . we . . . asked . . . one of our marketing assistants was begging, okay . . . he was begging us to let him try and reverse the chain. To try and find some answers."

"And? Mrs. Hanson?"

"We can't get hold of him," she said in a hiss across the phone.

"Since when?"

"Since yesterday afternoon. And that was before the interview. Oh, Jesus, we're scared out of our minds now . . . now that we know who's behind it. We just reported him as officially missing."

"His name?" Sam asked. "The marketing assistant?"

"Joseph Gerrard. He's twenty-three," she said. "I was told the FBI is trying to question Sal Batise now?"

Down the hallway, Sam saw an FBI man in a suit and tie waiting outside the door to Warden Wren's office, checking his watch, and now Sam felt the need to hurry Donna Hanson off the phone. FBI

Agent Givens had already been inside with Sal Batise once, but for only five minutes, the warden had told Sam, because Batise had refused to answer any questions without Sam Harper's presence in the room. In other words, whatever game Sal was playing, they were still in the middle of it.

Sam said over the phone, "I'm getting ready to go in with the FBI agent, yes."

"This is all so bizarre," she said.

"You don't know the half it," Sam said, motioning toward Agent Givens that he'd be off the phone in a minute.

"But can you ask him, I mean, where's the book? Has he even written it? Is he holding it hostage?"

"I'll ask him, Mrs. Hanson. And if I can get anything useful out of him, I'll get back with you."

"Thank you," she said. "Maybe we're being paranoid, and our assistant went out of town, camping without his phone, but—"

You're not paranoid, Sam thought, but didn't say. They had every right to be worried.

Donna, with sarcasm said, "Good thing his books never need any editing, I mean, if we do have to publish it in a hurry."

Intrigued by this, Sam said, "His novels don't need editing?"

She said, "No. Like I said earlier. His stories come in flawless. Character arcs, storylines, plot, dialogue . . . all of it. Up until now, Mr. Harper, I've had the easiest editing job in the history of publishing. I get the manuscript, read it, and I pass it along to production."

"So either Sal is a literary genius . . ."

"Or there's a secret editor in the chain who edits his books before I get them."

Sam digested this as he ended the call and handed the phone back to the guard, telling him he might need that number later. He shook hands with Agent Givens and did his best not to be starstruck by him. Agent Givens, along with local true crime blogger Ellie Isles, had headed the task force that had finally caught the I-64 killer, a.k.a. The Spider, a year ago. The story launched the popular true crime network now known as The Spider Web, which was where Carl, if he wasn't working or playing Dungeons & Dragons, spent most of his time. Agent Givens looked put-off at having to wait for Sam, but having already struck out with Batise minutes ago, he looked especially eager now for answers. The guard followed them inside the office, where Batise sat, as before, in his chair in the middle of the room, with two guards positioned in each corner along the back wall overlooking the prison yard below.

Sam sat awkwardly listening as Agent Givens questioned Batise about the disappearance of Joseph Gerrard. When Sal asked who that was, Agent Givens, already with a short fuse, told him that it was the name of a young marketing assistant from his publishing house, Quiver and Bow. Batise swore he knew no one by that name and then swore on his father's grave that he had nothing to do with any apparent disappearance of Joseph Gerrard. After a few terse questions about the bodies being unearthed across the country from the Mallard Malone books—they were up to four now, according to the latest reports, with a body recently dug up from an old plantation in Charleston, South Carolina—Agent Givens promised Batise he'd be back soon and abruptly left the room, leaving Sam, aside from the guards, alone again with Batise.

Sam said, "I talked to Donna Hanson on the phone." When Batise acted like he wasn't sure who that was, which Sam didn't believe for a second, he said, "Your editor. At Quiver and Bow."

"Oh," said Batise. "If you say so."

Sam checked his watch. "You do know you have less than twelve hours to live?"

"Quite aware, Sam Harper."

"Then it seems you'd start being more helpful."

"Is the governor here yet?"

"On his way."

"Ask me a question, and I'll see how helpful I can be."

"This is from your editor," Sam said. "She wants to know where the final book stands."

"Stands? What's that mean?"

"Has it been written, Sal?" Sam nearly shouted.

"That anger," Batise said, pointing at Sam, his chains rattling as he lowered his hands back to his lap. "Where does that come from?"

"Has the book been written?" Sam asked again, forcing himself to speak calmly.

"Yes."

"Where is it?"

"In a secret place."

Sam clenched his jaw, held his anger in check. It would be futile to ask him where that secret place was, because Sal obviously wasn't finished with being evasive.

Batise leaned forward. "The question you should be asking, Sam Harper, is when. When did I write the book?"

"Okay, Sal. Tell me. When did you write this final book?"

"How old are you, Sam?"

"Twenty-six."

"You were two years old."

"Excuse me?"

"When I wrote it," Batise said. "You were two years old."

"Are you telling me . . ."

"Yes. I wrote the book twenty-four years ago," he said. "And there's only one copy."

Sam tried to remain calm. 'Where is it? Where is the book?"

"It's buried in the ground," he said. "With another body."

Sam swallowed hard. "Which body?"

"Is the governor here yet?"

"I told you, he's on his way."

"Ask me the same question when he's here, and I'll give you an answer."

CHAPTER

24

BETH KNEW IT was coming.

Ever since she'd seen the drill bit come through the floor, she'd known it was coming, and it wasn't ten minutes later—ten minutes of Billy in the next room panicking through the hole in the wall, *what's going on over there, what's happening, Beth,* and her doing her best to calm him down—that the door to her room opened and Justice Minks walked in pulling a heavy chain across the floor behind him.

From her sitting position on the floor, he looked even taller than before; she didn't like him looming that large above her, but as soon as she made a move to stand, he said, "Stay there."

She froze, on her knees now, and did just that—she'd stayed there—but at least she was up higher than before, and in more of a position to move away from him should he come closer and try anything. Which, to her relief, he'd yet to do.

With the ease of connecting a swing set chain to the fixed hook on an overhead bar, he connected the chain he'd brought in with him to the one around her ankle. With tools latched to his belt, he hammered a sharp metal peg into the floor next to the far wall and attached both chains to it. She instantly thought of using that peg with the eyehole loop at the top as a weapon somehow, if she could wrench it from the floor after he left.

He then sank the new chain down through the hole in the floor, easing it through like a plumber using a mechanical snake until she heard the weight of it hit the floor in the room below.

Hardwood on that floor too, she thought, as Justice Minks silently went about his business, connecting chains inside his medieval torture house, what Billy Boyle earlier had referred to as a Chain House from the Mallard Malone novels. *The sick bastard.* And then her mind went to where it had minutes ago, when the hole had first been drilled—*Who was he putting down there? Who was next?*

Beth said, "You his biggest fan, Justice?"

Voice muffled behind the Guy Fawkes mask, he said, "Oliver Crown. Not Justice anymore."

"Is this all some big illusion for you . . . Oliver?" she asked, at the same time Billy Boyle shouted through the hole in the wall, "What's going on over there? Beth? What's going on?"

Minks said, "Shut him up."

Beth said, "Nothing's going on, Billy. Just relax."

"He's over there, isn't he?" Billy asked.

"Shut him the fuck up."

"Billy, stop talking, please."

It worked, for the moment, and Beth said to Minks, "Something missing from your childhood, Oliver? Something leading you to play out such . . . fantasies now, as a grown man?"

Ignoring her, Minks opened the door and left the room. He didn't close it, which she found odd. She considered running but knew it would be futile, connected to Billy as she was, and through a wall. Minks was still out there, his footsteps heavy on the floorboards, in what she assumed was a hallway. She heard another chain moving around out there and then seconds later saw the end of it come through a hole in the wall next to the door, a hole she didn't even know was there with the collage of book covers concealing it perfectly.

Dear God, she thought, as Minks reentered the room, walked directly to the end of the chain he'd just pushed through, and then walked it toward her. He connected it to the eyehole bolt he'd hammered into the floor. He stood, turned in a slow circle, as if surveying the room, maybe even visually measuring out what he'd done.

"How long have you known Sal Batise?" Beth asked.

Nothing.

"Are the two of you working together?" she asked. "Is this the end, Oliver? The end of some game you two started twenty years ago?"

He faced her but said nothing; she looked away because she couldn't look him in the eyes, couldn't mentally face that mask, not again—the PTSD came back in a flash of pain and horror, the corkscrew repeatedly plunged into her flesh.

"Why didn't you kill me back then, Oliver?" It dawned on her that he'd tried to do just that, and perhaps thought he had when he'd left her bleeding from so many violent wounds. She'd blacked out on the floor of the Hawthorne mansion and awoke in the hospital, remembering nothing in between. "Why did you wait twenty years to come after me again?"

He shocked her by answering, "He waited too long to die."

"Who? Batise? So this is about him?"

"Everything is about him," Minks said, but with obvious disdain, which instantly made her wonder if they really were working together. And if not, what was he trying to do? Minks said, "He has to die tonight, as planned."

"Or what?"

"You die."

As if part of her will to fight had left her with those words, she dropped back to her sitting position on the floor. But she wasn't finished. She couldn't escape physically, but it wouldn't stop her from trying to learn his mind. "What's wrong with your face, Oliver?"

"What's wrong with yours?" he asked, quickly, so quickly that she immediately tagged his response as reflexively juvenile.

"Is it a birth defect?" she asked. "A wound from later in life?"

"Stop talking."

"Did your parents beat you? Were you tortured as a child, Oliver?"

"Stop talking."

"What's happening over there?" Billy Boyle asked through the hole in the wall, in an obvious panic again.

Minks pointed at the wall behind her. "Shut him up."

She said, "Stop talking, Billy." But she, herself, couldn't stop. "Guy Fawkes, still . . . after all these years, Oliver? The mask," she said. "It's a symbol now . . . for protest. For resistance. Is that why you wear it? What are you protesting, Oliver? What have you been protesting for so long? You wore it then, and you're wearing it now."

"I like how it fits my face," he said.

But she couldn't tell if he was being serious or messing with her. She asked, "Are you Catholic, Oliver?"

"No. I'm nothing," he said. "And I'm everything."

"How did you meet Sal Batise? What brought you to him?"

"Same thing that brought everyone to him."

"His charisma?"

"He's the Breaker of Chains."

Beth needed time to digest this, but felt a more urgent need to keep him talking. "Guy Fawkes was an English Catholic. He was part of a group who—"

"I know who he is . . ."

She finished her thought anyway, "—who attempted to assassinate King James the First and blow up the English Parliament."

"In 1605," he added in a way that felt like he was trying to impress her.

She said, "So you know your history."

"I know the history that matters."

"What?" she said. "History of oppression? Resistance against authority? Is that what this is all about?" He watched her, his dark eyes wet behind the mask holes. She said, "On your mask, the mustache and goatee and eyebrows are prominent . . . why not grow your facial hair out on your own? Is your face so deformed that it wouldn't matter? Oliver? Or are you just scared to be noticed?"

"Stop talking."

"Leave the room then," she said. "Because I've nothing better to do in here than talk. Does Oliver Crown wear a mask? In the books? No? Then why do you?"

"The revolution is coming," he growled, widening his eyes.

"What revolution?"

"The uprising."

Just then something below tugged on the chain in the floor, moving her ankle along with it. She screamed, "What's going on?"

And that got Billy Boyle going again on the other side of the wall. "What was that? Beth, you're moving? What's going on?"

"Shut up," Minks shouted at the wall.

And through the floor, the chain tightened. Someone moved down there, and then, by the weighted pull on the chain around her ankle, she knew someone else had been attached to the chain below.

And then another male voice shouted from the room beneath her. "Help!"

A door slammed below.

Beth froze, her eyes on Minks. "Who's helping you?"

Maybe he smiled, she couldn't tell, but something in his expression shifted his mask, and from the next room, Billy Boyle lost it. "Beth? What's going on? Is he in there? Whoever you are . . . Oliver Crown, I mean . . . please . . . this is all a mistake. Please let me go."

"Shut him up," Minks said again.

Beth, still horrified by what was happening below her, screamed at Billy, "Shut up, Billy, please!"

But Billy only got louder: "I've got a wife and kids at home. Please. I didn't do anything wrong."

Minks stormed from the room, slammed the door behind him. Footsteps trailed down the hallway on the other side of the wall, and then the door opened in the neighboring room, Billy's room, and he screamed. He must have moved away because the tug on Beth's ankle was violent and immediate and the force of it pulled her a few feet across the room.

Heavy, angry footsteps sounded on the other side of the wall and Billy screamed, "No . . . please, no . . ."

The gunshot was so unexpected, Beth screamed again.

And so did the man in the room below.

The door slammed in Billy's room.

Minks's footfalls trailed away.

"Billy . . ." Crying now, Beth crawled as close to the wall as she could, but with the addition of the other two chains, she couldn't go as far as she'd previously been able to. "Billy? Oh God, please . . . Billy?"

Nothing.

And then the male voice from the hole in the floor said. "Who's up there?"

She crawled closer to that hole, but the chain wouldn't allow her to look down into it. Maybe it was better that way. She said, "I'm Beth. What's your name?"

"Joseph," he said. "Joseph Gerrard."

Beth rolled onto her back, stared at the plain white ceiling. And as if to normalize the situation for Jospeh as much as possible, she said, "And what do you do, Joseph?"

After a beat, where he seemed to be gathering his emotions, he said, "I'm a marketing assistant. At Quiver and Bow. Have you heard of it?"

"Yeah," she said, wiping her eyes.

Closing her eyes.

Swearing she could hear a typewriter pecking. Somewhere inside the house.

CHAPTER

25

TREVOR HARPER DROVE the speed limit, as he always did.

He wore his seatbelt. He used his turn signals. He stopped at every stop sign for three seconds, looked left and right and left again before turning out of the subdivision in which he'd lived for the past twenty years, wondering now if he'd ever return.

He wasn't driving like a man fleeing a crime scene. A murder scene. It wasn't even that he was telling himself to be calm, to stay calm, to drive in a way to not draw suspicion should he pass a police officer somewhere—this was just how Trevor Harper drove. And as he drove his burgundy 2017 Ford Escape, both hands on the wheel, south on Taylorsville Road, not knowing exactly where he was going but knowing this road was long enough to get him there, he was still in shock. First, because he'd just killed a man. Sure, he'd done it with honor, he thought, to protect a woman he'd admittedly developed feelings for over the years, but it didn't change the fact that he'd just killed a human being. And he wasn't driving alone. The dead man's wife—*now a widow*—was fleeing the scene with him. She, unlike Trevor, wore her shock quite openly and had yet to utter a word since getting into his car minutes ago and telling him, *Drive.*

When he'd asked, "Where are we going?"

She'd said, without looking at him, and in fact staring laser beams toward her house where Jake Hall lay dead inside, "Just drive, Trevor."

Eyes on the winding road, he periodically gave Lizzie a glance to see how she was doing. Her eyes stayed wide and worried; she appeared to be, at least in her mind's eye, still staring at her house. By now they were ten miles away and entering a portion of Taylorsville Road where stoplights and houses were scarce and nature had taken over. The only words he'd said to her since then were when he'd asked her to buckle her seatbelt, which she'd done without comment or hesitation, and apparently without blinking.

"You okay?" he asked with another glance as he drove.

She nodded.

He'd been wanting to ask her why she smelled of gasoline but couldn't get the words out. It was weird enough having the Louisville Slugger angled in between them, the knob inches away from the gear shift, the bat's barrel stained with a splattering of Jake Hall's blood just inches away from Lizzie's sandaled feet. He'd given that a few glances, too, each time looking back up to the road with thoughts of her white-painted toenails looming even larger than the bloodstain only inches away. He figured that if she'd noticed the bat—and how could she not?—and it bothered her, that she would have asked him to move it or done so herself. But something about it remaining where it was, where it had been when she'd so unexpectedly gotten into his car, spoke volumes. Like, they were fugitives together, and the baseball bat, the way it so casually and ceremoniously rested between them was now their bond.

If you only knew, Trevor thought, not only how long the bat had been one of his most treasured possessions, but how often he'd imagined using it just like he had on Jake Hall, *would you still be riding shotgun with me?* The killing of Jake Hall had not been premeditated, but in all his daydreams and imaginings, from all the way back when he was Tiny Tommy Batise, the bat's main purpose had never been hitting baseballs. In his mind, he'd imagined using it countless times as the weapon it had eventually become. As a club. Whether the grade school bullies at recess or the high school bullies in the hallways or the biggest, meanest bully, Justice Minks, back on the Freedom Ranch, he'd imagined bashing plenty of skulls in with his Louisville Slugger.

And those thoughts began as early as he could remember, back when he'd imagined becoming his own superhero to one day fight them all. Back when he'd imagined being The Raven, the boy who—just as he'd written in the thirty-seven issues of his own comic, *The Raven and The Mongoose*—after spending an evening inside an abandoned lighthouse with a raven who could talk and sing and who eventually bit him on the neck, acquired the power of flight at night. And when the boy became The Raven at night, he would fly around the city with his trusty baseball bat in its talon-like hands and swoop down and fight off any bully he could find. In the first issue, after fighting off a cluster of schoolyard bullies, The Raven finds a mongoose in danger of being eaten alive by a pack of wolves. The Raven, with his baseball bat, scares them all away, and he and the mongoose become instant best friends who make a vow to rid the world of bullies.

Up until now, the radio was on his favorite classic rock station and the music had been a pleasant diversion from the increasingly palpable anxiety hurrying him from home, but the host broke into the middle of his playing of Pink Floyd's *The Wall* in its entirety to give an update on all the bodies being found after Sal Batise's bombshell reveal that he was Mallard Malone. Trevor moved his right hand from the steering wheel long enough to turn up the volume, just as his favorite host read from his notes that nine bodies had been unearthed since this morning, all matching the supposed fictional burials in the Mallard Malone novels. All the victims were being attributed to the mysterious man once known as Justice Minks, and it was believed Minks may be responsible for the abductions and deaths of many more over the past twenty years.

Son of a bitch, Trevor thought, unknowingly increasing his speed toward Taylorsville, realizing now that, all long, he'd subconsciously been driving toward the abandoned wastelands that had once been the Freedom Ranch.

He'd known Justice Minks was the meanest, cruelest, most vile son of a bitch he'd ever encountered, even more so than his brother, the infamous Breaker of Chains, and, like many, had always assumed Minks was there the night of the Hawthorne murders.

That's bullshit, he told himself—*you knew he was there that night. You've known all along. And all it would have taken to corroborate Beth Hawthorne's account from that night back then would have been to open your fucking coward mouth*. And then maybe a more realistic hunt would have transpired for the man, and all of these murders might not have happened.

He shook it away.

No, this isn't on you.

But he'd been hand-delivered those sketches in secret that night from Jennifer, a sweet, innocent but brave-as-hell little girl. The sketches she'd given him in trust, of the three women and Justice Minks that night around the fire, with their machetes and the corkscrew in Minks's hand, the same sketches that had been used at trial to help put Sal's Angels away for life.

But the ones showing Minks?

Those had never been seen, had they, Trevor? Because you got rid of them. You burned them in your own little fire, didn't you?

Because you are a coward, Trevor.

No, he thought, as he drove, his speed increasing by the second. *You aren't a coward*. Minks had hissed in his ear that night to forget him. He could still feel the man's breath on his skin, his lips against his ear, because he'd taken the mask off to say it, to really get his message across.

> I was never here, Raven. And if you ever say my name, I'll come for you. I'll hunt you down and I'll chop your fake family up into pieces and feed them to you in a fucking stew. You understand me?

And Trevor had nodded and swore it and repeated it back and the threat had kept him quiet for twenty years. But these murders? The extent of Minks's true evil? Of that Trevor had no idea. *But deep down*, he thought, *you knew a man like Justice Minks wouldn't just then go become a pleasant member of society.*

And what would you have done, anyway? What would you have done?

His son's voice screamed at him. *At least I'm not all talk, Dad.*

Trevor clenched the wheel so hard now his knuckles had turned bone white.

"Slow down, Trevor, you'll get us killed," Lizzie stoically said beside him, the first words she'd spoken since getting in his car and telling him to drive.

Just drive, she'd said, him having stopped the car, backing out of his driveway in a hurry because he'd just killed a man, when he'd noticed her standing in the grass next to his driveway. Her opening the door. Him at first thinking she was going to retaliate because he'd just killed her husband, but instead she'd gotten in and closed the door and told him, drive, just drive, and now here they were, her still smelling oddly of gasoline with her white-painted toenails and short shorts and long legs and him finally slowing down so he wouldn't get them killed, him not daring to think that if she didn't want them getting killed that maybe they had some sort of a future.

And she said, "I burned the house down." He watched her as he drove, thinking, *The house was still standing when we left*, and maybe she could hear his thoughts because she went on: "I went outside to the garage and got the gas can."

That explained the gas smell.

"I snapped," she said. "I think. Or maybe I was wanting to do it for years, killing Jake and burning the house down with his body in it. It's probably burning pretty good by now."

He didn't know what to say to that and figured the moment maybe didn't need a response; in fact, maybe what she needed most was to not be judged, in favor or against, but either way, they were fugitives in this together, and with every square inch of road he put under his tires, further distancing himself from his previous life, his purpose in the next increased tenfold.

"Last night," she said. "You really . . . poured your soul out to me, Trevor. About who you were. The hell the world has given you. Those comics you did as a boy. But this morning, as soon as I got home, I Googled some things. And ravens," she said, for the first time giving him a glance. "I read that they're so intelligent that they can mimic human voices. They can gesture when they communicate.

They can remember faces, Trevor." She paused, as if for effect. "They have friends . . . and can have enemies."

Trevor knew all this, but that she now knew as well emboldened him somehow, and he felt like he'd never driven with so much confidence. "A group of ravens is called an unkindness," he told her.

She nodded, like maybe she'd learned that too from her morning Googling, right before the world, as she knew it, had been completely turned on its ass.

"The plural of mongoose is mongooses," she said, and he fucking loved her for it. "They're small but agile. They're fearless and can even take down a cobra snake." And when she asked, "Why are you smiling?"

He said, "I don't know."

But the truth was, he did; he was smiling because he was The Raven now and she was The Mongoose. He'd killed one bully and he wanted Justice Minks to be next.

As if reading his mind, she said, "Ravens are excellent hunters. They've been known to kill prey twice their size."

He nodded, tears in his eyes, thinking *Damn straight*, and also thinking of the last words his son had said to him. Well, he wasn't *all talk* anymore. Just ask Jake Hall.

Lizzie said, "So who we gonna get next?"

He hesitated, wondering if he'd heard her correctly. Not, what are we going to do next, but *who* are we gonna *get* next? As in . . .

As if they were The Raven and The Mongoose.

Those who fail to learn from history are doomed to repeat it. He'd said the famous quote often to his classes. But he'd learned enough from his own history by now to finally understand that's all he'd been doing, failing to learn, running and repeating, hiding and dodging, and this was the climaxed doom of it all.

Monsters don't go away until you face them head on. *Even if I die trying*, he thought.

Assuming he'd heard her correctly, he decided to answer her in turn. "You hear what they just said on the radio, about Justice Minks?"

"I did," she said.

"Then that's who we're getting next."

"That's exactly what I was hoping you'd say," she said, turning in her seat to face him, and he did his best not to notice how the seatbelt cut right between her breasts. She said, "Where to?"

"To the old Freedom Ranch," he said. "What's left of it."

"And then what?"

"I'll know when it comes to me."

CHAPTER

26

"YOU HAVE TO tell Sam," Carl said as he steered down the street.

"Me?" Jennifer asked from the passenger seat as they hurried away from Trevor Harper's house with the full stack of *The Raven and The Mongoose* comics in tow, along with a few pictures from the photo album she'd found open on the floor and the Mallard Malone novels she'd dropped on the professor's porch the day before. "How about *we*?"

"We, fine, whatever," Carl said, turning out of the subdivision, just as two fire trucks, lights flashing and sirens blaring, pulled in. "But he deserves to know."

"What, that his father isn't and never was who Sam thought he was?" Jennifer said. "That both his parents were members of The Collective? That they weren't even his real parents?"

Carl watched his rearview mirror. "We should have stayed."

"And done what?"

"I'm just saying, we called the fire department," Carl said. "We should have waited for them."

"And done what?"

He shrugged, like he didn't know, and who could blame him because she didn't know what they should be doing either. But she didn't want to get caught by the police and fire department, with questions she didn't know how to answer. Without sugarcoating it, they'd entered Trevor Harper's home without him there and walked out with armloads of his stuff. Carl was right, with what he'd said hurrying from the house, it did look like they were looting, especially as they noticed the billowing flames from the neighboring house. But Jennifer couldn't get past the notion that Trevor had left the door ajar on purpose, that he'd left the old comics on the kitchen table for someone to find. Maybe for Sam, to help explain things, but it also raised the question of why the professor had seemingly left in such a hurry that he'd be unable to explain things himself.

It seemed clear that Trevor Harper had been forced to leave in a hurry, and now she feared he was in danger.

She wished she had his phone number.

Sam would have it, of course. And everything happening now was connected to The Collective and the Freedom Ranch and Justice Minks, wherever he was, and she couldn't trust what Batise might be telling Sam now, inside the walls of that prison with—she checked her watch—only eight more hours to live.

"Where to?" Carl asked.

"I don't know," she said, staring at the picture she'd pulled from the photo album of Mr. and Mrs. Harper and their son Sam, but who were really The Raven and Yellow and, she felt certain now, the fifth kid on the farm. The boy she'd once seen in the upstairs window of the blue house. "Why did I erase him from the wall?"

"What are you talking about?" Carl asked.

"The wall," she said. "The closet wall. My stupid drawing. There were five stick figures, and one was erased. Why did I do that?"

"I don't know," Carl said. "But you really think Sam was the fifth kid on the ranch?"

"Yes," she said. "I know he was."

"But you don't remember him?"

"I was six, Carl. We were young. But no, I don't remember him. I don't even know if we ever met before everything went down, and the ranch was raided."

"What about the other kids . . . from the closet? You should see what they remember."

"I plan to call them." But then she was struck by another thought. "But why *did* Batise pick Sam? Of all the people trying to get that interview? He picked Sam . . ."

The same boy, she thought, closing her eyes for deeper concentration, the same boy her younger self had seen on the second floor of that house on the Freedom Ranch.

The same boy . . . who the other kids had thought had died because . . . because he'd gone into the woods where the demons lived. *But he never died. He never went into the woods.* That's just what they'd been told. He'd been taken into that house. Sal's main house.

"I've been thinking the same thing all day," Carl said.

"Because he knows him," Jennifer said, as it dawned on her like a lightning bolt. "He fucking knew him, Carl. He didn't pick him because he was an outlier, or to be difficult, or to shove it in the networks' faces. He knew exactly who he was picking," she said. "And why."

"Then why?"

"I don't know yet," she said, but thought maybe she did, and the thought sickened her. "Go back to the prison," she said. "It worked as a trigger this morning, and I need it to again."

Carl turned on his right blinker, changed lanes, turned around with a squealing of his tires, and began making his way toward the interstate like he couldn't wait to get there himself, to get back to his buddy. Still studying the picture on her lap, she said, "But if the plan was for it to be Sam all along, what would he have done if Sam hadn't put his name in to get the interview?"

"He would have revealed that he was Mallard Malone anyway," Carl said. "It was Batise's final card to play, no matter who he allowed in that room. He's only trying to stay alive."

He wasn't wrong, but Jennifer noticed that Carl's forehead, as he merged onto I-64, had broken out with some serious sweat. "You're sweating like a horse, Carl."

"Because it's fucking hot."

"No, it isn't, and you just got a little overly defensive, Carl." She watched him as he gripped and regripped the steering wheel, his chubby hands pink and seemingly void of any knuckles. "What aren't you telling me?"

"Nothing." He wiped his brow. "And do horses really sweat? I mean, what does that even mean?"

"*Carl.*"

"Fine . . . Sam had heard of the stupid contest to interview Sal Batise, but he initially didn't want to do it."

"Why?"

"Because he's Sam. That's not him, doing something like that."

"And then?"

"I talked him into it, okay?"

"Why?"

"He's doing this documentary thing, and I thought he should do it."

"Bullshit, Carl."

He clenched his jaw, punched the steering wheel with the padding of his right hand, but instead of making him look mad or tough, it came across as sad, and Jennifer felt instantly sorry for him. He was hiding something and scared. "Okay, so maybe it's bullshit," he said, "but it doesn't change that he needed to do it. He needed to grow a pair. Put on his big boy pants."

"Are you trying to make yourself feel better?"

He drove for thirty seconds in silence; she could tell he was building up to something, so she allowed him time to get to it. And finally, he said, "I was in Quills one morning, about three weeks ago. It's a coffee shop, our go-to. Mostly I work from my couch, but every Monday I go to Quills. Starts my week off right, you know? I'm there and I'm minding my own business, and all of a sudden, this dude, I've never seen him before, he sits down across from me, completely uninvited, and I'm like, hello? And he goes, you roommates with Sam Harper? Without thinking, I'm like, yeah, what about him? And he goes, I heard he's doing a documentary on Sal Batise. I concur, but I'm wondering where this is going." Carl kept glancing in his rearview mirror as he drove. "And then the dude tells me that Sam needs to put his name in. Like he knew he hadn't."

"Did he threaten you?"

"No," Carl said. "Not with any words, but it was clearly implied . . . just the way he looked at me. And everybody knows Batise has a web. He's got people all over, on the outside. He still has *followers*. Probably one of his old pals from prison."

Jennifer knew Sal Batise had done two stints in prison before starting The Collective. Two years for his first bit and one year for the second, the first for his role in a gas station robbery that left the clerk blind in one eye and the other for illegal prostitution and money laundering. It was thought by many—especially the ones who wrote the true crime books—that Batise had met Justice Minks during one of his stints in prison, although no Justice Minks had ever been found, which meant, just as everyone already knew, Justice Minks wasn't his real name.

Jennifer asked Carl, "What did he look like? This dude at the coffee shop."

"White guy. Dark hair. Pale. Greasy with a neck tat."

"Shit."

"What, you know him?"

"No, but like you said, it's probably one of his followers. Somebody continuing to do his bidding on the outside. But it's perfectly clear now that Batise wanted Sam from the start. And that scares the shit out of me."

"Me too," Carl said. "My stomach's been messed up for three weeks."

"Thanks for that."

"You asked."

"Did I?" she said. And then, "So how'd you convince Sam to contact the prison?"

"Just kept on him," he said. "Challenged his manhood. Do that enough to a dude, and he'll give in."

"Because men are still Neanderthals?"

"Yeah, I guess so. But just so you know . . . the perceived threat I felt in that coffee shop, it wasn't for me. It was for Sam. I was worried the threat was for him."

Jennifer watched him, thought the moment needed a quick punch of levity. "So that's the fuck, Carl?"

He smiled. "Yeah, that's the fuck, Jennifer."

He glanced in the rearview mirror again and his smile faded. "But I'm pretty sure somebody's been following us since we left the house."

CHAPTER

27

SAM HAD VOTED for Governor Hawthorne, both terms.

It was the first time Sam had ever voted. Truthfully, he'd gone into it blind that first time, voting for Gavin Hawthorne because he knew his father was, but by the second term it had been a no-brainer. Except for a few extremists on either side, the entire state of Kentucky loved Governor Hawthorne, and he rarely did anything to piss anyone off. And when it came to anything remotely controversial, like capital punishment, or extremely incendiary, like abortion, he had a way of answering questions that somehow appeased both sides. He was the Middle Man. The ex-professional athlete who still looked like he could take to the field. He was handsome and charming and charismatic and genuinely kind.

Sam, like he had with Sal Batise hours before, predicted he would be enamored by Governor Hawthorne's presence, if not starstruck, and maybe he would have been if the governor hadn't entered the prison looking like he hadn't slept in two days. But all Sam felt was sorrow, because the man was in clear pain and anguish, and the sight of it brought tears to Sam's own eyes when he shook the governor's hand, the man's grip strong and angry.

But what brought about Sam's sudden emotion was thinking of his own father, and how he'd left it with him yesterday, and he decided right then that he would call and apologize as soon as he got a chance.

"I'm sorry, sir," Sam said, letting go of the governor's hand, standing in a circle of men with whom he felt he had no business standing.

FBI Agent Givens. Warden Wren. Governor Hawthorne. Sam Harper.

Sam knew which one didn't belong, but he was far past wondering why at this point—the stakes had risen tenfold as soon as Governor Hawthorne entered the room, and Sam knew something was about to come to a head. He also knew, for whatever reason, that he was necessary, and he tried to stand as if he embraced it. He only wished Jennifer and Carl were with him—their mere presence would have been a boost.

Agent Givens said to the governor, "I heard Justice Minks finally made contact with you?"

Governor Hawthorne nodded, misty-eyed and clenching his chiseled jaw, which was dotted with dark stubble from having not shaved. "He has Beth. He says she's still alive. He's calling himself Oliver Crown now."

Sam assumed by their facial expressions that they all knew who Oliver Crown was and the significance of using that name.

Warden Wren folded his arms. "What does he want?"

Governor Hawthorne glanced at Agent Givens, like Givens already knew, and he probably did, and then said to Warden Wren, "He demands Sal Batise be killed as planned, no matter what happens in the hours leading up to midnight."

Sam could tell there was more.

Warden Wren said, "And?"

"His first demand is no lethal injection."

Warden Wren's face wrinkled in puzzlement. "What does he want?"

Governor Hawthorne said, "Firing squad."

The warden let out a disbelieving laugh. "You're kidding, right?"

"Does it look like I'm kidding?" said Governor Hawthorne.

"No," said the warden, straightening the lapels on his suit jacket. "I'm sorry . . . but . . . that's not possible."

"Make it possible," said the governor. "I'll shoot him myself if I have to."

Agent Givens ran a hand over his close-cropped black hair, as if what he was about to say even he couldn't believe. "But that's not all, Warden. He wants it done in the yard. On live TV."

Warden Wren stood speechless, glancing back and forth between the FBI agent and the governor like he was waiting for the cameraman to emerge from a secret hiding place, revealing that this was all a prank. But it wasn't, and everyone knew it.

Governor Hawthorne's strained eyes settled on Sam, sudden and hard. "What is it?"

Sam wondered if he was that easy to read, because it must have been obvious he was afraid to speak up, and when he did, his voice came out at first in a pathetic squeak. "I . . . Sal, he spoke of the book. The one that hasn't come out yet." He cleared his throat, sucked in a deep breath. "Evidently his publisher hasn't even seen it yet. Sal claims that he wrote it over twenty years ago. And there's only one copy."

"What's that have to do with anything?" Governor Hawthorne asked.

"I think," Sam said, "the book, and what happens in it, is important somehow."

"Where is it?" Governor Hawthorne asked. "The book?"

Agent Givens answered for Sam. "Batise claims it's buried with another body."

"What body?"

Sam said, "He's waiting for you, sir, before he tells us."

And with that, Governor Hawthorne stormed into Warden Wren's office.

Sam followed, as did Givens and Wren. A guard immediately closed the door behind them.

Batise made a theatrically sarcastic move up from his chair as if out of respect for the governor's appearance, but Warden Wren quickly said, "Sit down, Sal."

And Batise settled back into the chair in the middle of the office. "To what do I owe this honor, Governor Hawthorne?"

The governor looked like he was one word away from putting his hands around Batise's neck, but restrained himself by walking away, using the warden's desk as a physical barrier between them.

Agent Givens stood rigidly, arms folded. "The body, Mr. Batise."

"Don't call him *mister*," said Governor Hawthorne. "He's a monster." Rage flashed in the governor's eyes; he'd lost multiple family members in the massacre Batise had ordered that evening twenty years ago, and it was clear that time had done little to heal those wounds.

Batise said, "A monster you're going to want to keep alive, Governor, even after so many years of trying to end my life."

Warden Wren said, "Spill it, Sal."

"I want a promise first."

"You'll get no promise," said Agent Givens. "Tell us what you know."

Batise's gaze focused directly on Governor Hawthorne. "I want a stay of execution."

"Out of the question," said the governor.

"Then I'm sorry, I've got no body to divulge, and no book to be found," said Batise.

"What does the book have to do with this?" asked Agent Givens.

"Everything," said Batise, his eyes still on Governor Hawthorne, who'd turned away and was now watching out the window toward the yard, where Minks had demanded that Batise be executed by firing squad.

Sam got the sense the other three men were tiptoeing around their most recent information, so he spoke up. "Justice Minks has the governor's wife. He's calling himself Oliver Crown now. He's agreed to Beth Hawthorne's safety if and only if . . ." Suddenly Sam couldn't find himself able to say it.

Agent Givens stepped closer to Batise's chair. "He's demanding that not only are you to be executed on schedule, tonight at midnight, but he wants it done by firing squad."

Batise chuckled. "Does he now?" he said. And then softer, as if for his own ears, "Firing squad."

"This doesn't surprise you?" Agent Givens asked.

Batise straightened in his chair. "No . . . no, not really."

"Why not?" Warden Wren said, losing patience. "Firing squad is more archaic than the electric chair. We might as well hang you."

"I'd actually prefer that," said Batise. "The noose. Although the firing squad isn't as archaic as you think. Do your research. South Carolina. Last year."

"How do you know Justice Minks?" Agent Givens asked.

"No comment."

"Did you meet him during your two-year stint at Eddyville?"

"I'd like to call my lawyer."

Warden Wren said, "You *fired* your lawyer."

Sam said, "Why does this not surprise you? The demand for a firing squad?"

"Because, Sam Harper, that's exactly how it happens in the final book."

All eyes were back on Batise, not only because he'd finally answered the question, but because it was becoming increasingly evident that he was only being serious when it was Sam questioning him.

Sam told the other three men in the room, "In the final book, there's a cult leader named Malcolm Dodd, who is set to be executed. And it's only after this execution, evidently done by firing squad . . ."

"And televised," Batise added. "Don't forget that."

They all shared looks because they'd hadn't mentioned that part of the demand.

Once that sunk in, Sam finished: "And it's only after this execution that Oliver Crown gains his . . . stardom. But to ensure that Malcolm Dodd is executed, he holds the governor's wife as ransom."

"Well done," said Batise. "As I told Sam Harper earlier, Mr. Minks must be Mallard Malone's biggest fan. He sounds like an utter lunatic to me."

"In the book," Governor Hawthorne hissed. "Does she live? Does the governor's wife live?"

"Hmm, let me think," Batise said playfully. "I wrote it well over twenty years ago . . ."

"Cut the shit, Sal," said Warden Wren. "You have a photographic memory unlike anyone has seen before. You know damn well what's in the book."

"Temper yourself, Warden," said Batise. "A good poker player doesn't show all his cards."

And Sam noticed he'd said it in a way that insinuated Warden Wren didn't have any cards to play, and it was noticeable how quickly the warden tempered himself, backing down like a reprimanded dog.

Agent Givens said, "So you're Malcolm Dodd in this book. You're the cult leader on death row, and it's obvious you patterned this book on your life."

"I wrote the book well before I started The Collective," Batise said.

"Okay, so you used the book as a blueprint," added Givens. "Does Malcolm Dodd die by firing squad or not?"

"He does," said Batise. "Quite gruesomely, I might add. Took many bullets to finish him off. He was a very tough man."

"And then Oliver Crown rises from the ashes," Sam said. "What causes the ashes? In the book, what causes the country to crumble?"

"The *world* to crumble," he said, in amused correction. "The United States was just the first domino to fall, Sam Harper. And, like I said, it would be irresponsible of me to show all my cards now."

Governor Hawthorne stepped around the desk but stopped. "And I'm to assume this Malcolm Dodd, in the *book*, has pulled every trick known to the legal system to stay *his* execution, just like you, huh?"

"I learned from the best, Governor, and Malcolm Dodd was the—"

"Cut the bullshit," Governor Hawthorne screamed. "Why am I here?"

"Because it seems we have ourselves quite a conundrum, gentlemen." Batise shifted in his chair. "I'm doing everything in my power to stay alive while this Oliver Crown is doing everything in his power to see me die."

"Seems simple to me," Agent Givens said. "You die tonight as directed, and this all goes away."

"If you can trust Justice Minks, that is." Batise folded his hands on his lap, grinned.

Governor Hawthorne turned toward the door, and on his way, said to the warden, "Pick your firing squad, Adrian. Shoot him right out there in the yard at midnight. I'm done."

Before the governor reached the door, Batise called out, "My stay, Governor?"

Hawthorne ignored him, opened the door, his body language saying, *Fuck your stay*.

"I know where your sister is buried," Batise shouted.

Everyone froze.

Governor Hawthorne stood still, with his hand on the doorknob, but Sam could see it trembling. The governor's younger sister, Emily Hawthorne, had disappeared twenty-three years ago, without a trace, and no one had heard from her since. The family, Sam knew, had long considered her dead and had grieved her loss in a private ceremony ten years ago. But from everything Sam had read, there had been no closure for her big brother, and her loss—and the questions still circling from her loss—ate at him still, daily.

The governor's shoulders rose and fell, rose and fell, as he sucked in deep breath after deep breath. If this was a joke by Batise, it was the utmost cruelty—there was no closer nerve he could have struck with the governor. But as Sam studied the man's grinning face, he knew he was telling the truth. Batise knew something about Emily Hawthorne's disappearance, even though it had occurred three years before the Hawthorne massacre and by all accounts a year before The Collective was even formed.

"Emily Hawthorne," said Batise, like the governor needed reminding of his sister's name.

Governor Hawthorne turned slowly. "You evil motherfucker." He started toward Batise, but Agent Givens and Warden Wren held him back.

"Ignore him," said Givens. And then over his shoulder to Batise, "Start making sense or I'll shoot you myself."

"You killed my sister?" Gavin Hawthorne was larger and stronger, but Givens and Wren together managed to keep him away from Batise.

"I did no such thing," said Batise. "But I do know where she's buried. And the manuscript, the *only* copy, I might add, was buried with her."

"Why?" Sam asked, but his voice was drowned out by the commotion, by the struggle to keep Hawthorne back.

"Where is she?" Hawthorne screamed, beginning to calm, but still distraught. "Where is she? Please . . . where is she?"

"My stay, Governor."

"Fuck you."

"Stay my execution, Governor Gavin Hawthorne, and I'll give you her exact location."

CHAPTER

28

BETH'S BODY HURT everywhere.

Whatever pain meds he'd given her for the gunshot wound were wearing off, and her right calf was throbbing. Her hips and shoulders and knees hurt from the strain of the numerous chains holding her centered in the room.

Although the room was vast, she could only move within a five-foot radius in any direction before one of the chains stopped her.

She'd given up calling Billy's name through the wall, finally allowing her mind to go there—Billy Boyle was dead, and every time she gently tugged the chain that funneled through the hole in that wall, dead weight resisted her on the other side. As for Joseph Gerrard down below, her last few attempts at getting him to talk had fallen on deaf ears. Terrified ears, more like, because she knew he could hear her. She could hear him rustling down there. But for now, she'd leave him be.

The typing had stolen her attention, but in a good way.

Typing, even someone clacking away on what sounded like an old machine, was normal, when nothing else in the house was.

"Hello," she called out again toward the hole in the wall near the door, but to no avail. She felt sure there was a hallway out there, and if indeed that chain connected her to another prisoner, it was across that hallway and into another room. At first, she thought that was where the typing was coming from, but after more careful focus, it sounded farther away, and at times she'd thought it could be coming from outside, beyond the window's iron bars.

The door opened suddenly, and she screamed.

When Justice Minks entered she fell backward, painfully wrenching her shoulder on one of the chains. She'd been so preoccupied, she hadn't heard his footsteps in the hallway. He walked directly toward her, squatted down, pulled a cell phone from his pocket.

"What's your name?" he asked.

"You know what my name is."

"Say it."

"Bethany Hawthorne."

"What time is?" he asked, and at the same time showed her the watch on his left wrist.

What was this about? she thought, but read his watch. "Three . . . three-thirty-seven, or eight."

He touched the screen and her voice emerged from the iPhone: *You know what my name is . . . Say it . . . Bethany Hawthorne . . . What time is it . . . Three . . . three-thirty-seven . . . or eight . . .*

"That'll do." Minks pocketed the phone and stood from his crouch. "He needed to know you're still alive."

"Who?"

"Your husband."

Just the thought of Gavin brought tears to her eyes.

There was no way Minks was letting her go, no matter what Gavin did or didn't do.

On his way out of the room, Beth said, "Wait . . . please."

Minks stopped, turned.

"I hear someone typing," she said. "A typewriter." He stared at her, said nothing. She said, "At least tell me I'm hearing it and not going crazy."

He said, "My wife."

Your wife? Jesus Christ . . .

He said, "She's working on a book."

And then he closed the door and left the room.

CHAPTER

29

TREVOR WASN'T SURE why he needed to return to the old Freedom Ranch, but with Lizzie's full support, and not knowing where else to go, they'd headed straight there.

"It'll give us time to think," she'd said on the way. "And regroup." After a few minutes of driving in silence, she'd said, "I wonder if the house is burned down by now?"

He didn't know how to respond to that, so he'd just let her talk, let her get out whatever she needed to get out, and once she'd started talking, she talked until they arrived at the Freedom Ranch, or what was left of it. Bottom line was that after Trevor had fled her house with his bat in tow, she'd watched him go, thinking, *That man is a hero*. When Trevor laughed, she'd said, *I'm serious*, and then he'd gotten serious, too, because there wasn't much to laugh about with any of this. But Trevor also remembered when her husband had once told him heroes don't come in pint-size. And then Lizzie had gone on to say that as soon as Trevor had left with his bat, she'd gotten on her dead husband's cell phone and went scrolling, and after finding text chains from two different women she'd always thought he'd been tagging on the side, she'd gone straight out to the garage to get the gas can—as if beating the shit out of her wasn't enough, he'd been cheating on her, too, and she'd snapped. *I mean, I just snapped, Trevor*, she'd said from the passenger seat as he drove. *And now I guess I'm a fugitive, because it sure won't be hard to investigate that mess.* Even if the house hadn't burned down, Trevor thought, Jake's body would be, seeing as she'd apparently poured the can of gasoline over his dead body before striking the match.

The first thing he said to her when they arrived at the Freedom Ranch was, "We'll figure it all out." He'd thrown his stained Louisville Slugger over his shoulder. "I won't let anything happen to you, Lizzie." It felt odd saying it, given his passive history, but he'd so thoroughly stepped into the role of his own fictional childhood hero that now he felt indestructible, and as they walked toward the old, wooded ranch, where most of the barracks had either crumbled or been burned down or vandalized and completely overgrown, it dawned on him exactly why they'd naturally migrated toward the very place he once vowed never to return.

Because that's what The Raven would have done.

"The Raven," he told Lizzie as they walked the main trail leading into the camp, "in my comics, as a boy, he'd always fly somewhere and sit and think, to focus, and often it was to a place that had caused him pain. Because with pain often comes clarity. The Raven was always fueled by painful memories."

They approached the camp side by side, and for the first time Trevor noticed the handgun tucked into the waistline of her shorts. He wasn't familiar enough with guns to know what kind it was, but it looked good on her. Not out of place. In other words, unlike him, he felt sure she'd fired one before.

"It's registered," she said. "I have a license to carry."

"I'm not judging," he said, thinking, *If The Raven had a baseball bat, The Mongoose could have a gun.*

"Is that why we're here?" Lizzie asked. "So you can relive some painful memories?"

"Yes," he said with confidence, and at the same time trying to tamp down the anxiety the place was already stirring up inside him. He'd heard stories of what had happened here since the authorities had raided and the arrests followed. It had been under the watch of investigators as they collected their evidence for nearly a year, and then the long, slow process of decay and dilapidation took over, turning it into what it was now—an abandoned nightmare of memory. He'd heard it had morphed into a place for teenage dares and haunts and sex parties and drug deals, but it appeared as if all that had run its course and the surrounding forest had begun, in earnest, to reclaim what had once belonged to it.

It didn't surprise him to see that Sal Batise's main house, although weatherbeaten and overgrown with weeds and covered in graffiti, had somehow stood the tests of time. The blue paint had either faded or peeled away. Most of the windows had been shattered, and it appeared a portion of the roof had caved in on the right side near the chimney, where crows squawked and circled.

The front door was missing. Inside the opening, darkness reigned.

And frightened voices from twenty years ago sounded from within.

CHAPTER 30

Before

THEY'D BEEN WARNED.

It might be chaos when the authorities came. Iris had asked what *authorities* were.

Yellow said, *The police.*

Peter had asked Raven and Yellow what *chaos* was. Raven had said, *It's a state of utter confusion*, and then stammering . . . *lack of organization . . . lack of order.*

And then Yellow had said simply, *It's unpredictability.*

And now, as they hurried through the darkness of the Freedom Ranch, fleeing *from* the burning Kitchen House just as so many ran toward it with buckets of water, skirting the woods where she swore she saw demons watching from the shadows, Jennifer never could have predicted they'd be heading *into* the blue house, where they all knew the Breaker of Chains lived, and sometimes the man in the mask. But it was also the house she now knew with certainty another boy lived—Steven. The plan was to get him and go.

Earlier, Markie had asked what a *diversion* was, and things had been so tense and scary then that his question had gone unanswered, as he had asked it at the exact point flames began whooshing inside the Kitchen House. She knew it had been The Raven that started the fire, and now, as they hurried from the bright light and growing heat, she knew what a *diversion* was. And that's why they were entering the Blue House to get the other boy now.

The fire had been the diversion.

Last night, Jennifer had watched from her bed inside the barracks, knowing Raven had entered the Blue House. But he'd done so sneakily, because she also knew that the Breaker of Chains and the Man in the Mask weren't inside. *Maybe there'd been another diversion then*, Jennifer thought as they ran now, her with a pencil in one pocket and a small flashlight in the other, even though they'd been told not to bring anything with them—the kids holding each other's hands just as Raven and Yellow held theirs, creating their own chain of sorts, and they'd been warned to not break it, no matter what, just as they'd been warned not to look back, not to look at the woods, *not to let go!* And Jennifer thought back to last night, when she'd seen Raven leave the Blue House, closing the door all quiet-like, all while the boy watched him go from a window on the first floor this time. And before Raven had hurried back, he'd gone to the window where the boy was, and he'd placed his hand, fingers splayed against the glass in the window, just as the boy was doing on the other side, and Jennifer remembered thinking it looked like a mirrored reflection, except Raven was older.

Although not too much taller, Jennifer had thought, knowing Raven was the shortest man at the ranch. Shortest but also the nicest, and the way the two of them had held their hands pressed against the glass had made her cry.

Because how cool was that? To be so close as that boy must be to Raven. Almost like a father to a son.

CHAPTER 31

Although some reporters remained, the parking lot outside the Twisted Tree State Penitentiary gates had mostly thinned out since the morning's interview.

Even so, Carl parked his truck discreetly in the far back corner of the lot, next to a run of tall pine trees and behind a delivery truck.

Jennifer thought it best to confront Sam in person with the news of his father, but after Sam finally answered and told her too much shit was going on for him to leave now, going on about hanging with the governor and FBI agents and him being the middle man in it all, he convinced her to reveal what she needed to over the phone.

Politely ignoring Carl's suggestion that she stay in the vehicle so she wouldn't be seen, Jennifer got out of the truck and paced the grass next to it while she waited for Sam to respond to what she'd just told him, waited for him to say *something*. "Hello?" she said, prodding him, knowing he was still there; she could hear him breathing over the phone. "Sam?"

"I heard you," he said. "But . . . what do you mean he ran? From what?"

"I don't know," Jennifer said. "I just know his neighbor's house was on fire, his car was gone, his front door was open, the photo album—"

"I heard you," he said again, harsher this time. "But . . . what comics are you talking about? *The Raven and The Mongoose*?"

"Not published comics," she said. "Just little booklets he made as a kid."

"And he left them on the kitchen table?"

"Yes, I think for you to find, but . . . I have them, if you want them."

"What . . . no, not right now. This doesn't make any sense."

Jennifer took a deep breath. "Sam . . . he's The Raven. Your father. And your mom . . . she was Yellow."

"What are you talking about? Yellow and Raven, what the fuck, Jennifer?"

"They were both from the Freedom Ranch, Sam. They were members of The Collective."

"Bullshit."

"We were all kids on that ranch."

"You were," he said, "but . . . No, just, no. I wasn't there."

"I'm not saying they were bad, Sam. They saved us." *Saved you*, at least, she thought, as flashes of her time in the closet closed in on her. "They're the reason the Freedom Ranch was raided. They tried to get us out . . . they got you out, somehow."

"What are you saying?" he asked defensively. "That . . . they aren't even my real parents?"

"Just like mine aren't my real parents, Sam, maybe. I don't know . . . you were different from us. They treated you differently, so maybe you were . . . I don't know."

"This is too much . . . I gotta go."

"Call your dad, Sam."

"Is he even my dad, Jennifer? Is that what you're trying to tell me? This is bullshit."

"I'm sorry . . . I thought you needed to know before . . ."

"Before what?"

"I don't know what Batise is telling you in there," she said. "I don't trust him."

"Right now, I don't know who to trust," he said. "I gotta go."

"Sam, wait. Was it ever a thing, you and your father, placing your hand on a glass window . . . and he'd place his on the other side?"

Silence.

And then, with a weak voice, he said, "I gotta go."

And he hung up.

Jennifer stared at her phone for a beat before sliding it into the pocket of her pants. She wiped tears from her cheeks, got back into the truck.

Carl said, "You okay?"

"Yeah," she said, but it was clear she wasn't.

"I'll text him."

"Don't. He needs to process it."

Carl sighed, watched out his window, and then abruptly opened his door.

"What are you doing?" she asked.

"That car," he said, one leg outside the truck and one leg in. He nodded toward a car across the lot. "That's who was following us earlier. Son of a bitch."

Carl got out without closing his truck door and headed across the parking lot.

Jennifer ran to catch up with him; they didn't need the attention from a spontaneous parking lot confrontation. She didn't even know what car he was heading toward until a balding man with glasses, wearing a crisp white button-down tucked into belted blue jeans, got out of a forest-green Mercedes and stood with his hands up, as if cautioning Carl's aggressive approach.

"You following us?" Carl asked like he was heading straight for a punch.

Jennifer said, "Carl stop." Luckily, he did, because the other man now stood in a fighting stance of his own, albeit a rather pathetic one. Jennifer recognized him as the same man who had made a grab at Sam on his way into the prison before the interview. She stepped in front of Carl and said, "Down, Cujo." And to the man, "What do you want?"

"Look," he said, again holding up his hands as a peace offering. "My name is—"

"I know who you are," Jennifer said.

Carl said, "I don't."

Jennifer said, "Harold Martin. Wrote the book *Mastermind* . . . on Sal Batise." She thought about saying *bestselling* book but didn't want to give him the satisfaction. "Why are you following us?"

Harold scratched his scalp. "I don't know . . . I was desperate, I guess. If I'm being honest, I'm still ticked off I didn't get the interview."

"Because you consider yourself the foremost expert on The Collective and Sal Batise?"

He didn't deny it. "And I had to know . . . why he picked that kid."

"He's twenty-six," Jennifer said. "He's not a kid."

"And the dude has a name," Carl said. "It's Sam Harper. And his documentary is gonna swallow your book whole and shit it out into little pieces."

"Carl, please," Jennifer said, "this isn't a contest." She stepped toward Harold Martin, who appeared older and more defeated than he had seconds before. "Look," she said. "If you're here as a reporter, we've got nothing to say. If your feelings are hurt, I'm sorry. So if you'd kindly stop following us, it would be much appreciated."

She started to turn away, when Martin said, "I'm sorry to hear about your mom."

Jennifer froze. "What about my mom?"

"Oh," he said. "You haven't . . . never mind, I'm sorry."

"No, what the fuck are you talking about?"

"One of the bodies," Martin said, with a hint of satisfaction. "It was just on the news. Your biological mother . . ." And while hearing that gave her instant relief, she opened her eyes wide, demanding more. He said, "They just discovered her body in southern Indiana. Found evidence she was killed . . . twenty years ago, fleeing the ranch."

"What evidence?"

"There was a glass jar buried with her," he said with a gulp. "Inside the jar was a note."

"What did the note say?"

"*Killed by demons,*" he said. And then, with caution, "*Mother of Jennifer.*"

"You're lying," she said flatly.

"Why would I lie about that?"

Because you're a liar, she wanted to say, thinking of what she'd apparently written on the closet wall so long ago . . . *The Raven was here . . . The Raven is a lyer . . .*

Martin stammered, "And . . . that wasn't the only body with a glass jar buried with them. They also discovered, near Bowling Green, the man who must have been Iris's father. It said much the same. Killed by demons . . . I can't believe you hadn't heard . . ."

"We've been a little busy," Jennifer said, her voice heavy with sarcasm.

"And now we're going," Carl said with an attempt to coax Jennifer away.

But Jennifer stayed put. "So the children on the ranch weren't left there by parents who fled?"

"No," said Martin. "It looks like they were killed . . . for bringing kids onto the ranch. That broke one of the rules."

"Why would they be buried with glass jars, and notes, if not . . ." she trailed away.

"If not for a plan for them to be revealed at a certain time in the future?" Martin said. "And you've heard about the most recent fire?"

"What fire?" Jennifer asked, although she assumed he meant the fire they'd called in at the house of Trevor Harper's neighbor.

But that wasn't it.

"Barrett Goldsmith," Martin said. "It was reported an hour ago. Two buildings were burned to the ground on his horse farm, here in Twisted Tree."

"Why?"

He shrugged. "Don't know. But with the McFee mansion burned down this morning, and now this," Martin said, "it just gets me thinking . . . about the class war Batise always spoke of."

"What . . . to usher in his execution somehow?" Jennifer asked.

"Seems like an awfully big coincidence otherwise."

Jennifer thought back to their question to Batise that morning and his insistence he had nothing to do with the McFee mansion burning down. She'd believed him then but now wasn't so sure, and now, more than ever, feared for Sam's well-being inside that prison, with him.

"So what next?" Harold Martin asked, like they were now a team.

Jennifer glanced at Carl, then said to Martin, "Look, I think everyone's main concern right now should be finding Justice Minks and Beth Hawthorne. And not trying to find meat for your follow-up book."

"That's not what this is," Martin said softly, and somehow she believed him. "From what I hear, Governor Hawthorne is in quite a pickle."

"How so?" Carl asked.

"Again, from what I hear . . ."

Carl said, "You must have big ears."

"Batise isn't the only one with connections."

"What are you hearing?" Jennifer asked.

"That Minks is holding Beth Hawthorne for ransom, to ensure Batise is executed on schedule. And that Batise is claiming he knows where the governor's sister is buried, and he's holding that back to get another stay of execution."

"Nice," Jennifer said. "And you're staying mum on this bit of knowledge?"

"No," he said. "The news needs to be reported."

"Even if it means putting someone's life in danger?"

"Or it could help keep her alive," he said. "Two sides to every coin, Ms. Daley."

"More like the devil on one shoulder and the angel on the other," she said. She got out her phone and sent Sam a quick text: I know you hate me right now but someone inside the prison is leaking information.

She turned to go and again Martin's voice stopped her. "You managed to do something I have never been able to do in twenty years, Ms. Daley."

"And that is?"

"A personal interview with Sal Batise."

"I rode someone's coattails," she said.

"But deserving all the same," he said, as if for the first time throwing her an olive branch. But she hated olives. He said, "I've also never managed to get one-on-ones with any of Sal's Angels."

"Maybe it's your bedside manner," Carl said.

Martin ignored him. "Or maybe because I was never one of them."

"Just because I was on the ranch as a kid," Jennifer said defensively, "doesn't make me *one* of them. I wasn't there by choice."

"Of course not," he said. "I didn't mean to imply you were. All I'm saying is, you managed to get in with Batise this morning. If you want to know more about Justice Minks, you might see if you can talk to his Angels."

"What makes you think they'll let me in?"

"Because Beth Hawthorne's life is on the line," he said. "And I have a feeling one of them might talk to you."

"Who?"

"Nancy Tanner," he said. "At trial, she was the only one to speak of Justice Minks."

"Which is probably not even his real name."

"Of course it isn't," Martin said. "Nobody has ever been able to figure out who he was. But I saw your sketch of him on the news. And I think that's a start."

"What makes you think she'll talk to me?"

"She was always the weakest link of the three. She's had twenty years of multiple life sentences to think on it." He pulled a business card from his shirt pocket, held it out. "I want to help bring closure to this. I know Beth Hawthorne, and I want to see her back home alive."

She snatched the card and slid it into her pocket.

"And Minks," he said. "He's calling himself Oliver Crown now."

"Lovely," Jennifer said.

"And the final Mallard Malone novel—it's apparently buried with Emily Hawthorne's body, somewhere in New York. They're digging it up now."

"You know this how?"

Martin smiled. "Connections."

Jennifer said, "Did you know that Batise was Mallard Malone?"

"No. You think I would have sat on that if I did?"

"Figured you paid for that Mercedes somehow." *Couldn't have been on a small-town journalist salary*, she thought.

"I sold a lot of books," he said.

Jennifer turned to Carl. "Let's go."

Carl went, but before following her, he lunged at Harold Martin as if to strike, and the reporter jumped back.

And then Jennifer and Carl returned to his truck.

CHAPTER

32

SAM PACED THE hallway outside Warden Wren's office.

FBI Agent Givens said, "You okay?"

Sam nodded. He wondered how much of his conversation with Jennifer had been overheard, not only by Givens but by the guard posted outside Warden Wren's office. He wiped his eyes, tried to play it off like he was tired and not teary-eyed, but he knew Givens hadn't fallen for it.

So, Sam felt the need to add, "I'm fine, thanks."

But he was far from fine. And now Jennifer was texting him about a possible information leak in the warden's office somewhere? *Great*, he thought, pacing again, *just one more person to not trust*.

"Okay," Givens said. "Just that this is a lot for one person to take on."

Just say it, Sam thought. *You think I'm a kid. Nobody here likes playing second fiddle to a kid.* But it wasn't like he'd asked for this.

"And this isn't normal," added Givens. "None of this. I've probably broken protocol at least fifteen times in the past ten hours, but . . . Sal Batise has never been normal, has he?" Sam wondered if Agent Givens was somehow speaking in code. He was being sincere, he could tell, but Sam sensed an undercurrent of pressure being applied. It was clear the FBI agent didn't like being idle. And then Givens said, "He's only truly communicating with you, Sam." He checked his watch. "And we're running out of time."

Sam nodded again, thinking he understood what the agent was insinuating—maybe that it was time to get more aggressive—but knowing also that Agent Givens was on pins and needles as well. And, like Warden Wren, who'd been in and out of the hallway like a hummingbird at feeding time, they were both looking at their watches more than they weren't, all of them waiting any minute for word of Emily Hawthorne's discovered body, and the manuscript buried with it. If, indeed, the location Sal had given them was real. Not that any of them knew what that would then mean, or what Governor Hawthorne would ultimately do with it, but at least it meant another step toward a solution.

But what tortured Sam's mind now more than anything was the news of his father. Professor Trevor Harper. If that was even his name. The Raven and Yellow? *The Raven and The Mongoose*? What did any of it mean? Other than his parents weren't and never were who he thought they were. But how else could Jennifer have known about the hand thing—what he had done with his father for as far back as he could remember, whether on a car window or the window from their kitchen to the deck and even sometimes at bedtime, when he was a boy, he'd put his hand up in the air and his father would mimic it, pretending there was glass there, like they were reflections of one another. Who really knew when and why and how it had all started; all he cared about was that it was *their* thing, the equivalent of a secret handshake, and he had to rack his brain now to recall exactly when they'd *stopped* doing it. Teenage years no doubt, maybe even as early as puberty. But if Jennifer knew about it from the ranch, did it really mean he was there too? Part of him knew it had to be true because why would she make something like that up, but the bigger part of him flat-out didn't want it to be true.

He dialed his father's cellphone and found his hands shaking as it rang. It went to voice mail, so he tried his landline next. When that went to voice mail, he headed toward Warden Wren's office door and asked the security guard to let him in.

The curious glance Agent Givens shared with the guard didn't go unnoticed, but Sam wanted to tell them both to fuck off. *You suddenly have your life turned upside down and see how you react.* The door closed behind him and there, in the middle of the room, just as he'd been for most the day, was Sal Batise. This time he was eating what looked like a blueberry muffin, but as Sam walked closer he could tell from the smell that it was chocolate.

"Sam Harper," said Batise, gesturing toward what had throughout the day become Sam's chair, directly across from him.

Sam sat, but he wasn't happy about it. "Did you kill Emily Hawthorne?"

"No, I told you that."

"Minks?"

"Presumably."

"Because you ordered him to."

"Why would I do such a thing? And if so, why would I admit to it?" He pursed his lips. "Although . . . they can't kill me twice, no?"

"If the only copy of that manuscript was buried with Emily Hawthorne, how does Minks seem to know every detail of it?"

"It's obvious he read it before he buried it."

"And he has a memory like you? Never forgets a detail?"

Batise licked a finger, crumpled the muffin wrapper into a little ball. "Something is troubling you, Sam Harper. What knowledge have you stumbled upon since last we spoke . . ." He looked at an imaginary watch on his left arm. "Only thirty minutes ago."

Sam peered out the window overlooking the yard, but felt Batise's eyes on him, then felt his own jaw quivering.

"Tell me, son. What's bothering you?"

Sam turned on him, full of as much fuel and fire as he could muster. "Why?"

"Why . . . *what*?"

"Why me?"

"Sam and Sal . . . Sal and Sam . . ."

"Stop it."

But Batise had to say once more: "Sam and Sal."

"Did you know two people from the Freedom Ranch . . ."

"I knew everyone from the Freedom Ranch, Sam Harper. It was *my* ranch."

Sam went on as if he hadn't been interrupted. "Their names were Raven and Yellow."

Batise leaned back in his chair, folded his hands in his lap. "My father, from prison, he used to tell me, *Take care of your little brother. Take care of Tommy. Take care of Tiny Tommy Batise.*"

"Who is Tommy Batise?"

"Who do you think Tommy Batise is?"

"Your relative? Your brother?"

Batise pointed at him. "Very good. Now keep going."

"Your father asked you to take care of him because he's your *little* brother?"

"Right again," said Batise, "except in this case, my half brother. My father got around, and unlike me, he didn't always . . . pull out in time." Batise winked. "Most the time. But I was told time and time again to watch over Tommy because, yes, he was my little brother, but also so small, ya know? Do you know a grown man who has always seemed kind of . . . tiny, Sam Harper? Maybe even a grown man you seem to tower over and perhaps you've always wondered why?"

"Stop."

"You wanted to know why, so I'm telling you why. I haven't got much time left." He showed him the muffin wrapper balled in his hand. "I just had my *last* snack. Speaking of lasts, Sam Harper, I have requested you share in my last meal and it's been granted by Warden Adrian Wren. Steak and potatoes. My favorite."

"What do you know about my father?"

"I know when he was a little boy, his mind drifted toward the fantastical and the imaginative. He liked to make up his own stories and live in his own little world where he was a raven and he had a mongoose sidekick and together they hunted bad guys. *The Raven and The Mongoose*, Sam Harper . . . surely *Trevor* Harper has shown you the artwork from his childhood."

"You're lying," Sam said, but this was just as Jennifer had told him.

Batise said, "Who can you *trust*, Sam Harper? Your friends? Are they really your friends? Warden Wren? Agent Givens?" He grinned, said, "Your father? Can you even trust him?"

Sam stood so fast his chair toppled and the guard went on alert.

Batise, chains and all, held up a hand to the guard, as if to hold him off. "Your eyes twitch when you get mad, Sam Harper. They've done so ever since you were a boy . . ."

"How would . . ." Sam backed away.

"My father, from prison, begged me to take care of my little brother, of Tommy. And it turns out that Tiny Tommy took care of me."

"What are you talking about?"

"How do you think I was arrested? Who do you think called the police on his own brother? Tiny Tommy became the Tattler."

Sam shook his head, felt suddenly disoriented.

"Have you wondered why I have to keep saying your full name, Sam Harper?"

"Because . . ." Sam put a hand to his temple, nauseous as well as dizzy now. "Because . . ."

"Because I have to constantly remind myself that's your name now. Just as Trevor Harper and Annie Harper took new names, so should the boy they stole from my house."

"No . . ."

"The boy once named Steven Batise."

"No," Sam hissed, but at the same time knowing Batise was telling the truth. But when he looked up at Batise again and saw the man's right hand frozen, fingers splayed, up in the air, like he was waiting for Sam to give him a high five but was, in reality, making fun of a gesture he and his father—whoever the fuck he was—had always cherished, Sam lost it. The ball of fury in his gut rose like an erupting volcano and he saw dizzy and he saw blood and he charged at Batise like a bull loose in the streets of Pamplona. He placed his hands on the chained man's chest and pushed with all his strength and Batise went backward in his chair. Sam backed away as the guards leaped forward, one holding him back while the other helped Batise upright, and the fucker was laughing and saying he was okay, and all Sam could think of in that moment was Agent Givens—who was on his way into the room as well—telling him that none of this was normal.

None of this is normal, Sam.

Sam and Sal, Sal and Sam . . .

And then it dawned on Sam, as he was pulled from the office, how many times in the past few hours Sal Batise had referred to him as *son*. He'd thought it was just an older man speaking to the youth of the world, but the implication now made him want to throw up.

And Batise wasn't finished. He shouted toward the open door before they could get Sam through it. "You were in the closet, Sam Harper," he shouted. "I hear there were at one time five kids in that closet."

Warden Wren then entered his office. "Enough," he said to Batise.

Batise glared at the warden and then Agent Banks. "You all wanted to know who the Kentucky Cannibal was? Who the Kentucky Cannibal *is*, rather, so I'm telling you. He's out there, and it isn't Justice Minks." The next part he said directly to Sam. "You were in that closet, son. You were in that house. The Raven was there, right? The Kentucky Cannibal was there. And the Raven *IS* a liar."

CHAPTER

33

MAYBE IT WAS a mistake coming here, Trevor thought, after entering the kitchen of the dilapidated house and feeling his legs turn rubbery, like they no longer contained the necessary bones and muscle required to hold him upright.

Without warning, his body failed him; he dropped to both knees with a thud on the old linoleum floor, and the impact felt like it had shaken the house. Up until entering the kitchen, he'd been rejuvenated by returning to the past, because it was a past in which he'd too often felt like the hunted, like the prey, and he'd returned after so many years as a more emboldened hunter, the predator—The Raven. But all that had fallen by the wayside as soon as he entered the kitchen. It wasn't a kitchen he'd entered often during his time on the Freedom Ranch; he did his best to avoid the main house in general, just as he'd lived his life avoiding confrontation at every turn. But this had been his brother's house. This had been the house where Justice Minks, whenever he showed up, would stay, as he was the only member of The Collective seemingly able to come and go as he pleased. Which had often made Trevor wonder if Minks had ever truly been a member of the cult at all.

From his knees, he looked toward the stove, or rather, toward the gaping hole in the cabinetry where the stove had once been, the infamous stove where the authorities had found the even more infamous stew congealed in a pot on the front right burner. Vandals had no doubt taken the oven as a sick keepsake. Maybe they'd broken it down into parts and sold them on eBay as pieces of the stove used by the Kentucky Cannibal. The backsplash on the wall behind the oven was completely covered in graffiti, crude pictures of genitalia and laughing faces and bullets and knives and creepy blood splatter, all perfectly disguising the fact that the words—*The Kentucky Cannibal was here*—had ever been there at all. But Trevor didn't need the newspaper and television reports to tell him so, because he'd lived it. He'd watched Sal spray-paint the words on there while Justice Minks laughed, and even while Trevor knelt on the kitchen floor, twenty years later, the tears came. The tears came, and right along with them the fear and the fury in equal measure.

But what are you gonna do about it, Tommy, huh? Minks had hissed in his ear as he held a knife to his throat in one hand and with the other grasped his hair so tightly his scalp burned from the searing pain. *Nothing, because Tiny Tommy Batise is nothing . . . Your brother always told me you couldn't fend for yourself, so he always had to fend for you. That you don't know shit from Shinola. That he'd seen wet paper towels tougher than you, Tiny Tommy Batise.*

And Trevor cried now just as he'd cried then, except now it was no longer in shame, but from some kind of catharsis, churning in his gut and through his bloodstream and transforming him into the man he'd always wished he'd become. Because back then Annie had been hiding under a bed and he'd been scared for her, but even more scared for the children he'd hid upstairs in the closet, and he'd prayed they'd stay quiet because none of this was part of the plan, having to quickly hide them because their fire diversion hadn't diverted them long enough, and Sal and Justice had returned before they'd had a chance to fully escape with Steven and the other four kids. And Trevor—Tommy, back then, but known on the ranch as Raven—knew damn well what was really bubbling inside the pot atop the stove.

"Trevor?" Lizzie said behind him now.

But he barely heard her.

Because part of him was still back there, back *then*, and he wasn't about to tell them anything different from what he already had, that

Annie—Yellow, back then—had already taken all five kids into the woods and they were long gone by now, even though every one of them was still hiding inside the house, right under Sal's stupid fucking nose.

"Trevor," Lizzie said again, this time kneeling on the kitchen floor to embrace him, to wipe his tears. "What's wrong?" she asked.

And he stared at where the stove had been, his tears already drying, his eyes now as clear as his vision, as prevalent as the memory of that horrible night, and he said, "They made me eat it, Lizzie. He grabbed my hair. He forced my mouth open. I knew it was meat from a dead body in that pot . . . on the stove . . . and my brother, my own fucking brother, they made me do it. He was high . . . I could see it in his pupils, he was always high, Lizzie, just like everybody was always high, and he brought the big mixing spoon over from the stove, from the pot, some if it dripping on the floor, and he made me eat it." He gagged at the memory smells and could still feel the grit of it between his teeth and sliding down his throat. "They made me fucking eat it, Lizzie, and they laughed, but I wouldn't tell them where the kids were, I wouldn't give them up, and that was the right thing to do, right? That was brave, right?"

"That was brave," Lizzie said, gently touching his head of short hair, touching his cheek, "That was brave."

"And they called me a cannibal," Trevor said. "They thought it was funny. And Minks said that wasn't the first time I'd eaten human meat. The week before, one of the times Minks had stayed for a couple days straight, he'd offered me a quick dinner inside my brother's house, and maybe I thought it tasted funny even then, but a lot of times our meals tasted funny, Lizzie, because we cooked up whatever we could find in that forest. Maybe I should have known something was up because Minks was being nice to me for the first time ever and I'd convinced myself maybe a corner was being turned, but it wasn't, and that had never been truer than when they force-fed me that . . . that stew that night in the kitchen, *this* kitchen, Lizzie, and they called me the Kentucky Cannibal because of it and they spray-painted it on the wall above the stove."

He felt Lizzie's arms trembling as she held him, and he liked to think it was from rage over what had been done to him and not the fear of what he'd done. *Because you're not a cannibal if you didn't know, right? You're not a cannibal if they forced it down your throat.*

You're just a victim, and they're bullies.

And he said the next thought out loud: "It stops now, Lizzie."

And he knew that with her response he would either sink or sail, and when she said, "You're goddamn right," he thought he might cry all over again, because he was about to set sail and it wouldn't be alone. They stood together from the floor, didn't matter to him that she towered over him, especially in her heels, because nothing was going to stop him from finding Justice Minks now. Nothing was going to stop him from dancing on his brother's grave, because that clock had been ticking for way too long now and was finally about to run out.

He was The Raven, and she was The Mongoose.

And because his childhood heroes made decisions based on clues and facts and newly attained evidence, his heart swelled with pride when The Mongoose said, "There's something in the other room you need to see."

CHAPTER

34

BETH WAS EXHAUSTED.

Physically and emotionally exhausted.

But she'd refused to sleep. She couldn't defend herself if she was asleep. She laughed inwardly at that because she couldn't defend herself at all. But she'd give anything right now to be free of the chains. The weight of them was causing unbearable strain on her limbs and joints; so far she'd only discovered two positions where the strain was tolerable, but after a matter of minutes, even those positions hurt.

He was a madman to do this.

Or maybe Mallard Malone was a madman for thinking it up, these Chain Houses.

Earlier, she'd heard movement inside the neighboring room, what sounded like a body being dragged across a floor, and felt sure Billy Boyle's corpse had finally been removed. So far, no one else had been hooked to the chain to replace him, but when she pulled on the chain through that wall, the resistance was still heavy. Although not as heavy as Billy's dead body. She'd been able to move whatever it was attached to, but it had taken effort, and eventually the chain stopped again. By the sound of the heavy object scooting across the floor over there, she guessed it was a cinderblock, or maybe a boat anchor. Either way, the slight leeway granted by the change had allowed her to get closer to the hole in the floor, and after peering down into it, she'd been able to see Joseph Gerrard sleeping on the floor below. She feared for his state of mind. She'd tried getting him to talk and he either wouldn't or couldn't, but what disturbed her even more than his lack of response was that, aside from the wall with the window, he appeared to be chained in every direction available. A chain disappeared into the other three walls and another one disappeared into the floor next to where he lay curled into a ball, which meant there was either a room in the basement or this Chain House was three floors tall.

Refusing to stay idle and refusing to give in to her exhaustion, Beth had spent the past thirty minutes intermittently calling out her captor's name. Alternating between shouts of *Justice*, or *Minks*, or *Justice Minks*, or *Oliver*, hoping to lure him into her room, hoping to coax him into conversation, because she was a full believer in the idiom: *Better the devil you know than the devil you don't.* She stopped shouting when she heard footsteps thundering down the hallway outside her room, but when the door flew open so rapidly the knob punched a hole in the drywall, puncturing one of the book covers plastered there, she knew she was in trouble, because it wasn't Oliver Crown in his Guy Fawkes mask, but another man altogether, one she'd never seen before.

"You're gonna shut the fuck up, bitch, or I will shut you up." He was tall and thick with small eyes and a shaved head, dressed in army fatigues with big black shitkicker boots that ran halfway up the shins of his camo pants.

Beth scooted as far away as her chains would allow. Within seconds she realized her display of fear was a mistake, as his rage quickly morphed into something she could only construe to be lust. Like he was an animal with uncontrollable urges that needed to be sated now, and she cursed herself for poking the bear. She'd only made her situation worse.

The man, glancing over his shoulder toward the open door, acting as if his time might be limited, began undoing his belt, and before she knew it his pants were down around his ankles. Beth grabbed the chains around her, one in each hand, gritted her teeth, and hissed, "Try it, motherfucker."

He stepped forward, grinning, oblivious to another sound of footsteps approaching down the hallway, these angry as well, but somehow moving more methodically and controlled, and seconds later Justice Minks showed himself in the doorway, mask and all, a large gun in his right hand.

Beth's shaved-head assailant glanced over his shoulder and said in desperation, "It's not what you think, Justice . . ." But he barely had time to blink before Minks pointed the gun and blew the man's brains across the floor, against the wall.

Beth screamed, and her screaming acted like a trigger for the rest of those held captive inside the house, because a chain reaction of screaming soon followed, even from Joseph Gerrard directly below, and by the sound of the cacophony of fear resonating through the Chain House, through the walls and floors, Beth guessed the number of prisoners was close to a dozen, if not more. She looked away from the carnage, away from the sight of her assailant's body somehow still resting on his knees, mostly headless, before Minks kicked it over and the body landed with a loud, floor-shaking *thump* on the hardwood.

"He knew better," Minks said. If Beth had anything in her stomach, she would have thrown it up right then and there, especially as Minks squatted down with his eyes on her. "He'd been warned. Oliver Crown is a leader of the new world order. And they *don't* rape or pillage." His knees popped when he stood. He checked his watch. "Four hours now."

"Until what?"

"Batise is executed," he said. "By firing squad. On national television."

This was news to her. For the first time, she wondered how much the world had changed over the past thirty-six hours. "And then what? You'll let me go?"

He didn't answer, just stared at her with those dark eyes, and after forcing herself to investigate them, really focus deep into them, she realized she recognized those eyes from somewhere. From the horrors of the attack inside the Hawthorne mansion, yes, but perhaps even before then.

"Oliver," she said. "Take off the mask."

He watched her, said nothing, the gun hanging heavy as a boulder in his right hand, grip loose like he might accidentally drop it.

Beth adjusted her seat on the floor. "You said they've all been forced to read the books. All of them. Who is . . . all of them? Justice?"

"Oliver," he said. "I'm Oliver Crown now, and I'll soon be the leader of men and women."

"The new world order?"

"Don't mock me."

"Why am I here?"

"Because this is what happens in the book."

"What happens then . . . in the book . . . after the execution?"

"It's Malcolm Dodd," he said. "In the book. He's executed. By firing squad."

"On national television," she said, eager to show him she was listening and taking him seriously. "Is Sal Batise supposed to represent . . ."

"Malcolm Dodd."

"But what will happen after Batise is executed?"

"Then my army will create chaos," he said. "And Oliver Crown will rise from the ashes. It's all in the book."

"What book?"

He pointed to his head with the barrel of the gun. "It's in here."

"You've memorized it?"

He nodded. "But the original is downstairs. In a safe."

As calmly as she could, and without looking at the dead man's body to her right, Beth said, "You mentioned your wife?"

"She's off-limits."

"So I do . . . have limits?"

No answer.

"Can I . . . meet her. Your wife?"

He stared at her.

"What's her name? Oliver?"

"Her name is Elizabeth," he said. "Elizabeth Bennet."

Beth was familiar with the name, knew it from somewhere, and then it hit her. "The same name as the wife in *Pride and Prejudice*. By Jane Austen."

"I know who wrote it."

"You've read it?"

"Seven times," he said, and the revelation couldn't have shocked her more.

"And your wife's parents . . . they must have been . . . Jane Austen fans?"

"I don't know, were they?" he said, with snark. "But she *is* Elizabeth Bennet."

"And that would make you . . . Mr. Darcy?"

"When I'm with her, yes," he said.

"And when you aren't . . . with her?"

"I'm Oliver Crown."

He headed for the door, but she stopped him: "Oliver?"

"What?"

"Can I see your face?"

"No."

"Do I know you? From somewhere?"

After a beat, he said, "Yes."

And then he closed the door.

CHAPTER 35

Before

JENNIFER WASN'T THE oldest of the group, but she was the newest to the ranch—what was left of it—and therefore, in her mind, the least damaged.

Which also apparently made her the most equipped to handle their current circumstance, locked in the dark closet with a flashlight as their only source of light, and that had begun to flicker over the past thirty minutes.

The inconsistent light made it difficult to draw.

Iris said every time the light flickered it looked like the figures and shapes in her mural were moving.

The strobe effect, Jennifer had told her, smelling fresh urine from one of them having just gone in their pants. The five of them with an unspoken agreement not to ask who it was, perhaps in fear of them being the next one to have an accident.

The closet was completely empty, which Jennifer took to mean this was not the Breaker of Chains' bedroom, but instead a spare. Which meant, she hoped they'd be spared. The new boy's name was Steven. She wondered if he had a mother somewhere. He didn't talk much, and when he did, he had a nervous voice. Of course, he was new to her, but not to the rest of them. But in the weeks he'd been away from the children's barracks, it seemed an awkwardness had developed between them, and therefore little was said. Them thinking he'd been killed by demons, only for him to be alive inside the Blue House again, and now locked inside the closet with them, the five of them like the fingers of a hand, promising, in what few words they'd uttered since being ushered into the closet, to not be broken apart. *We're like a fist now*, Jennifer had told them in a hushed whisper as she drew on the wall, careful not to draw too hard in case someone would hear.

And she knew it was Steven who'd wet himself, and she felt sorry for him.

Had his mother gone into the woods too?

The sound of footsteps on the stairs rendered them still, ultra quiet, and when the footsteps came closer, across the floorboards and then stopping on the other side of the door, Markie started shivering from fright.

Jennifer gripped his sweaty hand, and he calmed a little.

A key unlocked the closet door, and along with the fresh air that whooshed in, The Raven's face showed in the opening. They were safe. But his face didn't show it; he was worried and rushed, and instead of looking for all of them, his eyes sought out only one of them. He reached for Steven and gently ushered him out.

The Raven said, "I can only take one of you now, but I'll be back. I promise." And then, "Stay quiet, just for a little longer."

The door closed, locked, his footsteps trailed away, back across the bedroom floor and down the distant stairs, and somewhere even more distant, a door closed.

Jennifer had Peter hold the flashlight on her mural. In large letters, she wrote *The Raven was here* across the wall.

And then she found the five stick figures she'd drawn inside the house in the middle of the wall and erased the fifth one.

CHAPTER 36

CARL WENT AS far as he was allowed inside the Kentucky Correctional Institution for Women, before telling Jennifer he'd see her back at the truck.

Carl being Carl, he took it in stride; he loved his truck and didn't mind sitting in it. And he promised to keep himself busy as he waited by scouring the Spider Web, the online true crime network he'd talked about all the way from the state penitentiary at Twisted Tree to the women's prison in Pewee Valley, with a quick stop at a Goodwill store along the way. After reading the visitor's dress code, Jennifer realized, in transit, that while her morning interview attire would suffice because it showed no shoulders or cleavage, her open-toe shoes would be out of compliance. It was something Sal's prison had either overlooked or had no rules against, but she wasn't taking any chances here. So instead of going out of their way to her apartment, she'd hurried into the thrift store and came out five minutes later with a pair of five-dollar closed-toed flats. By the time they'd pulled into the prison's parking lot, they'd heard news of yet another fire, this one set in Ransom, a town that neighbored Twisted Tree, at the home of millionaire Henry Hollingsworth. It was the third fire of the day, the victims all from the moneyed class, all in the same general area, and all were considered arson.

So Jennifer could tell Carl couldn't wait to get back to his truck to do his own bit of gumshoeing on the fires. Meanwhile, Jennifer did her best to prepare herself for another unprecedented interview. She was shocked she'd been able to jump through the numerous hoops of protocol to secure the visit with Nancy Tanner. It was a shot in the dark, spurred on by their confrontation with Harold Martin back at the state pen, but Warden Julia Bates, after putting her on hold for ten minutes, returned with the news that Nancy Tanner had agreed to speak with her within the hour. The female warden made it immediately known that this wasn't their typical protocol and then proceeded to list every rule she was about to break in allowing the visit.

They had visiting days, and this wasn't one of them. They had visiting hours, and even if this was the right day, that window had closed hours ago. And inmates in the Segregation Unit were required to have an appointment scheduled one week in advance, and then it was up to the inmate to schedule it with their caseworker, which Nancy Tanner had obviously not done. All visitors were supposed to be listed on the inmate's approved visiting list, which Jennifer clearly was not. All this, Jennifer knew, would have been impossible on such short notice, but with a resigned sigh, Warden Bates said, "Now, out of all three of the women mentioned, why is it Nancy Tanner you'd like to talk to?"

"Because I think back then, at trial, she truly had something to say . . . but was afraid to."

"And now?"

"Now, given what's going on with our state's First Lady, I'm hoping she can help us out."

"*Us*, meaning?"

"The authorities," Jennifer said. "The FBI."

"Of which you are neither," stated the warden.

"Correct," Jennifer said. "But—"

"I know who you are, Ms. Daley, which is why I even took the time to reach out to inmate Tanner in the first place. I thought perhaps she'd have a soft spot for you. None of Sal's "Angels," although they've been model prisoners, no doubt knowing they're all inches away from death row instead of lifers, have ever agreed to *any* interview over the past twenty years."

"That isn't what this is about," Jennifer said, thinking about the documentary. "I promise."

"I understand," said Warden Bates. "Which is why I'll allow you a few minutes. But all three women, their only visitors have been family and a few friends, and even those have dwindled over the past two decades. Inmate Tanner hasn't had a visitor for nine months, and of those on her short list of visitors, most haven't visited within the past five years. Look, I understand the urgency, and perhaps Nancy Tanner does, too, and maybe she still has some of her soul left . . . she only pondered it for a few seconds before telling me she'd see you."

And here Jennifer was, sitting on the opposite side of a glass partition, about to have a no-contact visit with a woman tried and found guilty of multiple murders inside the Hawthorne mansion that fateful night, her body shaking in anticipation and from the strenuous security checks to get here.

A minute later, a door in the room opposite opened, and escorted inside by a tall male prison guard was Nancy Tanner, wearing a khaki short-sleeved uniform, handcuffs, and a chain around her ankles that made her gait short and clunky as she approached Jennifer's window. Her long blond hair of yesteryear had been cut short and was all gray now. She took her seat on the opposite side of the glass, rested her cuffed hands on the small ledge in front of the opening, and leaned into Jennifer's view.

Jennifer, on instinct, learned back in her chair, which drew a short chortle from Nancy Tanner on the other side of the partition.

"Ugly up close, isn't it?" said Nancy, her voice deeper than what Jennifer remembered from past videos.

But she was right, it *was* ugly up close, the skin-puckered mass of wounds and scar tissue on the left side of her otherwise perfect nose. Jennifer *had* forgotten about the left eye, or the lack of one. And the reason it had been plucked out twenty years ago in the first place, in the days after the trial where she'd mistakenly invoked the name of Justice Minks on the stand.

Losing the eye had been her punishment for talking then.

Jennifer couldn't help but think what Nancy's punishment might be now.

CHAPTER 37

SAM DIDN'T KNOW what kind of room he was in, a lobby, an office, or whatever, other than it didn't have any windows but had a weird number of chairs and a stupid number of doors.

Four of them, in fact, one door for each wall, and other than the one he was facing now from his cushioned chair against the far wall, he didn't know to what or where any of the other doors led. But this was the room they'd taken him to after his outburst of aggression toward Sal Batise, what seemed like hours ago, but had been only a matter of minutes. He'd texted Jennifer, but when she didn't respond he texted Carl, and when Carl said that Jennifer was currently in a visit with Nancy Tanner—*the* Nancy Tanner—Sam didn't know what to think. Or what to do. They were out there with wings and he, for the first time all day, felt trapped. But his urgency to leave the prison paralleled his intense need to stay. After pushing Batise like he had, he doubted they'd even let him in the same room again.

For the fifth time since being escorted into this room, Sam got out his phone and stared at his dad's contact. At least, who he thought had been his dad, but now didn't know what to think or who to believe. During his flurry of texts with Carl, he became convinced, just as Jennifer and Carl evidently were, that Sam himself *had* been that fifth kid on the Freedom Ranch, the fifth stick figure represented on and then erased from that closet wall. And that Trevor Harper—the so-called Raven—had been on the ranch as well.

Although Sam remembered none of it. Or maybe he did, and perhaps, in the past had, but he'd confused it all with nightmares and dreams.

He finally hit the call button and paced the room as it rang on the other end. It went to voice mail; his next decision was whether to leave a message or not. He wanted to yell at Trevor but at the same time needed to know if he was okay. When Trevor Harper's voice came on asking the caller to leave a message at the beep, Sam nearly hung up, and then nearly said, *Dad, call me*, before swallowing the first word whole and going with, *Call me, it's Sam, we need to talk.*

And then he ended it, felt better for having done it.

The door to his left opened. He turned to find Agent Givens approaching. Sam said, "Did something happen?"

"No," Givens said. "But we did learn a little bit. I think we found someone who could be our Oliver Crown."

"What's his name?"

"That's where it gets a bit tricky," Givens said. "As you know, Batise was in and out of prison throughout his teens and twenties. During his longest bit, he was at Eddyville, two years, out on good behavior, and then he started The Collective soon thereafter. Anyway, we've always had a feeling if Minks did exist, that he'd possibly spent time in prison with Batise."

"They never found that connection before," Sam said.

"Yeah, but I think we might have now," Givens said. "And the guy *is* like a wisp of smoke, Jesus. We did find, at the same time Batise was there, a man named Jeffrey Justice. He got out five years ago after a twenty-year bit for armed robbery and vehicular manslaughter. This was flagged twenty years ago when the FBI investigated it, and Jeffrey Justice was questioned then, but didn't have much to say, and honestly it was flimsy to begin with. All the man had was a last name that matched our mystery man's first. They scoured the prison inmates for someone named Minks, thinking maybe our guy borrowed both names, but never found one, and soon the theory that Justice Minks might have been in prison with Sal Batise went by the wayside."

"And now?"

"We tracked Jeffrey Justice down. He didn't want to talk at first, just wanted to be left alone, trying to pick up the pieces and live a normal life, a second life, he said, after so thoroughly fucking up the first. But we asked him about his time at Eddyville, twenty-some-odd years ago. He recalled, of course, when the FBI had visited him back then, that he thought it odd they were questioning him. But seeing as he, in his second life, is now trying to do good for the world, he eventually talked, a couple hours ago. He spoke of a roommate he had at Eddyville, for roughly four months, whose name was Luther Wright. I asked him what Luther Wright looked like, and he laughed. Not in a joking way but more like he was afraid, even so many years later. He spoke of the scar across the man's face. Said it was hideous, and he did his best every day to never look at it, because if Luther ever caught anyone staring, he was quick to make a scene. That's how he put it: *quick to make a scene*. Now remember, back then, with Beth Hawthorne's testimony, she never saw his face, never saw his eyes, just the mask he was wearing, so we had nothing to go on. Back then, if the fourth murderer that evening *was* there, everyone always assumed he wore the mask, like Sal's Angels did with their balaclavas, to make sure their faces went unnoticed. Now we know our guy wears his mask because he's self-conscious about his butchered face. So Jeff Justice, even though he never had any true issues with this Luther Wright, whispers often enough to the guards he respects that his roommate creeps him out, and soon thereafter Luther Wright, without being told why, is moved to another room with another roommate. Justice did his best to act surprised and pissed about it, and he believes to this day Luther Wright believed his act."

"And the second roommate's name?"

"Mac Pritchard," said Givens. "Mac Michael Pritchard. Would have been convenient if his last name was Minks, right? But get this, Pritchard was a sexual deviant doing life in prison. He was questioned briefly back then but was useless as far as information. He's dead now. Died of natural causes inside Eddyville ten years ago. But we've got agents in there now asking around, seeing who remembers what from back then, and more than one remembered Pritchard and Luther Wright and said Pritchard was scared as hell of his new roommate. That's why he was silent when the FBI questioned him back then. His roommate was years gone by then, but still . . . the fear of getting got was real. Turns out Pritchard, as I said, sexual deviant, convicted rapist, had a fetish for, get this . . . mink coats. Naked women in mink coats, at first, all he needed to get off was a mink coat. And he had an extensive collection of them. Weird, right? But evidently Luther Wright catches wind of this and gives Pritchard a nickname."

"Minks?"

"Bingo," said Givens. "It wasn't like a prison-wide nickname, just one Luther Wright gave him, like a secret handshake almost, between them."

"So Luther Wright gets out of jail and steals the name Justice from roommate one and Minks from roommate number two?"

"Yes," said Givens. "And plenty of people have remembered seeing him often on the yard with Batise. And now that your friend's sketch of our man has gone viral, the prison easily looked back at their files from the nineties and found our Luther Wright."

"Are we even sure *that's* his name?"

"No, not certain, but we think so," he said. "Hoping so, the buck has to stop somewhere, right? But that's not all. Luther, we're finding out, while never once violent at Eddyville, was known for his . . . weirdness. For his face, yes, but more so because he just creeped people out. He never said much and was rarely seen without a book. Jeff Justice said he read all the time inside their cell. And he mostly didn't go by Luther. Got mad when people used his name."

"What did he go by?"

Givens smiled. "Edmond Dantes."

Sam looked confused.

Givens said, "From *The Count of Monte Cristo*?"

"Ah," Sam said, playing it off like he'd read it in high school like he was supposed to.

"You know the story, right?" Givens didn't give him time to respond. "Edmond Dantes, young sailor, wrongly accused of treason, falsely imprisoned. While in prison, he learns of a hidden treasure on the island of Monte Cristo. He escapes, acquires a fortune, and then seeks revenge on all those who wronged him."

"And now he's calling himself Oliver Crown . . ."

"Yet another fictional character, yes," Givens said.

"And how did Luther Wright leave Eddyville? If he escaped, that story would have had that face plastered all over the news."

"Early parole," Givens said. "Good behavior, if you can believe it. And after he walks free, he becomes our Justice Minks."

"Jesus," Sam said, his mind made up now, whether he was going to leave Batise to die alone or not, because he couldn't now walk away from this. He had a documentary to finish, but even more importantly, Beth Hawthorne was still out there, being held captive somewhere, and no matter how anxiously his mind was screaming for Sam to step away and go home and become boring Sam Harper again, to flee from this situation before he got truly burned, he couldn't.

Givens said, "Get this. When Luther got his walking papers, guess what name he signed."

"Edmond Dantes?"

"Yeah."

"And they allowed it?"

"No, they ripped it up, made him sign the papers again. Said if he tried that stunt again, they'd rip up the early parole papers too. But, from what we're hearing now from Eddyville, from those who were there back then, they were eager to see him go. But as soon as Jennifer's sketch of him went on TV and social media, they all remembered him as Luther Wright."

"Shouldn't you be telling this to Batise right now?"

"Already did. It's like talking to a wall. He still refuses to speak to anyone but you."

"He still wants me in there?"

"Yes." Givens nodded toward one of the doors. "So, if you're ready, let's get you back in there." He looked over his shoulder before opening the door. "You hungry?"

"Yeah," Sam said, although he didn't feel like eating anything.

"Good," Givens said. "Because there's a table set for two in there." When Sam paused, confused, Givens said, "Last meal. Remember?"

Yeah, thought Sam, *that's right . . . steak and potatoes.*

And he imagined Batise liked his steak rare.

C H A P T E R

38

TREVOR SLOWLY TURNED inside the circle of folding chairs, inside the old dining room of Sal Batise's Freedom Ranch house.

Lizzie, standing in the doorway, arms folded, said, "See what I mean?"

He nodded, took it all in like any good raven would, feeling like a different man now after whatever catharsis had happened between the two of them and his nightmare memories inside the kitchen moments ago. But she was right. It was clear. Not only was this house still being used, but a meeting of sorts had taken place here, recently. By the smell of cigarette smoke in the air, very recently. And as she'd pointed out, showing him through the window, where two of the four panes of glass had been shattered, the tall grass all around the cabin looked trampled under tire tracks. Several. And if all the chairs in the circle had been full, that meant ten people had met here to discuss something. An empty Sprite can sat next to the legs of one chair, a spent cigarette butt resting on top. Twelve Coors bottles rested in various spots around the circle of chairs, all of them dead soldiers except for one that was open and nearly full. The cardboard case they'd come in had been discarded and partially stomped in the far corner.

If only Trevor could have been a fly on the wall for whatever meeting this had been. But on the heels of what was about to happen with Sal Batise, his own brother, in less than four hours now, this location where a secret meeting had recently taken place, inside the very house Sal used to live, was too much of a coincidence. Everything he remembered of his brother, from childhood up to the day Trevor had turned him in, was cloaked in manipulation and anger. But beyond all, revenge. His brother spoke of revenge so often that Little Tommy Batise had eventually bought into it, fallen prey to it, and had been brainwashed by The Collective. He was the repressed, he was the slighted and the downtrodden, and they'd all been convinced they would not rest until the elite world was gone. He could remember Sal preaching to his followers, in these very woods, about the Haves and the Have-Nots . . .

. . . because even when the Haves show kindness, it's masked by pity and shame and disgust, and deep down they all secretly wish the guttersnipes would return to the gutters . . .

"And one day we'll have our revenge," Trevor said softly, to himself, using the same words his brother so often used, but he realized it all came back to revenge.

And Sal's voice from the past again returned in full . . .

. . . and there will be an event to change it all, a trigger, and every chain we've forged in life, every chain that had been thrust upon us by a society who has never cared, will be broken . . . and the Breaker of Chains will . . .

"Trevor," Lizzie said.

He turned to face her, saw she was holding a crumpled piece of paper.

"I found this on the floor." She held it out to him.

He took it with caution, turned it over. The words written on it revealed a list of eight names. His gut told him they were all wealthy men and women.

"The fires," Lizzie said.

Trevor nodded. Three of the eight names on the list had already fallen victim to arson in the past twelve hours, all around Twisted Tree and neighboring Ransom.

"He's got something planned," Trevor said of his brother.

"What?" Lizzie asked. "Class war?"

"Maybe," he said, thinking of the fire he and Annie had set to the Kitchen House twenty years ago before trying to flee with the children. "But I think these fires are just a diversion for something bigger."

"Like what?"

"I don't know," he said, holding up a hand to quiet her.

A vehicle had pulled up outside the house. Two car doors closed.

Out the window, Trevor saw two rough-looking men approaching the porch, one white and one Black. Both pulled handguns from their waistlines and seemed eager to get inside and see why there was an unknown car parked out front.

Trevor had the baseball bat, but it was no viable defense against real weapons held by two men who looked more than willing to use them.

A real Raven, he knew, would fly away.

He looked at Lizzie, who'd just removed her top and was standing in a bra and now stepping out of her shorts, quickly, one leg and then the other. "What are you *doing*?" Trevor whispered, just as the men's footsteps pressed heavy on the floors in the other room.

CHAPTER

39

DUSK CAME WITHOUT warning.

And through the bars of the window across the room, the flame-scorched sunset brought with it a sense of impending doom.

Her own.

Because who was she kidding? She was never getting out of here. What had seemed to her already as days passing had only been a bit over twenty-four hours, and within a few more Sal Batise would die, on schedule. But the notion of her then being set free, Beth knew, was a nonsensical one. She'd seen too many faces now, all rough-looking characters. A man and a woman had been in the room with her, just long enough to remove the body of the man Minks had shot and killed. As if they'd been trained, they didn't look at her, didn't speak to her, but the fact that they'd shown their faces sealed her doom.

And although blood and brains still stained the floor, the door was closed, and they'd been gone now for an hour, at least. She'd tried to get a reaction from Joseph in the room below, but he was catatonically unresponsive. But at least he was still alive, unlike Billy next door, who'd been removed hours ago and, to her knowledge, had yet to be replaced. But she felt certain now that the chain going through the wall next to the door, and probably across a hallway into another room, had someone attached to it now, because the chain had been moving a lot more in the past few minutes, tugging painfully at her ankle, and she could hear someone whimpering through the walls. To keep her fearful mind preoccupied, she returned to the puzzle.

A thousand pieces.

A winter landscape; the Alps, according to the box. The box she'd at first analyzed to see if she could somehow turn the corners into a weapon but now found herself glancing at every few minutes to compare the puzzle-piece border she was creating to the picture on the box. It proved to be a diversion she appreciated, yet deep down didn't fully trust, because after looking through the hole in the floor, Joseph had not been given a puzzle to help pass whatever time *he* had left.

The puzzle was specifically for her, which she'd known the instant when, right after they'd carted the dead body from the room, the woman had returned to slide the puzzle across the floor and telling her, *A gift from Oliver Crown*, before leaving.

As a child psychologist, Beth was big on puzzles, to the point that she considered it her thing. Often, when children refused to open up or were afraid to talk to her, she'd casually start placing pieces into whatever puzzle she had started on at the coffee table, and without fail, the child would inevitably become intrigued enough to start helping, and gentle conversation would typically start soon thereafter.

She'd asked Minks earlier what was wrong with his face, trying to get a rise out of him, not knowing if, in fact, he was wearing it for any reason other than disguising himself, but now as she looked up from the scattered puzzle pieces on the floor, having just snapped the final piece to complete the border, she knew he had some kind of facial disfigurement.

Because it suddenly dawned on her, like a lightning bolt of cold chills coursing over her skin, that she knew him.

She knew him from the attack inside the Hawthorne mansion twenty years ago, yes, but from many years before that.

Because he'd once been a patient, if only for a day. Because how could she ever forget that poor boy's face?

Luther Wright had called himself by another name then, as he was doing now.

CHAPTER 40

Before

BETH WATCHED THE young boy on the chair, the laces on his ragged sneakers untied.

It had broken her heart to see how dramatically he'd flinched when she'd scooted over to tie them for him. So, she'd left them alone.

Left him alone.

Laces untied.

Both knees scabbed, recently bruised, as was his right wrist, the bruise-ring around it so lurid it could have been mistaken for a bracelet from afar. He'd obviously been beaten, more than likely abused.

But his face. The poor child. The scar ran from his left eye, diagonally across the bridge of his nose, ending in a puckering starfish-shaped scar in the middle of his right cheek. Whatever had caused it, this horrible wound, the pain must have been brutal, the crude, unprofessional stitches seemingly having caused more harm than healing.

The boy, Luther Wright, was one of her first patients, thrust upon her by the state to analyze, and seeing him tugged at her heartstrings. But after ten minutes of trying to coax words from him, she'd stood from her chair, moved a few paces to her right, to the couch in front of the coffee table holding the scattered puzzle pieces that would eventually show a picture of the snowy Swiss Alps. After quietly working the puzzle for a few minutes, Luther stood, walked across to the opposite side of the coffee table, sat with his legs crossed, and within thirty seconds put a piece into place.

When he looked up at her and found her smiling, he showed the hint of one too and continued searching for the next piece.

"Well done," Beth told him. "You must be an expert at puzzles, Luther."

"I'm not Luther."

"Oh," she said, leaning forward, elbows on her knees, hands clasped and hovering over the puzzle. "Who are you, then?"

"I'm Holden," he said without looking up from the puzzle, his eyes homed in and darting from piece to piece. "Holden Caulfield."

"From *The Catcher in the Rye*?"

"Yes," he said. "That's me."

CHAPTER

41

"THANK YOU," JENNIFER said to Nancy Tanner. "For agreeing to speak to me on such short notice."

"You can't look at me, can you?"

Jennifer forced herself to look up to the clear partition, at Nancy's face looming on the other side of it, at the puckered wound of her missing eye. "I'm sorry."

"For what?" Nancy asked.

Jennifer let out a nervous laugh. "I don't even know."

"I know what they called me," Nancy said.

They called you a lot of things, Jennifer thought. *Pure evil. Full of malice. Soulless. The prettiest of all of Sal's Angels.* "The weakest link," Jennifer said.

"But they were wrong. I was the strongest . . . the only one willing to speak up at trial."

"And look what happened to you."

"And look what happened to me," she said, in agreement. "But do you know what? Do you want to know why I recanted my testimony?"

"Because you claimed to be high when you said it."

Nancy chewed on her lower lip, stared at Jennifer with her lone blue-gray eye. "You were a cute little girl. You've grown into a gorgeous young woman."

Jennifer didn't feel worthy of the flattery. "Were you? High . . . at trial?"

"We were all high, honey, on that ranch . . . all the time we were high. But at the trial . . . no. I spoke the truth about Justice Minks being there."

"Then why did you recant?"

"Do you know what would be worse than being in prison the rest of your life?"

"Death row?"

Nancy grinned. "No, that would have been preferred, to tell you the truth." Nancy leaned forward. Despite her changed appearance, the shorter, grayer hair, and the hideous wound where her eye had been, she was still pretty. "It's being completely blind in prison for the rest of your life. That's what would be worse than just *being* in prison. They already told me they were taking one eye. They said if I didn't recant, I'd lose both. So maybe I *was* the weakest link."

Jennifer almost said, *I'm sorry* again, but stopped herself. Nancy Tanner had slaughtered multiple people with a machete and then celebrated it with a drunken orgy around a campfire. She had put herself here. "So Minks *was* there that night," Jennifer said.

"Of course he was. He bragged about killing Beth Hawthorne with a wine bottle opener," Nancy said. "I forgive you, by the way. Those drawings you did of us. There was a time, at trial, where I would have cut your hands off for drawing them. For starting the ball rolling, really, for the ranch's demise."

Jennifer sat strong, rigid in her seat. "I think you all got the ball rolling plenty fast enough with what you all did that night."

"Would you believe me if I said I don't remember it?"

"No."

"I wouldn't either," she said with a grin. "But I don't."

"Because of the drugs?"

"Yeah," she said. "And time. Nightmares show me snippets. I choose not to believe them."

"What about remorse?"

"Would it bring them back?"

"No."

Nancy folded her arms on the ledge. "Yeah. I do. I do have remorse. I'm sorry for what I did."

"And the other two?"

Nancy smiled. "They're still drinking the juice, I'm afraid."

"Still followers?"

"Until their dying days, I assume."

"But not you?"

"No. I'll gladly admit to my atrocities."

"Do you see each other?"

"No," Nancy said. "They've kept us apart for a decade or more."

"Us children . . . on the ranch," Jennifer said. "Did you know our parents had been killed?"

"Yes," she said with a grin. "By demons, right?"

Jennifer didn't share her smile. "My mother was one of them."

"I know. I'm sorry."

"Did you kill her?"

"No."

"Who did?"

"Who do you think?"

"Minks?"

"Yeah," she said. "He did all of Sal's killing."

"Why did he specifically go for Beth Hawthorne that night?"

"You're a bright girl. You always were," Nancy said. "You know I kept you alive, don't you?"

"How?"

"It was chaos on the ranch," she said. "We knew the authorities were on the way. Minks was looking everywhere for you all."

"And The Raven hid us in a closet right under his nose."

"A closet Minks personally asked me to check, looking for you children," she said. "He asked me to check all the closets upstairs. I knew you all were in there. I heard you. Almost opened the door, but I didn't."

"Why not?"

"Even then, I wasn't real big on leading children to the slaughter."

"Minks would have slaughtered us?"

"In a heartbeat."

"Then why hasn't he done so over the past twenty years?" Jennifer asked.

"You'd have to ask him," Nancy said. "But if you want my opinion, he'd already scooted past the trial unscathed, and murdering you all would have only brought about unwanted attention."

"Makes sense," Jennifer said.

"I never said he wasn't smart."

"Back to my original question," Jennifer said. "Why did he specifically go after Beth Hawthorne that night?"

"Because Sal pulled him aside and told him to."

"Why?"

"I don't know. We weren't privy to everything said between those two."

"Why did he send you all to the Hawthorne mansion that night?"

Nancy blinked her eye, held it shut like she was trying hard to remember, or maybe contemplating whether she should. And when she opened it her eye looked wet, like a tear might soon come from it. Maybe she recalled more from that night than she was letting on. "The news and writers and books . . . haven't they all given that answer enough?"

"But I don't believe it was as simple as an attack against the Haves by the Have-Nots."

"It's what Charles Manson tried to do with Helter Skelter."

"Manson tried to start a race war."

"And this would have been a class war."

"And Manson was also deeply wounded by the fact he absolutely failed as a musician. Failed as a star. And Sal Batise has never shied away from how he'd emulated Manson."

"Clever girl," Nancy said. "I think you're almost there. What does the world know now that was never known about Sal before today?"

"You've heard?"

"You'd be amazed how many ears these walls have," Nancy said. "And do you think he just got a wild hair up his ass to start writing, as Mallard Malone, in prison? I'd imagine he'd been thinking of that series for decades."

"Did you know he was Mallard Malone?" Jennifer asked.

"No."

"Did Minks?"

"I assume so," Nancy said. "But apparently the final book in the series . . . Book One . . . he wrote decades ago and never found a publisher. In that sense, he *failed* as a writer."

Jennifer said, "Just like Manson was rejected by the music industry."

"And why were the Hawthornes having a celebration that night at the family mansion?"

"It was to—oh my God," Jennifer said, getting it now. "To celebrate the release of Justin Hawthorne's debut novel."

Nancy said, "*The Craze*, I believe it was called."

"So it came down to. . . . jealousy?"

"The root of many crimes."

"Did anyone know Sal Batise had written a book?" Jennifer asked.

"I suspect Minks at least *knew* of the book," Nancy said. "Even back then, on the Freedom Ranch, he always had a book with him. Odd trait for such a cold-blooded killer like him" She paused, as if to reminisce. "One day, I remember, maybe a month before the ranch was raided, Minks had misplaced the copy of *The Lord of the Flies* he'd brought with him. He had those smaller paperbacks so he could slide them into his back pocket. But he must have left it somewhere. He turned that main house up and down looking for it, and then did the same with the Kitchen House. He was so irate, he insisted Sal call everyone from the barracks and question them one by one."

Jennifer swallowed heavily, did her best to not show a reaction. She knew damn well where that copy of *The Lord of the Flies* was, and perhaps out of fear of Minks finding out—because these walls have ears—she restrained herself from telling Nancy Tanner that the book to which she was referring was sitting on the shelves of her childhood home, collecting dust.

"But no one told Sal Batise what to do," Nancy went on. "And that was one of many times he made it known who was in charge on that ranch. But Minks . . . he was a cold-blooded killer. A psychopath, sociopath, all those things, but you didn't fuck with his books, you know?"

Jennifer nodded like she knew, like she'd known even back then when she'd seen the worn paperback on the wooden bench inside the Kitchen House and taken it. She'd been only days into her stay and had thought it more of a free library grab, until she'd witnessed Minks's tirade that day and feared for her life should she admit to taking it. And so that book stayed hidden under her bed with all her drawings until the night they'd fled, and she'd taken it with her then, as well, hiding it in the waistband of her pants and keeping it there until the police pulled them out of the closet.

Jennifer fidgeted in her seat, under Nancy's watchful gaze, and for a moment she wondered if Nancy knew she had it.

But Nancy continued on: "Minks was a monster."

"He still is a monster."

Nancy held up a finger, like, *let me finish*, and said, "But he wasn't without his feelings. Throwing a fit like he did that day, over that book, like he was a child. A grown man acting like a child. I was with him that night. And he told me . . . it wasn't so much about the book itself, he was a fan of *The Lord of the Flies*, he'd read it multiple times, and often liked to *be* Ralph, you know, from the book, but that book was special to him because it had come from Mr. Mosby."

"Who was Mr. Mosby?" Jennifer asked, although the name seemed familiar.

"I don't know. When I asked, all Minks said was, the only man who ever showed him love. Apparently that's who gave him that book."

Jennifer let that sink in. "Nancy, do you have any idea where Justice Minks might be hiding right now? Where he might be keeping Beth Hawthorne captive?"

"I don't."

"Are you afraid to tell me, or you truly don't know?"

She smirked. "I'm not afraid of anything anymore. But I will say, if it's possible to admire someone twenty years your junior, I admire you. For what you did. What you're doing."

"But you can't help me?"

"I believe I already have," Nancy said. "All puzzles have pieces, Jennifer, and the putting of them together gains momentum as more of the picture comes to light."

Feeling a sudden need to speak to Sam so he could relay all this to the FBI, Jennifer slowly pushed away from the partition, gave the guard a glance, and then said to Nancy, "I've got to go. Thank you . . ."

"No," Nancy said. "Thank *you*."

"For what?"

"I'll be dead before sunrise."

Jennifer couldn't tell if she was joking, so she said nothing. Or maybe she *would* be dead before sunrise, because the walls have ears and this entire monstrosity had spun a web much wider than she knew. But whether she was being sarcastic in thanking her, Jennifer didn't know. Before Jennifer pushed her chair back in, she asked: "Why was Justice Minks allowed to come and go as he pleased from the Freedom Ranch?"

"There's an exception to every rule, Jennifer," Nancy said. "Sal Batise was a man of many sins, but murder, firsthand, to my knowledge, was never one of them. And a man who needs people murdered but is unable to do so himself, needs a man who is capable of murder."

"Where did Minks go?" Jennifer asked. "Whenever he left the Freedom Ranch, where would he go?"

"Home to his wife," Nancy said matter-of-factly.

Jennifer blinked. "But marriage was not allowed."

"Exceptions to every rule."

"But you were . . . and the other girls . . ."

"Yes," Nancy said, and Jennifer could tell she'd just read her mind. "I was intimate with Justice Minks, just as I was with Sal Batise, just as we all were with each other on the Freedom Ranch. We were completely broken of our chains." She let out a quick laugh again. "You think a man like Minks was beyond adultery?"

"Of course not," Jennifer said, feeling suddenly foolish now.

But then Nancy said, "Would you believe, and he told us this quite openly, that he'd never even screwed his wife? His own wife?"

"Why not?"

"Because she wouldn't have him," Nancy said. "She didn't love him in that way, he told us. Sad, almost. And get this, he of such noble character, would never force a woman to love him like that. That's how he said it, *like that*. He'd never force himself on a woman. So, he fucked us. Me and the other two, us *Angels*," she said, her words dripping with facetiousness. "We figured he was lying, anyway, about having a wife, and if that was the case, who really knew where he went when he wasn't on the Freedom Ranch?"

"Did you ever see him without the mask?"

"No," she said. "And he never got to know me without mine." She lowered her voice. "We all wore masks, Jennifer, they just weren't so outwardly visible. Good luck finding him. As you've probably discovered, he's a man of many names. The Count of Monte Cristo whenever he was feeling revengeful and mysterious. Holden Caulfield whenever he was feeling alienated. Mr. Darcy whenever he felt an urge to lean toward the aristocratic and aloof. Hannibal Lecter or Count Dracula whenever he lusted for blood. He's Shakespeare's Iago when he's bloated with malice. When he's especially cruel and arrogant and sadistic, he's Joffrey Baratheon. And Mr. Hyde . . . let's just say he was in there, too, always watching, observing . . ."

"Are you saying we're dealing with multiple personalities here? A dissociative disorder?"

"Or the ultimate plagiarism," Nancy said. "He didn't just steal these characters from the books he'd read, Jennifer. He truly believes he *became* them."

CHAPTER

42

THE STEAKS, BROUGHT in from a local high-end Twisted Tree steakhouse, were better than Sam had imagined a last meal could be, or should be, given the state of their situation, with two folding chairs on opposite sides of a flimsy-legged card table in the middle of Warden Wren's office, one of them shackled and chained, the other free to roam about; one hinting he was the other's father, and the other not knowing who to believe anymore.

Multiple times, Sam had been on the verge of asking who his mother was, but each time words failed him. The sun had set an hour ago, and something about the finality of this meal brought the execution to stage front-and-center. Sam also knew this was officially Batise's fourth final meal, and that he'd managed to acquire last-minute stays of execution on the previous three. But with Justice Minks applying the pressure, Sam saw no path out of this for Batise. There was the prospect of finding Emily Hawthorne's body, and the book along with it, but once the body was found, Sam wondered what leverage Batise would still have, and during their dinner, he'd asked Batise as much, and Batise had countered with, "My stay will come by what is learned from the book."

"So that's your play?" Sam asked. "Your life hangs in the balance of a book you wrote and buried over twenty years ago?"

Batise looked at his left wrist, as if checking a watch that wasn't there. "They better hurry."

"You don't seem worried," Sam said.

"This isn't my first rodeo, Sam Harper." Batise wiped his mouth with a cloth napkin and tossed it on an empty plate still swimming with blood from his rare steak. "Although I'd be lying if I said the firing squad doesn't give me pause."

"You're the one who wrote it in the book," Sam said. "Minks is just following your playbook."

"But I didn't think it would ever be done to me."

"So you aren't working together?"

"Do the feds think we are?"

"They aren't ruling that out."

"As they shouldn't."

"Are you?"

"No," Batise said. "The man truly wants me dead. He *needs* me dead. Or the series just wouldn't work. It's important for what happens in the next one."

"You mean the previous one?"

"Sure," he said, picking his teeth with a pinkie fingernail. "And no, I didn't name you."

Sam had raised the question earlier while they were eating—*Who named me?* And that he'd recently learned his *real* name was Steven Batise.

Batise had avoided answering the question then but answered it now: "Your mother named you."

"And who was my mother?" Sam asked, throat heavy with emotion, because he'd never consider anyone his mother other than Annie Harper.

"Her name was Jules Whitaker. She named you Steven Batise."

"Was she a member of the cult?"

"No . . . she was before The Collective," Batise said. "I didn't even know you were born."

"You've been on record, many times, and despite bragging about the thousands of women you've been with, you claimed to have never sired a child."

"And then Jules shows up on the Freedom Ranch with a little boy she claims was mine."

Sam's jaw tightened: "Am I? For sure . . . yours?"

"Nothing in this world is a certainty, Sam Harper."

Sam's cell phone started moving across the table with an incoming call. He turned it over, saw *DAD* on the screen, and then placed it facedown on the table again.

"You're not going to answer that?" Batise smirked. "I'm sure the two of you have much to discuss."

"And we will," Sam said.

"The Kentucky Cannibal . . ."

Sam ignored that, couldn't fathom it, and stayed focused on his most pressing concern. "Am I yours?" Deep down, he prayed he wasn't.

Batise answered, "I always pull out, Sam Harper."

Batise had said as much countless times during interviews. This wouldn't be the first incident where a woman came forth claiming she'd had Sal Batise's child; but not one, over the years, had ever matched to Sal's DNA, which had led authorities to believe, however basic his form of birth control was, that he was telling the truth.

"Then why was this Jules Whitaker so sure I was yours?"

"Because, perhaps, this one time I forgot," he said. "And maybe my . . . system isn't as reliable as I might have thought."

"And you cast her aside?"

"I moved on."

"And she what, heard about the Freedom Ranch and decided to have a family reunion?"

"Or she noticed my growing popularity and wanted a free place to stay."

"You got her pregnant," Sam said angrily. "You owed her that much."

"It takes two to tango, Sam Harper. What if I said she'd seduced me?"

"I find it difficult to believe you have ever been seduced by anyone."

"Justice Minks sure seems to be doing a job of it. Or Luther Wright, as he was called."

"Because that's his real name," Sam said.

"And Steven is yours."

"What happened to her?" Sam asked. "Jules Whitaker?"

"She passed away, unfortunately."

"How?"

"Soon after she arrived at the Freedom Ranch."

"I didn't ask when," Sam said. Batise smiled as they watched one another. Sam said, "What's funny?"

"Just that you definitely have some of her spunk. Some her grit. And I bet my brother would agree."

"What do you mean?"

"Tommy knew her as well," he said. "Or . . . I'm sorry, Trevor Harper. Professor Trevor Harper, rather. I hear he has a PhD now, with tenure. Yet he'll always be Tiny Tommy Batise to me."

"What was she to him?"

"Answer the phone next time he calls and ask him."

Sam had a notion of calling him right now but held off. "How did Jules Whitaker die?"

That smile again. "She went into the woods. She was killed by demons."

"You fucking murdered her."

"Rules in any cult have to be followed, Sam Harper," Batise said. "No children are to be brought to the ranch. And I am not a murderer."

"And neither was Hitler?"

"Not the first time I've heard the comparison."

"Was it Minks?"

"Of course it was."

"Is her body going to turn up with the rest of them being discovered right now?"

"Very likely," Batise said, staring out the window toward the sky. "Looks like a blood moon."

"How can you live with yourself?"

"How can *any* of us live with ourselves? We just do. And remembering our mothers isn't all it's cracked up to be."

Sam said, "I loved my mother."

"I hardly ever knew mine before she vanished and left us alone," Batise said. "And Annie Harper wasn't your mother."

"She raised me," he said. "Cancer took her. She was good through and through."

"She was a traitor just like my little brother."

Sam held himself back. Batise seemed to be amused by his apparent restraint, if not impressed.

Sam grabbed his phone, thumb-tapped a quick text to his father, to The Raven: Can't talk now but did you know a woman named Jules Whitaker?

"Before my father was incarcerated," Batise said, still staring at the moon, "and before my mother left us, we took a basket of food for a picnic lunch around a nearby lake. Tommy was only three. I was infatuated with the ducks. While Tommy fed them, I ran through them, scaring them into flight. And when they'd return I'd do it all over again, and at the same time I couldn't help wondering how they would taste, plucked free of their feathers and roasted over a fire, turning slowly on a spit. Tommy, at that point, of course, had not yet developed his tendencies toward human flesh . . ."

"Stop," Sam warned. "Finish your story."

"My father had a peculiar way of talking, Sam Harper. At dinner, instead of saying pass the ketchup, he'd say pass the Heinz. Or with mayonnaise, he'd say get the Hellmann's. Or with the baseball bat he'd say grab the Louisville Slugger and let's go hit some balls. Always the brand names instead of the thing itself. And that day he said, Sal, leave the goddamn mallards alone. And Tommy, who was young and thought it funny to repeat things, kept saying *mallards alone, mallards alone*, except he spoke a little funny, Sam Harper, and used to blend some of his words together, so his mallards alone sounded more like *mallards malone, mallards malone*, Mallard . . . Malone."

"So that's where your pen name came from," Sam said. "But I didn't ask that."

"But maybe you should have," said Batise.

Sam's phone vibrated—a long text from Jennifer: I was just with Nancy Tanner. Sal wrote the novel 23 years ago. He failed as a writer back then. Sam wasn't finished with the text but couldn't help looking up at Batise, who watched him quietly but with obvious curiosity, with one eyebrow raised in anticipation. Sam returned to the text: The Hawthorne massacre happened because of jealousy. Justin Hawthorne was celebrating the publication of his debut novel that night and Sal resented him for it. For their status, for his success . . .

Sam looked up from his phone when a door opened and FBI Agent Givens stormed in with Warden Wren. Sam stood. "What's wrong?"

Agent Givens ignored Sam and instead spoke to Batise. "There was no body there. And no book. No Emily Hawthorne. What the *fuck* is going on?"

Warden Wren and Agent Givens must have seen the look on Batise's face just as Sam did, because they shared a confused look and Givens backed off. It was clear that Batise was as shocked as they all were, and that he'd fully expected them to find a body, or, at least, bones, exactly where he'd told them.

For the first time all day, Sam saw worry in the eyes of Sal Batise, but then it quickly morphed into alarm, and then what looked like a revelation, when he turned to Agent Givens and said, "What if Emily Hawthorne is still alive?"

CHAPTER

43

TREVOR KNEW WHAT Lizzie was doing as soon as she pulled him to the floor and straddled his waist. He only wished he'd had time to undo his belt and at the very least unzip his pants to make their act more believable.

The Freedom Ranch had become many things over the past two decades of deterioration and decay, and one of them, as preposterously unclean as it was, was as a popular place for teens to hook up. They were far from teenagers, but it was worth a try. As the footsteps came closer, Lizzie leaned down and kissed Trevor on the lips, and then she started slowly grinding on him, stopping only when one of the two men said, "Well, what do we have here?"

Trevor's head rolled to the right just as Lizzie, above him, turned her head to the left, and they both did their best to act like they'd been unknowingly caught in the act, like they didn't know these two men were killers and more than likely linked to Minks. Trevor had been meaning to ask Lizzie more about her gun, and if she'd ever used one before, but at least they had one. Had something.

"Don't stop on our account," said the white man, who, underneath his fresh stubble and tatted arms and neck, was thin as a rail and tall as a beanstalk. He wore jeans and brown shitkicker boots, an unbuttoned flannel shirt, and a baseball cap pointed backward. He looked at his partner, who was built like The Rock but not nearly as tall. "What do you think, Ray, you think they should stop on our account?"

Ray's no-nonsense demeanor said clearly that he didn't want to be there, and he was in a hurry to go. "Let's just start unloading the shit and go. And don't be fuckin' saying my name, motherfucker."

The lanky white man laughed, pointed his gun lazily toward Ray. "He's a little uptight sometimes." He sat in one of the folding chairs that formed the circle around where Trevor and Lizzie lay on the floor and then jerked a nod. "Go on, get to fuckin.'"

Ray shook his head and walked out of the room. Seconds later Trevor heard him walking up the stairs, and then on the floorboards directly above them.

Their one-man audience looked up toward the footsteps on the ceiling. "Fucker sounds like he might come right through the floor up there."

Lizzie had begun to move from Trevor's waist, holding up a cautious hand in an apologetic, *we'll just get our clothes and get going* gesture, but the man wasn't having it. He pointed the gun directly at her. "I said, go on, get to fuckin.'" And moved the gun to Trevor. "And you . . . get your pants off." When Trevor didn't comply, the man said, "You deaf as well as a midget?"

"I heard you just fine," Trevor said, feeling the raven wings fluttering into a frenzy inside his chest. He glanced toward his bat on the floor across the room and then back to the man. Lizzie gently patted Trevor's chest, like she was telling him, *Stay still, I got this.* But he wondered, *How?* She was half-clothed, and the man was five feet away with a gun aimed at them. Then again, Trevor could feel how calm Lizzie was, straddling him.

"I said get your pants off," he said. "And you, with the tits, take that top off and show'm to me."

When Lizzie reached around to unlatch her bra, Trevor said, "Don't."

And the man laughed. He scratched the stubble on his cheek. "Got us a stubborn little man." He leaned forward. "Would you rather see her brains scattered all over the wall? Huh? And what the fuck you two doing in here, anyway? Don't you read signs . . . no trespassing?"

"Just wanted to relive some memories from years ago," Lizzie said. "That's all."

"What . . . did you lose your virginity in here, way back when?"

Ray was still walking on the floor above, and then he started scooting something heavy.

As soon as the man with the gun looked up toward the noise, Lizzie reached down toward where she'd kicked off her shorts and grabbed her gun. Before their man realized what she'd done she'd pulled the trigger, hesitating only slightly, blowing out the man's right kneecap in an explosion of bloody mist and bone. The man screamed, dropped his gun to the floor as his chair toppled. Above them, Ray's footfalls quickened, and it sounded like the ceiling might come down under his thunderous steps. Lizzie was quickly on her feet and following the sound of Ray's movement up above. She fired into the ceiling, once, and then a second time.

The second bullet must have hit him.

Ray screamed, landed somewhere above with a loud, house-shaking thud. By then, Trevor was on his feet, baseball bat in hand. The white man was screaming and reaching for a gun that wasn't there anymore because Lizzie had it in her other hand. Ray must have been trying to move up there, but it didn't go well, because next they heard him tumbling down the steps and landing on the bottom floor with an even louder thud than before.

Lizzie nodded toward the stairs in the other room and said to Trevor, "Go check on him."

Trevor looked at Lizzie in amazement.

She said, "I sneak out to the shooting range more than I let on. Just in case."

Trevor left the room, less surprised by Lizzie's apparent transformation than maybe he should have been. He knew firsthand how trauma could transform a person. He approached the stairs with caution. He had the bat positioned over his shoulder and ready to swing should Ray come at him. But when he turned the corner, Ray was an unmoving mess at the bottom of the steps, his arms and legs akimbo, his eyes unblinking as blood leaked from a bullet hole in a neck that looked broken.

Back in the dining room, the other man was still screaming, but with two guns Trevor trusted that Lizzie would be fine while he ran up the stairs to see what Ray had been doing.

It was the same room he'd hid the children in twenty years ago, and stepping into it was like stepping back in time. The closet no longer had a door on it, and if he were to look, he'd bet that Jennifer's mural had been covered in graffiti years ago, just like the rest of the room's walls. But what shook Trevor, other than the trail of Ray's blood across the old floorboards, was the dozens of crates full of weapons and ammunition that took up most of the floor.

They're preparing for a war, he thought as he removed his cell phone and snapped a few pictures. The man screamed again downstairs, and Trevor left the room in a hurry to join Lizzie. Back in the dining room, he found her standing above the man as he squirmed across the floor in a futile attempt to get away. But she followed, hovering above him, both guns aimed at him as he whimpered and begged for his life.

"Who do you work for?"

"Go fuck yourself, bitch."

"My husband said the same thing to me this morning," Lizzie told him. "And you know what? He's probably nothing but ash right now. Who do you work for?"

When the man didn't respond, Lizzie stepped on his shattered knee and he wailed, crying and slobbering on the floor, and then, without warning, vomited at the feet of one of the folding chairs. He looked up. "They're . . . coming."

Trevor stepped closer, squatting down with the bat resting on his shoulder. He realized there was still a spot of Jake Hall's blood on the barrel, and he hoped this bastard noticed it too. "Where is Beth Hawthorne?"

The man coughed, heaved, cried out again as Lizzie put more pressure on his knee.

"Where's Beth Hawthorne?" Trevor asked again.

"Ain't my lane," the man croaked.

"What are you planning with those weapons up there?"

Lizzie asked, "What weapons?"

"They're storing enough weapons for an army," Trevor told her, and at the same time reiterated his question to the man with a widening of his eyes. "Huh? If Beth Hawthorne isn't your lane, what is?"

"I'm just carving out my path, man."

"What path?" Lizzie raised her foot as a threat to bring it down on his knee again.

"In the world of Oliver Crown," the man said, as they all heard another vehicle approaching the house. And then multiple vehicles, some of them honking, and they heard hooting and hollering.

The man on the floor laughed. "You two came here to get it on . . . well, consider yourselves fucked now. Oliver Crown's army has arrived."

Trevor hoisted the bat over his shoulder, as if preparing to strike—and in his mind's eye saw the Louisville Slugger connecting with the man's face, busting teeth, splitting skin, splintering bone—but then he stopped. For a split second he thought of Sam. And what Sam might be thinking of him now. His grip eased on the bat's handle.

As if in response to Trevor's backing down, Lizzie aimed one of the guns at the man's face.

Trevor said, "No . . . don't."

"He can ID us, Trevor," she said. "He's a bully. Aren't you?" she said to the man. "You're a murderer and a bully. And who are we now, Trevor?"

"The Raven and The Mongoose," he said without hesitation, and it felt good. "But we aren't executioners." Trevor lowered her arm, the gun along with it. "Come on. Let's go."

Car doors opened and closed outside.

Lizzie yanked her clothes on, and together they fled out the back of the house just as a crowd of men entered the front.

CHAPTER

44

Before

BETH HAWTHORNE GATHERED her thoughts as she watched young Luther Wright place piece after piece of the puzzle together.

The boy truly thought he was Holden Caulfield, the protagonist of the classic novel. When she asked him if he'd read it, he gave her a look that said, *Of course I've read it. Who hasn't?* But he was far too young to read such a book, not only the level of reading but to understand the complexity of it: with the themes of alienation and lost innocence, it should have been too far over his head. And when she asked him if he understood what it was about, he gave her that same look of disdain, and, as he worked the puzzle on the coffee table, said, "Holden Caulfield was a cynical and rebellious teenager who was trying to find his place in a world of adults who were nothing but big fat phonies who wear masks."

"What masks?" Beth asked.

"Ones you can't see."

"Do you wish you could wear a mask? Luther?"

"Do you think I need to?"

"No. I think you look fine."

"That's what James says."

"Who is James?"

"James has a giant peach," he said as an answer.

"And where is James?" When he didn't answer, she asked, with trepidation and a quiver in her voice, "Are you sometimes James?"

"Yes," the boy said, rolling his eyes. "James taught me it's never too late to make friends. He taught me courage. And that family doesn't always have to be your family."

"Who can be your family then if not your family?" she asked.

"Regular people," he said without looking up. "Like you. Like Mr. Mosby."

"Who is Mr. Mosby?"

"He owns the used bookstore across the street from our apartment."

"Is that where you've . . . read all these books?"

"Yes. He lets me take them home. I hide them under my pillow."

"Why do you hide them?"

"Because Mom doesn't like Black people."

"Is Mr. Mosby Black?"

"Yes. And Dad says reading is for sissies."

Beth watched him work the puzzle, the scar so prominent across his face she wanted to cry. "Can we talk about how you got that scar?" He shook his head, kept working. She said, "Did your mom and dad do that to you? Did they hurt you?"

He shrugged, said, "Holden was often disillusioned."

Beth asked, "Do you think you are?"

"Are what?"

"Disillusioned?"

"No."

"Do you think you're a teenager?"

"Is Holden Caulfield a teenager?" he asked with sarcasm.

"In the book," she said. "Yes, he is."

"Then yes," he said. And then, "Do you have more puzzles at your house?"

"Yes . . . many more."

"Do you have heat in the winter?"

"Yes."

"And air in the summer?"

"Yes."

"Does your house have rats?"

"No, honey, it doesn't."

"Are there monsters in the mirrors?"

She wiped her eyes, said, "No. No monsters."

"Then I'll come live with you."

"I wish it were that easy."

"It can be."

"I'm on your side, Luther. I'll do whatever I can—"

"I'm not Luther," he said forcefully. "I told you that." In his eyes, she saw fury rising. And then he said, "If I can't live with you, I guess I'll have to kill you, Dr. Hawthorne."

She swallowed hard. "That sounds a little harsh . . . even for Holden Caulfield."

"That's because Holden didn't say it."

"Who said it?"

"That was Mr. Hyde."

CHAPTER

45

BETH KNEW SHE was taking a chance in calling out the name *Luther*.

Luther Wright.

The last time she'd screamed one of her captor's names, she'd nearly been attacked and raped by one of his men, before "Oliver Crown" himself had come to the rescue. But she also knew the name *Luther Wright* might trigger him somehow, hoping at the very least it would get him upstairs again and into her room. It might seem like a little victory to her, but if he was in here, if she had his attention, then he couldn't be elsewhere doing God only knew what to someone else.

What surprised her was how quickly he'd come, and the fact that he'd brought with him a chair to sit in. She'd called his name only three times, before she'd heard his footsteps in the hall and the doorknob turned. He didn't walk in angrily, she noticed, as he sat in the chair and faced her uncomfortable seat on the floor, but more like he was resigned. Or, perhaps, glad she'd finally figured it out. And before saying one word to her, he removed his Guy Fawkes mask and placed it delicately on the floor. His face was pale and scar-pocked, the mountain-range stitching lurid and raw. For a long beat, they stared at one another.

"So that's what this has been about all along?" she asked.

"Wrong."

"Why did you try to kill me twenty years ago, Luther?"

"Luther is dead," he said. "He died as a little boy . . . when his father took the red-hot iron poker from the fire and dragged it across my face."

"Why?"

"Because he didn't like me."

"Why didn't he like you?"

"Because he never wanted me."

Beth tried again. "Why did you try to kill me inside the Hawthorne mansion?"

"Because the Breaker of Chains told me too."

"And not because I wouldn't take you in as a boy?"

"No." He scratched the puckered wound on his cheek. "Although the bringing of us together again showed me quite plainly how small the world really is. Do you believe in fate?"

"I don't know," she said. "Is it fate that has me here . . . inside a Chain House?"

"You've read the books?"

"No," she said. "But Billy told me about them . . . before you murdered him."

"I told him to stop talking, and he didn't."

"Did that punishment fit his crime?"

He pointed to his scar. "Did this?"

"No, Luther, it didn't."

"Don't do that."

"Do what?"

"Don't call me *Luther*. Don't turn this into a doctor's visit. I know what you're trying to do, and this is why you're in the territory you're in. This is why you're with the Untrustables," he said. "Oliver Crown loathes them most of all. They're even worse than the rapists and molesters."

"As a boy, you spoke of a Mr. Mosby," she said. "You used to run away from home and take refuge inside his bookstore. He taught you how to read, right?" He nodded, and she went on. "He taught you how to immerse yourself in fictional worlds and how to forget the cruelty of the real world. He gave you a place to escape."

"What about him?"

"Please tell me . . . you didn't kill him."

"No . . . but I did take care of him. I love him still."

Beth licked her dry lips and craved water. She'd needed to pee for the past two hours but at the same time felt dehydrated. "What do you plan on doing?" she asked. "After Batise is killed."

"You'll see," he said.

"Will I? Will I still be alive to see? See what, Oliver?"

"See me rise from the ashes and become the leader of men."

"Does this not make you . . . disillusioned?"

He studied her like he felt sorry for her, or maybe pity, and then finally answered her earlier question. "I was there to kill you. Specifically you."

"Why?"

"Because I'm a killer."

"But why me, specifically?"

"Because he didn't like the way you and your sister-in-law laughed that day at lunch."

At the mention of Emily, her sister-in-law, Beth's heart skipped a beat.

He continued. "He knew I'd already taken care of Gavin Hawthorne's sister. Then why not take care of his wife too."

"You . . . what?" She felt the blood drain from her face. "What did you say?"

"Which part?"

"My sister," she said in a growl.

"In-law," he said, correcting her. "Sister-in-law."

"She was my best *friend*," Beth screamed, tears flowing suddenly. "What did you do to Emily Hawthorne?"

"It's more of what she did to Sal Batise."

"What did she do to poor Sal Batise?"

"She rejected his book," he said. "*The* book. Book One. He said it was his masterpiece, and it was to be the first book in a long series, but she rejected it. *Sorry, not for me, I wish you all the best with it elsewhere. And just FYI . . . I only typically take queries from agented authors, but for this I made an exception.*

"And?"

"He didn't want to send it elsewhere. He wanted Emily Hawthorne as his editor."

"Why?"

"Because she was perfect," he said. "He'd been researching her for weeks. She checked all the boxes. Her manuscript wish list. This should have been everything she'd dreamed of, and she rejected it. And by then he'd long day-dreamed about their partnership and perhaps even more because she was very easy on the eyes. His words, not mine."

"What did you do to her?"

"Sal was in New York, awaiting her response, and it came, quickly, as he'd assumed, because he was quite proud of the work, but it came quickly for the *wrong* reason, Doctor. As you can imagine, he was crushed. Beyond crushed, because he knew what he had . . . and look at it now . . . the world of Oliver Crown . . . who was wrong and who was right?"

Beth spoke quietly. "What did you do to her?"

"Sal followed her to a quaint little café, where Beth and Emily Hawthorne sat outside eating yogurt and muffins and drinking hot coffee with swirls of foam, and Sal took the table right behind them, ordering a coffee but bypassing the food menu, because he wasn't there to eat!" He stomped his foot at the word *eat*, as if to punctuate it. "He was there to listen. And listen he did, as Emily told you about a manuscript she'd just read by an unsolicited author that had come to her through the slush pile. She couldn't even remember his name. But it was so far-fetched, she barely got through it. And she said the writing was so masculine it bordered on sexist." He leaned forward, elbows on his knees, and only then did she realize how long his fingers were, hanging lazily down toward the floor. "So he asked me to take care of her. To kill her and bury her body and bury with it the only copy he had of the book he called *The Breakout*."

Beth was shaking all over, which made the chains connected to her start rattling on the floor, trembling on her wrist and ankle. She wanted to rip his eyes out. She wanted to open that scar on his face good and wide and scream right into his head. But she forced herself to calm, calm, calm, and then said, "Where is she? Where did you bury her?"

He grinned. "What if I never did? What if I kept the book," he said, gesturing toward the hundreds of Mallard Malone book covers fastened to the walls, "and became so infatuated with the world, and waited so patiently for it to all come out just as it did, that I set all this in motion for Oliver Crown to rise from the real ashes?"

"You're not sane."

"Not what a good doctor should say to a former patient, Beth," he said with a wry smile. "But what if I took care of her instead? And what if I've been taking care of her for twenty-three years now?"

Beth's eyes grew large, and her throat constricted to the point where her next words came out as a mere whisper. "She's alive?"

He gathered his mask from the floor, placed it over his damaged face, and stood from the chair.

From the neighboring room, where Billy had been, Beth heard a door open and multiple footsteps shuffling across the floorboards.

Beth panicked. "What's going on?"

"You heard the sound of a typewriter earlier." He gestured toward the hole in the wall and the chain running through it. That chain moved with a distinct tug against her ankle, and she knew now that she was connected again to another person. "So I figured I'd bring it closer to you."

She heard what sounded like furniture being positioned in the neighboring room, maybe a table or a desk, and then seconds later a chair was placed.

He said, "Wait for it." Beth waited. The sound of pecking keys resonated through the hole in the wall, and he smiled.

He lifted the chain from the metal post in the floor across the room, gave her a few more links of slack, and then reattached the chain to the post, allowing her to get closer to the wall.

CHAPTER

46

"YOU COMING?" JENNIFER asked Carl.

"Should I?"

"I've left you in the truck enough today," Jennifer said, with a nod toward her childhood home. "Come on, meet my parents."

Once inside, Jennifer was not surprised that Carl acted like the perfect gentleman, shaking her father's hand and calling her mother *ma'am*, before following Jennifer into her childhood bedroom.

She turned on the light, saw that it was exactly as it had been when she'd moved out years ago. She'd always had an irrational fear her parents would turn her room into something else as soon as she'd gone off to college, but here it was, down to the posters and pillows and stuffed animals, exactly as she'd left it. She took a beeline toward her old bookcase at the foot of the bed. She knelt, reached for the bottom shelf, and moved her row of Harry Potter books aside to get to where she'd hidden the copy of *The Lord of the Flies*. She still didn't know why she'd felt the need to hide it years ago, or to keep it hidden still, as an adult, other than being superstitious about moving it.

"One Direction?" Carl said. "Really?"

"Shut up," she said, with a glance toward Carl, who was looking at her posters. She pulled the book from the shelf and replaced the Harry Potter books.

Carl said, "I do like that 'Watermelon Sugar' song."

"That was Harry Styles," she said, standing so quickly it made her dizzy and reminded her that she'd hardly eaten anything all day. And even though she'd told her mother they were fine and that they couldn't stay long enough to eat, Jennifer could hear her in the kitchen preparing them something to go. And by the smell of what was warming in the microwave, she guessed it was lasagna, which she'd gladly take with her.

"Isn't Harry Styles in One Direction?" Carl asked.

"Was." Jennifer hit the light in her room. "But 'Watermelon Sugar' is from his solo career."

He followed her down the hallway. "I ever tell you I can sing solo?"

She looked over her shoulder. "No shit?"

"So low you can't hear me."

"You're an idiot, Carl."

"Now that's no way to speak to a friend," Jennifer's mom said, coming out of nowhere, or maybe it was the kitchen, with two Tupperware bowls stuffed full of lasagna.

"It's true though, Mrs. Daley. I am an idiot."

"Now I hardly believe that," she said with a smile.

Jennifer kissed her mother's cheek and thanked her for the food and promised they'd be careful, and that, yes, she'd fill her in on everything tomorrow. From the truck Carl waved, backed carefully out of the driveway, and Jennifer wondered, as her parents stood in the open doorway, waving back to Carl, if they now thought the two of them were dating.

Carl had the Tupperware bowl open and was already digging in as he steered down the road with his left knee. "This is delicious."

"She does make a mean lasagna." Jennifer turned on the dome light, opened the copy of *The Lord of the Flies*, and just as she'd recalled, on the top right corner of the title page was a sticker that had never meant anything to her until now.

Property of Leland Mosby
Twice-Told Used Bookstore
189 Butchertown Road
Lagrange, KY 40220

Jennifer read off the address and Carl claimed to know roughly where it was, and after punching it into the GPS on his phone, said they'd be there in ten minutes.

"It's ten o'clock," Carl said through another mouthful of lasagna. "Severely doubt it's open."

But she'd already Googled the bookstore and dialed the number. It said on her phone that it had closed two hours ago, but she felt she needed to try, even though she didn't know if Mr. Mosby was even still alive. She was about to end the call after the fourth ring when someone answered, and the voice of an older Black man said, "Hello, Twice-Told Used Books."

And Jennifer sighed relief into the phone. "Is Mr. Leland Mosby there?"

"This is he," the man said. "But who would this be?"

"My name is Jennifer," she said, almost in a panic. "Jennifer Daley. I'm sorry, I . . . I didn't think you'd pick up."

"A man who loves his books as I do, rarely leaves them. What can I do for you, Ms. Daley?"

Where to even start, she thought, but said, "Have you seen the news today?"

"I see the news on no days," he said. "Don't watch it anymore. Can't, rather, as it too often, and too quickly, brings about indigestion."

"You've heard that Beth Hawthorne was taken?"

"Yes, people in the store do chatter."

"And you know Sal Batise is set to be executed?"

"In just a couple hours, if I recall."

"Yes . . . well, we're pretty sure that the mystery man . . . from the Hawthorne massacre years ago, Justice Minks . . . that he has her. A man you knew as a child."

After a pause, he said, "You don't say? Are you police, Ms. Daley? FBI?"

"No, neither," she said. "But I was one of the children found in the closet . . . at the Freedom Ranch. Twenty years ago."

"Well, I'll be . . ."

"Is it okay if we stop by, please? I need to talk to you about Justice Minks."

"But I don't know him from Adam," he said. "And I'm closed until tomorrow morning. Maybe you could—"

"But you *do* know him, Mr. Mosby," she said. "I have a book you loaned him a long time ago. A paperback copy of *The Lord of the Flies*." Although he remained silent, she could tell he'd begun breathing harder, or deeper, and it was clear the mere mention of the book had struck a nerve. So, she said, "He was Luther back then. A little boy with a terrible scar on his face named Luther Wright."

After a pregnant beat and a deep breath, Mr. Mosby said, "How far away are you?"

She glanced at Carl's phone mounted on the dash. "Five minutes."

"The door will be unlocked when you get here."

CHAPTER

47

"KILL HIM NOW," Governor Gavin Hawthorne said inside what Sam had secretly named the War Room, the waiting room with the four doors.

He paced, red-faced and weary-eyed, having admittedly not slept a wink since his wife's abduction. With his shirt cuffs rolled to the elbows, Sam could still see the remnants of the professional athlete he'd been. Every time he clenched and unclenched his fists, his forearm flexed with ripe tendons and toned muscles.

Agent Givens said to Sam, "You saw his face in there when I told him. He was shocked." And then to the room, where Governor Hawthorne paced and Warden Wren sat in a chair staring at the carpeted floor: "He truly thought her body was going to be in the ground, exactly where he told us. And he hasn't been wrong on any of the other bodies he's given us today. So far, he's batting a hundred percent until now."

Governor Hawthorne spun toward him, eyes wet, voice soft. "So you think he's right? That my sister is still alive?"

"Either that or he was off on where her body was buried."

Warden Wren stood up. "Or he's lying."

Hawthorne said to Agent Givens, "You think he's lying?" His anger returned in a flash. "Is he just fucking with us?"

Sam took the moment to interject himself, and said with confidence, "I believe him."

"Because he's fucking with you too," Warden Wren said, and then softened his tone. "I'm sorry, Sam. I didn't mean to be so blunt. I've just known him longer than anyone, and I've rarely known him to be genuine."

"He's got less than two hours to live," Sam said.

"A position he's already been in three times and danced," the warden responded.

Hawthorne said, "Your firing squad ready?"

Warden Wren shook his head in disbelief. "Yes. I've got four guards willing to do it."

"And television?"

The warden sighed, nodded. "I really hope it doesn't come to that."

Hawthorne said, "I'm not taking a chance."

Agent Givens said, "And we don't typically negotiate with sociopaths."

Sam waited for a break to speak. "We're forgetting about the book. The buried book. If Minks . . . or Oliver Crown . . . is playing that book out exactly as it's written, *we need that book*."

Hawthorne looked at his watch. "We have ninety minutes to find it." And then, "Who am I kidding, the only way I'm going to see my wife again"—he pointed through the wall—"is if that motherfucker dies. On schedule."

Agent Givens said, "You really think he's going to give her back?"

Sam spoke up. "It depends on what happens in the book. I think Minks is that far out there in whatever fictional world he's living in that he'll do everything by the book."

Agent Givens said to Hawthorne, "And once Batise is dead, if your sister really is out there, Gavin, it might then become harder to find her."

Hawthorne said, "You're saying we need him?"

"And he knows it," said Warden Wren.

Agent Givens said, "But at this point we don't know if the two of them are working together in this, or if they want the other dead."

A thought struck Sam with sudden clarity, and he found himself moving quickly toward the door that led to Batise.

Givens said, "Where you going?"

"I just thought of something," Sam said, opening the hallway door, and the other three men followed. The guard outside the warden's office let them in, and Sam moved directly toward Batise. "You finished that book twenty-three years ago."

Batise visually took all the men in as they entered the room. "Yes."

"Emily Hawthorne disappeared twenty-three years ago."

"Yes."

"And you *thought* you knew where she was, because you arranged to have her killed. You told Justice Minks to kill her and bury your one copy of the book with her." Sam paused a beat. "But I think Minks didn't kill her at all—and maybe he still has her."

"My thoughts exactly," said Batise, without delay.

"Why did you order her killed?" Sam asked. "We already know the reason you ordered the murders at the Hawthorne mansion. You were jealous. You sent Emily Hawthorne your novel and she rejected it, didn't she?"

Batise grinned. "Clever like your father."

"How did you send it to her?" Sam asked. "Did you mail it or email it?"

"I emailed it," he said. "Unsolicited. Unagented. Slush pile. And she read it. And yes, the bitch rejected it."

Governor Hawthorne made a move, but Agent Givens held him back and told him, "You shouldn't be in here."

Batise said, "But I want Governor Gavin Hawthorne in here. He needs to hear this. About how wrong little sister was about the prospects for my series. For Oliver Crown."

"*Fuck you*," said Hawthorne.

"How professional," said Batise. "Although what would you expect from a tobacco-spitting dugout jock."

"If you emailed it then it could still be in her emails." Sam looked at the governor. "What happened to all her stuff? Her laptop?"

"We . . . we have it all," Hawthorne said, thinking. "Somewhere, in storage, but we kept it. We were allowed to keep everything from her office."

Sam said, "Can we get to it?"

"You have ninety minutes," Batise said. "Tick-tock, tick-tock."

Hawthorne ignored him, looked up suddenly and faced Agent Givens. "It's in her old room at the Hawthorne House. All her stuff is still in there. Two of my nephews moved it all about ten years ago. I think her laptop could still be in there."

Givens said, "I can have agents there in ten minutes."

"Do it."

Warden Wren turned toward Batise, sitting so smugly in his chair that even Sam wanted to strangle him. "Or you could save us the time, Sal, and just tell us exactly what's in the book that we need to know. Unless you want more deaths on your head."

"What's a few more, Warden? You can only kill me once."

Warden Wren raised his voice. "Tell us what's in the book!"

"Maybe if you tell the room you have a mistress."

Warden Wren stood rigid, backed away, giving Batise a look that said *how dare you*, and it was clear to Sam the two of them had had some kind of arrangement and Batise had just broken it.

Governor Hawthorne shook his head. "I couldn't give two fucks about your personal life, Warden." And then to Batise, "Tell me, in the book, the governor's wife is kidnapped by Oliver Crown. Does she live?"

"Is she in the next book?"

"I don't know," he said. "I haven't read them."

"Well, maybe you should," said Batise. "But no, she does not, because Oliver Crown, as I wrote him, will do anything to gain power. He will lie and cheat and murder anyone to get to the top."

"So he's going to kill her no matter what?"

"That would be my guess."

Hawthorne began pacing the room, flexing and unflexing his hands, seething with every step.

Batise said, "But it seems you've put more faith in the man out there than the one sitting right in front of you."

"And what can you offer me?"

"The location of Oliver Crown's house."

Agent Givens said, "Where is it?"

Batise grinned at Governor Hawthorne. "Grant my stay."

"I can't."

"Then we'll have to see if he keeps his word," Batise said. "And perhaps we'll never know if Emily Hawthorne still lives."

"You're going to burn in hell," Governor Hawthorne said.

"Maybe," said Batise. "But not yet. So trust him, Governor, or trust me. You've got ninety minutes. Tick-tock, tick-tock . . ."

Hawthorne stormed out of the room, and on his way out said to Sam, "Find out where Oliver Crown lives." And to Agent Givens, "Find her laptop."

CHAPTER

48

TREVOR WAS SURPRISED when his phone rang.

He'd hoped it was Sam, but when he saw the number wasn't in his contacts, he didn't answer.

He and Lizzie were already on edge, having, they thought, distanced themselves enough from the mob at the Freedom Ranch to relax from that danger, but the threat of the unknown loomed larger now that they were without a car and every step taken down the dark country road took them that much closer to midnight.

And, he feared, farther away from Justice Minks.

They'd been walking the road, throwing up thumbs to each passing vehicle, but after ten minutes, they'd had no luck. He didn't even know where they were heading even if a car should pull over for them.

His phone battery was down to 45 percent and he was trying to use it sparingly. They'd need it to track Lizzie's phone. It had been her idea, adding him to her Life360. That part was easy. The hard part had been escaping the house back at the ranch while the dozen or more men—and a few women, they'd noticed—had gone inside to discover two of their own, one dead and the other badly injured, one at the foot of the stairs with a gunshot wound and a broken neck and the other in the dining room with a blown-up knee. But when he and Lizzie were sure all the arrivals had gone into the house, probably upstairs to gather the ammunition and weapons, they had sneaked through the woods toward his car.

If it hadn't been boxed in, they might have tried to take it. But even if there had been a gap to get out, they feared being heard pulling away, and the last thing they wanted was to be pursued by a dozen vehicles who probably knew the roads much better than they did. So they'd moved as quietly as they could toward the cluster of vehicles parked around the house, a mixture of trucks and SUVs and Jeeps and sedans, and Lizzie had placed her phone, on silent, on the backseat floorboard of an extended truck. By the time she'd quietly closed the door, the dead body must have been discovered inside the house, because someone had started screaming, "Nooooooo," just as someone else repeatedly wailed Ray's name.

Trevor and Lizzie were deep into the shadows of the woods by the time four of the men stormed out of the house with what looked like AR-15s. Two broke off in opposite directions. The other two spotted Trevor's unfamiliar car and searched it, inside and out, before unloading countless bullets into the vehicle, walking away only after it had been reduced to a heap of hissing steam. They must have gone back inside to regroup and load what Trevor had seen in that upstairs bedroom earlier, because as he tracked Lizzie's phone, they were only now pulling away from the old ranch. At least, the truck with Lizzie's phone inside it was leaving.

And while they'd been hoping for headlights in either direction, hoping that next vehicle would be the one to stop and give them a ride, what Trevor sensed behind them was an army. He looked over his shoulder to see he was right, and then quickly led Lizzie toward the roadside trees to hide until they passed, which they did seconds later, in speeding blurs and loud engines and pissed-off drivers. Once their taillights faded into the dark tunnel of night ahead, Trevor and Lizzie stepped back out onto the road, at which point his phone rang again.

Same number as before, but this time he answered it. "Hello?"

"Professor Harper?"

He knew right away who it was and knew there was no good reason she could be calling. "Jennifer?"

"Yeah, it's me."

"Tell me nothing has happened to Sam. Please."

"Sam's fine," she said. "He's still at the prison. He's mad. He's confused."

"I can explain it all," Trevor said as they walked. "What can I do for you?"

"I . . . I know who you are," she said. "Who you were."

"I figured by now you would," he said. "Did you get my number from Sam?"

"No, from Carl," she said. "But we found the comics you left on the kitchen table."

"Did you take them?"

"Yes."

"Good."

"Where are you?" Jennifer asked.

"We on the same team here?"

"Yes . . ."

"We're outside the Freedom Ranch."

"Who is *we*?"

"I'm with a partner, and a friend."

"The Mongoose?"

Trevor laughed, and Lizzie beside him must have overheard because she laughed too. "Yes," he said, as big, bright headlights approached from the oncoming lane.

Beside him, Lizzie said, "I'll flag him down."

"What do we need to do next, Jennifer?" When she didn't answer, and in fact, with her anxious breathing over the phone, sounded afraid to, he said, "What *we* could use is a ride." And then after watching Lizzie stop what appeared to be a semi-truck by waving her arms in the middle of the road, he said, "Or maybe not. Might have just found us one. Where are you?"

"I'm on my way to a bookstore," she said. "To see someone who once knew Minks. Back when he was a boy named Luther Wright. That name ring a bell?"

"I wish it did, but it doesn't."

After a pause, Jennifer said, "I wasn't wrong, was I? Leaving the Mallard Malone novels on your porch."

He sighed and then acknowledged Lizzie up ahead; it appeared the truck was agreeing to give them a lift, and she was beckoning him on. "No, you were right. I knew right away after reading them, and maybe deep down I had a feeling all along it was my brother."

"It's all so unbelievable."

"Not if you lived it," he said, gesturing to Lizzie that he was coming; she'd already climbed into the truck, and he suddenly had a fear the driver would take off with her. "And Jennifer, we found a list. I'm going to screenshot it for you and I need you to call these names to 911, or something. They could be in danger of fire."

"There was another one," she said. "At the Culbertson mansion. Thirty minutes ago."

"Damn," he said, knowing the name was on the list. "They're all diversions. I think they're trying to pull the authorities away from something bigger, and it has everything to do with Sal's execution."

Jennifer sniffled over the phone. "A diversion . . . like you and Yellow did when we escaped from the ranch?"

He found himself choking up too. "Yeah, like that," he said, eager to change the conversation. "Jennifer, look, I don't know what Minks has planned, but we just found enough weapons and ammunition for an army to break into Fort Knox, and they just left here madder than hornets."

But it was like she hadn't heard that last part. She cleared her throat. "You never came back," she said, crying now. "You came for Sam. You saved Sam from the closet, but you never came back for us. You promised."

"I know I did."

"I pissed my pants in that closet. I became a different person inside that closet."

"I'm sorry . . ."

"You promised you'd come back to get the rest of us."

"I know it and there hasn't been a day gone by, ever since, that I haven't thought about it, Jennifer. I tried, believe me, I—"

"The Raven . . . is a liar," she said, interrupting him, and he could tell it took courage, like even though the words might have caused pain for both of them, they had to be said.

"I'm sorry . . . Jennifer, look, I gotta go, but we've got each other's numbers, and we'll figure this out. Okay?"

But she'd already ended the call.

CHAPTER

49

"HELLO?" BETH CALLED out, her lips an inch from the hole in the wall, close enough to smell the metal from the chain connecting her to the woman in the neighboring room.

Through the hole, she saw the woman sitting on a piano bench at a desk in the middle of the room, typing on an old, clunky typewriter. To her left was a stack of blank pages. To her right appeared to be a manuscript, three inches tall, and growing, page by page. Was this the woman he'd called his wife, when he'd referred to himself as Mr. Darcy and her as Elizabeth Bennet? Her chestnut brown hair showed hints of gray and was so long it nearly brushed the hardwood floor behind her.

"Hello," Beth called out again. "What's your name?"

The woman continued typing, like she was in a zone, until she reached the end of the page, at which point she pulled the page out and stacked it atop the manuscript to her right.

"Don't drink the wine," the woman said without turning around. She loaded another page. "And my name is Elizabeth," she said. "Elizabeth Bennet."

No, it's not, Beth wanted to tell her. *He's lying to you. He has you chained through a wall and he is not Mr. Darcy.* But instead, she said, "What are you working on?"

"A book."

No shit, Beth wanted to say, but at the same time thought, *I know your voice.* "What's it about?"

"Oliver Crown," she said without hesitation. "It will pick up where the first book left off. It'll be Book Nine. It's called *Oliver Crown Reborn.*"

Beth said, "Your name isn't Elizabeth Bennet. You know that, don't you?" When she didn't answer and resumed typing, Beth said, louder, "How long have you been held captive here?"

The woman paused in her typing, as if to ponder the simple question. Although if she'd been here a long time, as in months or years, then maybe it wasn't so simple. There was a hole in the far wall of the neighboring room, but no chain through it. But just that it was there meant someone had probably been in that room too. It appeared this woman was connected only to Beth. The woman had yet to resume typing since the last question. Her hands shook noticeably as they hovered over the keys.

When she finally spoke, her voice cracked, "I don't even know anymore."

"Can you turn around? So I can see you . . ."

The woman started typing again, maybe a line or two before stopping again. Her shoulders vibrated. She was crying. She said, "I know your voice. But it can't be . . ."

Beth's entire body began to hum like electric current ran through it instead of warm blood. Without explanation, her eyes welled with tears. "Please . . ."

The woman turned slowly on the bench, lifting the chain around her ankle so it didn't snag—she was clearly used to having it on. When the woman faced Beth, she at first kept her head down like she was ashamed to show her face.

When she looked up, Beth lost it, first crying and then sobbing—it was Emily, her husband's sister, abducted so many years ago.

CHAPTER

50

"I CAN'T BELIEVE THIS is happening," Warden Wren said inside the waiting room, with the same woeful expression Sam had seen on his face minutes earlier inside his office, when he'd watched out the window toward the yard as prison personnel readied the area for Sal Batise's execution.

The news crew, outside the window, seeming as anxious as the rest of them here on the inside, had been setting up cameras and testing microphones as Warden Wren watched from above, muttering the same thing he was now: *I can't believe this is happening.*

Governor Hawthorne had gotten a call thirty minutes before from the President of the United States, insisting to the governor and the warden that this could not happen. *You cannot go through with this, Governor. We can't have a death row inmate shot to death by firing squad on live television.* It was incomprehensible, he'd gone on to say, with Sam and the rest listening in disbelief on speakerphone. But when the President had urged them to allow the FBI to do their job and end this another way, Governor Hawthorne had blown up on the phone, telling the man in the White House who he'd voted for in both terms, that there was no other way, and that Justice Minks, the man they now knew was born Luther Wright, was enough of a psychopath to do anything to anyone. Maybe he was being naive, but as he'd told the President, *The only way my wife stays alive is if Batise goes down exactly as he said.*

We don't fall prey to ransom demands, the President had told him.

And Hawthorne had said, *With all due respect sir, I do, this time.*

Minutes ago, after waiving a chance to speak to a priest or preacher or spiritual supervisor, Batise had been taken away for a requested shower and shave, a change into fresh clothes, and what he'd called a thorough brushing of his teeth.

Now here they were—Sam, Warden Wren, Agent Givens, and Governor Hawthorne—inside what Sam had earlier dubbed the War Room, as the four tried to think a way out of this nightmare.

The only one of the four not sitting now was Agent Givens, who paced the windowless room, animatedly gyrating his left hand as he spoke to this person and that person, ending one call only to jump right into another, all of them waiting to see if Emily Hawthorne's laptop could be recovered from the Hawthorne mansion. The governor's cousin lived there now with her family, and Gavin had made the initial call, warning her that FBI agents would be there within minutes to search the upstairs room where he'd stored all of Emily's things, and to let them do anything they needed to do. His cousin, understanding the situation, said, *Of course, of course, Gavin . . .*

But that had been thirty minutes ago, if not more, and they'd yet to hear a word from that end. Governor Hawthorne looked like he might come apart at any moment. In the middle of the table, all seven of the Mallard Malone novels rested in a stack, not unlike Sam had seen at his father's house the day before, but even though the books had been brought for possible reference, they'd yet to be touched, and were mostly viewed by those in the room like they were cursed.

Governor Hawthorne reached across the table and grabbed the first book in the series, *Long Pale Moon*, from the top of the stack. He opened the cover, closed it, and said to Sam and Warden Wren, "My sister and I, when we were little, we both liked to read and write stories. She was much better, a faster reader, a better writer, for sure, but we used to, when we got bored, we'd play a stupid game. We'd take the first word from each chapter and combine them to see if they ever made sense as a sentence of their own."

Sam said, "Did they?"

He smiled longingly. "No. Maybe a few times there'd be a string of a few words that could make sense, but mostly it was nonsense. Just stupid, kid stuff." He sighed, clenched his jaw. "But it became our thing. She'd go to summer camp and she'd write me letters. Just checking in, telling me about her stay in the woods." He opened the book again, flipped a few pages, stopped, as if reading, but then looked up again. "She'd leave a hidden message in her letter, every time. The first word of every paragraph," Hawthorne said, sniffling. "Just stupid stuff, the letters were short, so the messages were short, but she'd sneak in something like, *your bedroom smells like farts*. Or *you will never be as smart as me*. And I'd write her back and attempt to do the same . . . she was better at it than me." As he spoke, he flipped through more pages, his eyes scanning. And then he flipped through another few pages, stopping again to scan. He looked up at Sam. "Can you hand me that pen and paper?"

Sam did as requested, asking, "What is it?"

"I don't know," said the governor, even as he wrote three words and skipped to what Sam assumed was the beginning of the next chapter. He wrote another word and sat straighter in his chair as he flipped through more pages, faster now, and with an urgency that brought Sam out of his chair in anticipation. The governor wrote another word and said, "Holy shit."

Warden Wren said it this time, "What is it? Gavin?"

Hawthorne's face had gone pale. "Emily's alive." He stood from the table, turned the sheet toward them. "Sam, you talked to Mallard Malone's editor? She said his books came in clean, like they didn't even need to be edited."

"Like they'd *already* been edited."

Governor Hawthorne turned the paper toward them so they could read the words he'd written. "The first words of the first six chapters."

Sam read.

I

Am

Alive
Please
Help
Me

Governor Hawthorne showed the first smile Sam had seen since he'd come into the prison hours ago. "That's her. That's my sister. She's alive." He looked at the warden. "Get Batise."

At that point, Agent Givens stepped toward the table with news of his own. After noticing their current reactions, he said, "What happened?"

"I'll tell you in a minute," Hawthorne said. "What do you have?"

Agent Givens said, "They located your sister's laptop and booted it up. Talk about a needle in a haystack, but they found Batise's manuscript submission attached to his query letter from twenty-three years ago. Oliver Crown is first introduced halfway through the book, as a new member of Malcolm Dodd's cult. Batise goes into detail where Oliver Crown lives. Like the burials in the other books, it seems like unnecessary detail, extraneous detail that probably should have been cut, but I've got a SWAT team on the way there now. They're ten minutes away. It may be his house."

Gavin nodded, still scared, Sam could tell, but also saw a hint of hope in his eyes.

Agent Givens said, "Now why do you all look like you've just seen a ghost?"

Before the governor could answer, the warden's secretary opened the door, poked his head inside the room, and said, "Governor Hawthorne . . . he's on the phone. Oliver Crown."

CHAPTER

51

LELAND MOSBY'S USED bookstore was larger than she'd thought, and Jennifer was surprised she'd never been here before.

But then again, the store—which appeared to take up two floors of a three-story residence—was outside the city limits in small-town Lagrange, which was closer to Twisted Tree than Louisville.

Carl followed the PARKING IN THE BACK sign to the lot behind the store and turned the truck's engine off. "You okay?"

Jennifer nodded, eager to get out but giving it a minute for her tears to dry. She hadn't intended to grow emotional calling Trevor Harper; she'd spoken to him before, and she'd taken his class for an entire semester, but the abruptness of her emotions had come out of nowhere. But now that the repressed anger had come out, she fought the urge to call him back and apologize for ending her call so abruptly. Even though she'd known who he was since they'd left his house hours ago with the Raven comics in tow, the *I know you from somewhere* feeling she'd had now for months had hit her full force.

Holding the copy of *The Lord of the Flies* she'd taken from her childhood bedroom had prompted the phone call while in transit from her parents' house to Mosby's bookstore. Holding it again had reminded her of her time in that closet, when she'd had it concealed under her shirt, tucked halfway into the waistline of her pants. *The Raven is a liar,* she'd thought before making the call, vaguely remembering writing it now, but recalling with clarity why she'd written it. Because he'd promised to come back, and he never did. He'd taken Sam and never came back for the rest of them. But she felt better now for having said it, and getting some of the anger out of her system.

On their way around the building toward the front of the store, Carl showed Jennifer his phone and she said, "What am I looking at?"

He pocketed his phone. "According to the Spider Web, there's been fifteen other fires reported across the country just since this morning."

"Fires happen all the time, Carl, everywhere," Jennifer said, looking up at the pitched roof of the three-story Victorian home that Mosby had converted into a bookstore. Lights shone through the windows of the first two floors, which made her wonder if Mosby lived on the third. "I'm sure there's never *not* a fire always going on, somewhere in the country."

Carl sidled up beside her, matching her pace as she closed in on the tall front door that looked like something out of Victorian England. "Every one of these fires was set at the home of a millionaire."

"I'm listening," she said, bounding up the wide concrete steps.

"That's all I got right now," he said. "But it's something, right?"

"Yeah," she said, and then under her breath, "something to follow." Without knocking, she opened the door and stepped inside the foyer, which held thousands of books, some on dark, wooden floor-to-ceiling shelves, but in every nook, cranny, and gap stood stacks of used books, hardcovers and paper alike, some of the stacks multiple rows deep, which made her wonder if the foyer was this packed what might the rest of the store look like. And as she called out Mr. Mosby's name and moved slowly down the narrow, book-choked hallway, she saw that in every room she passed that she was right. Books by the thousands, on wall shelves, books stacked on the floor and on tables, big and small, and some highlighted and propped on scattered column-like pedestals. "Mr. Mosby?"

Carl took it all in with equal amazement, and said softly, "Now *this* is the fuck, right?"

"Yeah," she said. And then, "Mr. Mosby?"

She didn't like the feeling she was getting, and the anxiety increased with every step taken without a response—she'd spoken to the man on the phone only a few minutes ago and he'd said the door would be open. Which it had been. But she'd taken that to mean he'd be here. He'd be expecting them, if not waiting eagerly for their arrival. Mentioning the name *Luther Wright* earlier had changed his tune in an instant.

"You think he fled?" Carl asked.

"Why would he flee?"

"I don't know," he said, ducking his head in to investigate another room as they turned down the octagonal hallway leading through the first-floor maze. Even the kitchen was full of books. The countertops were barely visible under the sheer number of volumes stacked atop them. An overflowing bookshelf stood where the oven should have been, and another where the refrigerator would have gone. "It's obvious he knew Luther Wright. And I would guess," he said, pausing as they turned another corner, his anxiety evident in how quickly he was breathing, "that anyone who knew Luther, and can remember his face, might be in more danger now than they'd been before your sketch hit the news."

"Thanks," Jennifer said.

"Just saying."

"I know," she said, but also knowing he was right, and she couldn't help but wonder if she'd brought trouble to Mr. Mosby's doorstep by reaching out to him. "But from what I could gather, it sounded like Luther loved Mr. Mosby."

"Desperate times," Carl said.

They jumped when a voice emerged from a shadowed hallway behind them, like an echo from a labyrinth. "There you are."

Jennifer turned to find who she assumed was Leland Mosby. She didn't know why she assumed by his deep, theatrical voice over the phone that he'd be tall, but she certainly hadn't expected him to be so short, like Trevor Harper short, and maybe even smaller.

In his arms he held a stack of a dozen books. His hair and beard were summer-cloud white, his skin the color of mahogany, and his smile broad and welcoming. He stepped farther out of the shadows, reached his right leg behind him to kick closed a door that Jennifer briefly saw led to a steep set of basement stairs. "Mice down there," said Mosby, breathing heavily, every bit of eighty years old, maybe older. "Gotta keep the door closed. The mice love books even more than my loyal customers, except my customers don't eat them." He handed the stack of books to Carl and wiped his hands of dust Jennifer couldn't see, because while the entire bookstore looked cluttered, it was noticeably clean. He offered his hand to Jennifer. "Leland Mosby, at your service." And then he nodded kindly to Carl, who had no free hand to shake.

His grip was much stronger than Jennifer would have imagined. As much as she'd instantly loved this magical place, this labyrinthine house of books, and even more so now wanted to get to know the man who owned it, she didn't have time to dawdle. She showed him the copy of *The Lord of the Flies* and said, "This came from your store, maybe decades ago."

"Ah, yes, back when my store was inside that little hovel across the street," he said. "It's a nice breakfast joint now, the biscuits and gravy are divine." He watched them both. "But I gather we're not here to discuss food, but Luther Wright." He shook his head sadly. "That poor, lost soul. Oh, Luther . . ."

"So you knew him?"

"Did I ever," said Mosby. "His family lived in one of the upstairs apartments next door to my shop. Every time he ran away, which was often, he'd come to my store. After the third time, I learned that he couldn't read, and that broke my heart, so I taught him. He caught on quickly—the boy was bright—and instantly to the books he would go, whether he was running away that day or not. I'd find him hiding in my aisles. Reading under stairwells. Under tables. Atop the tables. Behind my desk. We'd discuss every book when he was finished, and oftentimes I'd have to coax him out the door at closing time." At this point Mosby grew noticeably sad, his eyes filled with moisture. "The poor child was terrified of his home. He was abused, I knew that, and I called Protective Services more than once, but there the boy remained, until . . . that horrible face wound . . ."

"How did he get it?" Jennifer asked.

"I don't know for sure," he said, "but the first time I saw the wound, poorly tended to, I might add, and even more crudely stitched, I'm afraid, I was convinced, along with the massive cut, that it had involved burns as well. As if he'd been struck with something searingly hot." He sighed, wiped his eyes. "I'm sorry. After your call, I did spend a minute scouring my news feed. The bookstore is on Twitter, if you can believe that, or X, or whatever it's called now, and I saw the sketch you did. It's the same scar. It's the same boy, now a man, now Justice Minks, now Oliver Crown. And back then he'd become whatever protagonist, or even occasionally the antagonist, of whatever book he was reading." He turned to Jennifer. "I could see it in the eyes—you're quite the artist, Ms. Daley. So detailed it brought memories of Luther back with screaming vengeance. I'd always wondered what had become of him. I *feared* what had become of him. Of poor Luther Wright."

"And now we know," Carl said.

Mosby nodded. "I never dreamed he'd become this, if it is as they say."

Jennifer said, "We need your help finding him. He has the governor's wife. And we think he has something planned after Batise's execution."

"Yes, I've quickly caught myself up on the situation." He patted the top book of the stack Carl now held. "I've saved these for over thirty years, should Luther ever come back. These books were his favorites. He returned to them often, as you can see, by how worn they are."

After a quick perusal, Jennifer saw that Carl held a mix of paperbacks and hardcovers, as well as larger art-type books, or perhaps photography, and the pile had been stacked like a pyramid, largest books on the bottom, up to the small paperback of what she now realized was *The Grapes of Wrath*, and beneath that, stories from Edgar Allan Poe.

Mosby saw her looking at the top book, *The Grapes of Wrath*. "He went for a time convinced he was Tom Joad. Didn't matter that Luther was a boy and Tom Joad was a man." He shook his head sadly. "Even at that young age, he understood deeply the dynamic themes of that novel, and often ranted about that vast divide between the wealthy landowners and those who worked their land." He said to Carl, "Let me get you a box for those."

As they followed him back to the kitchen, Jennifer asked, "When was the last time you saw him?"

"Over thirty years ago," he said. "At least. It was not long after the wound on his face. Finally, by then it seemed Social Services had had enough, and into the system he went. I never heard from him again."

As Carl placed the books inside the box Mosby handed him, Jennifer asked, "When did you move across the street to this . . . house?"

"Seven years ago," Mosby said. "It had always been a dream, to turn this house into a bookstore. I live up on the third floor. I have many wealthy customers . . . but seven years ago, I received a very large anonymous donation for the bookstore, and I used it to purchase this house."

"And you don't know who it came from?" Jennifer asked.

"No, not really, although I could make a few guesses, and I've often wondered if it wasn't one particularly loyal book club, a group of women who all have money."

Carl and Jennifer shared a look.

Mosby said, "What am I missing?"

Jennifer said, "What if the anonymous donor was Luther?"

Mosby laughed, like that was ridiculous, and then his face changed to, perhaps, belief in the possibility.

Jennifer said, "If he was the secret mule between Batise and the publisher for the Mallard Malone novels, he could be worth millions of dollars, if not more."

Carl added, "The timing of it would coincide with an initial payment."

"Yes," Mosby said, still in obvious disbelief. "An advance for that first book. Dear God. Luther . . ."

"He's not Luther anymore," Jennifer said, before jumping at the sound of broken glass and rapidly fired bullets at the front of the bookstore.

CHAPTER

52

Before

LELAND MOSBY TOOK the paperback copy of *The Grapes of Wrath* back from the boy and placed it atop a nearby stack.

"You seem to have taken to the book, Luther," said Mr. Mosby. "Although it does sadden me that a boy your age should find empathy with the lifelong conflict between the powerful and the powerless." He patted the boy's head, careful not to stare at the angry scar running across Luther's face, the crude stitches as angry as the boy's eyes in the flickering candlelight. "How about something a touch lighter for your next read?"

The boy's expression didn't change. "What is *wrath*?"

As a man of words, Mr. Mosby, in any other moment, would not have hesitated in his answer, but the question, coming from the boy, now, gave him an anxious pause, if for no other reason than the fear of why he'd asked it. "Well," said Mr. Mosby. "It is an anger so great that it may express itself in an intense . . . desire to severely *punish* someone." The boy nodded, knowingly, almost, if not satisfied with something. Mr. Mosby didn't trust the *lack* of a look in the boy's glassy eyes, and said, "But I think what you're feeling, Luther, is anger, pure and simple. Mixed in with a bit of fear and confusion."

"No," Luther said, and then added so matter-of-factly that it turned Mr. Mosby's blood cold: "It's wrath."

CHAPTER

53

Oliver Crown sat on the folding chair he'd brought into the room with him, five feet away from where Beth sat on the floor with her back against the wall.

Behind her, the clacking of typewriter keys sounded again from the neighboring room, having resumed seconds ago, after Beth and her sister-in-law Emily had scrambled frantically upon hearing his heavy footfalls in the hallway; Emily back to her piano bench to write, Beth, back to her chains, still in shock that Emily was alive, after over two decades of captivity, no matter who she might have thought she was, or had been all these years.

He is not your husband, Emily, she'd hissed through the hole in the wall, peeking to see her sister-in-law, now in her late forties, crying in the other room, crying and confused like no rational adult should ever be confused, because it was her own identity at stake. She was not who she thought she was anymore, and Beth could tell in the few minutes they'd spoken that Emily not only recognized her and remembered her but knew exactly who she was. But at the same time, she was convinced she was a woman named Elizabeth Bennet, and her husband was Mr. Darcy. Horrifying thoughts traced like tattered ribbons over Beth's skin as she listened to the typing over there, knowing Emily was typing out of fear, typing out of such controlled habit that it tortured her to imagine what all her husband's sister had gone through over the past twenty-three years, to become the slack-jawed and lifeless-eyed woman she'd just witnessed through that hole in the wall.

But yet, Beth thought, as she stared at the phone Oliver Crown held out to her from his seat on the chair, Emily was alive and didn't look bruised or beaten or starved or malnourished, and if she was alive, there was hope. If she was alive, she could heal, she could be repaired, and Beth swore if they made it out, she would accept whatever percentage of Emily came back with them, because she knew over time she could find the rest of it, whatever was left of her dear, sweet friend and sister-in-law.

But if the phone in front of her wasn't enough, the gun in his other hand, pointed right at her, she thought, might do her in, especially so soon after hearing her husband's desperate, anguish-ridden voice at the other end of it, as her captor sat so smugly reiterating his insane demands for Sal Batise's execution, no matter what the mastermind tried in any last-second defense inside the prison.

"I need proof she's still alive," Governor Hawthorne said on the other end of the call.

"Very well," Minks said into the phone, before holding it out toward Beth.

Beth nodded toward the phone, and the gun pointed at her; the message was clear—behave, don't try anything stupid.

"Beth . . ." said her husband.

"Gavin," she said, staring at the book covers coating the walls. "It's me. Do as he says."

"Oh my God, Beth—are you hurt? They're saying you were shot."

"I'm fine . . ." she said, closing her eyes, thinking, *You're not fine, you're not fine, he's going to kill you either way, Beth, especially now that he's shown you Emily. He's going to kill you. You won't walk away from this, so . . .* She opened her eyes, stared at Minks, stared at the gun and the phone, and said, "Gavin, I love you . . . and he has me inside a large house with—"

Minks fired the gun.

Beth screamed.

CHAPTER 54

THE PURE TERROR in Governor Hawthorne's scream, after hearing what had to have been a gunshot over the phone, was unlike anything Sam had ever heard before, until an even louder, more guttural roar emerged when he yelled, "*Fuck!*" and hurled the phone across the room.

Agent Givens was quick to say, "She screamed, Gavin. You heard her. She screamed."

"He shot her!"

"Then she wouldn't have had time to scream."

Governor Hawthorne gasped for breath. He looked up, still seething, but starting to see reason, Sam could tell.

Sam said, "He's right. We heard the gunshot. She screamed. He was just trying to scare her."

Governor Hawthorne nodded, slowly composing himself. He looked at his watch. "Forty minutes."

Batise had yet to return from the shower and shave he'd requested. Sam still half expected him to go full-blown Houdini and somehow vanish from the prison. It was impossible though, he knew; there were always too many guards watching him, and outside, according to Warden Wren's latest report, was all set for the execution.

Governor Hawthorne ran a hand through his hair and said to Agent Givens, "Where are we at with the house?"

Givens's eyes were glued to the phone. "We got our warrant. They're there now. No one answered, so they're going in."

Governor Hawthorne closed his eyes.

Sam's cell phone rang. It was Jennifer. "Yeah?"

"Sam, we need help," she said frantically over the phone. "Now."

It sounded like they were in a car. "Where are you?"

"We're a mile away from you," she said. "We have a man with us. Leland Mosby. He knows Luther Wright. He knew him when he was a boy. We were just in his bookstore, and someone shot it up trying to get to him . . . or us . . . I don't know, but we need somewhere to go."

"They're following you?"

"We got out the back of the store but yes, we think at least one of them is following us."

Sam looked up to find Agent Givens staring wide-eyed, his phone to his ear, nodding and listening, and Governor Hawthorne—who'd been paying attention to Sam's call with Jennifer—must have noticed Agent Givens's bloodless face as well. "What happened?"

Sam said Jennifer: "Give me a second."

Agent Givens lowered his phone. "The house was a trap. Minks was expecting us. It just blew up, with four of our agents in it."

"Sam?" Jennifer shouted over the phone.

Agent Givens said, "Who is that?"

"Jennifer," Sam said, and then quickly told him the situation.

Agent Givens said, "This man Mosby knows Luther Wright?"

"Yes."

"I'll see that they get safe passage into the prison." And then he left the room.

Sam said, "Jennifer . . . stay on the line. Wait for my directions. We're getting you inside the prison."

He heard her urging Carl to go faster.

And then he heard Carl say, "I'm already going ninety-five. The truck is shaking."

Jennifer's voice returned, "Sam . . . you need to talk to your father. He's out there. He's trying to find Minks . . . Luther."

"And do what?"

"I don't know," she said. "He might not have been who you thought he was, Sam, but he's . . . he's always been what you needed, and you need him still, Sam. And he needs you."

"My life was a lie," Sam said. "My entire life, Jennifer. He's not even my father!"

"But he's your dad, Sam," she said. "Not Sal Batise. I don't care if he's your biological father, Sam. He doesn't care about you."

"He does," Sam said softly, but even as he said it he could hear the doubt in it, the pathetic false insistence of it.

"He's playing you, Sam. You can't trust anything he says."

"I'm seeing this to the end," he said. "I am all he has right now."

"He's a pathological narcissist, Sam. He doesn't give a fuck about anyone but himself," she said. "He uses his charisma and flair to control. He's making you feel special so he can control you."

"Bullshit," he said, but knew she was right.

"He divides people to control them," Jennifer said. "It's been less than a day, and he's got you under his thumb already. He's turning you away from your real family."

"I know who my mother is . . ."

"Sam, stop," she said. "Your true mother died of cancer when you were a boy, and she was a hero and her favorite color was yellow, and . . ."

Agent Givens returned into the room and said to Sam, "Tell them to pull around to the back. There's a sign for delivery trucks, a dirt road leading through the woods and around the back."

Sam relayed the message to Jennifer, told her he'd see her soon, and ended the call.

"The parking lot is full of reporters," Agent Givens said. "From all across the country."

Governor Hawthorne checked his watch. "Thirty minutes."

Warden Wren entered the room. "Batise is back in my office."

Agent Givens, still fuming from what had happened at the house, the loss of four of his agents, nodded toward Sam. "Let's go."

Sam didn't move. "Give me a second."

"I don't have a second," Givens said. "Those deaths are on his head."

"Give me a second," Sam said.

And then stepped out into the hallway to call his dad.

C H A P T E R

55

INSIDE THE CAB of the semi-truck, driven by a man named Todd, who had already gone way beyond the call of duty as they tracked Lizzie's moving cell phone east toward Simpsonville, Trevor Harper's phone vibrated with an incoming call.

When he saw it was Sam, his heart jumped.

"Answer it," Lizzie said from her seat between Trevor and Todd, a burly, bearded long- haul trucker with a kind heart and, to their luck, an even bigger love for the governor and his wife. And having already told Trevor and Lizzie that he'd take them wherever they needed to go, he also said to Trevor, "Answer it."

"I can't lose track of her phone."

Lizzie said, "Put in on speaker."

Trevor put it on speaker and accepted the call. "Sam?"

"Dad . . ."

Trevor didn't know how desperately he'd needed to hear that word until he'd heard it, and tears instantly formed in his eyes. "Son."

Sam sounded emotional over the phone as well. "Who is Jules Whitaker?"

Trevor immediately closed his eyes, conjured strength, he didn't have much time. When he felt Lizzie's hand on his arm, he opened his eyes with newfound courage and got right to the point. "She was once my fiancé, Sam."

"I . . . don't understand."

"Because you were never meant to know," Trevor said with a catch in his throat. "What has my brother told you?"

"That Jules is my mom," he said. "That Jules Whitaker is my biological mom. And that he was . . . with her. But how . . . if she was *your* fiancé?"

"We were to be married," Trevor said. "We were young. Naive. Sal . . . he . . . he found out . . ."

"Found out what?"

"That she was a virgin," Trevor said. "That I was . . ." Trevor shook his head, couldn't believe he was doing this in front of Lizzie and a virtual stranger in Todd, but to salvage his relationship with his son, he plowed on. "We were . . . saving ourselves for marriage. My brother, he found that out, he thought it was cute. He thought it was funny. He joked about us. And then one day I noticed Jules was beginning to change. Her innocent personality turned combative. She became quiet. Distant. Started doing drugs . . . with Sal. It wasn't long before she started to show."

"With me?"

"Yeah . . . with you. He'd seduced her," Trevor said, surprised by how easily the words had come from his mouth, given how many years it had taken for him to get over what she and Sal had done. "She admitted it . . . she'd fallen under his spell, Sam. Once Sal found out she was pregnant, he didn't want anything to do with her, and I was so mad I couldn't look at her. One night, she ran off. I never saw her again. Sal said she'd disappeared into the woods and was overwhelmed by demons. Her own, of course. But one day, out of the blue, when you were about five years old, she arrived at the Freedom Ranch. I think he had Minks kill her, Sam."

"But he left me alive?"

"Yeah, he did."

"And you watched over me?"

"Yes," he said. "Me and Annie." He laughed, wiped his eyes. "The Raven and Yellow. But Jules, with how easily he fooled her, how easily he seduced her . . . she was the one who . . . gave him the idea."

"For what?"

"To form the cult," he said. "She was the first member."

"But you joined too," Sam said, sounding confused and disbelieving.

"I was weak, son. Lost. So was Annie. We didn't see it at the time, nobody does when they're in one, but over time our eyes were opened, to all of it."

"And you brought it all down."

"Yes, we did."

"I don't think he's ever forgiven you."

"Just as I'll never forgive him, Sam."

They were silent for a beat.

"Dad . . . he called you the Kentucky Cannibal. Is it true?"

"No," Trevor said. "No . . . just something they called me. A cruel joke, nothing more."

"Okay," Sam said, still sounding confused, and so suddenly small. "I gotta go."

The call ended.

Lizzie's phone had entered Twisted Tree and was heading farther east toward Ransom, Kentucky. *Fitting*, Trevor thought, if that's where they were heading.

Toward Ransom.

CHAPTER 56

"I DON'T EVEN KNOW if hell is the right place for you," Agent Givens said.

And Batise, freshly scrubbed and shaved and now wearing the all-white uniform he would die in, stood in the middle of the warden's office, acting as if hadn't heard a word the FBI agent had said, before finally answering, "I had nothing to do with that house blowing up."

"Just as you had nothing to do with the nine murders inside the Hawthorne mansion twenty years ago."

"My thoughts and prayers—"

"Fuck your thoughts and prayers." Agent Givens took a deep breath, stared at Batise, who had not taken his eyes off the window overlooking the yard since his arrival back into the office. "You could have stopped it."

"But I didn't."

"No, you fucking didn't. Because you don't wish to show all your cards, you worthless piece of shit." He pointed out the window toward the yard where the armed guards had joined the news crew down there. "And you've got twenty minutes to live."

"Tick-tock, tick-tock . . ." Batise smiled, looked worriedly at Sam. "What is it, Sam Harper? What is it that has changed in you since we last spoke? Huh? You can no longer look at me? Your own flesh and blood?"

Sam thought of his conversations with Jennifer, and his dad, and refused to fall back under the man's spell.

Agent Givens must have sensed Sam's discomfort, because he steered Batise in another direction by showing him the first book in the Mallard Malone series.

"We think Minks has Emily Hawthorne as well, and that she is still alive." Agent Givens showed Batise the words Governor Hawthorne had written down minutes earlier. "They had a secret system of communicating as kids." He tapped the paper. "Look." Batise looked and appeared to have read the words, but Givens read them aloud anyway: "I am alive please help me."

"That means nothing to me."

"First words of the first six chapters."

"And that's it?"

"That's it," Givens said. "The rest made no sense, but by then she'd gotten her point across."

"It just took you eight years to find it."

"We had no reason to look," Givens said.

Sam jumped in: "Were you aware?"

Batise turned toward Sam. "He speaks again."

Sam stood strong. "Is that how you started those six chapters?"

"No," he said. "I wrote all the novels in third person, so there should be no I, unless the chapter started with dialogue, which I was not in the habit of doing."

"So someone changed what you'd written," Sam said.

"As editors tend to do," he said. "And with me being in here, I was never involved in the editing *process*."

Agent Givens said, "We think Emily Hawthorne edited all your novels before they went off to the publisher."

Batise grinned. "It appears she did a very good job." And then he changed the subject. "It was as surprising to me as it must have been to your men, FBI Agent Givens, I assure you. That house blowing up. I had nothing to—"

"Where is he?" Givens asked. "Minks? Luther Wright? Oliver fucking Crown? Huh? Where is he?"

"Tell the governor to grant my stay," Batise said. "When weighed against eternity, twenty minutes is still plenty of time to get that done." And then, "Have your men finished the book yet, Agent Givens? Seems they've found it on her old computer, which is how they found Oliver Crown's house, but have they finished it yet?"

"Not yet," Agent Givens said, "but you can save us the time. What do we need to know?"

"Spoiler alert?" asked Batise. "I think not."

The guard approached, gently clutched Batise's arm, and led him toward the door. "We're to take him down now," the guard said.

"Tick-tock," said Batise, and then, "But do let me know when they get to the good part of the book. It's quite crucial to the rest of the series."

Agent Givens gritted out, "What is going to happen?"

"Just make sure Governor Hawthorne knows the stakes," said Batise. "Killing me may or may not save his wife. But keeping me alive could save thousands. And Sam, don't stand too close to the windows."

CHAPTER

57

BETH COULD NO longer hear out of her right ear.

The bullet he'd fired had passed her head by inches and burrowed clear through the wall and into the neighboring room.

He'd stormed out soon thereafter and had yet to return.

Emily had screamed as well, but while the gunshot had temporarily paralyzed Beth, the ringing in her other ear still incessant, it had seemingly woken Emily from whatever stupor she'd been in, and for the first time since they'd spoken through the hole in the wall, Emily, on the other side of it, said Beth's name. Beth was so stunned by almost being shot in the face that she hadn't realized Emily had stopped typing again. And when Emily had called her name, it sounded like she was right on the other side of the wall, her lips to the hole.

"Beth, I left something for you. Hurry, grab it."

Footsteps approached in the hallway again. Beth could feel the footfalls as much as hear them. She turned, stared into the hole, and saw something metallic resting atop the chain that connected them. She grabbed it seconds before the door to her room opened and Minks, in his Guy Fawkes mask, stepped back inside, where he again placed a chair down and sat in it, facing her. He carried a bottle of what she assumed to be wine, except the dark bottle had no label on it. In his other hand he held a wine glass. He poured wine into it and handed it to her. When she wouldn't take it, he placed it on the floor next to her.

"From the Cask of Amontillado," he said.

CHAPTER

58

As soon as Jennifer and Carl entered the room inside the prison with Leland Mosby, she hugged Sam, hard and strong, and didn't want to let go.

They wasted no time introducing Mr. Mosby to Sam and Agent Givens and Governor Hawthorne, and by the time Jennifer stepped away from Sam's warm embrace, Mosby, in complete understanding of their time crunch, had already taken out the stack of books they'd brought from the store and was laying them all face up on the table.

"As you can see," Mosby said, gesturing toward the books before them, "Luther, even as a boy, had become weirdly fond of all things Italy." Jennifer quickly perused the table, seeing *The Grapes of Wrath*, as she had before at the store, but also a book of stories by Edgar Allan Poe, and the rest of the books, just as Mr. Mosby has suggested, had to do with Italy, and in particular, Italian wine making and grapes and vineyards. "He would tell me daily that one day he would live on a vineyard, inside a great stone house, one ripped straight out of Tuscany, he'd say. The boy, you see, had such a horrible childhood that he was forced to spend it imagining something better. This . . . this was always his better. An Italy he knew only from pictures but had come to adore in his mind."

Governor Hawthorne said, "So we look for a vineyard. A house that looks like . . ."

"These," Mosby said. "Yes." And then he opened the book of stories by Poe and pointed to a particular one halfway through the volume. "'The Cask of Amontillado' . . . have you read it?"

All of them shook their heads, no, except Agent Givens, who said he vaguely remembered it from high school.

"This was one of Luther's absolute favorites," Mosby said. "Published in November of 1846. Stripping it down to the bones, the story is about revenge and murder. It takes place in an unnamed Italian city and tells the story of a man named Montresor who takes revenge on a fellow nobleman named Fortunato. He uses the latter's love of wine to lure Fortunato into his cellar to try his Amontillado. He chains him and then kills him by building a wall around him, sealing him inside."

As Jennifer took it all in, she noticed Carl, in one of the chairs across the room, texting someone with furious intent, and at the same time keeping track of what Mosby was telling them.

Agent Givens said, "So we need to find a vineyard?"

"But this is horse and bourbon country, not wine," said the governor.

Agent Givens got on his phone, texted someone, and looked up again. "Anyone? Vineyards?"

"Give me a second," Sam said, also texting someone.

From behind them, Carl said, "Got it." When all eyes fixed on him, Carl stood from the chair and showed them a picture. "Martin just sent me this."

Agent Givens said, "Who is Martin? And what am I looking at? An old wine bottle?"

Jennifer said, "Harold Martin, the reporter. He wrote *Mastermind*, the bestselling true crime book on Sal Batise and his cult."

Carl said, "And this picture was from the initial investigations of the ranch after it was raided. It was one of many left out of his book, but he still had access to it. He found it immediately when I asked him about anything pertaining to wine and the Freedom Ranch."

Agent Givens looked at his watch. "Ten minutes."

Carl showed them the picture on his phone again. "Look at the bottle. LouTalia merlot. The bottle was found on a counter inside Sal's main house, next to the stove where they'd found the now infamous stew. It was believed the merlot was used in the cooking of that . . ."

"Stew," Agent Givens said. "Yeah, we got it, the human stew, get to the point."

"LouTalia was a local vineyard that combined the owner's love of Louisville with Italy. Italia. From all accounts, the wine was not very good. The company, after spending millions on their vineyard, folded after just three years, leaving a huge inventory behind. The farm was bought and sold, bought and sold, and then a fire destroyed the main house there . . ." Carl paused to read from his phone, and by the sound of the constant vibrations coming from it, Jennifer realized he was still getting texts from Martin as he spoke. His eyes flickered as he quickly read the incoming messages. "The house burned down thirty years ago. For years the property was abandoned and went into decay, until it was purchased twenty-five years ago for nearly nothing by a man . . ." Carl looked up, not for any kind of dramatic affect but in apparent disbelief. ". . . a man who went by the name Montresor Amontillado."

"Jesus Christ," Agent Givens said. "It's him. Where is the old LouTalia Vineyard?"

Carl looked up from his phone. "Ransom . . . Ransom, Kentucky. Deep in the woods."

Governor Hawthorne said, "Get your men there now."

Agent Givens shook his head. "We don't have time."

Sam said, "But my dad might."

"What?" Agent Givens said, confused.

"The Raven," Sam said with a proud smirk. "He just landed in Ransom. He's there, and he's getting ready to go in."

C H A P T E R

59

21 vehicles full of heavily armed men and woman left the old vineyard 15 minutes ago, heading west on I64.

Trevor hit Send, and off the message went to Sam inside the prison.

He quickly typed another message: We're tracking their destination, so I'll let you know ASAP where they're heading. He hit Send again and pocketed his phone.

Other than Todd, their new long-haul trucker friend who insisted on keeping his rig parked along the road leading into and out of the old LouTalia vineyard, Trevor and Lizzie were alone, hunkered atop a wooded hillside overlooking a rolling-hill valley seemingly mimicking a picturesque Italian countryside. Like something stolen from a book, stolen from Tuscany itself and plopped down in the middle of wooded nowhere. They'd traversed through woods and woods and more woods, and then *this* . . . a hidden gem of trellised gardens and rustic stone structures, rows upon rows of craggy grapevines full of robust green and purple fruit, and on the far side, as if carved into the hillside, were tiered olive groves. Center to all of it, resting in the middle of the valley like a beating heart, was a massive stone structure, Italianate in design, and sprawling, from an arial view, in the shape of an *L*. It was three levels tall with a steeply pitched red roof, below which rested dozens of windows spaced evenly throughout the sides of the house, on all three levels.

Dozens of rooms, thought Trevor as he and Lizzie—he with a baseball bat and she with a gun—carefully navigated the hillside that funneled majestically down toward the moonlit vineyards. He wondered if some of the Mallard Malone money had gone to create this.

This illusion.

But it was real.

And as they neared the bottom of the vineyard, where the sheer size of the house loomed even larger from below, Trevor saw that not only did each room glow with light, and some with moving shadows, but each open-air window was covered with vertical bars.

CHAPTER 60

BETH TRIED NOT to look at Minks.

Instead, she focused her gaze out the window toward the clear, moonlit night, and imagined she was a bird that could soar between the vertical prison bars to her freedom.

When she glanced his way, she saw him on the folding chair he'd brought in with him, watching her, his dark eyes probing alien-like at her through the holes of the Guy Fawkes mask, the unlabeled bottle of wine open and airing out on the floor beside his big, brown right boot. That boot was flat on the floor while his left leg was stretched out, his leaned-back posture like that of a Roman Caesar.

Her back felt aflame, in excruciating pain from sitting in such weird positions on the floor for so long. The bullet wound in her calf throbbed, like every pulse from her heart pushed blood directly down toward it.

But at least the ringing in her ear from the gunshot was subsiding. She could hear Emily typing again in the neighboring room.

Minks said, "Did you have a nice reunion?"

She ignored him.

"Look at me," he said.

She continued to stare out the window.

"This will soon be over."

"Kill me now," she said.

"Drink," he said, of the glass of wine he'd placed next to her. "It's my finest vintage."

Without drinking, without looking at him, without acknowledging that he'd even left the wine glass for her to consume, she said, "You've heard of Stockholm syndrome?"

"As an avid reader, I've heard of most things, Dr. Hawthorne," he said. "But that's not what this is."

"It's a psychological coping mechanism," she said. "It can develop in victims of captivity. Victims of abuse."

"Mr. Darcy has never once abused her."

"Causing them to identify with," Beth said, "and in some instances . . . develop positive feelings toward their captors."

"Mr. Darcy has never once harmed one hair on her head," he said. "And she is not a captive here."

"What would you call the chains, then?"

"For her own safety."

Finally, she looked at him, not because he'd asked her to but after what he'd said, she couldn't help it. "And I thought *you* were Mr. Darcy."

"I am, when I'm with her."

"And now . . . you're Oliver Crown?"

His mask shifted like he'd just smiled behind it. "No . . . no . . . now I am Montresor," he said. "Here, at night, on my vineyard, I am always Montresor. Luther built this for me, you know." He looked at his watch. "He'll be dead soon."

"Batise?"

"Yes."

"And then what?"

"Soon Oliver Crown will rise from the ashes and create the new world order."

"You say that as if you're jealous, Montresor . . ."

"Montresor is jealous of no one."

"Is Luther still in there?"

"Yes."

"Can I speak to him?"

He watched her, said nothing.

"Can he hear me?"

He leaned forward in his chair but didn't respond.

"Tell him I'm sorry. I'm sorry for everything that ever happened to him." From her left hand she revealed a puzzle piece. She showed him. "I'm sorry for not taking him in as a boy. I'm sorry he was beaten and abused, and no one ever did anything about it, but tell him I tried."

"He says you didn't try hard enough."

"I know that now," Beth said, holding out the puzzle piece, nodding toward the puzzle she'd been working on the floor. "Have Luther finish the border for me. I know he was good at puzzles."

Montresor, or whoever the fuck he was now, inched forward in his chair, and then stood.

Beth started crying; they weren't fake tears, because in an instant she was back inside her office as a young, new psychiatrist and Luther was a boy who was so damaged she didn't know what to do for him. Now she held out the puzzle piece to him, coaxing him closer, and in his movement, she could tell something had changed. He was no longer the cocky, confident man who'd been sitting in the chair seconds ago, but now appeared somehow smaller, like a Jekyll to the previous Hyde, like a passive boy instead of the monster she knew he was.

He knelt on the floor, took the puzzle piece from her, and moved it toward the lone gap in the Swiss Alps border.

And Beth, in her best child psychiatrist voice, said, "There you go. You're doing great."

He nodded.

And Beth said, "Luther?"

And when he turned, she clutched the bottom of the typewriter key Emily had given to her through the hole in the wall, as firmly as she could in her right hand—the letter ***Y***—and plunged into straight into his right eye.

He screamed as blood leaked from his eye socket.

And then a gunshot sounded from somewhere in the house.

And all the prisoners started screaming.

CHAPTER 61

NOW THAT BATISE had been escorted from the prison tower, they'd moved their group inside Warden Wren's office, as witnesses to the execution that was apparently going to take place despite the President's command.

Jennifer and Sam stood side by side at the window overlooking the yard. Down below, Warden Wren, along with a news camera crew, stood with dozens of prison guards, four of whom stood out from the rest as the assumed group who'd either volunteered for, or had been chosen as, the designated firing squad in Batise's execution.

Sam remembered Batise's last words to him, to stay away from the window, and that message, coupled with the bizarre scene emerging below, sent a wave of foreboding dread through him.

At the same time they were still trying to process—and no one more so than Governor Hawthorne, who'd been pacing since the news—what Agent Givens had told them minutes ago, after he'd ended his call with the fellow agent who'd been speed-reading the novel found on Emily Hawthorne's old computer. "Right after Malcolm Dodd's execution," he said, "in the book, all hell breaks loose at the prison. Inside and outside the prison. Half the guards in the prison are owned by Oliver Crown. The ones who aren't are quickly gunned down. It took them years to infiltrate the prison. Bottom line, in the novel, all the inmates break out."

Jennifer said, "We have to stop this."

"We can't," said Governor Hawthorne.

"Unfortunately, that doesn't even scratch the surface," Agent Givens said. "It happens all over the country. Simultaneous breakouts, all triggered by Malcolm Dodd's execution. Inmates and guards within, former inmates armed up on the outside."

"The chaos Batise spoke of," said Governor Hawthorne.

Under her breath, Jennifer said, "And Oliver Crown rises from the ashes."

"Jesus," Sam said, thinking out loud. "The caravan Dad saw leave that vineyard . . ."

"They're more than likely heading for the prison," Hawthorne said, finishing his thought. "And most of the law enforcement around here has been dealing with the fires all day."

"The diversion," Jennifer said.

Governor Hawthorne turned to Agent Givens: "How far out from the vineyard are your men?"

"Seven minutes."

"Too long," Hawthorne said. "It's five minutes until the execution."

"They aren't superheroes, Governor."

But my dad is, Sam thought, but said, "My dad's already in there."

"Your dad is an unarmed history professor," Agent Givens said. "Who weighs maybe one-forty soaking wet."

At the same time Carl, from the warden's desk, said, "Holy shit." Everyone in the room looked at him.

Sam and Jennifer simultaneously said, "What?"

Governor Hawthorne stopped pacing.

Agent Givens was on the phone, but his eyes swiveled toward Carl.

"Those fires I said earlier," Carl said. "That were being reported all over the country. Like the ones here. There are more coming in by the minute on the Spider Web." Atop the desk, Carl turned a paper so they could better see what he'd written. "So far, every one of the fires, what they're now calling the millionaire fires, has been set in a town or city near a state penitentiary. Fires near the Louisiana State

Penitentiary, Angola, the Alcatraz of the South. Some six thousand dangerous criminals. Maricopa County Jail in Phoenix. Nine thousand inmates. Fires near Harris County Jail in Houston. Upward of ten thousand inmates. Cook County Jail in Chicago, houses ten thousand inmates. Rikers, New York, upward of fifteen thousand inmates. Los Angeles County Jail, inmate population just under—"

"Fuck," Agent Givens said.

"Twenty thousand . . . inmates," Carl said, finishing anyway. "The list goes on, sir."

Agent Givens turned toward Governor Hawthorne. "The country is about to be thrown into complete chaos. We need to stay this execution."

Governor Hawthorne, his face bloodless, shook his head in shock, disbelief, and every emotion in between. "He'll kill her."

Agent Givens wanted to hold back, Sam could tell, but couldn't. "He's going to kill her anyway, Governor!"

At that, Governor Hawthorne clenched his jaw, stood firm, and said, "Then you better warn the White House."

CHAPTER 62

Right after Beth plunged the bottom of the typewriter key into Minks's eye, she used the next few seconds to grab the chain from the floor and wrap it around his neck.

Before he realized what she was doing, and while he was trying to pull the typewriter key from his blood-gorged eye, she'd placed her foot against his chest for leverage and started pulling on the chain, leaning back and pulling with all her strength, pulling despite how much the searing pain the exertion was causing on her wounded calf and strained back, pulling because her plan was working and maybe there was light at the end of this nightmarish tunnel, pulling because she just wanted this fucker to die.

Justice Minks—because maybe she'd just strangled the Montresor right out of him—bucked and flailed on the floor, choking and gasping for air, his mask now off his face from the fight, his neck strained and tendons tight as he'd given up on the protrusion in his eye to fight the chain around his neck.

Another gunshot sounded from somewhere in the house.

Beth flinched at the sound, and for the briefest of moments must have eased off on her grip. The chain slipped in her hands. He moved his right hand far enough to grab the wine bottle beside his chair, and then it came out of nowhere, crashing across her brow like the impact of a car wreck, and the bottle shattered and blood, mixed with merlot, sprayed across the floor.

CHAPTER

63

TREVOR KNEW INSTANTLY that the house wasn't right.

The inside appeared as meticulously kept and clean as the grounds outside. Not a crumb graced the shiny marble countertops. Not a grain of dust touched the baseboards or ceiling fans or the dozens of bookshelves that filled nearly every wall, inside the dining room and living room and study. The air smelled of potpourri and fresh chocolate chip cookies and flowering indoor plants.

But the chains connected to the walls weren't right, the way they lay, meandering, around the floors of each room like heavy lifeless snakes, the end of each chain marked by distinct ankle bracelets.

Lizzie had shot two men dead already, with no hesitation, as they'd emerged, one from a stairwell and the other from what Trevor assumed was a garage. It had been thirty seconds since she'd shot the second one and so far, no other captors had come at them. The rest, they assumed, had all left in the caravan.

But neither of the two men had been Justice Minks.

Perhaps he'd been in one of the fleeing caravans, but Trevor didn't think so. They heard a man scream, somewhere inside the house, soon after they'd entered it, and now, the walls seemed to be whimpering.

"You hear that?" Lizzie asked, gun poised. "Voices."

"Yeah," said Trevor, his bloody bat over one shoulder as he eased toward a room and nudged the door open with his foot to see a vast, high-ceilinged bedroom with a four-post king-size bed, the bedspread made and tucked, pillows stacked to perfection, the entire room like something out of a magazine.

"Trevor," Lizzie said from outside the bedroom.

Trevor ducked back into the hallway, where Lizzie had opened another door that led to a long hallway marked by numerous doors on either side.

And the whimpering grew louder.

It wasn't coming from the walls.

But the rooms.

So many rooms.

C H A P T E R

64

"DEAD MAN WALKING!" shouted a guard.

Sam stood with Jennifer at the window inside Warden Wren's office overlooking the yard, where guard towers cast angled beams of light toward the center of it all.

Two guards escorted Sal Batise toward the stone wall that bordered the basketball court and turned him to face his four executioners, four guards who stood fifteen paces away holding, what to Sam, looked like machine guns.

Words were exchanged between Warden Wren and the four executioners, and then between Warden Wren and the news crew, and then finally Warden Wren approached Sal Batise, and the two of them stood talking.

Batise looked up toward the center tower, toward the warden's office, toward Sam and Jennifer and Agent Givens and Governor Hawthorne at the window, and Sam froze.

Jennifer, beside him, grabbed his hand and held it.

Carl, behind them, didn't want to watch, and was still bringing in news of more diversion fires across the country. "ADX Florence in Colorado, the Alcatraz of the Rockies. Fires near USP Atlanta, San Quentin, Sing Sing . . ."

Agent Givens checked his watch. "Two minutes. Governor, you need to stop this."

C H A P T E R

65

TREVOR AND LIZZIE opened one door after the next, and to their horror, every room held a captive—male, female, didn't matter—with each one not only alive and in various conditions of declining health, both mental and physical, but chained to more than one anchor.

Each prisoner was shackled by chains that burrowed through walls and ceilings and floors, and they all begged for help.

Trevor and Lizzie promised they'd return, but first, they had to find Beth Hawthorne.

Now that their presence inside the horror house had been recognized, cries of help now sounded from each side of the hallway and from all three floors, and, perhaps, even a basement, because those chains going down into the floors had to lead somewhere, to someone.

"I'm going to throw up," Lizzie said as they navigated the hallway, turning at the *L* toward another hallway of doors and rooms, all of them unlocked and full of prisoners.

"It's a Chain House," Trevor said. "Have you read the Mallard Malone novels?"

"No," she said. "Not much of a reader."

"I've only read half of the first," he said. "It was enough. But in one of the territories, in this apocalyptic world, they hold their prisoners inside what they called Chain Houses. All the prisoners are connected to one another. And yeah," he said, approaching a stairwell. "I might throw up too."

They froze at the sound of someone coming down the nearby stairwell.

Stumbling was more like it.

And then, as if he'd been shot out of a cannon, a large man emerged from the stairwell and crashed into the wall.

It was Minks.

He straightened, moved like he was blind, and then Trevor saw why. There was something protruding from his right eye, which was a blood-oozing, gory mess, and his neck was red and scratched and bleeding in places as well, like he'd recently been choked by something. He gasped for air, struggled to breathe, but managed a grin when he saw his two intruders.

"Tiny Tommy . . . Batise," he said in a croak. "Come for dinner?"

And Lizzie, having seemingly seen enough, pulled the trigger. Once, then a second time—one for each knee, instead of kill shots. She was leaving it to him to finish the deal.

Trevor clutched the bat, moved forward, and brought it down with all his strength.

CHAPTER

66

Minks is dead.

Sam showed the text message from his father to Agent Givens and Governor Hawthorne, who immediately said, "Beth? Emily?"

Sam said, "I don't know yet, but Minks is dead."

Agent Givens turned to Hawthorne. "Governor, you've got one minute." He pointed toward the window and yard below. "There's a chance if he's killed, the country is overrun by criminals."

"The President knows the threat."

"And he won't have time to stop it at this point."

Governor Hawthorne nodded, like he knew it, and then said, "I'll grant the stay."

Agent Givens pounded on the office window to try and get the warden's attention, but they were up too high. He sprinted from the room.

Governor Hawthorne jumped on the phone to call his office.

Sam knew this wasn't how it was supposed to go. Papers needed to be signed. Protocol needed to be followed. This wouldn't do.

Carl sat wide-eyed and quiet at the warden's desk.

Sam and Jennifer watched out the window as Sal spoke what might have been his last words.

CHAPTER

67

BETH SCREAMED, "HELP!"

In reality, she feared her voice was barely audible. Her vision was blurry. She felt certain the blow she'd taken from the wine bottle had given her a concussion.

"Beth . . . Can you hear me?"

I can hear you, she thought. Emily's voice through the wall. But was it real? Was any of this real?

"Beth . . ."

Her voice was different from her late twenties' voice from decades ago, deeper, a bit rawer, but it was her.

She was alive.

"You're alive, Beth. Get up. Get up and scream for help before he comes back."

"Help!"

It came out louder this time, like some of the fog had been shaken off. "Help. My name is Beth Hawthorne!"

CHAPTER

68

TREVOR AND LIZZIE followed the voice.

Too many voices cried for help at once, from every direction, but it was the voice that had just announced herself as Beth Hawthorne that they followed first, and with haste, ducking under and stepping over chains that ran across the hallways like tripwires and limbo poles, opening every door until they found her in one of the end rooms off the third-floor hallway.

She was wobbly on her feet, and bleeding from a head wound at her temple.

"Beth Hawthorne," Trevor said, still gripping the baseball bat.

"Yes," Beth said weakly. "And Emily . . . she's alive . . . in the next room."

CHAPTER

69

SAM SAID, "THEY have her, Governor. Beth is safe. And your sister. She's alive too."

Governor Hawthorne collapsed to his knees, crying.

Another text came in from Sam's father: The vehicles that left here, it looks like they're less than a mile from the prison at Twisted Tree.

"Shit," Sam said, showing the text to Jennifer, and then the governor, who'd made it to his feet again and now looked ready to tackle a heavyweight prize fight.

"We'll see what the government's response is," said Hawthorne. "And how quickly it comes." He stood with them at the window overlooking the execution, where Agent Givens was running across the yard, shouting toward Warden Wren, who turned toward the commotion. Governor Hawthorne checked his watch. "Thirty seconds."

But it was only five seconds later before the first shot was fired.

Early.

CHAPTER

70

TREVOR DIDN'T KNOW how much time they had before anyone might return, but he wasn't leaving here without freeing every one of the prisoners.

To their relief, they found three keys hanging on hooks inside the spotless kitchen, and what had apparently made their captor's life easier, having one universal key per floor, with several copies of each, made their job of freeing the prisoners that much faster, and one by one they unlocked the padlocks on the chains, starting with Beth and Emily Hawthorne and working their way down the hallway and down to the lower floors.

Those who could walk, walked. Those who couldn't were helped.

Trevor thought, *Who's the Breaker of Chains now, big brother?*

And then he wondered if Sal was still alive.

Midnight had passed thirty seconds ago.

He'd worry about that later. Now, he needed a way to get these people to freedom.

Trevor called their trucker friend Todd, who had promised to wait up next to the highway in his rig, and asked for one more favor.

CHAPTER

71

IT WAS LIKE a car wreck.

Sam knew he shouldn't look, but he couldn't *not* look.

He knew he should have moved away from the glass—he'd been told, warned—but none of them moved.

They'd all stood stunned for too long—if seconds could be considered too long—before ducking or diving or running like they should have done.

And by then, the bullet—or maybe it was shattered glass—had struck Sam in the shoulder and neck area, spinning him away from the chaos down below and onto the carpeted floor, with Jennifer yelling his name and coming to his aid.

Him bleeding on the floor, losing consciousness, his mind replaying what he'd just witnessed in the yard below.

CHAPTER

72

Seconds before

THE FIRST GUNSHOT had been premature, too early, and not aimed at Sal Batise.

One of the four guards, in the exact moment after Sal had spoken something to the cameras and Warden Wren, turned toward the warden and fired, blowing the man back across the lawn. Sam, at that point, while Jennifer screamed in horror and Governor Hawthorne shouted, *Noooooo,* saw Agent Givens drop to the ground, not because he'd been hit but to avoid the gunfire that had begun spraying across the yard from every direction. From the towers, from the walls. Because the first shooter was not the only guard turned traitor. Guards fired at guards. Guards fired at the camera crew. Guards fired and prison workers fled from the madness, and soon, alarms were blaring, and lights were flashing, and walls were breached, and prisoners were escaping from cells.

And then, when Sam should have been taking cover—Jennifer had literally been trying to pull him to the ground, where Carl and Governor Hawthorne lay covering their heads—Sam saw Sal Batise, hunkered down and moving through the very chaos he'd predicted, looking for cover, looking for his way out.

Then Sam saw Agent Givens, kneeling down and aiming, the barrel of his gun tracking Batise's every step. He pulled the trigger at the same time he, himself, was hit by a bullet in the chest. Agent Givens was blown back on the grass and Batise, across the yard, had gone down on one knee, before standing again and limping away. He'd been shot in the leg but was still alive, and Sam couldn't stop watching, couldn't stop . . .

Couldn't stop.

And then suddenly Batise, only steps away from an open door and perhaps his ultimate freedom, was shot multiple times from somewhere, from someone, or from several at once, his body riddled with bullets and dancing like a bloody puppet maneuvered by invisible marionette strings.

And then the window in front of Sam shattered, and he went down in a shower of glass.

After

HAMMERING ECHOED OVER the front yard, and the air smelled of fresh wood.

The framing of the house next door was going up quickly, Sam thought on his way to his father's front porch, still, even six months later, in disbelief that after all the time they'd lived next door to the Halls, after all the time his father had spent secretly and silently pining over Lizzie Hall, in particular, that they were now off somewhere living together.

Exactly where that was, Sam didn't yet know but felt secure in his dad's promise that one day soon, he would. They'd send word, an exact address, but for now—it was better if Sam was in the dark, just in case the police came back with new questions about the fire that had occurred next door six months ago, and the fact that Jake Hall, a fireman, had died in the conflagration, his body too scorched for an autopsy no one was eager to conduct. But as Trevor had told Sam on the phone months ago, it's easier to say "I don't know" when you truly don't know.

And so far, although it was clear the fire had been started by gasoline, too many of Jake's fellow firefighters had concurred that Jake had been acting odd of late, and maybe they should have seen it coming, but as one of the men said, *We just didn't think he'd do it by fire.*

Sam called bullshit on all of it, and could only gather from those firemen's comments that none of them really liked Jake Hall to begin with, and that they'd suspected for some time that he was abusing his wife, and they'd concocted a suicide story for Lizzie with a little bit of, *Good for you, Lizzie Hall, sorry we didn't help out sooner.* And so Lizzie, even before any investigation from the life insurance policy had been completed, had the quarter acre cleared and construction on a new home started from afar. A home she planned on putting on the market as soon as there were new floors down.

And now, as Sam and Jennifer and Carl went back to work for their fourth straight day of rooting through Professor Harper's house, getting it ready to sell, Sam thought why not get the same realtor and put them up together.

A package deal, just like his father and Lizzie seemed to be.

Sam had thought often in the six months since his release from the hospital, with everything that had happened that night and afterward, with thousands of unaccounted-for prison inmates still on the loose after their escapes from forty-seven prisons around the country, no one gave a shit about something as small as Jake Hall possibly perishing in a fire. Whether he'd died by baseball bat or flames, the local authorities didn't have the bandwidth to deal with it when they were still trying to round up the nearly two thousand inmates who'd escaped from Twisted Tree State Penitentiary that night.

Nowadays, with a curfew that had started as temporary and now seemed permanent, at least until the inmates were caught, everyone carried a gun, just in case. Even Carl and Jennifer had handguns now. Jennifer had bought hers the day after what the media had dubbed The Great Breakout, and then bought extra ammunition when she learned Nancy Tanner, within hours of their visit that night inside the women's prison, was killed inside her segregation unit cell.

Working on the never-ending documentary consumed their time.

Going through Trevor Harper's house helped take their mind off things going on *out there*, and as life tended to do after chaos, it went on. The final Mallard Malone novel, found edited in typed manuscript form inside a bedroom of that horrible Chain House, was set to come out in two weeks' time.

Sam had started working through the drawers and closets of his father's bedroom, the same room that had at one time belonged to his father and Annie, before taking a break and leaving for a quick lunch. Now that they'd returned, Sam went back to work on the closet, where he'd been pulling out boxes and files and clothes and junk. He pulled out a Nike box and opened it, and was a bit taken back by what was inside it.

College brochures from SCAD in Savannah. The University of Kentucky. The University of Virginia, and finally, a stack from Centre College in Kentucky.

Sam leafed through them, knowing, except for SCAD, that he'd not applied to any of these colleges. So why did his father have them? Although Jennifer *had* gone to SCAD. He turned toward the open door and called out her name. She was working in the kitchen, and Carl was going through the hallway closet. It didn't surprise Sam to see Carl come into the bedroom along with Jennifer. Even though Sam and Jennifer had gotten close in the past weeks, close enough to definitely say they were dating, he often wondered if he'd ever get as close to her as Carl seemed to be.

"What is it, Sammy?" Jennifer had begun calling him Sammy, for whatever reason, inside the hospital, when for nearly forty-eight hours, they weren't sure if he'd make it, before bam, one morning, his eyes had popped open and he'd asked for some oatmeal, and Carl, at his bedside, had wiped his tears and told Jennifer, beside him, *Now that's the fuck. That's the fucking fuckity fuck, right there, Sammy boy.*

So maybe that's where it started.

Sammy.

And he liked it.

He waved the two of them over. Still self-conscious of his scars, Sam turned his good side toward Jennifer, even though two nights ago she'd kissed the scars on his neck, and then his cheek, and the one that had put a permanent dimple at the top corner of his lip.

Carl had his phone out. "Check it," he said, showing them his screen. "Look who's running for President."

"Governor Hawthorne?" Sam asked.

"Nope," Carl said. "Beth."

Jennifer said, "Even better. We need her." And then to Sam, "What's up?"

Before showing her the shoe box and what was in it, he asked, "Where did Markie go to college?"

"Markie from the closet?" she asked.

"How many Markies do you know?" Carl asked.

She flipped Carl the middle finger without looking at him. "Centre College, why?"

"And Iris?"

"Virginia."

Sam swallowed hard. "And Peter, he went to UK?"

"Yeah," she said, sitting on the edge of the bed. "What's this about?"

He showed her the shoe box. "Found this." He showed her the brochures. "Found these."

"Why would he have them?" Jennifer asked.

"He obviously never lost track of any of you," Sam said.

"Oh damn," Carl said. "What if it's more than that?"

"More than what?" Jennifer asked.

"I don't know," Carl said, thinking out loud. "But . . ."

"But what, Carl?"

"You said yourself, Jennifer, that your family . . . they were great and all, like really great . . . your parents, but . . ."

"Get to the point, dork."

"You were poor as fuck," Carl said. "So how did your parents pay for SCAD?"

"Financial aid," she said quickly, defensively, and at the same time had her phone to her ear and they could hear it ringing. When a woman's voice answered, Jennifer said, "Hey, Mom. Quick question, how did you and Dad afford SCAD, really? Don't mess with me."

Her mother stammered, "We just . . . you know . . . made ends meet."

"Did someone pay for my education at SCAD?" she asked bluntly. "It's okay, Mom, I just want to know."

"Yes," her mother said after a moment.

"Was it Professor Harper?"

After a beat, her mother said, "Yes." And then she started crying. "He never wanted you to know. He never wanted any of you . . ."

"Mom?"

"I gotta go."

Jennifer laughed. "No, you don't. Come on, tell me. He paid for all our educations, didn't he? Me, Markie, Iris . . . Peter. All four of us, from the closet?"

"Yes, dear." A heavy sigh. "He did. And we were all sworn to secrecy. So . . . can you please not tell the other three?"

"That's fine, Mom. I won't. Love you. Gotta go." Jennifer ended the call, wiped tears from her cheeks. "Well, son of a bitch."

Sam watched her, sat on the bed and hugged her, rubbed her back.

"Get a room," Carl said, before sitting on the opposite side and hugging Jennifer too.

It didn't need to be said that Trevor Harper had never gotten over the guilt of leaving those four in the closet, for grabbing Sam but not being able to rescue the other four.

Jennifer pulled away, wiped her eyes again, and stared Sam in the face.

Sam said, "What?"

She reached out, gently rubbed her thumb over one of his cheek scars from the exploded glass. "Your father . . . he was at the hospital."

Sam perked up; he hadn't seen his father since the day he'd walked out of this house questioning his manhood. "When?"

"You were . . . you were out," she said. "It was during those two days where it was . . . tenuous. I was in the room with you. Your dad . . . what a goofball, it was like he was there incognito, like a ninja or something, dressed in a baseball hat and a sweatsuit, like something he'd never wear in his previous life."

"Which one?"

"Good point," she said. "His professor life. But he—" Jennifer started crying again. "He watched you from the window and he . . . he put his hand up against the glass . . . to your hospital room." She inhaled a deep breath and let it out, and by now, Sam was crying too. "Like a starfish, right on the glass, just like the two of you would do when you were little."

Sam wiped his eyes. "I didn't know."

"But you did, dude," Carl said. "You smiled, in the bed."

"I did."

"You fucking did, dude."

Jennifer said, "That's when we knew. That's what gave us hope. And then I turned to look, and your dad was gone."

Carl said, "Like a fart in the wind."

"Like he came and did what he needed to do and then went back into whatever hiding he felt he needed to do."

"The Raven," Sam said softly, thinking again of what Agent Givens had told him the day Sam was released from the hospital; the day Sam realized Agent Givens had survived, that he'd had a vest on that night when he'd been shot in the chest. But he'd thought Sam might want to know Batise's last words: *Tell my brother Tommy, he did good, and the seed might turn a man into a father, but the true growth comes from the dad.*

Sam smiled, stared out the window as the framing on Lizzie's house went up outside. He laughed. When Jennifer asked what was funny, he said, "Oh . . . nothing." But it wasn't true.

He'd just recalled the image that had gone viral on the internet months ago, when Luther Wright's hidden Italian villa "paradise"—his horrifying Chain House—had been all over the news and online, on every form of social media known to man. Specifically, he remembered the words written in black Sharpie on the stone backsplash behind the kitchen stove.

The Raven was here!

And below it.

And so was The Mongoose!

ACKNOWLEDGMENTS

I CAN'T BELIEVE WE'RE at the end of another book, my second book of 2026, in fact, which makes it the first year where I had two releases. Hopefully the first of many double-release years. To borrow the line from Wrigley's DOUBLEMINT GUM, *double your pleasure, double your fun* . . . so I hope you had fun with both *Dig* and *The Chain House* this year, because I gotta say, out of all the novels I've written, *The Chain House* just might be, if not my favorite, the book I had the most fun writing. The idea came to me quickly, and the writing of it came just the same—one, because the story genuinely cooked, but two, and more glaringly, because I really had trouble getting this one out of my head when I called it quits each day, which meant it caused me sleep issues, and so I had no choice but to write it as quickly as possible, if for no other reason than to be able to sleep again. And it worked. I finished the first draft in two months and was finally able to sleep a little bit, without the fear of Justice Minks and Sal Batise torturing my brain at night, as they'd been doing for weeks, near the end of the first draft. But the finishing of any book, as always, doesn't come about without the support and guidance of so many. My friends are absolutely the best, and I don't have to name you all—you know who you are—and thank you. To everyone at Crooked Lane Books for making my work stand out, from editing to cover design, I thank you. But a special thanks goes out to my editor Sara J. Henry (our 6th novel together!) for constantly making me toe the line and reprimanding me when I go over it, and to my publisher, Matt Martz, for so thoroughly believing in my work. My agent, Alice Speilburg, is as good as it gets, and my thanks to you goes on and on. To my kids, keep making me proud. Maybe stop growing up so fast, but keep making me proud. And to Tracy, my wife of 27 years, thank you for your belief in me, and for allowing me to so stubbornly continue to chase a dream.

Continuously onward and upward . . .

James